BEACH TOWN

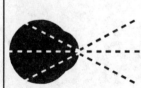

This Large Print Book carries the
Seal of Approval of N.A.V.H.

BEACH TOWN

MARY KAY ANDREWS

WHEELER PUBLISHING
A part of Gale, Cengage Learning

GALE
CENGAGE Learning®

Farmington Hills, Mich • San Francisco • New York • Waterville, Maine
Meriden, Conn • Mason, Ohio • Chicago

GALE
CENGAGE Learning

Copyright © 2015 by Whodunnit, Inc.
Wheeler Publishing, a part of Gale, Cengage Learning.

ALL RIGHTS RESERVED

Wheeler Publishing Large Print Hardcover.
The text of this Large Print edition is unabridged.
Other aspects of the book may vary from the original edition.
Set in 16 pt. Plantin.

LIBRARY OF CONGRESS CATALOGING-IN-PUBLICATION DATA

Andrews, Mary Kay, 1954-
    Beach town / Mary Kay Andrews. — Large print edition.
      pages cm. — (Wheeler Publishing large print hardcover)
    ISBN 978-1-4104-7745-3 (hardback) — ISBN 1-4104-7745-2 (hardcover)
    1. Large type books. I. Title.
PS3570.R587B43 2015b
813'.54—dc23   2015013864

Published in 2015 by arrangement with St. Martin's Press, LLC

Printed in the United States of America
1 2 3 4 5 6 7 19 18 17 16 15

32007 8965

Dedicated with love to Katie and Mark,
best daughter and son-in-law on earth!

ACKNOWLEDGMENTS

The former journalist in me loves doing research for my novels, and I can't thank the following people enough for their time, advice, and help. Any inaccuracies or mis-statements of fact are all mine.

Brian Albertsman of Atlanta is a real-life film location manager and a world-class gentleman who answered all my dumb questions and allowed me to tag along after him on the job. Kai Thorpe answered more location scout questions, as did Becky Ollinger. My dear friend and junk buddy, Ki Nassauer, was my personal California research connection, driving me around L.A. and environs, and introducing me to people like hair and makeup genius J Money, Ben and Dan Newmark of Grandma's House Entertainment, Marla Schlom and Susan Lorenzana, and Kevin Beers. Susi Fuller and The Three Speckled Hens in Paso Robles treated us to the best overnight visit ever at Proulx Wineries. Patti Callahan Henry helped out with emergency medicine information and Gwinnett Superior Court Judge Warren Davis and Busy Belden were lifesavers when it came to untangling my legal questions.

I must give huge credit and thanks to everybody on Team MKA, including the invaluable Grace Quinn, Katie Trocheck Abel, Jersey Meg, aka Meghan Walker of Tandem Literary, and Red Meg, aka Meg Reggie of Meg Reggie Public Relations.

As always, all praise goes to the best damn agent in the universe, Stuart Krichevsky, and his team at SKLA, including Shana Cohen and Ross Harris.

My publishing family at St. Martin's Press is simply the best — starting with my endlessly patient and wise editor, Jennifer Enderlin and her assistant Caitlin Darreff. I am perpetually grateful to my publisher, Sally Richardson and the rest of the Flatiron Building gang, including but not limited to Tracy Guest, John Karle, Jessica Lawrence, Jeanne-Marie Hudson, Stephanie Davis, Anne Marie Tallberg, Jeff Dodes, Talia Sherer, and Michael Storrings.

Back at home are the people who matter the most; my family, including Tom, Katie, Mark, and Andy. Their love and support keep me going — even during those dreaded flabby middles.

And thanks again, dear readers, for buying

the books that allow me to buy junk and pursue all my dreams!

1

Greer Hennessy needed palm trees. She needed Technicolor green fronds swaying in wind machine–enhanced breezes, with some Dolby-sound crashing waves. And was it too much to ask for a Panavision wide shot of a sun-kissed beach? Wasn't this Florida?

Instead, the only trees she spied through the bug-spattered windshield of her rented Kia were part of an endless wall of tall spindly pines, underplanted with miles of palmetto clumps. She'd landed in Panama City three days earlier.

Before leaving L.A., she had browsed the Florida film and television commission website, which featured photos of every imaginable kind of scenery in the state, from the dark brown ribbon of the Suwannee River lazing through the northern edge of the state, to the green pastures of Ocala horse farms, all the way down to the funky conch cottages and banana palms of the Florida Keys.

Day one of her journey, she'd taken one

look at the wall-to-wall high-rise hotels and condo towers lining Panama City Beach and headed west on US 98, and then over to 30A. She'd found palm trees, yes, but also an infestation of cuteness in planned beach communities with picturesque names like Seaside, Rosemary Beach, and Watercolor, which hugged both sides of the road on 30A and reeked of taste and money. The houses were as colorful as the community names and oozed magazine cover potential.

Pretty it was. Sleepy it wasn't. The beach roads were clogged with BMWs and big SUVs, the highways crowded with outlet malls, convenience stores, and strip shopping centers.

The Gulf of Mexico, or what she could glimpse of it, was pretty enough, textbook turquoise, contrasted against sugar-white sand. Perfect for a chamber of commerce brochure but lousy for the kind of gritty location she was seeking.

At the overpriced condo she'd rented that second night in Destin, she asked around about nearby beach communities. Greer usually divulged her occupation and mission only when absolutely necessary.

"I'm looking for someplace quiet," she'd said to the waitress at a pseudo-quaint breakfast place called Eggs 'n' Joe. "Maybe a place with old-timey mom-and-pop motels? And, like, shrimp boats maybe?"

"Mexico Beach," the waitress said, presenting her with a fourteen-dollar check for a bagel sandwich.

But Mexico Beach wasn't it.

Apalachicola was next. Plenty of shrimp boats and oyster boats. She parked and walked around a bustling marina that even had a pier, snapping photos with her cell phone.

Not what I had in mind, Bryce Levy texted back.

Greer got in the Kia and drove, following the coastal Florida highway as it headed south and east.

She had high hopes for a place called Saint George Island. There she found a general store, a couple of motels, and a few scattered T-shirt shops. Sandy roads traversed the island, and large multistory houses stood silhouetted against sea oats and sand dunes.

She shot photos of the beach, one of the motels, and the entrance to the state park and e-mailed them to the producer/director. Her phone dinged a moment later with his text.

No.

She thought again about the one brief meeting she'd had, two weeks earlier, with Bryce Levy, the newly anointed boy wonder of Hollywood.

Her best friend, CeeJay, was in the honeymoon phase of her fling with Bryce and had somehow managed to convince her new boyfriend that Greer was the only location manager experienced enough for his next big film project.

This despite the fact that Greer's last location scouting job had literally ended up in highly publicized flames — with lawsuits and finger pointing and a near-fatal blot on her previously flourishing career.

CeeJay herself had driven Greer to the meeting with Bryce, which he'd insisted had to take place in total secrecy in his leased Brentwood mansion.

The producer wasn't what she expected. CeeJay's usual type was the hot, young starving artist, complete with black leather and body piercings.

Bryce Levy was none of these things. He was much older than CeeJay's usual men. He was casually dressed, in an open-necked white dress shirt, the sleeves rolled up to expose muscled forearms. He had a high forehead and a full crop of wiry blond hair. Wire-rimmed glasses sat atop a generous nose. He had expressive blue eyes and was laughing explosively at something his caller was saying. She guessed his age as late forties to early fifties. Except for the nose, which looked like it had been broken a few times, he was matinee idol handsome.

"This is a really high-concept piece," Bryce said, settling back in his chair. "Action, some romance, with thriller elements. And I've signed two great leads. Adelyn Davis, you know her work, of course. And the male lead? Off the chain! It's the guy's first film, but he's gonna be box office gold, I know."

"You'll die when you hear," CeeJay said, eyes dancing with excitement.

"Ceej . . ." Bryce said, giving her a stern look.

"Okay, I'm not saying a word."

"What can you tell me about the setting?" Greer asked.

"That part's easy. It's a beach town. A real sleepy, backwater kind of place. East Coast definitely. I need you to find me a place with a look that's a cross between *Body Heat* and the town in *Jaws*."

Greer blinked. "You want a cross between Florida and Nantucket?"

He nodded rapidly. "Yeah. I see palm trees. Long stretches of deserted beaches, some dunes with those wavy wheat-looking things . . ."

"Sea oats," CeeJay said.

"Yeah. Sea oats. And then there should be trees with that Spanish moss stuff hanging down, beat-up old fishing boats. Atmospheric, you know?"

Greer nodded, her mind racing. Dunes, palm trees, shrimp boats, Spanish moss? He

15

was definitely talking about a Southern beach.

"It should have a real throwback feeling, like the kind of town the world forgot about. We'll need an old-school motel. Not a movie set, but an honest-to-God fleabag motel. No high-rise condos, fast-food joints, nothing that would suggest it's a tourist trap, or that Walt Disney even exists. And we're also gonna need a cool old building that can be exploded during the movie's climax."

She was taking notes while Bryce described the project.

"Any specific kind of old building?"

"I can visualize it, but I can't really describe it," he said. "It needs to have this iconic look — say, like, the Parthenon, or the Alamo. Like that."

"But the movie is set in contemporary time?" Greer asked.

"Of course. It's just — like I said, this beach town, it's like a total throwback. See, that's where the conflict comes in. Our guy rides into town, kinda like a modern-day Shane. He's back from active duty in Afghanistan, come home to his loving wife, only she's not so loving, and nothing is the same. And did I mention he's ex–Navy SEAL?"

"Got it," Greer said. Although she wasn't sure she actually did get it. Not without a script, or at least a treatment.

"Am I allowed to know the name of the

16

project?"

Bryce and CeeJay exchanged knowing glances.

"Beach Town," Bryce said. "Dynamite, huh?"

The problem was that, for this project, Bryce wanted a look that was a cross between two movies that had been shot more than thirty-five years earlier. He didn't know or care that the Florida of his imagination no longer existed — if it ever had. He just wanted palm trees and Spanish moss and rusty shrimp boats. And an Alamo that he could blow up.

She picked up her phone and sent another text:

Not finding the exact combination of sleepy fishing village/beach. Maybe do beach shoots at state park in Panhandle, and village exteriors someplace else?

Bryce's reply was terse, as usual.

Keep looking.

As she was putting her phone back into the cup holder in the Kia's console, she remembered the slip of paper Lise had pressed into her hand a lifetime ago, back in L.A. On a whim, she pulled the paper from her purse and stared at it.

Give him a call, her mother had urged. He'd get a kick out of hearing from you.

Greer wasn't so sure.

Sitting at the departure gate back at LAX, she'd had an hour to kill. She was updating her Facebook page, flicking dispassionately through her feed, when she gave in to the urge she'd been fighting since packing up Lise's apartment.

There were three Clint Hennessys on Facebook, but only one who lived in Florida, and only one whose profile picture showed an intensely tanned guy with a white handlebar mustache, grinning through the open window of an orange Charger emblazoned with a huge Confederate flag across the roof.

She found herself holding her breath as she stared down at the photo of her long-gone father. His eyes were the same blazing blue she remembered, the mustache drooping below thin lips stretched wide into a guileless smile. He wore the same kind of sleeveless "wife beater" T-shirt he'd always favored, and Greer was surprised to note his leathery, still muscular biceps.

The father of her memory was perpetually laughing down at her, tugging at one of her pigtails, teasing her about her missing front teeth, offering a stick of his ever-present Juicy Fruit gum. It was a funny thing about her memories of Clint. He was always grinning, laughing at some private joke. But Lise never seemed to find her stunt-driver father funny. Even as a five-year-old, Greer sensed the tension between her parents.

After he'd gone, Lise sold the two-bedroom ranch house in the Valley and they'd moved in with her grandmother, sharing Dearie's tiny one-bedroom apartment until Lise got the part in *Neighborhood Menace,* and they'd moved into a house in Hancock Park.

"Give him a call," Lise had urged, as they'd sat in the oncologist's reception area, waiting for yet another set of test results. "We both know how this is going to end. After I'm gone, he'll be all the family you have left."

"You're not going anywhere," Greer had insisted, wanting it to be true. "I'll still have Dearie. And anyway, he's not my family."

Maybe that's when it finally began to sink in for Greer — that Lise had resigned herself to dying, because she'd stopped holding grudges.

"Call your dad," Lise repeated, propped up in bed at home. "He wants to see you. And you need to see him."

"I don't need a father." Greer had inherited her mother's stubborn streak.

Maybe she could have used a father when she was ten and had to take one of Lise's boyfriends to the father–daughter dance at school. Maybe Clint could have helped her out when she was fifteen and learning to drive in Dearie's yacht-sized Bonneville. Or maybe, yeah, he could have helped out by steering her away from the legions of wrong guys she'd dated over the years.

Maybe if Clint had any interest in his only child he would have taken the trouble to show up at Lise's funeral.

He hadn't done any of those things. And it was too late now. Greer crumpled the slip of paper, thought about tossing it in the trash, but at the last minute, as her flight was boarding, she'd tucked it back into her purse.

Somewhere south of Steinhatchee and west of Gainesville she pulled up to a restaurant she'd seen advertised on faded billboards for the past fifty miles.

Little Buddy's BBQ was a low-slung wooden shack perched in the middle of a pothole-pitted crushed oyster shell parking lot crowded with pickup trucks and big American sedans. A thick hickory-scented cloud hovered over a huge black smoker off to the east side of the restaurant.

All good signs, Greer thought, as she pushed through the screen door to observe the crowded dining room. She'd done quite a bit of location scouting in the South in recent years, and one thing she'd learned early: if you wanted to do beta research there, the local barbecue joint was the best place to start.

Scouting thoughts were laid aside when a paper plate loaded with chopped pork, coleslaw, potato salad, and a single slice of garlic-toasted white bread was plopped down in front of her, along with a quart-size plastic tumbler of iced tea so sweet it could have been dessert.

She was using the bread to mop up the last drop of barbecue sauce when the counter guy slid her check across the counter. "Anything else? Some pie, maybe?"

"No pie," Greer said with a groan. "I'm stuffed. But I could use some help."

"How's that?" He was a skinny, older man, in his late sixties, she thought, with thinning gray hair cut in a military-style flat-top crew cut.

"I'm looking for the perfect beach town."

He shifted from one foot to the other. "Destin's a few hours north of here. Saint Pete's a couple hours south."

Greer shook her head. "Yeah, I know about both of them. But I'm looking for something quieter. Picturesque, but not touristy, if you get what I mean. An old-timey-looking beach. A small town with palm trees, white sand, fishing boats."

"Sounds a lot like Cypress Key," the counter guy said. "I ain't been in a few years, but the last time I was there it was pretty much like you just described."

She tipped him ten bucks and headed out to find Cypress Key.

2

"Proceed to the route!"

The disembodied voice on Greer's GPS was maddeningly vague about which exact route she should take. Against her better judgment, she'd turned off US 98 and on to a county road that looked like it might lead her straight into *The Blair Witch Project*.

Since she didn't have a road map, she'd have to rely on the magic of some mystical satellite high up in the blazing blue Florida sky. She only prayed it knew where she was supposed to go.

It had rained so hard the night before, Greer had awakened with a start in her cheap motel room, startled by the steady rattle on the roof and at the windows of the cinder block room. She'd been living in drought-stricken California for so long, she suddenly realized, she'd forgotten what rain sounded like.

She'd called Dearie before leaving the motel. There hadn't been time to stop by to see her before leaving Los Angeles. Her eighty-seven-year-old grandmother kept bizarre hours, often sleeping during the day and watching television most of the night.

"Dearie? How are you?"

"Who is this?" Dearie demanded.

"Who else calls you at five o'clock in the morning, Pacific time?"

"Sometimes the people at that Prayer Cathedral call. They seem nice."

"You're not still sending them money, right?"

"Not since you cut back on me," Dearie said accusingly. "Say, where are you?"

"I told you, I'm down in Florida, scouting for a film."

"That's right. Well, have a nice time. And don't forget my money. We're supposed to take a bus trip to Knott's Berry Farm this week. Or maybe next week. Anyway, I'll need a little extra for that."

The sides of the pancake-flat blacktop road were still awash in puddles, and the air was syrupy thick with heat and humidity. Green walls of palmettos, stick-thin pine trees, and scrub oaks draped with Spanish moss were a blur as the Kia sped down the county road.

She glanced nervously at the GPS, which claimed she should arrive at Cypress Key in 14.2 miles, and again at the dashboard, where the needle of the fuel gauge hovered dangerously below the quarter-full mark. She'd had

23

zero bars on her cell phone for the last forty miles. If she ran out of gas on this godforsaken edge of nowhere, she was certain she'd be eaten alive either by the swarms of mosquitoes or by one of the black bears whose silhouette was featured on ominous-looking BEAR CROSSING signs posted every few miles.

Finally, she began to see billboards. They urged her to eat at Tony's — home of three-time world champion award-winning clam chowder. Or take a swamp boat ride. *As if!* Or stay at a motel called the Silver Sands, which boasted forty-two modern rooms, air conditioning, tile baths, and free television.

Five minutes later she breathed a sigh of relief after spotting the CYPRESS KEY 5 MILES marker. The landscape changed suddenly. In the distance she saw the gleam of water, a swath of sand, and a metal bridge.

Ahead, she saw a stretch of waterfront, with docks jutting out into what a sign told her was Choklawassee Bay. Fishing trawlers and sailboats bobbed in the calm water. Rooftops peeked above the tree line, and she spotted a handful of shrimp boats, far out on the horizon, in the Gulf.

Spanish moss, shrimp boats, palm trees, and a beach. She felt the familiar serotonin buzz starting at the back of her skull, the one that told her she was onto something. *Proceed to the route.*

■ ■ ■ ■

She pulled into the first gas station convenience store she found, filled up the Kia and,
noting that she now had two bars on her
phone, pulled up the Cypress Key Chamber
of Commerce website. There were half a
dozen motels in town, which came as a relief.
Bryce's assistant had e-mailed that she'd
need to find housing for a cast and crew of at
least sixty people.

The Buccaneer Bay Motel consisted of a
cluster of faded A-frame cedar units gathered
around a cracked and drained swimming
pool. There were four beat-up cars in the
parking lot and a faded VACANCY sign swinging from another faded billboard leading to
the motel's entrance. She drove on, past a
couple of ramshackle seafood processing
plants. Promising, she thought. Totally gritty
and atmospheric.

A heavy chain-link fence with a NO TRES-
PASSING sign surrounded the Stephen Foster
Memorial Elementary School, an Art Deco-
era stucco building with a red tile roof and
boarded-up windows. Rusting swings sat in a
weed-covered playground.

Two blocks over, she hit pay dirt.

Cypress Key's Main Street reminded her of
a relic from an old Bogart movie. Was it *Key
Largo* or *To Have and Have Not*? Two-story

stucco and wood-framed buildings with rickety-looking balconies and front porches stretched for three blocks. There was a library, a barber shop, an old bank, and many vacant storefronts. But the Hometown Market lights were on and its plate glass windows promised fish bait, cold beer, milk, and Boar's Head deli products. There was even a welcome center in the former movie house.

Greer pulled to the curb, which she happily noted was free of parking meters, jumped out of the Kia, and began snapping photos, stopping only to e-mail them off to Bryce Levy.

She pressed her face to the glass of what had most recently been the Smart Shoppe Women's Boutique. The walls were bare and the floors littered with trash, but they were wooden, and if she stood back a ways, she saw that the high ceilings were made of pressed tin panels. She snapped a picture of the real estate sign in the window.

FOR LEASE: CALL THIBADEAUX REALTY

Her cell phone dinged and she smiled as she read the text message.

LOVE IT LOVE IT LOVE IT. SEND MORE PIX ASAP. ART DIRECTOR IS DROOLING.

She walked back to the welcome center and tugged at the door. Locked. A sign on the door indicated that the center was only open Thursday through Saturday, 10:00 a.m. to

2:00 p.m. But a wooden rack held an assortment of maps and brochures for local businesses. Greer helped herself and kept walking.

When she came to a street marker for Pier Street, she inhaled a lungful of salt air. She followed the street for two blocks, past pastel-painted wooden cottages and yards full of exotic greenery spilling from every corner. Ahead, she saw the bay. And sure enough, the street narrowed and then morphed into a wooden pier.

A handful of businesses, wooden huts, really, lined both sides of the pier. There was a kayak rental stand, a bait shack, a dock for Cypress Key boat tours, and another for golf cart rentals. She clicked off photos as she walked, pausing to e-mail them to Bryce and his art director.

She had only the sketchiest sort of treatment for this movie, and Bryce hadn't bothered to give her a list of sets he wanted, but Greer's location scout antennae were beeping away. Every instinct she possessed told her she'd found exactly what Bryce didn't even know he was seeking.

The pier ended abruptly in yet another chain-link fence. But behind it she saw a hulking white elephant of a building, crouching at the water's edge.

Built in the same stucco design as the old elementary school, this building was much bigger, shaped almost like a Quonset hut, with a red tile roof and creamy yellow stucco walls. Big picture windows looked out on the pier at the front of the building, barely shaded by red and white striped canvas awnings, the frayed fabric flapping in the breeze coming off the bay. A fanciful crenellated parapet jutted out from the building's front, and a pair of raggedy but still towering palm trees grew from stucco planters on either side of the entry.

The red neon sign above the parapet was rusting, but the lettering was still readable. The sign said Cypress Key Casino, but Greer knew she'd found her director's Alamo.

She snapped away, e-mailed, and did her own abbreviated version of the happy dance when Bryce texted back immediately.

Awesome! Send interiors!

It was close to six o'clock, but heat still shimmered off the concrete pier. Small groups of fishermen were knotted about, but they were concentrating on their quest for trout and redfish, not on her. She glanced back toward the waterfront. Children were playing along the narrow sand beach, splashing in the limpid waves while parents lolled on chairs.

Greer strolled casually to the far edge of the chain-link fence. It wasn't terribly high, but it was high enough that she'd definitely attract attention if she attempted to scale it. She leaned as far over the edge of the wooden safety railing as she could, and for the first time noticed that a short dock jutted out from the side of the casino. A small aluminum fishing boat bobbed at its mooring, alongside a weather-beaten sailboat.

Five minutes later she handed her credit card and driver's license to the teenager who was running the kayak rental stand.

"Ever been in a kayak before?" the kid asked, looking her up and down.

She wasn't exactly dressed for a boating expedition. She wore white capris, a black sleeveless T-shirt, and her red Keds. She tucked her credit card in her pocket and her cell phone in her bra.

"Lots of times," she lied. He shrugged, handed her a neon orange life vest and an aluminum double-edged paddle. "We close at seven. If you're not tied up here by ten of, I gotta charge another seventy-five bucks."

"I just want to take a little spin around, get my bearings for the week."

He hefted a kayak off the aluminum rack, dumped it in the water, and helped her climb down into what looked like nothing more than a pregnant blue banana.

The kayak wobbled wildly, and she had to clamp her lips together to keep from screeching. He stuck his foot onto the end of it, steadying it. "Lots of times, huh?"

"I've seen it done lots of times," she said lamely.

He gave her the short course on balancing and paddling. Ten minutes later, she was making for the end of the pier, glancing over her shoulder, praying the water would stay calm and that she wouldn't be seen.

As she nudged the kayak up to the landing, a huge pelican squawked and took off, landing a few yards away, giving her a malevolent stare. She paddled close to the pier, stood up, and the kayak began to wobble crazily.

She dove desperately for the concrete pier, and somehow made an imperfect landing.

Greer sat on the pier for a moment, gathering her wits and her courage. She checked her tied line to make sure it was secure, then dashed toward the casino building. A rope was stretched across the stairs leading up to the casino deck, and a faded NO TRESPASSING sign was fastened to it.

She stepped nimbly over the rope and scampered up the steps. She was on the side of the building, in a sort of open-air pavilion. Round concrete picnic tables and concrete benches were spattered with bird droppings, and another faded red and white awning shaded what was left of a refreshment stand. But the windows were boarded up now. A plate glass door to the left of the stand had sheets of plywood nailed across it. She stood on tiptoes but couldn't see inside.

A narrow wooden catwalk ran across the back side of the casino, with large bay windows overlooking the water. Two windows had been broken out and ineffectively patched over with peeling strips of silver duct tape. She pulled at a strip and it came off in her hand.

The window jamb was a good four feet up from the floor of the catwalk. The stucco walls offered no hint of a handhold, and it was definitely too high to jump. She walked a few yards down the catwalk, to a service door. Two galvanized steel trash cans were bolted to the wall, and a collection of old wooden milk crates was haphazardly stacked in the alcove that sheltered the door.

She grabbed two crates. Using them as a step stool, she vaulted over the windowsill without looking, and promptly fell flat on her ass on the wooden floor, a good five feet below.

If Greer hadn't already had the breath knocked out by her fall, the interior of the Cypress Key Casino would have done the trick.

She crawled to her hands and knees, and stood slowly. The late afternoon sunlight streamed through salt-streaked windows, casting a moody golden glow on the cracked plaster walls.

This had once been a grand old place, Greer realized. The high, vaulted ceiling was set off by heavily carved wooden beams, and dust-covered ceiling fans hung from long metal rods. The floors beneath her feet were scarred and littered with what looked like more bird droppings, but at one time this had been a highly polished maple dance floor.

On the south side of the cavernous room was a raised bandstand, with a threadbare fringed and swagged red velvet curtain pushed to one side. Behind the bandstand was an impressionistic painted pastel mural of jazz musicians, reminiscent of pre-Castro Havana.

On the north wall, opposite the bandstand, stood a varnished dark wooden bar. Yellowing signs tacked to the wall behind it advertised snacks, sandwiches, beer, and something called setups. Nothing on the menu board cost more than fifty cents.

Greer pulled her phone from her bra and began clicking photos, mindful of the time and the waning light. At first, she concentrated on the bandstand and its mural, and then the bar.

When she rotated around to capture the rest of the ballroom, she noticed a large illuminated sign hanging by chains from the ceiling on the north end of the building — a sign for bingo. Thus explaining why this was called a casino.

Rows of round wooden tabletops with fold-up legs, and wooden folding chairs, were stacked against the wall beneath the BINGO sign.

On the opposite side of the room she spotted a door with an inset glass window. Crossing to it, she peered inside and glimpsed what must have been the casino's office. A large metal desk stood on one wall, and in the middle of the room stood a rolling metal cart holding a huge, old-school movie projector. She spun around and saw that, mounted on the wall high above the bandstand mural, was what looked like a pull-down movie screen.

At one time, this must have been the epicenter of culture for the community of Cypress Key.

For a moment, she stood in the empty old building, imagining it in its heyday, picturing couples who looked suspiciously like Bogie and Bacall, or even Spencer Tracy and Katharine Hepburn, dancing cheek to cheek as an orchestra played big band tunes of the era.

The light in the room changed, flaring orange. Alarmed, Greer glanced down at her phone. She had ten minutes to get back to the dock. She clicked off a few more photos on her phone and then, regretfully, pulled a folding chair up to the window to make her escape.

3

Job one was to find housing — for herself
and the cast and crew of *Beach Town*. Cypress
Key was only about a mile long, with two
motels and a couple of condo complexes with
several vacation rental signs posted out front.

The Silver Sands looked like it might fit the
bill.

It wasn't much to look at. A trio of mint-
colored two-story concrete block units
formed a horseshoe surrounding a courtyard
with a small garden and an even smaller pool.
But it was right on the Gulf, which was a
plus, and it had a blinking neon VACANCY
sign, which sealed the deal, since it was starting to get dark and she was hungry and tired.
She snapped some photos and texted them
to Bryce.

She followed a wooden sign pointing to the
motel's office, which looked like it had actually been carved out of the last two ground-
floor units on the far end of the motel.

A buzzer sounded as she pushed open the

door, and a silver-haired woman seated behind the desk looked up from the paperback book she'd been reading.

"Need a room?"

"Yes, please," Greer said. "Just a single."

"Traveling alone?"

"That's right."

"In for the weekend?" The woman turned to an old-fashioned wooden mail rack mounted on the wall, and studied the numbers. "I don't have anything right now with a Gulf view."

"That's all right," Greer said wearily. "I mostly just want a clean bed and a hot shower. Do you have a weekly rate?"

"I can give you the AAA rate. That's four hundred ninety dollars."

"Really?" Greer tried not to look shocked She'd paid half that for a single night back in Destin. "Okay, that would be fine."

She handed over her American Express card, but the woman shook her head. "We don't take that one."

"Visa?"

"That'll work. I'll need a driver's license too."

Greer studied the older woman as she took down her billing information. She was rail thin, with leathery skin that bespoke a life spent in the Florida sun. Her silver hair was cropped in a pixie cut, and her gray eyes were flinty behind a pair of steel-rimmed glasses.

She was dressed in a sleeveless white cotton blouse and neatly pressed blue jeans.

"You got a car?"

"Yes, a Kia."

She handed Greer a hot pink paper parking pass. "Put that on your windshield."

"Will do."

Now the woman passed her a clipboard with a single sheet of paper, which appeared to be a hundredth-generation photocopy. She tapped four different spaces on the paper. "Initial here, here, and here, and sign here, that you understand the rules."

Greer scanned the page, then initialed a statement that pledged that she was over the age of twenty-one, would not allow more than four guests to sleep in her room, would not smoke in her room or play loud music after 10:00 p.m. Lastly, she pledged not to clean fish anyplace other than the designated fish cleaning station.

"College kids," the woman said, by way of explanation.

She handed Greer a key with a plastic Silver Sands Motel fob. "I'm Ginny Buckalew, the owner, manager, and head housekeeper."

"And I'm Greer. Is there a place nearby that I can get a quick dinner?"

"Walk up one block and over another, and that's Tony's. Good clam chowder. Another block over, you got Wong's, which is so-called Chinese. I never seen anybody Chinese coming or going from that place, so I'd skip it if I were you. Right next to them is the pizza place. It's fast and it's cheap and that's the best thing I can say for it. Captain Jack's has decent seafood, but they water down the drinks. The Cypress Key Inn probably has the best food, but it's not cheap."

"Where do you like to eat around town?" Greer asked.

"At home," Ginny said. And for a moment, Greer could swear the older woman cracked a smile.

"Anyplace else?"

"Captain Jack's is okay," Ginny relented. "And it's fast. But they close at nine on weeknights, so you'd better get going if you want dinner."

"Got it," Greer said.

She was halfway down the walk toward her car, but doubled back to the office.

"One more thing, Ginny. You've got Wi-Fi, right?"

"Wi-Fi? We don't even have caller ID."

Room number seven was what some people would call Spartan. Ceramic tile floor, cinder block walls. Aluminum-framed jalousie windows looked out onto the courtyard, with a hulking air conditioner poking out the middle window.

The decor was early thrift shop: a double bed with a polyester quilt in a Day-Glo floral pattern, mismatched brown laminate night-stands. A triple dresser held a television so old it actually had rabbit ear antennae. There was an Early American–style desk with a rickety wooden kitchen chair, and beside the desk stood a rusty dorm-size refrigerator topped with a microwave oven and a doll-sized coffeepot.

Equally style impaired was the bathroom, with bubblegum pink tile floors, a turquoise sink and commode, and a narrow shower stall.

Still, the room was scrupulously clean. She turned the faucet in the bathroom, and five minutes later the water got hot. She scrubbed her face and looked in the mirror. The humidity had turned her dark blond hair into a frizzy puffball. She pulled it into a tight ponytail and jammed a baseball cap on her head. Her career had taken her to lots of much better hotels, and a few that were much worse than this.

At Captain Jack's she ordered broiled red-fish, which the menu promised was locally caught, with sides of coleslaw and hush pup-pies and, mindful of Ginny's warning, two glasses of the house white wine. She had the restaurant almost to herself, with only two other tables still occupied.

While she waited for her dinner, she checked her e-mail. There were three new

38

messages from Bryce Levy, wanting to know how soon she could have her locations locked in.

"Soon," Greer muttered to herself.

There was an e-mail from CeeJay too.

Bryce showed me the pix. Gonna be an amazing project. Guess who's doing the hair and makeup for Beach Town? Uh-huh. Together again.

Having CeeJay on location would be great. She and Claudia Jean Antinori had met years earlier, back when Lise had gotten Greer a gig buying props for a short-lived Disney Channel sitcom and CeeJay was working her first job as a hairstylist on the same show, a puerile piece of crap called *Hall Monitor*. She'd bonded instantly with the loud-mouthed purple-haired chick from Traverse City, Michigan. This was even before Claudia Jean had morphed into CeeJay Magic, one of the most in-demand hair and makeup artists in Hollywood.

There was a second e-mail from CeeJay, with a PS on the subject line.

Make sure you book us a decent place to stay. Bryce is kinda picky about this kind of stuff.

Greer wondered how Bryce would feel

about signing an affidavit that he wouldn't clean fish in his motel room.

She was about to put her phone away when a new e-mail appeared in her in-box. The sender was somebody called MotorMouth. Just more spam, she thought, but as she was about to hit the Delete button, she saw the subject line and froze.

From your dad, Clint Hennessy

Not tonight, she thought, hitting the Save as New icon on her phone. She'd had a long day, a long week, a longer month. Whatever he wanted, it could wait. Like she'd waited, all those years when it mattered.

She finished her dinner, declined coffee or dessert, paid her tab, and walked outside.

Cypress Key rolled up its sidewalks early on weeknights. When she left the Inn, the pizza place still had a lit OPEN sign. A few people strolled past, but otherwise it seemed to her that she had the town all to herself.

All that would change very soon, she thought, once the circus came to town.

The motel pool was an eerie turquoise-glowing blob in the darkened courtyard. The smell of chlorine mixed with the heady scent of a waxy-petaled white flowering vine twining around the wrought iron porch posts. A couple of children splashed in the pool's shal-

40

low end, their parents perched nearby on cheap vinyl chairs, sipping beers and talking quietly.

Greer was tired, but not sleepy. She unlocked her room, threw her purse on the chair, and looked around. Nothing in the room to read. She turned on the television, flicked channels. No cable. Her viewing choices were two lame network sitcoms and a reality weight-loss show.

She tucked her key in her pocket and walked out into the courtyard. It was after ten, but the temperature and humidity seemingly hadn't dropped a single degree. When the grass of the courtyard gave way to the white sand beach, Greer abandoned her shoes.

The moon was half full, but the skies were clear and a light breeze raised small whitecaps on the waves lapping at the shore. She rolled up her pants-legs and waded into the lukewarm water, digging into the sand with her toes.

"Feels good, doesn't it?"

She turned to find the source of the voice, and gradually noticed a small orange glow coming from the shade of a banana palm. As she grew closer, Greer recognized the motel owner. She was seated at a picnic table, her head wreathed with a thin plume of cheap-smelling tobacco smoke.

Ginny Buckalew tapped the ash from a

skinny brown cigar into a plastic ashtray. A box of Swisher Sweets rested on the table, along with a cell phone.

"How was dinner?"

"Pretty good," Greer said. "I took your advice and went to Captain Jack's."

"Smart girl." Ginny nodded at the bench opposite hers. "Have a seat?"

"Thanks."

"You being from California, I guess you probably don't smoke," the old lady observed, before inhaling deeply.

"Not really."

"Me neither. As far as my family knows, anyway."

Greer laughed politely. The two women sat silently in the dark, staring off at the navy blue sky.

"What're you doing here, all the way from California, anyway?"

"I'm a film location scout," Greer said. "I've been all over the Panhandle the past few days, looking for just the right old-timey beach town."

"And you picked Cypress Key? Why not Destin, or Panama City? Or Sarasota? It's on down the coast a way, but people seem to like it."

"I found this place by accident," Greer admitted. "But it's perfect for what we need. No high-rises, no outlet malls or miniature golf courses. No golden arches. The director who hired me? I've been taking pictures all over town today, e-mailing them to him. He's crazy for Cypress Key."

"And so you want to make a movie here?" Ginny shook her head. "I like it, but then I've never lived anyplace else. We get folks who come back every year, but they're mostly fishermen, some snowbirds who come down for the winter from up North, a few families." She nodded toward the shoreline. "That's the only real stretch of beach on the island. Most tourists, they're looking for something bigger, flashier."

"This director doesn't want flashy for his movie," Greer said. She looked out at the beach, then turned on the bench and gestured at the turquoise glow in the motel courtyard. "He wants this."

"What? A Hollywood movie guy wants to stay here? At the Silver Sands?"

"I'm guessing he'll end up renting a house on the island. But he loves the look of the motel. So Old Florida. He wants to shoot part of the movie here, at your motel."

Ginny narrowed her eyes and exhaled another stream of smoke. "And you'd pay for that, right?"

"Absolutely."

"What about my guests? They might not like being in a movie."

"We'd rent out the whole place from you,

for as long as it takes to shoot the film," Greer said.

"How long would that be?"

"I haven't actually seen the shooting schedule," Greer said. "But from what the director has told me, it would probably be about six weeks, give or take. Starting next week."

"I've got forty two rooms here," Ginny said.

"We'll rent 'em all. Probably most of the crew and maybe a few cast members, too, would stay here."

"This time of year, rack rate for some of the bigger rooms is ninety dollars a night," Ginny warned.

Greer smiled. She'd counted the number of cars in the parking lot. Only six cars other than her own rented Kia. Business wasn't exactly booming at the Silver Sands. Ginny Buckalew was already doing the math in her head. She was hooked.

"I was thinking you'd give us the AAA rate. Eighty a night, okay?"

"Eighty-five," Ginny said. She stubbed out her cigarillo in the ashtray. She gave a furtive glance over her shoulder, as though she feared being overheard. "And that's the cash rate. No credit card."

"Done." Greer said. She suppressed a yawn and stood to go. "G'night."

"Just one more thing," Ginny called after her. "Your people can have every unit in the motel. Except my apartment. I live here, and

I'm going nowhere."

"Deal," Greer called back.

4

Room seven was stifling. Greer fiddled with the air conditioner's thermostat, turning it down from seventy-eight to seventy-two, but there was no appreciable drop in temperature. It was after eleven, and she was finally sleepy.

She brushed her teeth and released her hair from the confines of the ponytail. It cascaded around her shoulders, like some wild native shrub with a life of its own. Stripped down to nothing but a pair of panties, she climbed between the sheets, which thankfully were clean and smelled like bleach.

It was still hot. Her skin grew clammy with perspiration.

She got out of bed, turned the thermostat down to sixty-eight, fell back onto the lumpy mattress, closed her eyes, and somehow managed to doze off.

Two hours later she awoke, drenched in sweat, to the metallic rattling of the air conditioner against the aluminum window frame. Condensation dripped down the wall and onto the pile of clothing Greer had discarded onto the floor.

"Shit," she muttered, stumbling into the bathroom. She turned on the shower and stood under the trickle of cold water for at least thirty minutes. Finally, when her skin was shriveled and her body temperature had dropped sufficiently, she stepped out, pulled an oversize T-shirt over her still-wet body, and dropped back onto the bed, covered only with a tissue-thin top sheet. She fell into a sleep that felt more like a coma.

The faintest rays of light shone through a bent slat in the metal blinds of room seven. The air conditioner wheezed ineffectively. Greer was not even half awake when she felt something brush against her cheek.

She swiped her right hand across her face, then opened her eyes and spied a huge black roach scuttling across her pillow.

Greer let out a scream worthy of a Hitchcock ingenue, but the roach took no notice. She screamed again, clenched her teeth, and batted at it, at which point it took flight, winging its way across the room.

She stared at the bug in open-mouthed horror as it lighted atop the nightstand. A flying cockroach? When the roach flew onto the foot of her bed, she'd had enough.

She opened the door of her room and groggily considered her next move.

Squinting into the blinding morning sunlight, she spied a male figure three doors down from her own, pushing a laundry cart mounded with linens.

He was wearing a sweat-stained T-shirt with cutoff sleeves, baggy shorts, and flip-flops. His hair was as rumpled as the linens on his cart, and a pair of tortoise-shell glasses perched on the end of a nose that was sunburned and peeling.

"Hey! Do you work here?"

He rolled the cart toward her. "Huh?"

She grabbed a handful of his shirt and dragged him toward her room. "Get in here and get it."

He poked his head in the doorway. The room was dimly lit. "Get what?" He didn't seem to understand the urgency of the situation.

"That!" Greer pointed at the roach, which was now perched on the lamp on her nightstand. "That thing. That roach. It flew. It flew directly at me."

"That? That's just a little ol' palmetto bug."

"It's a roach. But Jesus H. Christ on a crutch, I've never seen one that big. In my life."

"It's a palmetto bug." He took a broom from the cart and raised it over his head.

"Don't kill it!"

"Why not?" He took a swing with the broom, but the roach flew across the room again, landing on the television.

"What the hell? Do you not understand? Just get it out of here. Take it outside and let it go. I don't want a stinky dead roach in here."

The janitor stared at the crazed, half-naked stranger, and the gray eyes behind those glasses crinkled in amusement.

For the first time, Greer realized how she must look. She tugged at the hem of her T-shirt, which barely reached midthigh.

"Don't look at me! Just do what I say and get rid of that bug before I call the front office. It's disgusting."

He shrugged and turned for the door. "Go ahead and call. If you don't want to kill the palmetto bug, my work here is done."

She picked up the phone. "I'm reporting you."

He laughed. "Report away."

She was getting nowhere with this rube. She sighed, dug a twenty-dollar bill from her pocketbook, and flung it at him. Twenties were the international currency of efficiency. Even the dimmest bulb could get behind one. "Get rid of that bug, okay? But don't kill it. Understand? Do. Not. Kill."

"Do not kill." He tucked the bill carefully into the pocket of his shorts, picked up a sheaf of papers from the dresser, and advanced on the hapless insect.

"Not with that!" Greer screamed. "My film

49

treatment. What the hell is wrong with you?" She snatched the treatment away from him and replaced it with a spiral-bound booklet that comprised the town's telephone directory, which was half the thickness of Bryce Levy's abbreviated film treatment.

"Here. And be quick. And then I'm gonna need you to fix that damned air conditioner too. It's like a sauna in this place."

The janitor nodded thoughtfully. He took the phone directory and gently slid it under the roach, folding the ends envelope style. He walked over to Greer's open suitcase, shook the bug out, and quickly zipped the suitcase shut.

For the first time in her life, Greer found herself stunned speechless. She stood there, wide eyed, slack jawed.

"Anything else?" He turned and headed for the door, but not before giving her a thorough up-and-down look, his gray eyes sparkling with mischief.

Greer narrowed her eyes. "Very funny. What? You're also the town comedian?"

"Nope." His hand was on the door.

"What about the air conditioner? It doesn't cool for worth a damn. And it's leaking all over the floor."

"Hmm." He walked over, squatted down beside the air conditioner, ignoring the pool of water on the tile floor.

Greer took the opportunity to size him up.

He was medium tall, a shade over six feet, mid- to late thirties, with a build that said he was active but not a fanatic. He didn't look like her idea of a typical maintenance man, but this was Florida. People came to this state with all kinds of agendas. He switched the air conditioner off, then on again. The window rattling started up again. "Sounds okay to me. But I'm no mechanic."

"What the hell kind of piss-poor maintenance man are you, then?"

"Not much. I can do a little plumbing, unstop a sink, like that. You need any towels?" He nodded toward the cart in the open doorway. "I got plenty of towels."

"Just get out," Greer snapped.

"Okay." He gave her a quick salute. "One more thing, though."

"What?"

He pointed toward her suitcase. "Since you're so into bugs and all, you should know that that palmetto bug in your suitcase there is a female. And right about now she's probably laying eggs all over the place."

Greer shrieked. She ran to the suitcase, unzipped it, and began flinging clothes onto the floor. When the cockroach scuttled away, she hesitated only a second before slapping it flat with her rubber flip-flop.

She heard the door close noisily, and then, unmistakably, she heard him chuckle as he trundled the cart back down the corridor.

■ ■ ■ ■

He pushed the cart into the laundry room and began shoving towels into one of the big commercial washing machines. He punched the On button, and as hot water began flowing into the big stainless steel drum he leaned against the folding table and thought idly of the flaky woman in room seven.

She wasn't your usual Silver Sands guest. Crazy curly blond hair, nice legs, and when she'd bent over to kill the roach he'd been rewarded with a glimpse of a very nice-looking butt in some skimpy leopard-print panties. He decided she looked more the type for Miami, or maybe Longboat Key or Palm Beach. What was she doing this far off the beaten path in Cypress Key? He'd checked for a wedding band, but she wasn't wearing one. No fishing tackle in the room, and only one suitcase. She was single, traveling alone, and she damn sure wasn't chasing trophy tarpon, that was for sure. So what was she chasing?

A rented Kia with Tampa license plates was parked outside her room. Maybe he'd get the chief to run the tag number and find out what she was up to.

He was so busy pondering the mysteries of guest number seven that he almost forgot to add the detergent and bleach before the spin cycle began.

5

Greer was halfway to the motel office, intent on lodging an official complaint with management, when her cell phone rang.

"Hi, Greer. This is Bennett Wheeler. I'm Bryce Levy's assistant. We met the other day at the house?"

"Oh, hi, Bennett."

"Did you get any of my e-mails?" Bennett sounded slightly peeved.

"No. Sorry. The motel where I'm staying doesn't have Wi-Fi. I was just going into town to try and check my e-mail."

"No Wi-Fi?" He sounded as incredulous as Greer felt.

"Bryce told me to let you know that he'll be out there on Monday, at which point he'd like to be able to tour all the locations you've set up."

"Monday?" Greer felt a rising sense of panic. "But today's Friday. And I just got here yesterday."

"Right. Bryce is eager to get started. Um,

about Cypress Key. How exactly does one get there?" Bennett asked.

"I suppose the nearest airport is in Gainesville. I'm not sure which airlines fly there from L.A., though."

"Oh, Bryce never flies commercial. Just let me know which local airport can accommodate a Gulfstream G650."

"I'll check on that."

"Great. Now, about housing?"

"I've arranged to lease a motel here on Cypress Key for the locations, and I think it'll work for most of the cast and crew as well," Greer said.

"I'm sure your motel is *perfectly* sweet, but Bryce will need a private residence. Minimum four bedrooms, four baths. A pool, of course. A screening room and hot tub would be nice. . . ."

Greer thought about what she'd seen of the island so far. The waterfront to the north and the south of the Silver Sands was studded with modest woodframe cottages. Nothing she'd seen would meet the standards of a man who lived like a pasha back in L.A.

"I'll find a real estate agent and see what's available," Greer promised. "But Cypress Key isn't Brentwood. There aren't a lot of properties like what you've described. And this is pretty short notice."

"CeeJay says you're a miracle worker," Bennett said blithely. "Also, Kregg and his

55

people are going need a house. You don't have to worry about Adelyn Davis. Her assistant made housing arrangements for her just down the coast from the shoot."

"Wait. Kregg? As in, *the* Kregg? He's the male lead?"

Greer didn't listen to a lot of hip-hop, but even she was aware that the twenty-four-year-old artist formerly known as Craig White had two certified platinum albums and had been heavily courted by every studio in town, all anxious to provide him with a star vehicle and thus to cash in on his newfound fame.

"Consider yourself sworn to secrecy," the assistant said. "Bryce wants to start rehearsing him right away. We've only got Kregg for four weeks before he goes out on his summer concert tour. His people are going to need six bedrooms. Security is going to be an issue, so a gated property is a must. A pool, of course, and a basketball court. That's how he likes to unwind. . . ."

"Bennett? The thing is, I'm pretty sure a house like that doesn't exist here."

"You're kidding."

"I'm really not," Greer assured him. "Tell Bryce I'll see what I can do. No promises, though."

Ginny Buckalew looked up from her paperback as Greer entered the office. "Morning. Everything okay with the room?"

"Now that you mention it . . ." Greer hesitated, not wanting to alienate the older woman. She was going to need an ally these next few weeks.

"What?"

"Well, the air conditioner doesn't seem to be working properly. It leaks, and rattles, but it doesn't really cool the room. My television only gets three channels, and they're pretty fuzzy. And there was a huge roach in my room this morning. It landed right on my pillow! And since you asked, I have to say, your maintenance guy is a rude jerk."

Ginny nodded as Greer enumerated her complaints. She got up and left the room. Two minutes later she returned and plopped a twelve-inch-tall electric fan on the counter. Beside it she placed a plastic flyswatter and a can of Black Flag.

"This is Florida," Ginny said. "The Silver Sands was built by my dad in 1946. It's hot. We got bugs. Deal with it."

Greer opened her mouth to protest, but thought better of it. With Bryce Levy and his entourage arriving in three days, she had other, more pressing concerns.

"Listen, Ginny, what can you tell me about that old closed-up casino at the end of the pier?"

"It's closed," Ginny said.

"Yes, I realize that. But what's the status on it? It would make an incredible location for

57

the film I'm working on. Do you know who owns it?"

"Talk to Eb," Ginny said.

"Who's Eb?"

"The mayor."

"Does he own it?"

"You'll have to talk to Eb about that."

"How do I reach him?"

Ginny opened the office door and pointed down toward the end of the corridor. For the first time, Greer noticed that a small wooden shingle was mounted outside one of the motel units, but she couldn't read the type from where she stood.

"That's his office," Ginny said.

The end unit wasn't like the other motel units. It had a plate glass door, but the interior of the office was obscured by a tightly drawn shade. The wooden shingle proclaimed this Thibadeaux Realty — Eben Thibadeaux, Realtor-Broker.

A hand-lettered sign taped to the door read "Gone out. Back later."

A bulletin board mounted to the wall beside the door held thumbtacked flyers for various homes on the market.

There were half a dozen advertisements for unpretentious-looking shacks labeled Cracker Cottages, none of them listed for more than $150,000. There were downtown commercial properties, a closed-up restaurant, a former art gallery, even the women's boutique Greer had photographed the day before.

She took special notice of three imposing-looking multiple-story waterfront houses located in a gated community called Bluewater Bay. No sale price was listed, but the flyers showed photos of swimming pools, huge state-of-the-art kitchens, and cathedral-ceilinged great rooms with spectacular water-front views.

She plucked the flyers from the bulletin board and headed back to the office.

"Eb's not there," she reported.

"You could try the store," Ginny said, clearly not interested in Eben Thibadeaux's whereabouts.

"Which store?" She wondered if the Ginny got a thrill from being deliberately cryptic and unhelpful.

"Hometown Market," Ginny replied. "Three blocks up, turn right, you can't miss it."

"Haven't seen him," the cashier at the super-market said. "Try city hall."

The clerk at city hall smiled apologetically. "You just missed him." She turned to a young man with muttonchop sideburns who was busily tapping away on a computer keyboard. "Did Eb say where he was headed when he left here?"

"I think he was gonna show one of those

condos over on the south end."

"Could you give me his cell number?" Greer asked politely. "I really need to speak to him."

The two clerks conferred quietly. "I guess that'd be okay," the woman said. "He usually likes to be accessible to constituents."

Greer found that if she stood on the top step outside city hall, her phone got exactly one bar.

And she was not surprised when the mayor's phone went directly to voice mail.

"Hi, Eben," she said brightly. "My name is Greer Hennessy. I'm a film location scout and I'd love to talk to you about using Cypress Key for the film we're going to be shooting in this area very soon. It's a terrific opportunity for your beautiful little community to really shine for the whole world to see. But it's urgent that I meet with you today. I'm staying at the Silver Sands Motel, but you can reach me at this number, at any time. Looking forward to meeting you!"

She popped her head back into city hall. The clerk gave her an expectant look.

"I left the mayor a voice mail. Any other guesses as to where he might be?"

"Well-l-l . . . it's Friday, and it's lunchtime, so if I had to guess, I'd say he's either at the Deck or the Boathouse."

"Those are local restaurants?"

"The Deck is. It's on the bayside, right after you come across Kiss-Me-Quick."

Greer's face showed her confusion.

The girl smiled. "Kiss-Me-Quick is the last bridge after you come over the causeway from the mainland. The Deck is on the right side of the road. You'll see all the trucks out front. Today's Friday, all-you-can-eat shrimp boil."

Greer nodded her understanding. "What about the Boathouse? What's the special there?"

"No special. It's just where Eb keeps his boat when it's not running, which it usually isn't. Keep going on the state route, after you've crossed Kiss-Me-Quick. The sign is so faded you can't hardly read it anymore, but I think it says Maring Marina. That's on the right side of the road, before you cross the humpback bridge."

Greer found the Deck with little trouble, and just as the clerk had predicted, the sandy parking lot was crowded. The restaurant was a low, rambling affair, a faded driftwood building surrounded on two sides by decks that looked out on the bay.

Inside she was greeted with the sharp scent of spicy seafood boil, fried fish, and beer. As she glanced around the crowded room, she realized she had no idea what Eben Thibadeaux looked like.

A hostess looked up from behind the cash

register near the door. She was young and pretty, with short, pale blond hair tucked behind one ear and a tiny gold ring piercing her left nostril. "How many in your party?"

"Just one, but, uh, I'm actually looking for somebody. The mayor? Is he here?"

"Eb?" She glanced looked over her shoulder, and then back at Greer. "Nah. He's not here."

She left another message on Eben Thibadeaux's voice mail, then drove three miles up the state route, following the city clerk's directions.

The boathouse was right where it was supposed to be. Greer took out her phone and began snapping photos. Even if Eben Thibadeaux was still MIA, this might make a great location for the film.

The building was made of sun-bleached wood and salt-corroded galvanized tin. MARING MARINA — DRYDOCK, MACHINE SHOP, WELDING — the sign's wording was so faded it was barely visible. There were three vehicles parked in the lot — two pickup trucks and a tired-looking blue sedan with four flattened tires.

Seagulls plucked dispiritedly at what looked like a piece of hamburger bun near the office door, but didn't budge as she walked past. The door creaked on its hinges. A high wooden counter faced the door, and behind it stood a desk — that was empty.

"Hello?" Greer walked around the counter and peeked into an inner office furnished with an old metal tanker desk and a file cabinet of similar vintage. Papers and catalogs and cardboard boxes of engine parts spilled across the desktop, but there was no sign of its occupant.

She returned to the outer office and pushed through a swinging door that led her out into a dank building that smelled like decaying fish and motor oil. It took a minute for her eyes to adjust to the dimness.

When they did, she saw that she was in a cavernous warehouse, with rows and rows of boats suspended from harnesses, three high, all the way up to the ceiling. A piece of heavy equipment that resembled a forklift was parked in the middle of a walkway that bisected the room.

"Hello?" Her voice echoed in the darkness. At the far end of the warehouse, a half-open roll-up door emitted a bright shaft of light.

She followed the light, walked out the door, and finally saw her first sign of life. A man stood just outside the door, bent over a pair of sawhorses that held a large, black outboard motor. His back was to her, but he wore a white T-shirt, blue jeans, and a baseball cap.

"Hey there," Greer called. "I'm looking for Eben Thibadeaux?"

"Hang on a minute," the man muttered.

He tinkered with the motor a little bit, dropped something on the pavement, and swore softly.

"Yes?" His face was sweaty and streaked with grease. He pushed the tortoise-shell glasses back from the bridge of his sunburned nose, and when he saw his visitor, frowned.

It was the surly maintenance man she'd encountered back at the Silver Sands Motel. "Christ. What now?"

"You!" Greer squinted into the sunlight.

"Yes, me." He took a blue bandana from the back pocket of his jeans and wiped his hands before shoving it back into his pocket.

"You're Eben Thibadeaux? The maintenance man at the motel? You sell real estate? And you're the mayor?"

"You left out grocery store owner," Eb Thibadeaux said. He pointed at the outboard motor. "And failed boat mechanic. To what do I owe the pleasure of this visit?"

6

"I've been trying to track you down all morning. I've driven all over town, been to city hall twice, and I've left three different messages on your voice mail," Greer said.

He frowned, patted his back pocket, and came up empty. "Sorry. Guess I left my phone in my truck. What's so important?"

"You're really the mayor?" She couldn't help herself. Eben Thibadeaux was the least mayoral looking person she'd ever encountered.

"So they tell me. The people's choice and all, although, I should tell you, I ran unopposed."

She sighed and was conscious of the sweat trickling down her own face, and the fact that her shirt was sticking to her back. It was easily ninety degrees on this black asphalt lot.

"Could we maybe go inside where it's cooler? I've got a business proposition to discuss with you."

"City business or personal business?"

"Both, actually."

She followed him through the dry-dock area and into the inner office, where he seated himself behind the desk and pointed her toward the only other seat in the room, a high-backed metal chair.

"I'm listening," Eb said.

She took a deep breath. "About this morning. Look, I'm sorry. I had a long drive down here, and I was tired, and hot, and, well . . . I guess I sort of made an ass of myself over that roach."

"Yep."

"The point is, I'd like to apologize."

"Okay."

"But you weren't exactly helpful, you know," she said. "Or polite. What does Ginny think of the way you interact with her guests?"

He chuckled. "She's used to it. What kind of business proposition are we talking about?"

"I should probably introduce myself. My name is Greer Hennessy."

"From Los Angeles. You're driving a rented Kia, and you've rented out the entire motel for, what, six weeks?"

"Who told you that?" Greer asked, stunned.

"My aunt. Ginny Buckalew."

"Wait. Ginny is your aunt? The same Ginny that owns the motel?"

"Co-owns it," he said. "With me."

"I should have known," Greer said. "Did

66

Ginny also tell you why I'm here?"

"Something about a movie you supposedly want to film here in Cypress Key?"

"Not supposedly. We definitely want to film here. Your town has everything we need. It's quaint and picturesque, it has that Old Florida, pre-Disney look that's impossible to find anymore. I know, because I just spent two days driving the Panhandle."

"There's lots of other places in Florida," Thibadeaux pointed out. "It's a big state. We got nothing but beaches and coastline. Have you seen Sarasota? Or Naples? How about Vero Beach, over on the east coast?"

"Are you trying to sell me on someplace else?" Greer asked, puzzled. "Look, I know we didn't exactly get off on the right foot this morning, but personalities aside, this film is the real deal. It's a big-budget, major motion picture with a director whose last movie was nominated for an Oscar."

He wasn't jumping up and down. Yet.

"We're talking about a six-week shoot," she continued, "most of it done right here in Cypress Key. It's a huge win for your town. In terms of local motels, restaurants, bars, and jobs, it's at least a million dollars in revenue."

"Interesting," he said, picking up a catalog and leafing through it. He looked anything but interested in her proposal.

But she had to keep trying.

"My director is flying in Monday, and he's bringing the male lead in the movie," Greer said. "And that's another reason I need to see you. The crew and most of the cast will stay at the Silver Sands and the other motels in town, if we need them, but we'll need to lease a couple private residences for the director and the principal actors."

He looked up. "What sort of residences?"

"High-end, luxury homes," Greer said. "The director needs at least four bedrooms, and as many baths, and a swimming pool."

"I think I could find something like that," Thibadeaux said. "We've got three properties for sale, out in Bluewater Bay. Spec houses. I'd have to see if the developer would be interested in a short-term lease."

"For the male lead, we'll need six bedrooms, and a pool. And a private basketball court."

"You're kidding."

"Unfortunately, I'm not. It's apparently in his contract."

"Who is this guy? George Clooney?"

"I'm not at liberty to say. But security is going to be an issue for him. His fans are totally rabid. I'm assuming this Bluewater Bay place is gated — with guards?"

Thibadeaux laughed. "Yeah, there's a gate, of sorts. And the developer built a guardhouse but, as far as I know, the gates have never been operational, and there sure as hell has never been anything like a security guard over there. You gotta understand something, Miss Hennessy. This isn't Miami. People here don't even lock their doors, let alone live behind a fence."

"How nice for them," Greer snapped. She was starting to lose her patience. The guy was doing everything he could to talk her out of using his town for the movie shoot.

"Look, Mr. Thibadeaux —"

"It's Eb."

"Okay. Eb. I've driven all over Cypress Key. I've looked at your business district, and the houses here, and I hope you'll forgive me for saying so, but it seems to me that this is sort of an economically disadvantaged community. You've got a charming Main Street, but more than half the old buildings are vacant. And the rest of the town isn't much better. There's a beautiful white sand beach on the Gulf, but the Silver Sands is the only motel where people can stay there, and even you would have to admit it's not exactly the Ritz. But once the movie is out and people see how charming your town is, tourism is going to pick up. Businesses will follow. I've seen it time and again. This movie will be a boon to your community."

"A boon." Thibadeaux set aside the catalog.

"Exactly."

His gray eyes stared her down. "And who guarantees that?"

"Guarantees? We'll have legally executed documents for all the locations we use for the shoot, if that's what you mean. Our production company will lease the motel and whatever private residences we need for the cast and crew. For a production this size, we'll be hiring locals — short term, it's true, but we'll need drivers, caterers, electricians, laborers to help build sets, security guards. And extras, of course."

"Of course," he said mockingly.

That did it for Greer. "What the hell is with you?" she demanded. "Most towns, if they were offered a big-budget production like this, they'd jump at the chance. But you act like I'm trying to put up a toxic waste dump or something. You've done everything but tell me to take my movie and get the hell out of Dodge."

He leaned across the desk. "Miss Hennessy?"

"Greer."

"Right. Greer, do you know anything about the history of Cypress Key? Have any idea why we are, as you say, an economically disadvantaged community?"

"Not really."

The chair squeaked loudly as he sat back. Eb Thibadeaux seemed to fill the chair — and the room, come to think of it. He was a shade north of six feet tall, not matinee idol handsome but undeniably intriguing, with the scholarly look of a professor — a professor who spent a lot of time outside.

"You mentioned a toxic waste dump, and I know you were joking, but that's essentially what we had here for the past sixty years. Only they didn't call it that. They called it the Cypress Key Paper Plant."

"A paper mill? Here? I haven't seen anything that looks like that," Greer said.

"That's because the Peninsula Paper Company, which owned and operated the Cypress Key plant, stopped operating here more than a decade ago. But for fifty years before that, three shifts a day, 364 days a year — they closed Christmas Day — that plant manufactured cardboard boxes. Six hundred jobs, that's what that plant meant."

"I'm sensing an unhappy ending," Greer said quietly.

"You could call it that. All those years, the foul-smelling smoke that poured out of there? Environmentalists called it pollution. Locals, like my dad, said it was the smell of money."

Thibadeaux swiveled around in his chair and, with his finger, stabbed at a point on the large map pinned to the wall behind his desk.

"The plant was right here. Its discharge pipes emptied directly into Horseshoe Creek." He dragged his fingertip a few inches to the right. "Two miles downstream, that creek flows into Choklawassee Bay."

He swiveled back around until he was fac-

71

ing Greer. "Ever hear of Choklawassee oysters?"

"I'm from California. But no, I never have."

"They used to be famous. When my dad was a kid, oysters from Choklawassee Bay were just as famous as Apalachicola's. Chocky oysters, that's what they were called, were shipped up and down the Eastern seaboard, to the finest restaurants around. But it wasn't just oysters that came out of the bay. Blue crabs, stone crabs, scallops . . . we had one of the finest fisheries on the central Gulf Coast of the state, right outside this old boathouse."

"Until?" Greer asked.

"Until we didn't. Until the catches got smaller and smaller, and somebody from the Feds finally thought to test the water quality of Choklawassee and immediately closed the bay for any kind of commercial fishing."

"Why didn't they just make the paper plant clean up its act?" she asked.

"Because at the time, back in the nineties, the Peninsula Paper Company owned more land in Florida than the State of Florida owned in Florida. They also owned enough politicians to keep the environmentalists off their backs," Eb said matter-of-factly. "For a while, anyway. Eventually the EPA came in and mandated all kinds of pollution abatement regulations. And at that point, ten years ago, Peninsula decided it was just cheaper to shutter the plant."

72

"And?"

"And nothing," Thibadeaux said. "More than four hundred folks lost their jobs. Peninsula abandoned the plant, and five years ago it burned to the ground. Arson, the state fire marshal said. Doesn't matter. We're a small town. You can imagine the hit to the economy. Commercial fishing was already all but dead. Families moved off, went on welfare. Those shops you saw on Main Street — the hardware store, the ice cream parlor, the diner, the shoe store — they all died a slow death."

"But you're still here," Greer pointed out. "You don't seem to have done so badly for yourself."

"Oh yeah," he said easily. "I'm what passes for a land baron in Cypress Key. I own half the Silver Sands, which as you saw, is a total gold mine. And the Hometown Market."

"And this boathouse?"

"Left to me by my grandfather and worth millions and millions, as you can see by the thriving business we do here," Thibadeaux said. "I'm probably the biggest thousandaire in town."

He opened the desk drawer, took out a paper napkin, and used it to polish his glasses. Which left Greer an opening for her last pitch.

"None of what you've just told me explains why you don't want us to make a movie here.

We can help this town. So why are you so opposed to this project?"

"Opposed? I never said I was opposed. I just expressed a degree of healthy realism."

"More like pessimism," Greer said.

"Whatever. You're not the first rodeo to come to town, you know. Two years ago, some high-tech outfit came in, sniffed around, and made a lot of noise about opening a customer service call center here. They promised to hire one hundred fifty people for twenty-three dollars an hour. Hell, I would have applied for a job paying that. The county offered them two million dollars' worth of tax incentives, the governor helicoptered in for a photo op. And then nothing. I heard they ended up building in New Jersey. The year before that, it was Chinese investors, saying they were gonna start clam farming and build a high-tech cannery. Three years later? Turns out it was all a scam."

He peered at Greer over the rim of his glasses. "So you'll have to excuse me if I don't jump for joy at the news that an unnamed director with an unnamed star might make a 'major motion picture' right here in sleepy little Cypress Key."

Greer nodded slowly. "Okay. I get it. You've been burned before. You don't know me from Adam, and it's true, right now I can't give you a lot of information about the project. But how about this?"

She pulled the film company's checkbook from her pocketbook, wrote out a check for ten thousand dollars, and placed it on the desktop. "I've left the payee blank. This is the amount we're paying to lease your motel. Call the bank, see if the funds are there. The director's name is Bryce Levy. You can Google him. I can give you his production assistant's phone number in L.A. and you can talk to him."

Thibadeaux glanced down at the check and shrugged. "Money talks, Miss Hennessy."

7

"I'm so glad we speak the same language," Greer said, giving him her best close-the-deal smile. "Now that you understand I'm not some fly-by-night huckster, let's discuss the Cypress Key Casino."

Thibadeaux frowned. "The old casino on the pier? What would you want with that?"

"There's a crucial scene in the film that would take place there," Greer said. "I've been specifically looking for just the right location and architecture, and that casino is it. Nothing else I've scouted even comes close. I know it's closed currently, and it looks like it's about to fall to pieces, which is perfect for our story line, because the script calls for it to be destroyed in an explosion. What's the story there? Who do I need to contact?"

"You're looking at him," Eb said.

"You own the casino too?"

"The city is the current leaseholder. I'm the mayor."

"Great," Greer said. "I love one-stop shopping. How much would the city take to lease it and then blow it up for the film?"

"Nothing."

She blinked. "You're not going to charge us to use the casino?"

"It's not for rent," he said.

"Why not? It's just sitting there empty. I think I can probably get the director to authorize, say, one thousand dollars a day for the filming? I'm not certain how long the scenes will take, but from the treatment I've read, at least five, six days."

"The casino is not for rent," he repeated. "It might look like a candidate for the scrap heap to you, but to us it's a local landmark."

"Okay," she said slowly, her mind racing. He was in the real estate business, and he was used to negotiating. She had to have the casino. "Two thousand a day. And I'll talk to my people about some up-front money to outright buy the building, demo it, and then haul it off. If it's a public safety concern, I can assure you we'll be hiring the best special effects professionals in the business. This could be a win-win for everybody."

"Sorry," Thibadeaux said, as he stood. "It's not a money thing." He gestured toward the door. "Do you want to go see those houses now? I'll have to pick up a key at my office."

"Wait. That's it? Just, no? Because you're the mayor and you said so?"

"Pretty much," he said cheerfully. He held the office door open for her and brought a key ring from his pockets. "I probably ought to lock up before we leave. Not that there's anything here worth stealing."

"What about the town council?" Greer asked, grasping at straws. "If it's city property, don't you have to put something like this to a vote? Isn't there a committee or something?"

"Oh sure. I guess that would come under the Ways and Means committee."

"Great. Who's on that committee? And when do they meet?"

He thought about it for a moment. "Let's see. Ways and Means? That'd be Ginny Buckalew. And Dr. Borden. And me. Ways and Means meets the first Monday of the month, which was this past week."

"Let's go look at houses," Greer said wearily. This was not surrender, she vowed to herself. More like a temporary retreat.

She followed Thibadeaux back to the Silver Sands and waited for him outside his office. He pointed at a blue golf cart parked in the lot. "Might as well ride over there with me."

Greer climbed into the passenger seat without comment. As they puttered along the quiet downtown streets, the mayor waved and nodded and greeted his constituents by name as his passenger quietly fumed and plotted her next move.

"Hey, Bernice," he called to an elderly woman driving a golf cart with a large black dog belted into the passenger seat. The driver of a rusting brown Chevy pickup with the bed loaded with crab traps beeped his horn and leaned his head out the open window. "Hey there, Eb."

"How ya doin', Kenny? Catching anything?" the mayor hollered.

A pair of oversize stucco columns flanked the entrance to the subdivision, which looked more like the entrance to a weedy meadow. The plaque on the columns read Bluewater Bay Luxury Residences.

"There's where the guard shack was going to be," Eb pointed.

Greer studied the road. "Hmm. Wonder how quickly we could get some gates and a shack built?"

"You'd need a variance," he said.

"Let me guess. That has to be approved by the mayor?"

"Actually, no. That's the city clerk's job."

"And is the city clerk by any chance related to you?"

He laughed. "She was — by marriage. But she got smart and dumped my cousin Butch."

At first glance, Bluewater Bay didn't exactly live up to its name. She saw no signs of either blue water, bay, or luxury. Asphalt roads looped through a landscape dominated by sand, scrub oaks, and clumps of palmetto.

Every few yards a forlorn-looking FOR SALE sign poked up from the sandspurs.

Thibadeaux saw Greer's look of dismay. "It gets better down at the cul-de-sac. All this land used to belong to the paper company. They bought it for the timber, logged it, and kept it, because that's how they ran their business. Then, after they closed the box mill, they decided to get into real estate development. Four years ago they came in, clear-cut this parcel, and subdivided it. The idea was to sell waterfront lots to builders for spec homes. Only problem was, by that time, the economy sucked. They finally ended up selling the lots for next to nothing. Milo Beckman, a local builder, built four houses. He lives in one, and he managed to sell one to a retired couple from upstate New York, but the other two houses have just been sitting here."

The street came to a Y in the road and Thibadeaux veered off to the right. As promised, at the end of the cul-de-sac she spied four large houses situated on large, nicely landscaped lots.

"This is the four bedroom one I told you about," Thibadeaux said, as he pulled the cart into the driveway of a vaguely Cape Cod–inspired white frame house raised up on concrete block pilings. "Milo hired an interior designer from Gainesville to decorate them as model homes, and the furniture is still here."

Greer followed him up the wood-plank steps. He unlocked the door, then stepped aside to allow her to enter.

"Killer views," he said.

Which was an understatement. They were standing in a vaulted-ceilinged great room with a back wall made up of three sets of French doors. There was a deck outside, and beyond that she saw a small swimming pool surrounded by a white concrete deck. Just past that sparkled the very blue waters of Choklawassee Bay. A squadron of pelicans flew past in V formation and, below, she saw the gray back of a dolphin as it coursed through the waves.

"Wow," Greer said, moving toward the French doors. Her footsteps on the wooden floors echoed through the high-ceilinged rooms. The furnishings were what you'd expect: large sofas, rooms decorated in beachy green and blue hues. Nothing spectacular, but nothing obnoxious either. She did a quick walk-through, shooting pictures with her cell phone, and e-mailed them off to Bryce Levy's assistant. When she returned to the living room she found Thibadeaux reading e-mails on his own phone.

"The house is great," she said. "Decent kitchen, nice-sized bedrooms and baths. Is the other house about the same?"

"Two more bedrooms, three baths, plus a half bath in the, uh, pool house, I guess you'd call it," Thibadeaux said.

She nodded thoughtfully. "But no basketball court?"

"There's one at the city park, on Pine Street," he offered. "The locals play pickup games most weekends."

"Not sure Kregg is going to like that idea," Greer mused.

"Who?"

She clapped her hand over her mouth. "Damn. Nobody's supposed to know it's him. Pretend you didn't hear that," she said quickly.

"Did you say Kregg? That's a person?"

"Obviously you're not a big hip-hop fan. You really never heard of Kregg? As in *Wannabe Crazy* or *Lies, Spies and Killa Highs*?" Greer asked. "The guy is huge. He's on the cover of this month's *Rolling Stone*. What century are you living in?"

"This one," Thibadeaux said with a shrug. "I mostly listen to country music. With a little alternative rock thrown in, just to prove to my niece that I'm not a complete troglodyte."

"How old is your niece?"

"Allie is seventeen. She lives with Ginny, but I guess you'd say I'm sort of her guardian."

"And how old are you?" Greer asked.

"How old are you?" he countered.

"I asked first."

"Forty-one," he said. "Yourself?"

"Midthirties," she admitted.

"No wedding ring?"

"No." She left it at that. She and Sawyer had lived together on and off, mostly off, and although she'd secretly fantasized about marriage, she'd somehow known from the beginning that Sawyer Pratt was a pathological bachelor.

Anyway, that was a long time ago.

Eb Thibadeaux wasn't done with his cross-examination.

"How old is 'midthirties'?"

"Thirty-five. Okay?"

He pondered that nugget of information. "About what I figured. And you actually listen to that hip-hop crap?"

"I'm in the entertainment industry," Greer reminded him. "Pop culture awareness is part of my job. As for Kregg? His stuff isn't *that* bad. He's kind of cute, if you're into that sort of look."

"Which look?"

"Oh, you know, the usual. Tattoos, scruffy beard, ripped jeans, soulful, urban, wounded, self-absorbed. Like that."

"I'm sure that's catnip for girls Allie's age."

Greer clutched his arm. "You can't tell her Kregg is coming here, Eb. You can't tell anybody."

"Cypress Key is two square miles. You've

seen what people on this island look like. Don't you think somebody is going to notice when this Kregg character shows up in his ripped jeans and urban, wounded soul patch? So, what's the big deal anyway? A few girls squeal a little and ask for an autograph?"

"You don't understand," Greer said. "It's not just a couple of girls. Kregg is a huge deal. This is his first movie. If word gets out that he's here, this place will be swarmed with fans. Crazed, obsessed fans who will stop at nothing to take a selfie with him."

"And that's a bad thing?"

"It is if you're trying to make a movie. You have no idea of the security hassles involved with a star of Kregg's magnitude. They'll show up on the set and disrupt filming. They'll stalk him, follow him to restaurants, the gym, home, pester him until he signs their CDs or allows a photo. And it's not just the fans. Once word gets out, we'll have the media here too. And that's another whole layer of trouble."

"Okay. I'll keep it to myself. About the houses? Yes, or no? I'll need to talk to Milo to make sure he's okay with a short-term lease, but I'm thinking they've been on the market long enough, he'd just like to see some positive cash flow."

Greer heard her phone bing, notifying her of an incoming text message. She glanced down, then nodded. "That was from the director's assistant. Yes on both houses. But we'll need a guarantee that security will be in place by the time Kregg gets here Monday. So, can you do that? Get a variance from the city clerk and get some kind of gatehouse erected by then?"

"I'll talk to Milo," Thibadeaux repeated. "Not sure about the timing of building the gatehouse. Tell you what I can do, though. There's only one street coming in and out of the subdivision. I'll ask the chief of police to station an officer out here to keep folks from coming in."

"That would be perfect," Greer said.

"It's gonna cost you," Thibadeaux warned. "We've only got six officers on the force. You'll have to pay for an off-duty officer."

"Of course," Greer said. "We'll need security for the duration of the shoot anyway."

"You can take that up with the chief," Thibadeaux said. "Her office is back at city hall."

"I'm headed that way as soon as I get my car from the motel," Greer said.

8

The police chief was an imposing-looking black woman named Arnelle Bottoms. "So y'all want to make a movie. Right here in Cypress Key? Are you sure?"

"Very sure," Greer said. "Eb Thibadeaux suggested I talk to you about security during the shoot. We anticipate being here about five or six weeks, and we need to make sure we don't have people wandering onto the set or bothering the cast, especially our male star, once everybody gets here."

Arnelle Bottoms was probably in her early forties, Greer decided. She wore her hair short and natural and her lipstick fuchsia. There was an engagement ring and wedding band on her left hand, and a pair of framed photographs on her desk showed two children — a teenage girl and a boy of probably ten or twelve. Her blue uniform fit a little snug through her ample bosom, and a small American flag brooch was pinned to her lapel.

Chief Bottoms pulled a yellow legal pad

from her top desk drawer and started jotting notes. "Mmm-hmm. So we'll need, what, one or two officers to secure the perimeter of your area. Any idea how many hours a day, that kind of thing?"

"The script is sort of a work in progress," Greer said. "I should have a better feel for it once the director and his folks arrive Monday, but usually they try not to work longer than eight hours, although that can vary. And from what I've seen of the film treatment, there will definitely be some night shoots."

"All right," the chief murmured. She looked up. "You said something about security for your male star?"

"Yes. He travels with his own security people, but we'll need somebody to guard the street leading into Bluewater Bay, where he'll be staying, to turn away fans and media people. The mayor promised he'd talk to the owner of the subdivision about building a guard shack and a gate. Until that gets done, we'll need an off-duty officer."

"You mind my asking who the star is?" the chief asked.

"I can tell you, but we're hoping to keep it on the down-low for as long as we can," Greer said. "He's a hip-hop artist named Kregg."

"Kregg!" the chief exclaimed. "For real? *The* Kregg is gonna be right here in Cypress key?"

"So you've heard of him?"

"Girl, my kids have played 'Wannabe Crazy' so many times I could sing it in my sleep," the chief said. "My daughter Tasha and her friends are gonna be so excited when they hear this. . . ."

"But not until we have all the security lined up, please," Greer reminded her. "Since you know how huge Kregg is, you get that his people are concerned about security. From what I've been told, his fans can get really crazy."

"Not on my watch they won't be," Chief Bottoms said firmly

Her phone dinged to indicate an incoming text. She glanced at the screen.

Hi Greer. It's your dad. So sorry to hear about your mom. We really need to talk. Please call me if you get this.

The hell she would. She wondered how he'd heard about Lise, wondered if her mother had given Clint her phone number and e-mail address. Not that it mattered.

She got out of the Kia and slammed the door. She headed back into city hall to do her job — without any annoying family distractions.

"Hi, Cindy. I'm ba-ack."

It was a play she'd learned all those years ago as a baby P.A. on her first television shoot. Learn people's names and use them. Everybody likes to think they matter. And everybody likes to think they have the inside scoop.

The city clerk looked up from her computer monitor and smiled.

"So I see. Did you ever track Eb down?"

"I actually did, thanks to you," Greer said.

"What can I do for you now?" Cindy asked.

"Um, well, I'm interested in doing . . . what would you call it? A title search? I need to find out who owns a piece of property I'm interested in for the film shoot."

"Film shoot?" Cindy turned from her monitor. "How exciting! So that's why you were looking for Eb?"

"Yup," Greer said. She leaned across the front counter. "It's supposed to be on the down-low. You know, sort of a not-so-secret secret."

Cindy nodded. "My lips are sealed. But I'm afraid you can't do a title search here. Property tax records are kept in the county courthouse, not here."

"Oh. Where's the courthouse?"

"It's in Ducktown. That's our county seat."

"And how far away is that?"

"Hmm. Depends on traffic."

Greer crinkled her brow in surprise. "Really?"

"Nah. Just kidding," Cindy said with a laugh. "The only time we have any traffic around here is when a log truck gets stuck on the railroad tracks. Ducktown's about fifteen minutes away from here. Straight down Ducktown Road."

Greer laughed at herself now. "Okay. So I guess I'll head down there."

"Exactly what property are you interested in? I've lived here all my life. Maybe I can help."

Greer leaned toward her and lowered her voice. "It's the old casino building. Your mayor told me the city has a long-term lease on it, but I need to know who owns it."

"Really? But that place is falling apart."

"That's exactly why it works for the movie," Greer confided. "That decrepit look fits right in with the plot."

"That's an easy one. The Littrells own the building. So I guess you'd need to talk to Vanessa."

"Does she live in Cypress Key?"

"Actually, she lives on Seahorse Key. That's a sort of island on the far south end of the island."

"She lives on her own private island?"

"There's a little causeway that goes over there, but yeah, I guess you'd say it's hers, since there aren't any other houses out there. As far as I know, the Littrells have owned Seahorse for, like, ever. I guess they've lived around here at least as long as the Thiba-deauxs."

"What can you tell me about this Vanessa Littrell?" Greer asked in her best conspiratorial tone.

"She's rich as sin, for one," Cindy said, wrinkling her nose in distaste. "The Littrells own almost as much stuff around here as the paper company. Vanessa was the only child, and her daddy's only brother died in Vietnam, so her daddy was sort of an only child."

"I take it you don't care for Vanessa."

"Does it show?" Cindy giggled. "We went all through school together, till her mama shipped her off to boarding school in Jacksonville her senior year of high school. Vanessa was always kind of snooty. Back then, she was nothing to look at. Kinda skinny. She had bad acne, and a real honker of a nose. My mama used to say Vanessa looked just like her daddy, 'bless her heart.' She never dated at all when she was in high school."

"And then?" Greer raised an eyebrow.

"When she came home from boarding school at Christmas break, she had bandages clear across her face. She told everybody she'd been in a bad car wreck and nearly died. Big surprise, when the bandages came off, she had the cutest brand-new little nose you've ever seen."

"And her popularity soared?" Greer asked.

"Oh yeah," Cindy said dryly. "When she

91

got home that summer before she went away to college, I think she dated every boy in town. Twice."

"Did she by any chance date Eb Thibadeaux?" Greer asked casually.

"Sure did," Cindy said. "All the girls in town were crazy for Eb."

"Including you?" Greer asked.

"I might have had a little bitty crush on him," Cindy admitted. "But I never would have had a chance with a big stud like Eb. So instead I went and fell for his dumb-ass cousin Butch. Big mistake. My mama talked till she was blue in the face, but I wouldn't listen. Married him instead of going to junior college."

"And in the meantime? Did Eb and Vanessa stick?"

"Oh no," Cindy said. "He had a full scholarship to engineering school up North somewhere. Maybe Purdue? And Vanessa went to Alabama, where she majored in sorority with a minor in beauty pageant."

"She sounds like a real piece of work."

"She is that," Cindy said. "Born rich, and got richer. She's been married a couple times, but she's been back here in Cypress Key for a couple years now, living at the Littrell home place on Seahorse. The thing I can't figure out is why."

"Why what?"

"Vanessa Littrell has enough money she

could live anywhere, do anything she wants. So why is she hanging out here in Podunky Cypress Key, Florida?"

"Maybe I'll just drive on over to Seahorse Key and ask her," Greer said. "But there is one more thing I need to see about here. The mayor says you're the one to talk to for a variance to build a guard shack and security gate for Bluewater Bay?"

Cindy nodded. "Do you mind if I ask why they need a security gate out there for Milo's empty houses?"

Greer just smiled. "Movie stuff."

"Ooh. Those are the nicest houses on the island. That must be where you're going to stash the stars, right?"

Greer winked. "Can't say."

"Fair enough," Cindy said. "You can't file for the request for the variance. It has to be the landowner. But you can tell Milo to call when he's ready for the permit. Shouldn't be any problem getting it done."

9

Greer had no trouble finding the causeway to Seahorse Key. Along the way, she took a call from Milo, the owner of the Bluewater Bay houses, who agreed to rent both furnished houses for the length of the movie shoot, and to start work immediately on getting the security gate erected.

"Just one thing, Miss Hennessy," he said, after they'd agreed to the deal. "These folks, they won't be having any of those wild Hollywood parties you hear about, right? I mean, I'll be glad to finally make a little bit of money off of 'em, but after your folks are gone, I need to be able to sell those houses. Which I can't do if they've been trashed. You understand what I mean?"

"Yes sir, I do," Greer said. "The director of the film only has about six weeks to get this movie shot on location before his star has to be available for another commitment. I seriously doubt he'll have time for any wild parties. Beyond that, we'll take out renters insurance on your houses, so if there were any damage, which there won't be, the insurance would take care of that."

"Fair enough," Milo said. "I'll have a cleaning service run out there this weekend and get both places spiffed up and ready before your folks come in."

She had a phone number for Vanessa Littrell, thanks to the city clerk, but Greer had already decided to pay a personal visit to Cypress Key's richest citizen. It was always her policy to do business face-to-face, and anyway, she found herself intensely curious about the woman.

Her Kia's air conditioner was no match for the heat of a swampy Gulf Coast late spring afternoon. Greer guessed the temperature was probably hovering in the nineties. She tilted the air vents toward her face and prayed she wouldn't look like a melted snow cone by the time she reached her destination.

This meeting could be the key to getting *Beach Town* made here. And if that happened, maybe her career could be resurrected. Her last job — the Paso Robles fire, all of that — would be forgotten, and forgiven. In Hollywood, you were only as good as your last job. This job — and *Beach Town* — would make people forget.

The causeway to Seahorse Key was actually nothing more than a narrow sandy road with a wooden trestle bridge crossing a tidal creek. Marshland lined both sides of the road, and once she'd crossed the bridge, a weathered sign announced she was on Seahorse Key.

She chose to ignore the PRIVATE PROPERTY–NO HUNTING signs, but it was hard to ignore the pair of large golden retrievers that ran alongside the Kia barking a nonstop alarm as she drove up to a sprawling house set in the shade of a grove of towering oak trees.

The main house was two stories high, constructed of silvery cedar planks and raised up on a foundation of white-painted brick. One-story wings sprouted at right angles to the main residence. The house reminded Greer of photos she'd seen of plantations in the Low Country of Georgia and South Carolina. The vibe was casual, moneyed elegance.

The woman walking toward her now, with a small white terrier tucked under one arm, gave off a similar vibe.

She was petite, with glossy dark hair in a chin-length bob, and the tank top, spandex shorts, and running shoes she wore obviously weren't just for show.

"Can I help you?" the woman called, a questioning expression on her face.

"Hi there," Greer said, staying by the Kia and gesturing toward the dogs, who though sitting, seemed to be on full alert, their ears quivering with intensity. "Are these guys friendly?"

"Depends on what you want," the woman said.

Gnats swarmed around Greer's face, and her face and neck were already slick with sweat. One of the dogs, the slightly larger of the two, emitted a low growl. The smaller one seemed intent on sniffing Greer's crotch.

"My name is Greer Hennessy, and I'm a film location scout. We're going to be filming a movie here in the next couple months, and if you're Vanessa Littrell, I'm interested in talking to you about the old casino."

"Here? On Seahorse Key?"

"Here, as in Cypress Key," Greer corrected herself.

"Luke! Owen!" Vanessa Littrell called sharply. "Here!"

The dogs happily trotted over to their mistress, who rewarded them each with head pats. "Come on inside then," she said, turning and walking toward the front door. The dogs and Greer trotted along behind her.

The interior of Vanessa Littrell's home was distinctly masculine. The dark wood floors were covered with worn Oriental rugs in reds and blues, and the sofa in the living room where she seated Greer was leather. The walls were paneled with knotty pine and dotted with sporting art, featuring paintings of dogs and horses and dead game. A portrait over the fireplace showed a handsome silver-haired man, holding a breached shotgun over his shoulder, with a hand poised on the head of a golden retriever that might have been a twin to the ones that now lolled at Vanessa Littrell's feet.

Greer wasted no time laying out her proposition.

"Your casino is a key location for this film. It's the right age and look. It's on a pier. It's as though the screenwriter wrote the film to go with your building."

"I see," Vanessa said, absentmindedly stroking the white dog she held in her lap. "And I'd like to help you, but at the moment the City of Cypress Key has a long-term lease on the building."

"Yes, the mayor told me that already," Greer said. "To be honest, I spoke to him first about leasing the casino, but when I told him the script calls for the building to be destroyed in an explosion, he made it very clear that he doesn't think it's in the city's best interest. Because it's a historic building."

Vanessa rolled her eyes. "That sounds like Eb, all right."

"I came out here to talk to you because I thought maybe, if you were interested, there could be a way to make this work, despite the mayor."

"If it were up to me, I'd say you can do whatever you want with the place," Vanessa said, frowning. "It's in deplorable condition, hasn't been used in three or four years, and honestly, it would probably take at least a million dollars in improvements — a million dollars the city doesn't have, by the way — to make it habitable again."

"But?" Greer asked.

"Eb Thibadeaux and a few busybodies in town have some pie-in-the-sky idea about making the casino into a community center. They've supposedly applied for some state and federal grants, but who in their right minds is going to hand this town a million bucks for improvements to a building the city doesn't even own?"

"You wouldn't consider selling it to the city?" Greer asked.

"The short answer is no. They don't have the money, anyway. Look, that's waterfront property. If it weren't for that damned crumbling white elephant of a casino, it would be prime for a mixed-use development. As it is — right now? It's worth zero."

"Except to the producers of this movie," Greer added. "You know, we'd actually pay *you* to let us blow it up."

"Suddenly, this is all very fascinating." Vanessa stood abruptly, setting the terrier on the floor. "Would you want to join me for a drink? It's five o'clock somewhere."

"Why not?"

"Stay!" Vanessa said sternly. Greer looked up, surprised.

"Not you," Vanessa said. She pointed at the terrier. "Stay, Izzy." The labs wagged their tails in united agreement.

Vanessa came back from the kitchen with a tarnished silver tray holding two heavy cut-glass tumblers, a bucket of crushed ice, a bottle of bourbon, and a pitcher of water. A plate held some sliced cheese and crackers.

"I'm out of white wine, and I don't care for beer," she told Greer, setting the tray on the coffee table. "Unless you like bourbon, I'm afraid you're out of luck." She poured a couple fingers of the amber liquid over ice in her own glass, and offered the bottle to Greer, who poured herself the same drink.

"Cheers." Vanessa took a sip and nodded at Greer. "I'm curious. Who told you I own the casino? Not Eb, I bet."

"Eb actually refused to tell me who owned it," Greer agreed. "It was Cindy, the town clerk, who suggested I come talk to you about the pier and the casino."

"Oh yes. Cindy Thibadeaux. We went to high school together. Not my biggest fan. I bet she told you about my nose job, right?"

Greer blushed.

"Ancient history," Vanessa assured her,

100

knocking her drink back in three gulps. "I get it. I was always the rich bitch in Cypress Key."

She poured herself another two fingers of bourbon and jiggled the ice in her glass. "When I was in school here, the cute, popular girls — Cindy and her crowd — they wouldn't give me the time of day because I had that hideous schnoz. And the guys wouldn't look twice because, well, I was friggin' ugly. Then, once I went away to boarding school and had dermabrasion and a nose job, the girls felt threatened and the guys were fascinated. I probably didn't do myself any favors, either, dating every guy who asked."

"Including Eb Thibadeaux," Greer said, swirling the bourbon in the thick cut-glass tumbler.

"Especially Eb," Vanessa said, with a sigh. She gave Greer an assessing look. "You're a pretty girl. You've probably been in a similar situation, where there's this one guy — the only one you think you want, and the only one who doesn't even know you're alive. So it's like a challenge — to make him want you."

Greer thought fleetingly of Sawyer, the improbable circumstances of their meeting, and how desperately in love with him she'd been, and how desperately unhappy she'd been almost the whole time they'd been together.

"Sometimes the one thing you want is the one thing that's no good for you," she said softly.

Without warning, the terrier jumped up into Greer's lap. She scratched Izzy's ears and the dog promptly rolled over onto its back. So she scratched its warm pink belly.

"Ah. I see you've been there too. Want to talk about it?" Vanessa asked, nibbling on a cracker and then washing it down with another generous gulp of whiskey.

She really didn't want to talk about her latest, greatest romantic failure, especially with a woman she'd just met, but if her heartbreak evinced some empathy from Vanessa Littrell, she would force herself to share a heavily edited version of the story.

"We met through work. Sawyer is an attorney, and different studios retain him when we're doing complicated leasing arrangements for location shoots. I fell hard for him, he fell indifferent."

Vanessa smiled ruefully. "Been there."

Greer scratched Izzy's throat and the dog gurgled in delight. "I travel a lot for my job — like, all the time — which means it was several months before I discovered he was cheating with me on his longtime girlfriend. I broke it off, he swore they were over, so I took him back. My best friend used to call him Ping-Pong Boy, because that's what our relationship was like. Every time I thought I was over him, he'd somehow charm his way back into my bed. And then he'd cheat on me. Most miserable, toxic relationship. Ever."

It was time to change the subject, Greer decided. Even a casual discussion of Sawyer Pratt made her feel dirty and degraded.

She looked around the room, appreciating the way the waning afternoon sun left streaks on the dark, polished floors. Izzy nudged her hand, to remind her that the dog had other territory that needed petting or scratching.

"Your home is lovely," she said, stroking the dog's ears.

"Lovely? Not sure that's the word I'd use for it," Vanessa said. She gestured at her surroundings. "My dad's been dead for years, but somehow I just haven't gotten around to redecorating."

"You've lived right here — your whole life?"

"Mostly. Except for both of my relatively brief, unhappy marriages." She held up a finger. "Husband number one was an architect in Birmingham. Well, he *said* he was. My folks supported us most of the time." She held up a second finger. "Husband number two was a stockbroker from Kansas City. Ha! My grandma knew more about picking stocks than that loser."

Vanessa pointed with her glass toward the portrait over the mantel. "Shoulda listened to dear old Dad and stayed single. Or just shacked up. Right? Who needs a cow when the milk is free?"

"I guess. But I'm probably no expert," Greer admitted.

"For real? You've never been married?"

"Nope." Greer took a swallow of bourbon, knowing it was already going to her head, but not caring. It had been a long week.

"Smart girl," Vanessa said, nodding her approval. "I tell ya, Gretta —"

"It's Greer."

"Right. Sorry. Anyway, in my wildest imagination, I never thought I'd end up back here in Cypress Key. It's pathetic — ya know?"

"If you dislike it so much, why live here? Your friend Cindy thinks you have enough money you could live anywhere you like."

Vanessa threw her head back and brayed at that notion, and the goldens lying on the carpet at her feet startled slightly.

"Everybody in this damn town knows so much about my business. Or thinks they do. What they don't realize is that none of the Littrells ever believed in selling land. Buying it? Oh, hell yeah. My father would go out to buy a six-pack, see a FOR SALE sign on a corner, and end up making a handshake deal to buy it. Even when it turned out the deal was a bad one, Dad would never just cut his losses and sell. Nosirreebob, not my old man. Consequently, I'm land rich and cash poor."

"But not . . . poverty-stricken poor," Greer suggested.

"No. I'm definitely not going hungry. But if I could just unload that damn casino, I would totally blow this town. For good."

"Really? You hate it here that much?"

Vanessa upended the bourbon bottle and emptied it into her glass. She tucked a strand of hair behind her left ear. "There is nothing left for me here," she said flatly. "My family's mostly gone. I have a few cousins on my mother's side, but we were never close. Friends? C'mon — do I look like the type to hang out at the Friday night fish fry at the fire station? You know what I do for fun? I work out. I run, or drive to Gainesville to play tennis with a couple of my old sorority sisters. And forget about dating. I've slept with all the eligible men in town, and honey, there's not a single one I'd let hang his jeans on my bedpost a second time."

She put an arm around each of the goldens and hugged them to her chest. "These guys are the only men in my life these days."

Vanessa released the dogs, then pulled herself slowly up from the leather armchair, stumbling a bit on the edge of a rug before steadying herself. "Wow." She grinned and held up the empty bottle. "There's more where this came from. You in?"

Greer put her half-empty glass back on the silver tray. "No, sorry. I've still got to drive back to the Silver Sands, and make some calls to the coast. My people are coming to town

Monday, and I've still got a lot of loose ends to tie up."

"You sure?" Vanessa asked, obviously disappointed. "It's Friday night. You don't necessarily have to go back to that dump hotel." She waved her arms expansively. "I've got plenty of room right here. You can have your own wing."

"Maybe a rain check," Greer said, moving toward the front door. Izzy followed along, nipping at her heels.

"Stop, Izz," Vanessa ordered. She scooped the dog up into her arms.

"But about the casino — I'm not giving up on that," Greer said. "If you're serious about wanting to let us demolish it for the film, I'll keep working on the mayor. Or maybe another member of the city council. There's got to be a way around Eb Thibadeaux."

Vanessa laughed that braying laugh, and Izzy barked. "So you're a schemer. Good. I like that in a woman."

10

She had a restless night. The room was a little cooler, but the air conditioner still rattled in the window, and although she'd sprayed the entire can of Ginny Buckalew's insecticide around the perimeter of the space, she awoke at least three times in the night, flailing her arms to ward off imaginary cockroaches.

At 7:15 a.m. she got up and, ignoring the tiny, cheap, one-cup machine on the bathroom vanity, went looking for coffee and food.

Greer walked a block up from the Silver Sands, and turned right on Pine Street. Cypress Key's main business thoroughfare was quiet this Saturday morning. A truck drove by, trailing a long, white fishing boat. The driver lifted one finger from the steering wheel in a casual wave. Greer nodded and kept walking.

She'd spotted the Coffee Mug the previous day, on her way to city hall. The lights were on inside, and she saw the back of a man sitting at a long counter.

Inside, she sat at the opposite end of the counter, placed her cell phone on the counter, and looked up at the menu scrawled on a wall-mounted blackboard. The waitress, a young woman barely out of her teens, wore jeans and a faded green Coffee Mug T-shirt. She stood poised with an outstretched pot of steaming coffee.

"Yes, please," Greer said, holding out the empty mug at her place.

The woman filled her cup. "Anything to eat this morning?"

"One egg, poached, over toast. Do you have multigrain bread?"

"We got white and we got wheat."

"Wheat, then."

"Bacon or sausage?"

"Bacon."

"Grits?"

"No thanks," Greer said quickly. "But do you have any fruit?"

"Nope, but I got some good-looking tomatoes I can slice up for you. Local grown, if you care about that stuff."

"I do," Greer said, surprised. "Tomatoes would be good."

Her food arrived ten minutes later. The egg was cooked nicely, the wheat toast was still warm, and the bacon was crisp and salty. The tomato slices were a deep, meaty red, the best Greer had eaten in a long time.

She hadn't had any real dinner the night before, settling for a bag of microwaved popcorn she'd picked up at a gas station convenience store on her way back from Seahorse Key.

While she ate, she leafed through a newspaper somebody had left on the counter.

The *Cypress Key Citizen* wasn't exactly the Sunday *New York Times.* It consisted of six pages. The front-page lead story was about the local high school cheerleading squad's thrilling third-place finish in something called the Sunshine State Cheer-off. It was accompanied by four photographs of the squad, and jumped to page three of the paper.

Right below the cheerleading story was a headline that promised *Major Hollywood Film Comes to Community.* But it was the sub-headline that made Greer want to slam her head down on the countertop.

HIP-HOP MEGAHIT KREGG WILL STAR, STAY IN CYPRESS KEY

Informed officials confirmed to *The Citizen* this week that a big-budget movie will be filmed in and around Cypress Key in the coming weeks, bringing millions of dollars of revenue — along with Grammy Award–winning pop vocalist Kregg, who will make his acting debut in the as-yet unnamed movie.

In an exclusive interview with *The Citizen,* Cypress Key Mayor Eb Thibadeaux confirmed Friday that a California-based location scout has been in the community this week, making arrangements for the film, which is expected to start shooting next week.

"We look forward to working with the production company and have been promised that Cypress Key will be prominently featured in the film," Thibadeaux said. He added that many of the cast and crew members will stay at the Silver Sands Motel, which was chosen because of its beachfront location and luxury accommodations.

"Luxury my ass," Greer muttered, pushing aside her empty plate in order to turn the page.

In addition, *The Citizen* has learned that the film scout, Greer Hennessy, of Los Angeles, has leased two homes in the exclusive Bluewater Bay subdivision, where the movie's producer-director, Oscar-nominated Bryce Levy, and his young star, Kregg, will live during the filming. Sources confirmed exclusively that work has already begun on a security gate and guardhouse at the entrance to the subdivision.

"Dammit." Greer shoved her coffee mug so

hard it splashed coffee all over the page. "So much for secrecy."

She heard a buzzing, and the screen of her phone lit up. The caller's number and area code were not ones she recognized. She hesitated, then pushed the Connect button.

"Hello?" she said warily.

"Hi. Is this Greer Hennessy?"

"It is," Greer said. "Who is this?"

"Hi, Greer. This is Cathryn Mitchell with *Entertainment Weekly's* Atlanta bureau. We understand you're down in Florida — in a place called Cypress Key — is that correct? I was wondering when you expect Kregg and his people to arrive down there for your upcoming project?"

Greer felt her face flush. "What's your name again? And how did you get this number?"

"Cathryn Mitchell. Spelled with a Y. You know how this business works, we have sources. Speaking of sources, I'm looking at an Associated Press story quoting the mayor of Cypress Key as confirming that shooting starts next week, and that Kregg is definitely lined up to star, with Bryce Levy set to produce and direct. Can you tell me who the female lead is? Help me out here, okay?"

"No way." Greer clicked the Disconnect button.

Her phone rang again, and the caller ID panel listed a number with an L.A. area code.

She let it go to voice mail. She didn't need to know who called. It would be another reporter — *Variety, The Hollywood Reporter,* the *L.A. Times.* Didn't matter which, because she didn't intend to speak to any of them.

The waitress hurried over to mop up the spilled coffee and refill her cup.

She gestured at the newspaper's ruined front page. "I guess you saw the big news, huh? We're fixing to have a movie made here. Hey. Maybe Kregg will come in here for breakfast. I mean, we're the only place in town open for breakfast, so there's a good chance, right?"

"Right," Greer said.

As if.

"I hear sometimes they hire extras when they make movies. That'd be a blast, wouldn't it, being in a movie with Kregg? My girlfriend and me, last year drove all the way down to Miami to see him in concert. We paid two hundred dollars apiece for those tickets, and you know what? If I had the money, I'd do it again in a heartbeat. He is one fine-looking dude. Know what I mean?"

"Mmm-hmm," Greer said, trying to sound noncommittal.

"I know right where that house is at where he's stayin'," the waitress continued. "Me and my old boyfriend used to kinda break into those houses and, uh, you know. . . ."

To forestall any more alarming confidences, Greer grabbed the check, tucked a five-dollar bill under her plate, and darted toward the door. She couldn't wait to track down Eb Thibadeaux and chew him out for spilling the beans about the upcoming movie shoot.

Her cell phone rang just as she stepped out onto the curb. A glance at the caller ID screen told her she wouldn't need to wait to blast the mayor — because it was the mayor calling.

"You!" she said accusingly. "You just had to go and talk to the damn press, didn't you? Couldn't wait to blab the news about Kregg."

"Where are you?" Eb Thibadeaux asked. "I knocked on your door just now. If you'll let me explain —"

"I just left the Coffee Mug," Greer said, her voice icy. "The waitress there knows exactly where Kregg is staying. Apparently, everybody in town knows now too. And not just people in Cypress Key. A reporter from *Entertainment Weekly* called too. The story is on the newswires, which means it's everywhere."

"Let's not do this over the phone, okay? Are you headed back to the motel?"

"You mean to the luxurious Silver Sands? Yes. I'll be there in five minutes, but I doubt anything you can say is going to change my opinion of you as a double-crossing blabbermouth."

"I don't give a goddamn about your opinion of me," he said heatedly. "But I would like the opportunity to clear the air."

"Whatever."

She clicked the Disconnect button and accelerated her pace from stroll to stride. While she walked, her phone continued to ring, until she finally turned it off.

Eb was standing outside of the Silver Sands office when she got back to the motel. He was dressed as he'd been the first time she'd seen him, when she mistook him for a maintenance worker — sweat-soaked white T-shirt, cargo shorts, running shoes. He had what looked like a two-day growth of beard, and an expression of barely contained rage.

"We can talk in my office," he said, pointing down the breezeway.

The door of a room opened, and a mother shepherded out two small children dressed in bathing suits and smeared with white sunblock. "Why don't we just talk out here?" Greer said loudly. "You don't seem to have a problem with oversharing. Why not let all six other guests here in on the source of our disagreement?"

The mother shot them an anxious glance, then hurried her children off in the opposite direction.

Eb clenched and unclenched his jaw. "Can we please just have a rational discussion in

114

my office?"

The door to the Thibadeaux Realty office was open, so she marched in and found herself a seat. The mayor launched himself into the remaining chair, behind a large wooden desk.

He leaned across the desk and looked Greer squarely in the face. "I'll tell you again. I had nothing to do with that story. The reporter called me repeatedly yesterday, and I purposely did not return her calls. Finally, she did what you did. She tracked me down — at the grocery store. There was no way to escape her."

"So you say," Greer replied, crossing her arms over her chest. "And yet, this morning, I read all about it in the local newspaper."

The room got very quiet. His gray eyes narrowed. "Are you calling me a liar?"

"I'm saying you've made it clear from the start that you wanted nothing to do with having a film made here, and now you've conveniently managed to sabotage it by leaking confidential information about the project," Greer said, feeling the heat rising in her face.

"I leaked nothing. The reporter already knew all the details when she called me. Including which houses you'd rented."

"But you didn't try to scare her off the story, right? No way you could just tell her she had her facts wrong? You just had to be a big shot and comment. . . ."

"Despite what you think, I'm not in the habit of lying. To anybody, for any purpose," Eb said. "She asked me point blank if what she had was factual. I asked her not to run the story, and I explained that you and your people had real security concerns about Kregg. I even hinted that if she went ahead with the story it could actually jeopardize chances that the movie will get made. Which, apparently, made her all the more eager to run with the story."

"Well, if you didn't tell this reporter, who did?" Greer asked.

"I don't know," he said sharply "Word travels fast. And you've talked to a lot of people locally. The chief of police, Milo, the clerk's office . . ."

"I swore all of them to secrecy," Greer said, knowing it sounded lame.

"And they probably turned right around and swore somebody else to secrecy too — and that's how the coconut telegraph works on a small island."

Greer took a deep breath. "So. I guess maybe I owe you an apology?"

"I guess," Eb said. "But what would be better is if, since you're apparently going to be around town for the next six weeks or so, you didn't treat me like your sworn enemy."

"I don't think that," Greer said. "It's just — I've got a job to do, and frankly, I could lose my job over a leak like this — and I can't afford to lose a job right now. Especially this one. Nothing personal, you know?"

"Of course not," Eb said. The phone on his desk rang, and he peered down at the digital screen and sighed. "This is the *Tampa Bay Times.* I think maybe I'll just let it roll over to voice mail."

11

Greer's phone was still blowing up with calls, text messages, and e-mails — all from the media, all wanting details about Kregg's participation in *Beach Town.* She ignored all of them — until Bryce Levy called, or rather, CeeJay called to warn her that Bryce would be calling.

As usual, her best friend got right down to business. "Girl — are you nuts? Leaking the fact that Kregg signed to do Bryce's movie?"

Greer felt the heat rising in her cheeks. This was it. Bryce was using CeeJay to do his dirty work. Probably her replacement was already on the way to Florida right now. If she lost this job, it really would be all over.

"You know me better than that," Greer said. "I told maybe three people, all of whom were definitely on a need-to-know basis, including the police chief and the mayor. Somebody talked — I'm not sure who, but the mayor swears he wasn't the one, and I'm inclined to believe him. Cypress Key is this tiny little flyspeck of a place. This is the biggest thing to hit the town since the last big hurricane. It's impossible to keep secrets here."

"Well, somebody started a real shit storm," CeeJay said. "And Bryce is not happy. He's had the media calling his office all day. And, of course, Kregg's manager went ballistic when the media started calling him. He even threatened to pull out of the movie."

"He can't really do that, can he?"

"Nah. Bryce has him under contract, and anyway, his manager knows this is a great start for Kregg's transition from music to movies. The guy's just blowing smoke, I think."

"Oh God. You don't think Bryce is gonna fire me, do you? I need this job, CeeJay."

"I think he just needs to blow off some steam," CeeJay said. "He's not gonna pull you off the project before it even really gets under way. Just tell him what you told me. I already told him there's no way you would have deliberately let the cat out of the bag. He'll probably yell and raise hell with you, and that'll be it."

"Hope so."

"You leave him to me," CeeJay said. "I gotta get back to packing. Did I tell ya, when we get back from Florida, Bryce wants me to move into the big house with him?"

"That's great, CeeJay. Out of the garage

119

apartment and into the house. I guess that means things are going good between the two of you?"

"I hate to jinx it, but yeah, things are great. His ex has a new boyfriend, so she's kind of taking a break from squeezing his balls, which is nice."

"Has he filed for divorce yet?"

Silence.

"CeeJay?"

"Look. You know how messed up legal shit is. His ex wants to clean him out and take half of everything. It's ridiculous that he should have to fork over a pile of money to that bitch. You know she's never had a job? In, like, ever? All she does all day is go to yoga and shop. Bryce's lawyers are trying to figure out how to keep her from taking him to the cleaners. It takes time. Right?"

"I guess."

"Don't use that tone with me, young lady."

Greer laughed. "I'm not judging. I just want you to be happy. You deserve somebody wonderful, who wants to be with you. That's all I'm sayin'."

"Quit worrying about me. I can take care of myself. You hear? I am happy. Bryce is amazeballs. We are going to make a kick-ass movie and all will be well. See you Monday, right?"

"Right."

■ ■ ■ ■

She waited all day for the other shoe to drop. Finally, since it was Saturday night and she was weary of microwaved popcorn and take-out pizza, she decided to treat herself to a real dinner — at what Ginny promised was the best restaurant in town.

For the first time all week, Greer took some pains with her appearance. She blew her hair dry to straighten out some of the curl and applied a bit of brown eyeliner and mascara. Most of the clothes she'd packed were strictly utilitarian — jeans and T-shirts, some capris and tank tops, but she had thought to throw a dress in her suitcase.

It was an old dress of her mother's, actually. Greer had liberated the Mexican cotton wedding dress while sorting through her mother's clothes. Most of Lise's clothes had been too flashy for Greer's taste, but there was something endearing about the simplicity of this piece.

The dress, a seventies throwback, was a fine white cotton minidress with a scooped, drawstring neckline, hand-embroidered bodice, and loose, bell-shaped sleeves. She added a string of turquoise and coral beads she'd picked up during a shoot in Santa Fe, and some turquoise and silver drop earrings, and slid her feet into a pair of leather sandals.

She set out to walk to the Cypress Key Inn, feeling oddly self-conscious in the short dress and jewelry.

Saturday night was apparently the hot night in town. Cars and trucks lined Pine Street, and diners sat at tables on the sidewalk in front of the pizza parlor. She heard the heavy bass thump of music coming from a place called the Crow's Nest, which, by the looks of the Harleys parked out front, constituted the local biker bar, and through the open door at Castaways she saw young families waiting to be seated for the chalkboard-advertised seafood buffet.

The scent of shrimp boil drifted on to the sidewalk. An older-model sedan rolled slowly past on the street, and a horn honked, followed by a low wolf whistle.

She allowed herself a small, secret smile, then walked a little faster.

The Cypress Key Inn was a white two-story wood-frame building with a wraparound porch furnished with wide-bottomed rocking chairs, wicker settees, and huge, leafy ferns. A pair of gas lanterns marked the front door, and Greer was charmed even before she walked inside.

The hotel lobby was dimly lit, but she could make out dark varnished wood floors, white plank walls, and a few pieces of ornate Victorian furniture. Behind the high-topped reception desk a staircase curved upward to the second floor. It looked like a movie set — in fact, it would be perfect for the film, and she wondered why she hadn't found this place earlier.

An elaborately carved bar stretched along one side of the lobby, and every stool was full. Sitting in the stool right in the center, looking up at the wall-mounted television showing a baseball game, was Eb Thibadeaux.

Greer stepped neatly into the dining room, hoping to avoid another encounter with Cypress Key's mayor.

There was a hostess stand located a few feet inside the door. The blond girl manning the stand was naturally pretty, but she'd given herself the dramatic Katy Perry eye makeup treatment in a failed attempt to make herself look older. Despite the navy shadow, the shiny black eyeliner, and the short, sleeveless black dress, it was obvious that she couldn't have been more than eighteen.

"Dinner?" the girl asked, gazing over Greer's shoulder to see if she had a date.

"Yes, please. Table for one."

The girl frowned and looked down at the open book on her stand before glancing into the dining room just beyond the doorway. The room held a dozen or so tables, and at least three were vacant. But the tables were candlelit, with pale pink starched tablecloths and small vases of flowers, and the diners were dressed up, for Cypress Key, which meant collared shirts for the men, a scattered few sport coats, and dresses on the women.

"Do you have a reservation?"

"No. Do I need one?"

"Not really. I'm just supposed to ask, because it sounds fancier." The girl giggled, grabbed a menu, and motioned for Greer to follow.

She seated her at a table on the enclosed porch, by a window. "How's this?"

"Great."

The girl looked around for a moment. "Okay, um, well, we're kind of shorthanded tonight. Do you want something to drink?"

Greer scanned the abbreviated wine list and ordered what she hoped was a safe choice — the house white — then went back to reading the menu.

"Everything's really good," the hostess offered. "Like, the grouper came off a boat just a little while ago, so it's fresh, and so is the redfish, but it's kind of spicy. The fried shrimp is my favorite, but some people like the linguine with clam sauce. We farm the clams locally, you know. And uh, well, you can always get the chicken or a steak. We only have one special tonight, the soft-shell crabs. They're sautéed in butter and wine, and served over potatoes and some kind of spinach stuff."

"Soft-shell crabs," Greer said quickly.

Her food arrived, and she had to agree with the recommendation that the Inn actually did have the best food in town. In fact, it was the best she'd had in a long time. She nibbled at her salad, sipped her wine, and savored the sweet crabmeat and buttery, salty potatoes.

The room began to clear out, and soon, even though it was barely nine o'clock, Greer realized she was the only diner still eating. But she was determined not to cut short her only night out on the town.

She glanced out the window at the alley just outside and spied the young hostess.

The girl was standing under a streetlight, having what looked like a fairly heated conversation with a young man who looked about her age.

He was muscular looking, tanned, with short, spiky dark hair and dressed in a white T-shirt, navy baseball pants, and cleats, and to Greer's eyes it looked like he and the girl were having a fight. At one point he grabbed the girl's arm, but she quickly wrested it away from him.

There was another sharp exchange and the girl stalked off, while the baseball player stood for a moment, watching her go.

"Young love," Greer murmured, returning to her dinner.

She was just finishing up her crab when a

shadow fell over the table. Eb Thibadeaux stood looking down at her.

"I thought that was you," Eb Thibadeaux said.

"Yep," Greer agreed. "It's me."

"I just finished dinner at the bar," he said, glancing at her nearly empty plate. "You had the soft-shells? Great choice."

"Best ever," Greer said. She was feeling surprisingly mellow — maybe because of the wine, maybe because she'd finally had a decent dinner. "Care to join me?" she asked. "If I can manage to flag down the waitress, I'm going to get coffee."

"I'll get her," he said, and turning toward the hostess stand, he called, "Allie?"

The waitress hustled over to the table, her face flushed.

"Hi, Uncle Eb."

"Could you bring the lady a cup of coffee? And I'll have a Fat Tire, okay?"

"No problem," the girl said.

Greer watched her speed in the direction of the bar.

"That's your niece? Allie?"

"Yep, that's our Allie."

"Pretty girl," Greer said.

"Too pretty." He frowned.

"Probably has a lot of boyfriends, huh?"

"Just one that I know of."

"The baseball player? I saw them a minute ago, standing outside. It looked like they were

126

having words."

"Great," Eb said, looking gloomy. "Now she'll be in one of her moods all week. Bart's not a bad kid. He's the catcher on the high school team. And a senior, which I'm not crazy about. Allie's a year younger."

Allie arrived back at the table, carefully placing Eb's beer on the table in front of him and a cup of coffee at Greer's place.

"Thanks, kiddo," Eb said. "Kind of quiet tonight, huh?"

Allie nodded. "If nobody else shows up in the next fifteen minutes, Rebecca says I can go ahead and clock out."

"You going out with Bart tonight?"

"No way," she said scornfully. "I'll probably just go hang out over at Tristin's house for a while." She paused. "If that's okay with you."

Eb gave his niece an appraising look. "Are Tristin's parents home tonight? I can call and check, you know."

Allie rolled her eyes and gave a dramatic sigh. "God! Yes, they're home. You can call and check all you like. Jeez. It was just that one time. Can you please cut me some slack?"

"Yeah. I'll cut you some slack when you're twenty-one," Eb said.

The girl scowled, then flounced away.

"God help me, she looks just like Amanda when she does that," Eb said softly, shaking his head.

"Amanda. Is that her mom?"

"Afraid so." He sipped his beer.

"And is Amanda your sister?"

"Thankfully, no." He set his glass down abruptly. "As screwed up as the Thibadeaux family is, I'm proud to say that Amanda is not blood kin. She's my sister-in-law. Well, ex."

Allie was back.

"Okay, Rebecca says she'll close everything down, so I'm going over to Triss's now. A bunch of other girls are coming too, and we're going to sleep over. Triss's mom says it's all right with her. And you can call her if you don't believe me."

"Don't worry, I will," Eb said. "And if Chief Bottoms sees any carloads of girls joyriding around town in a certain red Camaro, she knows to call me, too. Understand?"

"Whatever," Allie rolled her eyes again, then leaned in and gave her uncle a quick peck on the cheek. "G'night, boss man."

12

Greer studied Eb Thibadeaux over the rim of her coffee cup. He still needed a shave, but tonight he was somewhat dressed up, and he looked, she allowed, fairly presentable in a pale blue oxford cloth button-down shirt with rolled-up sleeves and navy slacks. She'd noticed when he walked that he wore loafers but no socks. This, she guessed, was the equivalent of black tie in Cypress Key.

He appeared to be studying her too.

"You look kinda nice tonight," he offered.

"Was that a compliment? It sounded semi-complimentary."

"It was definitely a compliment. I like your dress. You've got good legs, you know?

Greer tugged self-consciously at her hem and decided to change the subject.

"Do you mind if I ask where Allie's parents are?"

"I don't mind. Like I said, Jared, my brother, and Amanda are divorced. They split up years ago. I'm not real sure where Amanda is these days. Her folks are both dead. She drifts in and out of town, and sees Allie when it suits her. To tell you the truth, I think Allie's a little bit relieved when her mom isn't around."

"And Jared?"

"Jared." He took a long drink of beer.

"My older brother Jared is currently a guest of the State of Florida at the Starke correctional institution."

"Oh." Common sense, or decency, suggested she should drop this line of questioning. But now she was curious. And Eb didn't seem disinclined to shut her down. "That's a prison?"

"It is. If you're inclined to visit, it's in the northeast corner of the state. But I'm going to guess the state isn't going to encourage you to scout it for a movie location."

"Nope. Usually we only shoot at abandoned prisons. And then we blow them up."

"Touché." He smiled. "Would you like to know what Jared's in for? That's what everybody wants to know."

"If you don't mind telling me."

"I don't mind," Eb said. "Jared is currently incarcerated for possession with intent to distribute Schedule II narcotics."

"Oh."

"He was running a pill mill," Eb said abruptly. "OxyContin, Percocet, Darvocet. Whatever kind of pocket rockets you wanted, my big brother was happy to prescribe."

Greer's eyes widened. "He was a doctor?"

"No, but he was good at pretending. Jared graduated from an offshore medical school in Spain, did some kind of residency in the British Virgin Islands, but never quite managed to pass his boards in the States. Which never stopped him from practicing medicine."

Eb tapped the side of his half-empty beer glass. "He's quite a resourceful guy, my brother."

She was at a loss for words. "I hear there's a big black market for pain pills. It's quite a racket back in California."

"It's quite a racket in Florida, too," Eb said. "Big business, baby. Which is why hucksters like Jared get into it."

"But if he never passed his state boards, how did he get certified to practice medicine?"

"He was never certified. After he failed his state boards a second time, Jared was working as an EMT in Jacksonville. By that time, he and Amanda were split up. She had custody of Allie and was still living in Cypress Key, but Jared had bigger plans. In Jacksonville he met a guy — I think he was officially an ear, nose, and throat doc who was up for charges up North somewhere. Some kind of sexual harassment thing. They hooked up, and this doc suggested that they become partners in a promising new enterprise. They opened a string of these 'pain clinics' in small towns in north Florida — places where they figured the local cops weren't sophisticated enough to figure out what they were up to."

"And they got caught," Greer said.

"Yes they did. The local cops might not have noticed, but a couple of pharmacists got suspicious about the number of controlled substance scrips being written by these little clinics. They tipped off the FDLE, that's the Florida Department of Law Enforcement, and the FDLE sent in a couple of undercover narcs, who visited Jared and his buddy and made it plain they were looking to score Oxy. Bam! Now Jared is looking fine in an orange jumpsuit."

"And you're raising his daughter."

"Well. Ginny and I are raising her. It takes a village, you know. Or so I hear."

"She seems like a nice girl," Greer said.

"Allie's great. Got her head on straight, despite her screwed-up parents, which is a major miracle. She makes pretty good grades in school, and she's been waitressing since she was fifteen, trying to save up for her first car."

"How did you happen to become her guardian? Her grandparents aren't in the picture anymore?"

"Like I said, Amanda's parents are gone. My folks are both retired and in their seventies. They live in one of those retirement villages near Ocala. Dad has Alzheimer's, and there's no way my mom could handle a teenager. So that leaves me and Ginny."

He smiled. "Poor girl."

"You can't be doing that bad a job. You said yourself she's a good kid, works hard, and makes decent grades. How long have you had her?"

He considered the question. "She's seventeen now, and she came to live with Gin and me when she was thirteen, I guess. Nearly four years. It's not always hearts and flowers. I wouldn't wish a teenage girl on my worst enemy."

"And yet?" The question hung in the air.

"She has her moments," Eb admitted. He looked around the empty dining room and spotted the manager, Rebecca, counting out the cash register. He motioned to her and she came over.

"Rebecca, is it too late for another beer for me?" He glanced at Greer. "You want another coffee? Or some kind of after-dinner drink?"

"I can do that," Rebecca said. Turning to Greer, she asked, "Anything?"

"Maybe a sambuca?"

"Be right back," Rebecca said.

While they were waiting for their drinks, Eb tried to analyze why he was feeling this nagging attraction for Greer Hennessy, who was already becoming a major annoyance in his life.

She was beautiful, yes, but not in an obvious way. He liked her thick mane of curly, dark blond hair, especially the way she was wearing it tonight, falling loose around her shoulders. She had wide, intelligent brown eyes that seemed to take in everything, a generous mouth, and a genuine smile. Greer wasn't a fussy girly-girl but she knew how to dress, and he especially liked the way her skin glowed against the white cotton dress she was wearing tonight, and the way the loosely tied drawstring neckline kept slipping dangerously off her shoulder.

Their drinks arrived, along with their checks. Greer handed Rebecca her credit card, and Eb sat back in his chair and stretched out his legs. "So. You've heard enough of my dysfunctional family history. Tell me about you. How'd a nice girl like you get in a racket like this? I mean, movie location scout — is that something you study in college?"

"On this project I'm actually location manager as well as scout. I guess you could say it's a job I was born to do."

"How's that?"

"I grew up in L.A. Which is still very much a company town. I'm the third generation in my family to be in the business. My grandmother started out as a bit player in the late forties and ended up working as a seamstress in studio costume departments. My mom was an actress, mostly television."

"And your father?" Eb asked. "Was he in the business too?"

Her smile dimmed a little. "I guess. He was a stuntman. But my mother was the one who pushed me into the business. One day she mentioned that they were looking for a location to shoot a scene at her character's kid's school, and I volunteered to get the principal of my elementary school to allow them to shoot in our cafeteria. I got paid a hundred dollar finder's fee. After that, I was hooked."

"You were never interested in acting? You're certainly pretty enough."

"Thanks, but no, I'm not pretty enough. Just pretty doesn't cut it in the business. You've got to be beautiful. The camera has to love you. And you have to love it back. Seeing how hard my mom had to work at *getting* work over the years, and then worrying about aging? That life never appealed to me."

"Would I have heard of your mom? I mean, is she famous?"

"She certainly thought so," Greer said wryly. "She died a couple months ago. Her name was Lise Grant. She played the mom for a couple seasons in an eighties sitcom called *The Neighborhood Menace.*"

Eb scrunched up his face, searching his memory bank. "Sorry. About your mom and the fact that I don't think I ever saw her show."

"Thanks," Greer said. "I guess I got my real start ten years ago, working as a production assistant on a music video shoot."

"Which is what?"

"A P.A. is a glorified gofer. They do whatever needs doing, from fetching coffee to driving another crew member to running errands. The pay is crap, but you meet a lot of people, and if you're willing to do anything, and work under any circumstances, you can work your way up the ladder. That's what I did, and that's how I ended up here in Cypress Key, scouting for *Beach Town*."

"You never really told me exactly how you found us," Eb reminded her. "We're not exactly on the beaten path."

"Sometimes I just get a vibe for a place and I know it's right. And when I drove into Cypress Key and saw the pier, and the casino, I knew."

"Are you and Vanessa Littrell now conspiring against me?"

"I wouldn't call it a conspiracy," Greer said, choosing her words carefully. "Let's just say we agree that you're all wrong on the matter of the casino. Seriously wrong. The city isn't using the place, and face it, it's crumbling, even as we speak. But if you'll allow us to use it for the film we'll pay you enough in fees that you'll be able to get a start on a new

136

building on the city's own land. One that people can actually use."

"And how do you know so much about the condition of the casino?"

"I've studied it with binoculars. Seen all the seagulls perching on the roof, which is damaged and sagging badly, and anybody can see several of the windows are busted out. The place is structurally unsound and you know it."

"Bullshit," he said, and the wooden chair squeaked as he shifted his weight to lean forward. "You've been in there, haven't you?"

"Who me?"

"There are NO TRESPASSING signs posted all over the place. If you broke in there, you're breaking the law."

"Who says I broke in?" Greer sipped her sambuca and tried to look innocent.

"You must have, otherwise you wouldn't know what kind of shape the casino is in. C'mon. Fess up."

"Only if you swear not to have me arrested," Greer retorted.

He raised both hands in a surrender gesture.

"Swear it," Greer said. "On your honor, as the mayor."

"I swear I won't have your cute butt arrested and thrown in the pokey."

"I *might* have figured a way to take a tour of the casino," Greer admitted. "It's a beautiful old building. Such a shame for it to sit there, boarded up. How old is it, exactly?"

"Construction started in the teens but stopped when the first builder went bust. Finally, Manning Littrell — he was Vanessa's great-grandfather — finished it and opened it for business in 1923."

"Was it actually a gambling casino? I didn't know gambling was ever legal in Florida."

"It wasn't that kind of casino," Eb explained. "That was just a popular term during the time. It was originally a dance hall. Littrell brought in bands of the era for weekly dances and parties, and people came to Cypress Key from all over to dance. The rumor is that, during Prohibition, Chicago mobsters shipped hooch in here from Cuba and you could buy it under the counter. The casino was really big with servicemen during the war years, when guys home from leave would go to meet girls. In the fifties, the Littrells added a bowling alley on the second floor, but there was a big hurricane a few years later that literally blew the roof off the place, and they never rebuilt the top floor. Later on, in the sixties and seventies, rock bands played there. My parents actually met at there at a Tams concert. At some point in the seventies, Vanessa's parents turned it into a roller rink. And eventually it morphed into a bingo parlor and then, when the city leased it, a senior center."

"If it's such a big part of the city's history, why close it?" Greer asked.

"The roof," Eb said. "When the Littrells removed the second story, they just slapped a new roof on the first floor and called it a day. Over the years, other roofs were added on top of the original one. Now you've got fifty years' worth of roofs and fifty years' worth of saltwater intrusion from storms, and sagging, compromised ceiling beams, not to mention mold issues in the old stucco walls. The casino is structurally unsafe. That's why it's closed."

"Vanessa says you've applied for grants to restore the casino. Even though you don't own it? What are the chances you could get any grant money? I mean, wouldn't it cost millions to restore? Again, why not just make money on it while you can?"

"You mean, why not just give up the lease and let Vanessa Littrell tear down the casino so it can be redeveloped?" Eb brushed his hair back from his forehead.

"Look, Greer, I can't bring you up to speed in a few minutes on what amounts to a decades-long fight between the city and the Littrell family. But I can tell you that Vanessa Littrell cares only about herself — and the bottom line. We've had a feasibility study done, and we firmly believe there's a good chance the city will win enough grant money to buy the pier and the casino — and restore it to what it should be. But that's not what Vanessa wants. She wants to sell out to the highest bidder and make a quick buck and be done with it. And that's not in the community's best interest. No matter what she tells you."

He pushed his half-empty beer across the table and reached for his billfold.

"Hey," Greer said. "You don't have to get all mad about it. It's just that I happen to disagree with you about the casino. This could be a win for everybody."

Eb was counting out bills. "Don't take this the wrong way, but the answer is still no. The casino is a historically sensitive building. As long as I'm mayor, I'm going to protect it any way I can."

"And I'm going to try to find a way around you, any way I can," Greer said. "And I warn you, I can be very, very persuasive when I need to be. That said, it's been nice chatting with you tonight. And I enjoyed meeting your niece." She smiled her pretty, deliberately disarming smile and walked out of the dining room.

Eb watched her leave. Greer Hennessy was disruptive and annoying, and she had just announced that she had every intention of fighting him tooth and nail. So why was he already regretting he hadn't found an excuse to pick another fight with her — just to prolong the evening?

13

On Monday afternoon, Greer stood on Main Street at 2:23 p.m., anxiously shifting from one foot to the other, alternating between staring at her phone, willing it to ring, and watching the street, wondering if Bryce Levy and his colleagues had somehow managed to get lost after leaving the Gainesville airport three hours earlier.

It wasn't cool to be this apprehensive. She shouldn't be this apprehensive. How many films had she worked on over the years? What was there to worry about? Oh yeah. Only everything.

The call from Bryce that she'd been dreading had never come. She'd had an early-morning text from CeeJay, telling her they were about to board the flight from L.A., but that was all she knew.

She turned around again and examined the dusty plate glass window of the empty storefront she'd rented for the *Beach Town* production offices. According to Eb Thibadeaux, the space had last been used as a bookstore, a business called Tiny Tales, "back when people in Cypress Key had money to buy books."

The interior had pinkish-tan faux wood-grain paneling, a dropped ceiling of yellowed ceiling tiles, chipped linoleum floors, and zero aesthetic appeal. But, due to some fevered efforts on Greer's part, it did have two dozen rented desks and chairs, two working bathrooms, Wi-Fi, lots and lots of electrical and phone outlets, a brand-new copy machine, and most importantly, a three-hundred-dollar espresso machine.

Its most attractive asset was its huge dedicated parking lot in the rear of the building, a lot that would hold all the tractor trailers necessary for the movie's base camp.

"C'mon, c'mon," she muttered under her breath. Time was short. Bryce's most recent e-mail had made this clear. This afternoon his agenda included tours of all the locations, including a boat ride on the Choklawassee, a meeting with the town council, and in between, back-to-back production meetings.

Finally, a gleaming black Lincoln Navigator came into sight, trailing two more identical Navigators in its wake.

Greer waved frantically. The lead Navigator's headlights blinked. She inhaled sharply. The circus had come to town.

Bryce climbed down from the driver's seat of the Navigator. It was the first time she'd seen him since their top-secret meeting at the Brentwood mansion. Back in L.A. he'd looked like a successful businessman. For the Florida trip he'd gone rockabilly casual, with black snakeskin cowboy boots, worn blue jeans, a black pearl-snap Western-style shirt, and Ray-Ban Wayfarers. CeeJay's influence, Greer was sure.

He stood, stretched, did a 360-degree turn, taking in all of Cypress Key's historic downtown in one panoramic view. The Navigator's passenger-side door opened and CeeJay stepped out, wearing a black tank top and skinny black jeans. Her hair was stuffed under a black denim newsboy cap, and she clutched a huge Starbucks cup in her right hand.

"Greer!" Bryce folded her into a bear hug, then held her at arm's length. "This place is great," he said, beaming. "I can already feel it. It's great."

Greer felt her stomach unknot just a little. "Hope so," she said.

Greer was at the wheel of Bryce's Navigator. Bryce was in the passenger seat, with Stephen, the production designer, and Alex, the art director, in the rear seats. CeeJay was wedged in between the two men in the back.

Greer steered the Navigator slowly down Main, pointing out the coffee shop, the Cypress Key Inn, city hall, and the bars.

"Love it," Alex whispered, pressing his face to the glass. "It just reeks of failure and desperation."

Greer pressed her lips together and said nothing. *Failure and desperation? Not exactly a chamber of commerce promotional pamphlet.*

"The moral decay is a palpable presence here," Bryce agreed. "It reminds me of, oh, what's the film? Stephen? You know, Bogdanovich's masterpiece?"

"You mean *Last Picture Show*?" The production designer nodded emphatically.

"That's it!" Bryce said.

"Absolutely," Alex said. "If only we could shoot in black-and-white."

"Never get away with it," Bryce said. "But it would be fabulous. Maybe we could manage a black-and-white trailer?"

An hour later, after stops at the boatyard, the Silver Sands Motel, and the adjacent beach, Greer parked the Navigator in back of the store.

"I've lined up a charter captain to take you guys down the Choklawassee in an hour," Greer told Bryce. "There are a couple of small keys, owned by the state, that we can use for the island scenes, but since I still haven't seen a working script, I don't have a

144

clear handle on what else we need."

"Terry's working on fleshing it out," Bryce said. "He'll stay at the house you've rented for me, so I can keep my eye on him, and I intend to lock his ass in his room until he comes up with an ending. Once he's here, he can get a real feel for the setting. I think he's really, really close to finishing."

"He's not finished with the script? Not even a first draft?" Greer felt a chill go down her spine.

"Do you know Terry?"

"Only by reputation," Greer said.

"Great guy. Genius. We're like brothers," Bryce said. "He had a slip, that's all. But it's all good now."

"A slip?"

"Like a relapse. A little one. Anyway, the good news is we're out in the middle of nowhere. I'll put a lock on the liquor cabinet, and he won't have a car, so he won't be able to get to a store. Right?"

"Uh . . ."

CeeJay walked out to the parking lot, talking on her cell phone. Bryce hurried toward her, then stopped.

"I'll get CeeJay to drop me off at the dock for the boat ride," Bryce said. "And we can hook back up later this afternoon. You'll take us over to the pier and casino, right? We want to walk it, get an idea of the light, camera angles, all that."

Greer flinched. "About the casino. We've got a slight hitch."

"You'll work it out," Bryce assured her. He hooked a hand around CeeJay's elbow and guided her toward the Navigator. Watching them go, Greer was struck by the fact that Bryce was a good four inches shorter than his new lady love.

"Work it out," Greer muttered, watching them drive off. "Yeah. I'll work it out."

14

The *Beach Town* crew had been on location for a week, but today was the first day the film's principals would be on set. Greer had been up since 3:30 a.m., mainlining coffee, a machine in motion, directing the location of the trailers at the base camp, coordinating with the transportation drivers and the off-duty cops who were securing the perimeter of the shoot, and supplying answers to all sixty crew members who'd converged on Cypress Key at exactly the same moment.

Now, though, there was a temporary lull in the chaos, and she'd decided to reward herself with breakfast at the Coffee Mug.

Greer was considering the bowl of grits. It was steaming hot, flecked with chunks of bacon, and a half-dollar-size pat of golden yellow butter was slowly melting in the middle. Just this one portion of grits probably contained two bajillion calories. She lifted the spoon to her lips and, after a taste, decided this bajillion calories would be worth it.

"You're really gonna eat that whole bowl?" CeeJay asked, wrinkling her nose.

Greer yawned widely. "I'm gonna eat it, and then I'm probably gonna lick the bowl."

CeeJay speared a strawberry from her own virtuous bowl of fruit, and chewed slowly. "Gross."

"These grits are not gross. They are the holy grail of corn, bacon, and butter," Greer countered.

"No, I meant this strawberry. I think I just ate some pesticide." CeeJay chugged from her own bottle of Smartwater.

Now that the sun was up, the sidewalk outside the Coffee Mug was uncharacteristically crowded. Every table on the patio was full, and across the street, the Crow's Nest's front doors were open and she could see people seated at the bar and lounging on the benches on the sidewalk outside.

"What are all these people doing here? It's only eight o'clock in the morning."

"Yeah, I was just wondering about that too," Greer agreed. "This is the most people I've ever seen all at one time in this town, outside of Friday night, when all the bars were hopping."

Their waitress appeared with the coffeepot. "Did y'all see him yet?" she asked, craning her neck and staring out the window at the street.

"Who?" CeeJay asked.

"Kregg, silly," the girl said. "Y'all didn't see the paper today?"

"No-o-o," Greer said slowly. "What did the paper say?"

"He's supposed to be getting into town today," the girl said, her cheeks flushed with excitement. "My Aunt Cindy works at city hall, and she does all the permitting and stuff, and she told me they're gonna start shooting on that movie today. They've already got the beach at the Silver Sands roped off, but my best friend's brother has a boat, and when I get off work in an hour we're taking the boat over to Little Key, so we can watch."

"Good thinking," CeeJay drawled. "I'll bet you can get a good look at him from there."

The girl was staring out the window again.

"Oh my God!" She sat the coffeepot down on the table and covered her mouth with both hands. "There he is!"

CeeJay and Greer followed her gaze. A gleaming black stretch Hummer zoomed past the restaurant, followed by two black Escalades.

"That's Kregg!" the girl said. "In the Hummer. I mean, the windows were tinted and all, but I'd know him anywhere. I swear, that was him."

"Yeah, I heard he usually travels incognito

149

like that," Greer said.

The walkie-talkie she'd laid on the tabletop squawked. "Greer?" It was Zena, her assistant location manager.

"I'm here, Zena."

"We've got an issue. There's like a giant dead shark washed up down here on the beach."

"I'm on my way. In the meantime, get a couple of the grips to haul it off on one of the carts."

"Haul it off where? Just down the beach?"

"No! It'll just wash back up on the set. Tell them to take it over to the seawall on the bayside, near that old oyster cannery. Got it? Not the beach. The bay."

"Got it. Golf cart. Seawall. Cannery. Not the beach."

"I'll be there in five," Greer added.

CeeJay sighed and pushed her breakfast berries away. "Guess we better get back to work, huh?"

The off-duty cop waved their golf cart past the aluminum traffic barriers blocking access to the motel. A crowd had gathered there too, teenage girls, mostly, standing in knots, chattering and feverishly texting on their cell phones.

"I guess good old Aunt Cindy must have let everybody in town know we'd start shooting Kregg's scenes today," Greer said, scowling.

"Well, that and the newspaper." CeeJay held up the discarded copy of the *Cypress Key Citizen* they'd picked up from a table at the café. "Hmm. 'According to informed sources, Kregg was delayed by a week because he was in the studio working on his new album,' " CeeJay said, reading aloud. " 'But *Beach Town* producer/director Bryce Levy was happy to work around his young star's schedule.' "

"Happy? I wonder if that reporter has any idea how much money Kregg's little rehab spa week just cost the production company."

"Yeah, I don't know how these unit publicists look themselves in the mirror every morning, with all the bullshit they have to shovel every day," CeeJay said.

"What else does the paper say?" Greer asked, steering the cart past the trucks and crew vans parked in the Silver Sand's parking lot. Thick black cables snaked over the pavement, and generators were already humming.

"Here's where it gets interesting," CeeJay said. " 'Unnamed local officials say a special called meeting of the City Commission is scheduled for tonight, because Vanessa Littrell, president of Littrell Properties, which owns the Cypress Key Pier and Casino buildings, has filed a petition asking the council to

151

overrule Mayor Eben Thibadeaux's decision not to allow filming at the casino.' "

"Re-heally!" Greer allowed herself a smug smile, which CeeJay didn't miss.

"Your idea, right? Going over the mayor's head and directly to the council?"

Greer shrugged. "Oh, I don't know. Vanessa Littrell is a pretty savvy negotiator. She probably would have come up with the idea sooner or later on her own. I just maybe nudged her along because we're running out of time. If we can get permission to use the casino, the construction guys are still going to have a ton of work to do to get it stabilized before the set dressers can even get started."

"At least we've finally got our star in the same zip code," CeeJay said. "I swear, last week, Bryce was this close to flying to New Mexico and personally abducting Kregg from that clinic."

Greer pulled the cart in front of the Silver Sands office, into a slot she'd cordoned off with orange traffic cones and pink surveyor's tape. Suddenly, they heard a roar of high-pitched squeals, screams, and excited voices, followed by applause. A moment later, the black stretch Hummer rolled past.

"Speak of the devil. I think Kregg is officially in the house."

One of the P.A.s handed her a clipboard of the day's shot schedule. No surprises here.

Crews were already setting up on the beach for the scene where Kregg's character, Nick, would first meet Danielle, his love interest and the film's leading lady.

Casting was definitely not her department, but Greer always had opinions, and this time around Greer thought Bryce had cast exactly the right actress to play Danielle.

Adelyn Davis was only twenty-five, looked eighteen, but was already a seasoned screen veteran — she'd won her first television role as a four-year-old. In the years since her acting debut, she'd aced increasingly challenging roles, starred in her last two movies, and had even taken time off from acting to graduate from the Yale School of Drama.

Addie had reported to work the previous week, her lines memorized. She was annoyed, but unfazed, by her costar's absence.

She stood in the open doorway of her trailer now, made up, with hot rollers in her long, blond hair, a pink bathrobe thrown over her costume, daintily sipping from a mug of tea, watching the hubbub surrounding Kregg's arrival on set.

A heavyset young black man with a headful of dreadlocks clambered down from the driver's side of the Hummer, hitched up his sagging jeans, and sauntered around to the passenger side.

Craig White, aka Kregg, stepped out into the already blinding Florida sunlight, lowered his sunglasses, and blinked. Heavy-lidded pale blue eyes gazed around the crowded mini-village that had been erected overnight in the motel parking lot.

He was taller than Greer had expected, probably six five, and whip thin. The skin on the spaghetti-like arms hanging from the short-sleeved black T-shirt was the color of nonfat milk, so pale it was almost blue, and his dark hair fell limply around a narrow, angular face dotted crimson with what looked like a raging case of acne. He wore tight jeans and metal-studded black knee-high boots.

"Oh Jesus," CeeJay said. "I'm supposed to make this guy look like a Navy SEAL?"

The back doors of the Hummer and the two Escalades were flung open, and the rest of the star's black-clad entourage tumbled out, eight in all.

Bryce Levy pushed his way through the crowd with his arms extended. "Kregg!" he exclaimed. "Welcome to *Beach Town.*"

Kregg took a hasty step backwards. "Cool," he mumbled, eluding the director's embrace. "Very cool."

Greer looked down at her watch. It would take a good two hours to get Kregg through hair, makeup, and costume. She was assessing the possibility of a nap, when her assistant materialized at her side.

Zena was a stunner, in her early twenties,

tall and lithe, with huge dark eyes, olive skin, and long dark hair that hung nearly to her waist. They'd worked together a couple years previously on a short-lived reality show. Zena wasn't terribly good with independent thinking, but she was pleasant and good with details. Most importantly, she always showed up on time. Always. That made her golden in Greer's world.

"All good?" she asked her assistant. "No more Jaws?"

"The shark is history," Zena assured her.

"How's it looking down on the beach?"

"The shrimp boats you hired are anchored out near the sandbar. They look awesome."

"They should, for what I had to pay. How about Nick's boat? Has it been delivered yet?"

"Got here about thirty minutes ago."

"How's it look? Did they paint it the right shade of red? Has Alex seen it?"

"Alex says the red looks fine, but he's having the painters stripe the front of the boat. What's that called?"

"The bow. Does the boat actually run?"

"Yeah. The stunt driver checked it out. It runs fine. And the boats for the camera crews are here too."

Greer yawned again. "Okay. Can you take over for an hour or so? I'm dead on my feet."

"Yeah, wow, you look kinda washed out," Zena said. "Go ahead. I got this."

Greer unlocked the door to her motel

room. It was depressingly hot. She turned the dial on the air conditioner down to Eskimo level, inspected the room for renegade cockroaches, and yanked the venetian blind cord. It came away in her hand.

"Shit." She found a bath towel and draped it over the window. Finally, with the room dark and somewhat cool, she tumbled into the bed.

Two hours or two days later, the walkie-talkie on her nightstand squawked. "Greer?"

She struggled to an upright position and groped blindly in the dark for the radio.

"I'm here, Zena. What is it?"

"Sorry to bother you. Hey, the caterers just radioed me from base camp. Something's wrong with the generator, and they don't have power."

"God. What time is it?"

"Eleven thirty. They're going apeshit because lunch break is in thirty minutes and they've got seventy-five people to feed."

"So tell them to fix peanut butter and jelly."

"Really?"

"No, Zena. I'm kidding. Get one of the P.A.s to check to make sure there's gas in the generator, and that somebody didn't accidentally unplug one of the cables. I'll be over there in five minutes, but go ahead and give them the number of the pizza place for takeout, just in case."

Greer used one hand to clamp the bill of her baseball cap and keep it from flying away in the wind while, with the other, she trained the binoculars toward the beach as the wooden skiff bobbed at anchor in the surf.

The actors were standing in ankle-deep water. Kregg was stripped to the waist, and it looked like CeeJay had used a gallon of self-tanner to dispel his pasty complexion. She'd also shaved off most of his hair. Addie wore a gauzy white dress, which was plastered to her damp body. They were surrounded by cameramen and boom mikes and half a dozen crew members. Bryce Levy was seated on the end of a boom, just out of camera angle, waving his arms and screaming something Greer couldn't make out.

She glanced behind her and saw the source of the director's agitation. Bearing directly down on them was a yellow speedboat, loaded down with half a dozen bikini-clad teenage girls. Following it were two more boats.

The boat sped closer and closer to shore, and then slowed. Greer could hear their high-pitched squeals. "Kregg! Kregg! Hey, Kregg! Hey, Addie!"

Greer reached for her radio and sighed. "Officer Jackson? Yellow boat at four o'clock.

157

Two more following. Can you intercept?"

The radio squawked. "We got it."

A moment later she saw a black and tan craft with a local law enforcement insignia, in pursuit, with a loud, blaring siren mounted to the bow. Within twenty minutes the boats had been dispersed, but the damage had already been done.

It was almost four o'clock. Filming had already been disrupted twice by similar intrusions from enthusiastic fans zooming in and out of camera range. Each time the off-duty cops had chased them off, but each incident had cost valuable time.

Now, dark clouds were looming on the horizon. Overcast skies were actually better for lighting, but these clouds had an ominous look to them. Suddenly, a streak of lightning danced in the distance and a hard rain began to pelt the water's surface.

Bryce was waving his arms again. The actors hurried out of the surf, and assistants scurried to move the equipment out of the rain. The shoot was over, nearly as soon as it had begun.

"Let's get out of here," Greer told her assistant. Zena nodded and reached over and yanked the starter cord.

15

Greer wanted a shower. And air conditioning. And a very cold glass of wine. And dinner. Because the bowl of grits she'd inhaled hours earlier had been her only food all day, and she was hot and salt soaked and exhausted. She was on her way back to her room after the last production meeting of the day when her cell phone pinged.

The text message was from Vanessa Littrell.

SEE YOU AT THE COUNCIL MEETING IN 15 MINUTES. YES?

"No," Greer moaned. "No, no, no, no."

Before she could respond to the text, Bryce clamped a hand over her sunburned shoulder. "Good work today."

She winced and turned around to speak to her producer/director.

In contrast to her own grubby appearance, Bryce's hair was still wet from a recent shower, his clothes were pristine, and he smelled of aftershave.

"I'm glad you thought so," Greer said. "Tomorrow, I promise we'll get a better handle on all the gawkers and rubberneckers. I've already arranged for a couple more off-duty cops with boats."

"Fantastic. Look, one of the publicists . . . what's her name? Um, yeah, Meg, the one with the red hair? She just left me word that there's a city council meeting tonight. . . ."

"Right," Greer said cautiously.

"Something about a problem with permits to use the casino as a location? Meg says it's sort of a command performance. Goodwill in the community and all. The thing is, I really don't have time tonight for a dog and pony show. I've got a conference call to the coast, and then CeeJay and I are having dinner with Kregg and his people. So I was thinking, you should go."

Greer's heart sank. "Me?"

"Absolutely! You're the face of *Beach Town* with these people anyway. They'll love it. Right?"

"But the meeting starts in fifteen minutes." She took a step backwards, gesturing at her navy tank top, salt-crusted capris, and red Keds. "I've been on a boat all afternoon. Look at me, Bryce. I'm sweaty and stinky. I can't represent the film looking like this."

"You look fabulous, babe. Just do what you do." He leaned over, planted a kiss on her cheek. "We'll catch up in the morning."

Greer's phone dinged to alert her to a follow-up text from Vanessa.

"Coming?"

"*YES*," she typed. "*See you there.*"

She just barely had enough time to stop by her room, drag a brush through her unruly mop of blond curls, and change into a dry pair of pants and shoes.

The buzz of conversation was audible as soon as she entered city hall. She followed the voices till she found a large, high-ceilinged room packed with citizens sitting on what looked like straight-backed wooden church pews. The wood-paneled walls were lined with old black-and-white photos of past mayors, and the current mayor and council were seated on a raised dais at the front of the room. A ceiling fan whirred lazily overhead, barely stirring up enough cool air to make a difference.

"Greer!"

Vanessa Littrell was sitting in an aisle seat in the next-to-last row in the room, gesturing to her to take the seat beside hers.

"Is it always like this at these council meetings?" Greer asked, looking around the room. People were jammed into the pews, and more were standing along the back and side walls.

"No," Vanessa said, her eyes narrowed. "I

161

only come to council meetings two or three times a year, and usually you get maybe half a dozen people. That story in today's paper must have people riled up."

"For which side?"

Eb Thibadeaux started up the aisle, spotted her, and stopped, extending a hand to Vanessa.

"Ladies." He nodded his head briefly at Greer and made his way to the dais.

Cindy the city clerk stood at the podium, awkwardly reading aloud from a printed document.

"What's going on?" Greer whispered.

"I think you're about to get some kind of special award," Vanessa replied.

"Whereas the City of Cypress Key welcomes the cast and crew of *Beach Town* to the friendliest city in Florida, and whereas the city recognizes the positive recognition such a film will bring to our city, and whereas . . ."

Cindy's voice, low pitched and monotonous, dragged on with additional whereases, and Greer felt her breathing slow and her eyelids fluttering. A moment later, Vanessa nudged her in the ribs. "That's your cue."

Greer walked to the dais amid polite applause. Eb Thibadeaux gestured for her to join him at the podium, at which point he thrust a three-foot plastic replica of a key into

162

her arms.

"Smile," he instructed as Cindy snapped photos. He slung an arm over Greer's shoulder and drew her to his side, a little closer than was strictly necessary, she thought.

He placed his lips near her ear. "Resistance is useless."

"What's that supposed to mean?"

"Keep smiling," Eb said, barely moving his lips. "It means you can't win on this issue. It means Vanessa is wasting her time. And yours."

She looked up. He looked down. Directly into her cleavage.

Greer yanked at the neckline of her tank top.

"We'll see," Greer said. She tucked her giant plastic key under her arm and returned to the next-to-last row.

Cindy the clerk worked her way through the city council's agenda. There was old business to discuss: the purchase of new boots for the fire department, a report on landscaping progress in front of the town's veterans monument, a discussion of the cost for new bike racks at the beach crossover.

The room was stifling. Greer's eyelids fluttered and finally closed. Vanessa nudged her again. "Showtime," she whispered.

"At this time we have only one more matter of new business to discuss, and it is the

163

subject of this called meeting," Cindy announced.

"Mr. Mayor, Board of Commissioners? We have a citizen's request for an appeal from Mayor Thibadeaux's denial of a filming permit at the old Cypress Key Casino property. The citizen is Ms. Vanessa Littrell, who is the owner of that parcel."

Eb smiled blandly and spoke into his mike. "Why don't we hear from Ms. Littrell then?"

Vanessa walked briskly to the front of the room, where a microphone stand had been placed. She looked intelligent and competent in conservative black slacks, a high-necked, short-sleeved black top, and tiny gold hoop earrings. The showy diamonds she'd worn the last time Greer had met with her were noticeably absent.

"Ms. Littrell, would you state your name and address for the benefit of the minutes, and then the nature of your business before the council?" Eb said.

"My name is Vanessa Littrell, of number one, Seahorse Key, and I'm appearing before the council tonight not just as the owner of record of the Cypress Key Casino but also as a taxpayer and a fourth-generation resident of this town," Vanessa said, her voice low and calm.

She looked up at the council members on the dais, and then around at the audience in the room.

164

"I recently became aware that Ms. Greer Hennessy, who the council just presented with the key to the city, arrived in Cypress Key a week ago, to secure locations for the filming of a big-budget Hollywood film. One of the main places Ms. Hennessy sought to film was the casino building, which my family owns but which is under a long-term lease arrangement with the city."

Vanessa paused. "As everybody in this room knows, although the city continues to pay rent on the casino, it has been closed for many years, and its condition has deteriorated during that time."

One of the council members, an elderly man with a silvery Dutch boy haircut and thick-lensed glasses, raised a liver-spotted hand. "Ms. Littrell, are you accusing the city of negligence in maintaining your property? Is that why you're here?"

"No sir," Vanessa shot back. "I'm here because I'm dismayed by the mayor's outright refusal to accept an extremely attractive offer from these filmmakers to use the casino. It's my understanding that Ms. Hennessy made a generous cash offer, and in addition, her company would be willing to demolish the building and clear the property to ready it for new development."

She glared at Eb Thibadeaux. "I'd like to ask the mayor how this is not a win-win for the City of Cypress Key?"

A heavyset black woman wearing a black blouse and a clerical collar, on the far left side of the dais, raised her hand.

"Reverend Maynard?" Eb said politely. "You have a question?"

"Yes. Can I ask how much money these movie people were offering?"

Eb Thibadeaux shrugged and pulled the mike forward. "There were a couple numbers thrown around. I think the offer went as high as fifty thousand dollars." He pointed toward Greer. "Is that accurate, Ms. Hennessy?"

Greer stood. "Yes, that's the amount we are offering."

Rowena Maynard whistled softly. "That's an interesting offer, Eb."

"It certainly sounds good to me," Vanessa agreed.

Ginny Buckalew leaned forward. "Eb, did I understand correctly? The movie people want to tear the casino down? Can that be right?"

"That's what I was told," the mayor replied. "In fact, Ms. Hennessy personally admitted to me that they plan to blow it up for the movie."

The audience erupted in a ripple of concern. "No way!" a voice called from the back.

"It's already falling down," Vanessa protested.

Eb banged his gavel on the table.

"Thanks, Ms. Littrell," he said.

Vanessa returned to her seat in the audience.

Eb looked around the room. A low buzz of conversation had broken out. "I'm going to reserve my rebuttal until we hear from any other interested citizens." He looked around the room. "Would anybody else like to speak on this matter?"

At the front of the room, a thin black man rose slowly to his feet and inched toward the microphone.

He had a high, gleaming dark forehead with salt-and-pepper hair and was dressed, Greer thought, for church, in neatly pressed dark slacks, a yellowing starched dress shirt, and a bright purple bow tie — appropriate, since they were all seated in pews.

"Mr. Samuels," Eb said, beaming at his constituent. "Happy to see you, sir."

The old man cleared his throat nervously. "Yessir. My name is Solomon Samuels and I live at 614 and a half Oak Street. I was born right here in this county in 1937. I am a Korean War veteran and a registered Democrat. And I'd just like to tell these two ladies here . . ." He bowed slightly in Vanessa and Greer's direction. "As pretty as they are, I don't want no kind of jackleg Hollywood movie folk messing around with our casino. And I sure as goodness don't want 'em blowing it up, neither."

Applause rippled through the audience.

167

Solomon Samuels removed his wire-rimmed glasses and polished them with a starched handkerchief he pulled from his trouser pocket.

He smiled shyly. "No sir. Like a lot of folks here, that casino is a special place to me. Maybe a little more special to my people, and to me, because I met the future Mrs. Samuels there." He took a deep breath and continued.

"It was 1965, and me and my friends, we wanted to see Little Anthony and the Imperials. Y'all are mostly too young to remember 'Tears on My Pillow' or 'Shimmy, Shimmy, Ko-Ko-Bop,' but those were some mighty popular songs back then. They were going to put on a show at the casino, and that was the first time that black folk could see a show at the casino, or any place around here. Before that, black folk couldn't mix with whites. Mr. Lloyd Littrell, who I reckon was Ms. Littrell's granddaddy, he just up and decided he would sell tickets to who anybody who wanted to come."

Greer gave Vanessa a sideways glance, but Vanessa's face remained impassive.

"Anyway, we went to that show, and at intermission I went to the snack bar, and I met this pretty little old gal, her name was June, and that was the girl I come to marry. And for a long time after that, every year, me and my gal, we went to the casino for our anniversary. Didn't matter if we went to a show, or roller-skating, or later on, bingo. That was our special place. The casino's been shut up for a while now, but the mayor, Mr. Thibadeaux, he says he's gonna get the state or the Congress or somebody to give us some money to fix it up and make it a center for seniors like me. And I just think we don't need to be messin' round with no movie people who we don't know."

He gave an apologetic half-bow in Greer's direction. "No offense or nothin', but if the mayor says he's gonna get the casino fixed up, I say we don't let nobody blow it up, for no amount of money."

Solomon Samuels bowed again. The audience clapped its approval, and he sat down with that same shy smile.

Before the old man could be seated, Ginny Buckalew was speaking.

"Mr. Mayor, fellow commissioners, I see a lot of folks here tonight, but for myself, I believe I've made up my mind on this matter. I'd like to call for a vote."

"Big surprise," Vanessa muttered.

"I'd like to propose a vote to affirm Mayor Thibadeaux's decision to deny a permit to film at the casino," Ginny said.

The city clerk spoke into her mike. "All in favor?"

Each of the commissioners raised a hand.

"The motion is affirmed," Cindy said. The

room erupted in applause, cheers, and loud chatter.

Vanessa jumped to her feet and turned to Greer. "Unbelievable. I need a drink. C'mon. Let's head over to the Inn."

16

Vanessa and Greer found a table in the main dining room, and before Greer could object, Vanessa ordered a pitcher of martinis.

Greer eyed her glass with longing. Condensation beaded on the outside. Two plump olives rested on a spear. "I shouldn't," she said with a groan. "We've got a four a.m. call."

Vanessa knocked back her own drink in one swallow and poured herself a second. "Oh, come on. One won't hurt. Especially after that freak show we just endured."

Greer took a cautious sip. The cold temporarily froze her brain. She set the glass back down on the tabletop and reached for the bread basket. "That's all for me until I get something to eat."

When the waitress came, Vanessa ordered broiled flounder and steamed broccoli. "I'm absolutely famished," Greer apologized, before ordering herself a filet mignon, medium rare, baked potato with everything, sautéed spinach, and a Caesar salad.

She buttered a roll and watched while Vanessa sipped her martini. "Looks like round one of the Battle of the Casino went to the mayor," she observed.

Vanessa fished an olive from her glass. "This was only the beginning. I'm not giving up yet. There's too much at stake to just walk away. Anyway, Eb Thibadeaux does not know who he is messing with."

Greer's stomach growled loudly. She looked around the dining room, forcing herself not to gobble the roll in one bite.

"Speak of the devil," she said, watching the mayor stroll into the room.

Vanessa turned to get a look. Her face flushed pink. "Dammit. He saw us." She tossed back the rest of her martini, poured herself another, and topped off Greer's barely touched glass.

Eb lingered at the bar, got a bottle of beer, and chatted briefly with two men sitting at a nearby table, slapping one on the back. He table-hopped around the room, stopping at a long table of middle-aged women and joining in to sing "Happy Birthday" when a candle-topped cake arrived.

"What's he doing?" Vanessa asked, staring down at her glass as she chewed her olive.

"Glad-handing."

"Asshole," Vanessa said, fuming.

Greer was just about to cut into her steak

when Eb Thibadeaux arrived tableside.

"Ladies," he said jovially, pulling up a chair from a vacant nearby table. "Mind if I join you?"

"Beat it, Eb." Vanessa glared at him with undisguised loathing.

He threw his head back and laughed loudly. "Aw come on, Vanessa. Don't be such a sore loser. No hard feelings, right?"

Greer took a bite of her steak. It was salty and greasy and rich with a mushroom wine glaze, and she nearly swooned with happiness. She chewed slowly, watching while her tablemate slowly went ballistic.

"The hell you say." Vanessa nearly spat the words. "I'm sick to death of your regressive, antibusiness tactics. You're so terrified of progress coming to this burg, you can't see that the town is dying." She gestured toward the street outside.

"Look around, Eb. More than half the buildings out there are empty. That casino building is crumbling even as you sit here with that big goofy grin on your face. You just turned down fifty thousand dollars in cold, hard cash. When's the last time anybody made the city an offer like that? You keep talking about preserving our community's heritage. I got news for you, buddy. There's nothing left to save. It's gone. What business in its right mind is going to come in here? Who's going to bring jobs that pay more than

173

minimum wage?"

Eb shook his head impatiently. "Despite what you believe, Vanessa, we're not just sitting around, waiting for the casino to fall into the bay. We've had a feasibility study done, and right now we have three major grant proposals pending with the state and the Feds. That money will let us purchase and restore the casino for a community center that'll be worth ten times the money these film people are offering."

"Pipe dreams!" Vanessa said, waving a dismissive hand.

"It's not a pipe dream," he insisted. "We can restore the casino and redevelop the whole pier district, and that will bring in real growth and clean businesses that we can sustain." He glanced over at Greer. "It's tempting to want to grab the quick buck, but that's happened way too often in Cypress Key. We believed the paper company when they said they were going to be good corporate citizens and do the responsible thing, and where did that leave us? Right where we are today.

"I know what you're up to here, Vanessa. These movie people think you're on their side, but they don't know you like I do. You'll sell this town and that casino out to the highest bidder in a heartbeat, and never look back."

"You're forgetting one thing, Eb," Vanessa

said heatedly. "I still own the building, and I have no intentions of selling it. Not to the city, anyway."

Eb took a sip of his beer. "I have two words for you, Vanessa. Think about them." He held up two fingers of his right hand. "Eminent. Domain."

Vanessa's eyes bulged. "Fuck you, Eb Thibadeaux!" She shoved her chair back from the table. "You think the city can just condemn my property and take it without a fight? Hell no."

She tossed the last remaining drops of her martini into the mayor's face and stomped out of the dining room, with every eye in the room following her progress.

Greer handed Eb her linen napkin, and while he mopped his face with it she sighed and took another bite of her baked potato.

Eb eyed her curiously. "What about you? Don't you want to throw something at me? Maybe organize a lynch mob of your cohorts to come after me?"

Greer finished chewing and took another dainty sip of her martini. But it had lost its chill, and therefore its charm.

"Nope."

"You agree with me?"

"Nope." Greer reached over and snagged a spear of broccoli from the plate Vanessa had abandoned. "I still think you're dead wrong about the casino. But I can't figure out your motive in all this."

"You think I have some kind of ulterior motive?" he asked, obviously amused.

"Everybody has an ulterior motive," Greer said.

"What's yours?"

She chewed and thought, then dabbed her napkin to her lips.

"Me? My motives are pretty transparent. I want to get this movie made. I want *Beach Town* to be such a huge success that I'll never have to look for work again."

Eb sat back in his chair. "That's all you care about? Work? Getting this movie made, and then the next and the next?"

"You make it sound like I don't have a life," Greer protested.

"Do you?"

"I love my work, okay? But I have a life. I have friends."

"What do you do for fun?" Eb asked.

"I make movies. I love what I do. I love films, and despite all the craziness involved, I love making them."

"Seriously. If you had a day off, right now, today, how would you spend it?"

She shrugged. "Today? I guess I'd go hang out at the beach. I like being on the water. Or I might meet CeeJay for lunch, maybe hit the Rose Bowl Flea Market, if the timing's right. Or I might just catch a movie."

"CeeJay. Is that your boyfriend?"

"My best friend. Short for Claudia Jean. She's a hair and makeup artist, and she's actually here, working on *Beach Town*."

"And what do you buy at this flea market?"

She considered him. "Old stuff. I like mid-century California art pottery. CeeJay buys girly stuff like compacts and sterling silver hair brushes."

"So you actually go to the movies — even though you're in the business?"

The question took her by surprise. "Of course. Why else would I be in the business, if I didn't love movies? You ask a lot of questions, don't you?"

"I'm interested in you," Eb said.

"Why? I'm not that fascinating."

"Sure you are. You're cute, you're smart, you have an interesting job. And you don't back down easily. I don't meet a lot of women like that around here."

"You do realize I can't be charmed out of doing my job, right? And my job is locking down the casino for the film, so that we can blow it up in a few weeks."

Greer took another sip of the martini, then pushed it away and grimaced.

He noticed. "You want something else to drink?" He turned and waved the waitress over.

"I'll have another beer. You like red wine?" he asked, looking over at her nearly empty plate. "Burgundy? Merlot? I'm a little hesitant

177

ordering wine for a California girl. What would you like?"

"I'm no wine snob," Greer assured him. "Maybe just a glass of rosé? I actually shouldn't have anything else to drink. We've got an early call."

When the waitress returned with their drinks, Greer decided to turn the tables on him.

"Okay, I told you my motives. Now you tell me yours. You're obviously an educated guy. You've got some business savvy, owning a motel and the grocery store and that boat-yard. I know you're the mayor and this is your hometown and all, but what the hell are you doing here in the middle of nowhere?"

He threw his head back and laughed that laugh again. It was a good laugh. Not phony. Not ironic. Nothing held back. You didn't hear a lot of laughs like that in her line of work.

"You don't beat around the bush, do you? Not exactly a very Southern way to phrase a question," Ebb said.

'I'm not Southern.'

"I'm here because . . . I want to be, I guess," Eb said soberly. "Fifteen years ago, if you'd told me I'd be living in Cypress Key again, doing what I'm doing, I would have laughed my ass off."

"So . . . this is all an accident?" she asked.

"Not really. I did move away after college. I

178

went to engineering school on a scholarship from the paper company, got an MBA for lack of a better idea, then kicked around the country for a while. I worked in Texas, California, the Cayman Islands. I spent the longest winter of my life in Buffalo." He shivered.

"And then you ended up right back where you started," Greer said. "Why?"

"One of my early mentors at the paper company called and offered me too much money to ignore. I was freezing my ass off in Buffalo, and Florida sounded pretty good right then."

"Even if it was Cypress Key, Florida?"

"Jared had just gotten arrested," he said quietly. "My father hadn't been diagnosed with Alzheimer's at that point, but it was pretty obvious to my mom that he was slipping. So I came home."

He spun the beer bottle on the tabletop. "The company gave me all kinds of vague descriptions of what my job would entail, but when I'd been back here for three months they let me in on what I was really hired to do."

"Which was?"

"Get the plant ready to close down. I was supposed to quietly start making arrangements to sell off the equipment, slow down production from three shifts to one, get rid of the most expensive employees — anybody

179

over the age of forty-five, women, like that."

"That must have been brutal."

"I'm a coward," Eb said. "I couldn't do it. I quit."

"I wouldn't call that cowardly," Greer said. "You did stay around to help your family, right?"

"As much as I could. I'd always lived pretty lean, so I bought out my dad's interest in the Silver Sands, thinking I could help Ginny make a go of it."

"You haven't mentioned a wife or a girl-friend in any of this," Greer said flippantly. "What happened? Did she get fed up and split?"

"Not exactly. She died."

Greer clapped her hands over her mouth. "Oh my God. I didn't know. I'm so sorry. . . ."

"Not your fault," Eb said. "It was a long time ago." He looked down at his watch. "Come to think of it, in August it will be ten years."

"Wow. She must have been so young. . . ." Greer's voice trailed off.

"She was only twenty-seven. Breast cancer. Sarah was diagnosed right after we got back from our honeymoon. It was already stage two. She had surgery, chemo, radiation. Drug trials. We were up and down. Three years after she found the lump, she was gone."

"My mom died of breast cancer, two months ago," Greer said quietly. "I guess, in

180

a way, she was lucky. By the time they discovered it, the cancer had metastasized. It was too late for chemo or radiation, or any of it." Greer blinked back unexpected tears for a woman she'd never met, and for Lise, who'd been so alive. Until, suddenly, she wasn't. "That is just so . . ."

"Tragic," Eb said. He took another drink of beer. "Really, really tragic. And sucky. For Sarah. And your mom."

He gazed at her over the rim of the beer bottle. "What about you? No time for men in your life?"

"Not currently," Greer said.

"Currently? That implies there was somebody, recently?"

"Why do I feel like I'm being interrogated here?" Greer asked.

"You haven't answered my question," Eb reminded her.

"I was in a . . . relationship. But that's been over for a while now. It's not easy to date in my line of work. I travel all the time, and most of the men I meet are in the business. It's easy to hook up with somebody when you're all working so intensely on a film. You're thrown together for what feels like twenty-four hours a day. And then the movie wraps and everybody moves on to the next show. I'll admit, I did that, back when I was a newbie. But I found out fast it's not for me."

Greer stared down into her wineglass. "Lise used to say my relationships were always doomed because I saw too many movies. Like, real-life men could never measure up to the heroes in movies."

"No Prince Charming, huh?"

"I'm not looking for a prince. Actually, I'm not looking, period."

"Your last 'relationship,' " he said, making finger quotes. "Was the guy in the movies?"

Greer shook her head. "You just don't give up, do you? Okay, he was a lawyer. We met through work. He was older, and he seemed more mature than most of the men I've dated, which was refreshing."

"But it's not refreshing anymore?"

"No," she said succinctly. "Look, it's getting late, and I have to be bright-eyed and bushy-tailed at four a.m." She looked around the room and motioned for the waitress to bring her check.

Eb waited while she settled her tab. "Can I walk you back to the hotel?"

"Four blocks? Sure."

They stood in the restaurant's doorway, looking down the street. Rain pelted the roof of the tin awning, and the wind whipped the palm trees lining Pine Street. The temperature had dropped dramatically, too. Greer folded her bare arms across her chest and shivered.

182

"You didn't happen to bring an umbrella, did you?" Eb asked.

"The storm had let up by the time I walked over to city hall." She shifted her stance and a stream of rainwater ran down her neck.

"Dammit," she muttered, stepping sideways.

"I can borrow an umbrella from the restaurant," he offered.

"It's not that. If this weather keeps up, we won't be able to shoot in the morning. We've got all the beach scenes to do, and we can't do that in a storm."

"I can't do anything about the weather, but we could go back to my place to wait out the rain if you want."

She gave him a puzzled look. "Your place? You don't live at the motel, like Ginny?"

"Nope. Got my own pied-à-terre, just two doors down." He jerked his thumb toward the right. Toward the Hometown Market.

"You live at the grocery store? For real? What department? Frozen foods?"

"I live above the store, on the second floor." He turned around and took a few paces, walking backwards. "Don't you want to see?"

17

Greer stood in the Inn's doorway, watching Eb Thibadeaux go splashing down the covered sidewalk, momentarily paralyzed by indecision. It was after ten, and she had to be back at work in five hours. But the idea of being closed up in her dank motel room, with the wheezy air conditioner, alone again on a rainy night like this, was just too depressing to contemplate.

"Hey, wait up," she called. Eb turned around, and as he stood under the streetlight she saw his broad, easy smile. He was beaming.

Totally beaming. Ear to ear. Had any man ever smiled at her like that before?

Eb had the grocery store door unlocked by time she caught up to him. He flipped a switch and the overhead fluorescents lit up the market.

"Right this way," he said, directing her toward the back of the store, down the cereal aisle, and around the seafood cooler. She stepped around a long, stainless steel work-table and dodged a stack of waxed cardboard boxes, nearly slipping on the damp tile floor.

He fit a key into a door recessed into the wall behind the counter and flipped another switch, which illuminated a wide stairway.

The landing at the top of the stairs faced a tall set of heavy wooden barn-type sliding doors. Eb yanked a metal handle and the door rolled back. He flipped another switch and gestured inside.

"My crib."

She was looking at a long, wide, open space. If they'd been in Greenwich Village she'd have called it a loft. But here, in Cypress Key, it was just the space above the Hometown Market.

The walls were of exposed, whitewashed brick with plaster still clinging to some por-tions. The floors were of wide dark pine planks, and were gouged and scratched and grease stained in spots.

Stuff was everywhere. The walls held at least a dozen worn and rusted metal trade signs. A huge, billboard-sized yellow and red SUNBEAM bread sign was tacked to the wall just inside the door. She spotted a four-foot-diameter COKE button sign, a neon-scripted advertisement for Salem cigarettes, and a large wooden cutout of an ice-cream cone, listing eight different flavors.

Greer turned to Eb. "I'm speechless."

He shrugged. "I guess you could say I'm a pack rat."

She walked around the room, pausing to take it all in. In front of a black potbellied stove, a pair of tufted black leather Chesterfield sofas faced each other across an Oriental rug so worn you could see patches of floor in some places. The coffee table was a stack of wooden pallets topped with a thick slab of irregularly shaped marble. Lamp tables were made of what looked like upended wooden produce crates.

"Where?" Greer asked. "Where did you get all this amazing stuff? You've got an entire movie prop house, just in this living room."

"Most of it's just junk," Eb said. "Lots of times, when I sell a house, the owners just give me stuff they don't want to take with them. Or people leave stuff in rental houses when they move. That rug there, I found rolled up underneath an abandoned house. The signs, most of them were behind the market, in a storage shed, when I bought the place. The COKE sign was downstairs in the market, but people kept bugging me to sell it, so I finally brought it up here."

Greer set her hand lightly on a vintage milk glass Sinclair gas pump with the original green dinosaur logo. "How on earth did you get this up here?"

He pointed to another doorway she hadn't

even noticed, at the back of the room. "That's the old freight elevator. Comes in handy."

She ran her fingers across the buttery leather of a sofa. "You didn't find this in a shed."

"No," he said ruefully. "I had to buy it. Aside from my mattress, I think that's the only new furniture up here."

Adjacent to the living room was a rectangular oak table, its top deeply scarred and marred with cigarette burns and carved graffiti. Arranged around the table were five high-backed rolling stools.

"There must be a story behind this," Greer said.

"The library was getting ready to throw out the table, so I took it. I bought the chemistry lab stools for five bucks apiece right before they tore down the old high school."

Greer sat on one of the stools and swirled around on it until it faced the kitchen. There were no real cabinets in the space. An industrial stainless steel counter contained an integrated sink, and above it, Eb's thick white dishes were arrayed on simple wooden shelves. There was a commercial glass-front refrigerator, and a hulking fifties-vintage white porcelain stove with double ovens, six burners, and gleaming chrome knobs. An old wooden ladder was suspended by chains from the ceiling, and a battered assortment of pots and pans hung from it.

"Did you build all this?" she asked.

"Nah," Eb said. "I mean, I dragged the boards up here from the boatyard and nailed them to cleats on the wall for shelves, yeah."

"And everything else?" Greer asked.

"I got the sink and counter and refrigerator from the plant cafeteria, when the paper company shut down. I think I paid a hundred bucks for all of it."

"Tell me about this stove." Greer bent over to read the chrome nameplate. "Wedgewood? They made stoves?"

"I found that at the dump when I was hauling off some ruined wall-to-wall carpet from a rental house. Took me a week to get all the grease and rust off of it. It cleaned up all right."

"It's amazing," Greer said. "I've seen stoves like this at the Rose Bowl, fully restored, for like two thousand dollars. Does this one work?"

"Oh yeah," Eb said. He walked over and turned a knob, and a blue flame sputtered to life. "It runs on propane." He held up a copper teakettle. "How about a cup of tea?"

While they waited for the kettle to boil, Greer stood in front of a bank of steel-frame windows that looked out on an alley. The rain pounded on the roof and lightning crackled in the navy blue sky.

She heard the clicking of nails and looked

down. A plump black and tan dachshund with a graying muzzle waddled across the floor, stood at her feet, and barked furiously.

"Who's this?" Greer called to her host.

Eb peered out from the kitchen partition. "Oh, that's Gunter. He's nearly deaf, but I guess the lightning woke him up. Just ignore him, okay?"

Greer bent down, extended her hand, palm forward, and the dog sniffed suspiciously. She scratched his ears, and when he wagged his tail his whole body followed suit.

She walked into the kitchen with Gunter sniffing at her ankles. Eb had two thick white mugs on the counter and was digging around in a large glass Planters peanuts jar for tea bags. He plunked a bag in each mug.

"Funny. You don't strike me as a dachshund kind of guy."

"Gunter's cool. And he's low maintenance. Mostly he eats and sleeps and farts. He'll take a walk every day, if I really insist."

The dog sat down on Greer's shoe-top, looked up at her, and whined.

Eb sighed and flipped him a dog biscuit, which the dog greedily inhaled.

"Just how old is he?" Greer asked.

"Maybe nine or ten?"

"You don't know how old your own dog is? What kind of dachshund guy are you?"

"Not a very good one. Gunter's kind of a rescue. I found him last winter, rooting around in the trash behind the store. I tried to find his owner, or give him away, but he had mange and some other unpleasant issues, which makes for a lousy adoption candidate. You want some cookies or something? I could go downstairs and grab something. One of the perks of living above the store."

"No thanks." Greer wiggled her toes, and gently bumped the elderly dog off her sandal. She looked around the loft. "So. You rescue motels and old stoves and dogs. And casinos. Very noble."

Gunter whined again, thumped his tail on the floor, and looked up hopefully at Greer with large, sincere brown eyes.

"No more," Eb said sternly. "You're supposed to be on a diet."

The dog stood up, gave three short barks, and ran a couple of slow, sloppy circles around Greer's ankles, yipping and barking as he went.

"Ignore him," Eb said.

"Aww. Why would I do that? He's adorable." She picked up the dog and cradled him in her arms.

Suddenly she felt something wet and warm on her shirt.

"Oh no!" she cried, looking down at the yellow puddle on the floor.

Eb gently took the dog from her, set him on the floor, and fetched a roll of paper towels.

"Gunter also has what the vet calls situational incontinency. Which means, when he gets excited, he piddles. Sorry about that."

He took a paper towel and dabbed gingerly at the growing damp spot on her chest. But when his hand brushed her right nipple, he blushed beet red and jerked his hand back as though he'd touched a hot stove.

"Christ! Sorry. I swear, that was an accident."

Greer narrowed her eyes. "That's what they all say." And then she burst into a fit of uncontrollable giggles. Gunter sat back on his haunches, looked up, and gave a sharp bark of disapproval, which made her laugh that much harder. Eb started to laugh, too, which somehow tickled her even more. He threw his head back and straight-on guffawed. Gunter was not amused. He barked furiously and began running circles around them, peeing as he went.

Greer laughed until tears streamed down her face. She laughed until her sides ached, and she stumbled toward one of the lab stools, but when she went to sit down, the chair went spinning out from under her and she fell flat on the floor.

"I can't . . ." she sputtered, fighting to catch her breath, "stop . . ."

Before she knew it, Eb sprawled down on the floor beside her, gathered her into his arms, and kissed her hard. His lips were warm. Greer was so surprised she stopped laughing and kissed him back.

She felt a little dizzy. Martinis did that to her. Or maybe it was just having Eb Thibadeaux kissing her stupid. Greer decided she didn't care which it was, because it felt so damned good.

She wound her arms around his neck, and he gently pushed her backwards until she was flat on the floor. He stretched out beside her, kissing her again, working his tongue into her mouth and his knee between her legs. At some point she heard a thud, as he kicked off his loafers.

Greer ran her hands beneath his shirt, sliding them from his narrow waist to his shoulders, feeling the muscles flex as he turned toward her. His lips wandered away from hers as he nuzzled her ear, then dropped lower, feathering kisses on her neck, her shoulder, her collarbone.

"You smell nice," he whispered in her ear, running one hand beneath her damp top.

"Motel soap," she whispered back. "Courtesy of the Silver Sands."

His thumb brushed her nipple, came back, brushed again, and she arched her back in pleasure, so he did it again.

"That was no accident."

"Definitely not." He pushed the lace of her bra aside, found her nipple, and teased it with his tongue. "Neither is this."

She sucked in her breath, let it out slowly. "Allie."

"Hmm?" He raised his head and gave her a quizzical look.

"Your niece. What about Allie?"

Eb kissed the tip of her nose. "Relax. She lives with Ginny. We've got all night." He returned to what he'd been doing earlier.

Greer dug her fingers into his shoulders. He slid one hand down her belly and expertly unzipped her capris. He worked the waistband of her panties slowly downward, touched her tentatively, and then again, stroking inside her, as she gasped from the ripples of pleasure.

"Wait." She pushed herself away from him, hurriedly unbuttoning his shirt, sliding the sleeves from his shoulders. She kicked off her shoes, while she was at it.

When she turned back she found that Gunter had wedged himself between them. He licked her arm.

"Go away," Eb said. "Get your own girl." He scooted the dog backwards and reached for Greer, tugging her top over her head. He frowned when he saw the camisole she wore beneath the tank. "What's this? Two tops?"

"It's a conspiracy," Greer said, with a throaty laugh that died down as his lips found hers and his hands worked at undressing her. She propped herself up on her elbows and he pulled the lacy camisole over her head.

She ran her hands up his chest, teasing his nipples with her fingertips, and he pulled her closer, so his warm flesh was touching hers. He kissed her, and she inhaled the scent of him, something salty, something cedar-like. With a finger, he traced the outline of her lips.

"Anybody ever tell you that you have great lips?" he whispered. "I've been wondering since the first morning we met if they'd taste as good as they look."

She flicked her tongue inside his mouth. "And?"

"Better." He worked his hands down her hips, pushing at her capris for a moment, then stopping to bring his hands up, stroking her back.

In the dimmest recesses of her mind it occurred to Greer that things were getting out of hand here. Literally.

But it felt too good to stop. Eb suckled her nipples, and she groaned with pleasure

He kissed his way south, the stubble of his beard rasping on the tender skin of her abdomen. She curled her fingers into his hair as he licked into her and she felt an electric warmth flooding her body.

At some point she heard the teakettle whistling.

"Eb?"

He nipped her with his teeth, licked again, and she forgot all about the tea.

She worked her hands around to his waist and lowered the zipper on his fly with one hand as she tugged his briefs downward with her other, struggling to free the fabric from his impressive erection.

"Oh God," Eb moaned, pushing her hand away.

"What?" She looked up at him in surprise.

"Condoms."

"Oh God," she moaned. She sat up. "Absolutely."

He raised one eyebrow. "I don't suppose you . . ."

"What? Keep a stash of condoms in my purse when I go to a city council meeting, just in case I decide to sleep with the mayor?"

He sighed and reached for his discarded pants.

"Where are you going?" She pushed a stray curl out of her eyes.

He kissed her and brushed his fingertip against her jaw before standing and pulling on his slacks.

"Downstairs. Aisle six. Top shelf. One of the perks of living above the store."

She smiled. "I could make the tea while you're gone." She searched around on the floor for her clothes.

"The hell with the tea. I'll be back in two minutes. Stay right there."

She shook her head and stood up. "This is a terrible idea."

His face fell.

"That floor is cold and hard, and I've already got a splinter in my butt. Don't you have a bed or something a little softer?"

That big grin creased his face. He pointed toward the living room. "Right behind that sliding barn door. Two minutes. I swear."

He was halfway to the door.

"Eb?"

He turned, a wary look on his face.

"You mentioned cookies?"

"You got it."

He left the front door ajar and she heard him, taking the stairs two at a time, chanting "Cookies and condoms" under his breath.

18

Gunter whined and waddled toward the door Eb had left ajar. His tail switched slowly as he stared down the darkened hallway. The old dog gave one short, anxious bark.

"It's okay, buddy," Greer said as she gathered up her scattered clothing. "He'll be right back."

She found a paper towel in the kitchen, dampened it, and mopped up the puddle Gunter had left on the floor, then tossed him a treat from the jar on the kitchen counter.

The sliding barn door was heavy and she had to use both hands to yank it aside. She couldn't find a light switch, so she stumbled into the dim room, toward the bed and a nightstand with a lamp.

"Wow," she breathed, gazing around the room. The bedroom had exposed brick walls, too, and a battered wooden floor and high ceilings.

Eb was a typical straight, single male. Piles of discarded clothing littered the bare floor.

A worn pair of jeans hung on the footboard of a massive wrought iron bed frame. She ran her hand over the cool iron and decided it must have been made from salvage. The bed was unmade, with rumpled sheets and a plain quilted cotton blanket that looked suspiciously like a movers pad. A ceiling fan whirred lazily overhead. The swing arm lamps on either side of the bed were tarnished brass pharmacy lamps. There was a huge Victorian mahogany wardrobe in one corner of the room, which obviously stood in as Eb's closet, and beside it stood a makeshift dresser fashioned from an old wire-frame bread rack with a faded Merita Bread and Cakes logo.

Another large bank of steel-frame windows was curtainless, and she could see and hear the rain slashing outside. The sky lit up again with jagged strikes of lightning.

She switched on the bathroom light. More surprises here. The walls were of rough whitewashed shiplap lumber, but the floor was old black and white penny tile. A sink vanity had been fashioned from a vintage oak dresser, and its matching cheval mirror reflected Greer's messy blond curls and cheeks stained red from beard burn. She blushed when she realized she'd gone to the city council meeting earlier straight from a long day's work.

A claw-foot bathtub rigged out with a showerhead stood in a corner of the bathroom, which had been lined with sheets of corrugated tin. Impulsively, Greer turned on the water, dropped her clothes, and stepped in.

She let the hot water stream over her skin. Clouds of steam fogged the room, and she groped around the tub until she found a bar of Irish Spring soap on a block of wood nailed to the tin sheathing.

"Hey!" The voice startled her so badly she dropped the soap. She peeked around the shower curtain to see Eb Thibadeaux, bare chested, standing in the bathroom doorway.

"You don't mind, do you? I'm positively crusty from working all day."

He took a step forward and pulled the shower curtain aside, taking in her water-slicked pink body. She blushed and yanked the curtain closed. "I'll be out in just a minute."

Eb took a seat on the commode. "I can wait."

She peeked around the curtain again. "Out!"

She found a tiny bottle of hotel shampoo on the same ledge where the soap had been. She worked it into a lather and rubbed it into her scalp. The shampoo was the same cheap stuff stocked at the Silver Sands. Her hair would look like steel wool when it dried, but at least it would be clean steel wool. While she massaged her scalp, the thought occurred to her that she was taking a shower in a strange man's bathroom, after thirty minutes of fairly intense foreplay. He had every expectation that things were going to escalate. She had actually encouraged those expectations.

In fact, she wanted Eb Thibadeaux more than she'd wanted any man in a really long time. But what the hell was she thinking? She wasn't like CeeJay or the other women she worked with in the film business. They might hook up with a guy during a shoot, just for convenience — shack up for a few weeks, screw each other's brains out, then part without a backward glance. That wasn't Greer. And this wasn't just any casual crew screw. Eb was the mayor of Cypress Key. The mayor! Who was standing between her and getting her job done. What the hell?

She stood under the showerhead and rinsed her hair. She thought of how his hands had felt on her body, his lips on hers. They had come very, very close back there on his dining room floor. But not close enough. She hadn't been with a man since Sawyer, which meant it was nearly two years now.

CeeJay claimed that made Greer a born-again virgin.

"You about done in there?" Eb called, bringing her back to the here and now. "Need anything scrubbed?"

"Stay where you are." She squeezed the

excess water from her hair. Close was not enough. She wanted it all. She wanted Eb Thibadeaux hot and throbbing inside her, and the hell with the consequences.

She stepped out of the tub, wrapped a towel around herself, and wiped enough condensation from the fogged-up mirror to get a look at herself. Her hair looked like Medusa's — wet, wiry coils springing everywhere. She searched the bathroom, hoping for something like moisturizer, or a hairbrush, or any kind of beauty aid. She hesitated for a moment, glanced toward the bathroom door, and slowly opened the medicine cabinet.

Nothing promising — or surprising — here. A bottle of aspirin, a box of Q-tips, a tube of deodorant, and some antacids. She quietly closed the cabinet and hurriedly dragged a comb through her tangled locks.

The bathroom door opened slowly, and her first impulse was to hide. But then she saw his face, lit up like a Christmas candle.

He tucked a strand of her hair behind her ear and traced a drop of water down her cheek with his fingertip, his touch light and caressing. "Hello, beautiful."

She took his hand and followed him into the darkened bedroom.

He'd left just one lamp burning. Greer saw a forty-count box of Trojans on the bedside table and barely managed to suppress a giggle. He obviously had big plans for this evening. She stood in a pool of golden light beside the bed and looked at him expectantly. Eb hooked one finger under the edge of the towel and it fell to the floor.

"God, Greer," he breathed. She felt herself blush deeply and wanted to grab for something, anything, to hide her body. But Eb didn't give her a chance. He leaned forward and kissed her, lightly at first. He ran his hands down her back, and she shivered, so he pulled her closer, smoothing his hands under her butt cheeks, resting them there, pushing himself up against her.

His lips and hands wandered as he found her nipples, sucking one, then the other, while he stroked within her, until she was weak with needing more.

She unzipped his fly and pushed his pants and briefs down, over his narrow hips, then lower still. He took a step backwards and kicked free of them.

In the dim lamplight she took a moment to appreciate his physique. Eb's chest was smoothly muscled, with dark hair curling on his chest and groin. He was deeply tanned, with thick thighs and powerful calves.

He was backing her slowly toward the bed. She tumbled onto it and pulled him down with her. They lay facing each other, touching and kissing, stroking and licking, exploring each other's bodies until Greer thought she would lose her mind.

She straddled him and lowered herself slowly, savoring every inch of him, the palms of her hands braced against his chest. Every nerve in her body was taut. He caught her breast in his hand, stroked the nipple with the pad of his thumb, and she heard herself gasp with pleasure.

"Good?"

She kissed him in answer. "So good."

A few more thrusts, then he abruptly rolled away from her, groping in the dark for the condoms, smiling with his entire body.

Eb Thibadeaux was a man who took things slow. He teased her with his body, entering, stroking, withholding, smiling at her with his entire body.

Finally, when she was drenched with sweat and her entire body was writhing with need, she felt herself catching the sweetest wave of pleasure, and now they were surfing the wave together.

Afterwards, she rested her cheek on his chest, listening to the rain outside.

"I should go," she muttered.

"Why?" He was stroking her back, drawing lazy circles with his forefinger.

"We have an early-morning call. I have to be at the motel at four. I've got to get some sleep."

"They can't film in this storm, right?"

"Not if the rain doesn't let up, no," she admitted. "But I should go anyway."

The room was quiet. And then they heard soft snoring coming from the corner, where Gunter was sprawled on his back in a bed made out of an old wooden Coke crate.

"I think you should stay. We haven't even touched the cookies."

She propped herself up on one elbow. "I forgot about the cookies."

"I didn't."

He slid out from the covers and grabbed a plastic sack she hadn't noticed earlier.

He dealt the packages out onto the quilt. "I wasn't sure what kind you like, so I got some of everything we had. Oreos. Pecan Sandies. Fig Newtons —"

"Eww." She shuddered. "No Fig Newtons."

"Check. I'll make a note of that." He continued with the inventory. "Nilla Wafers. Nutter Butters. Chips Ahoy —"

"Chips Ahoy? Oh my God! The kind with the M&Ms?"

"You like 'em too? They're my favorites."

Eb opened the bag and offered her the first cookie. She leaned in and grabbed it with her teeth, then plopped back against the pillows and chewed happily, brushing at the crumbs that rained down on the sheets. He took a cookie, reclined on the pillow next to hers, and did the same.

Fifteen minutes later the blue bag was

empty and the sheets were strewn with cookie crumbs and the brightly colored shards of the M&Ms.

Greer sighed deeply. "That was amazing."

"Me? Or the cookies?"

"You. Definitely," Greer said, stretching and yawning. "The cookies were just an added bonus."

He pulled the sheet away from her bare breasts and leered. "And just think. I own a whole store *full* of cookies. Shelves and shelves of them. We can do this anytime you like."

"Are you trying to bribe me with Chips Ahoy?" Greer slid her feet onto the ground.

Eb grabbed for her but missed. "Come on, don't go just when we were having so much fun."

"Eb. I told you I have to work."

"Are you going to walk back to the motel in this rain?" He pointed out the window.

"I thought maybe you'd loan me an umbrella." She retrieved the towel she'd abandoned earlier and wrapped it around herself.

"Stay until the rain stops. Then I'll take you home in my golf cart."

A smile played across her lips. He wanted her to stay. He wanted her to sleep with him, which was the sweetest thing she could imagine. Sawyer never spent the night with her after they'd made love. Not in all the eighteen months they'd been together.

A wicked streak of lightning rattled the steel window frame, and she jumped.

"See?" He sensed she was on the fence about leaving, and tugged her hand. "C'mon. Just until the rain stops."

With a sigh she dropped the towel and climbed back into the bed. And Eb's arms.

19

The alarm chime on her phone rang quietly but insistently. Greer sat up in bed, momentarily disoriented.

Then she heard the sound of soft snoring, saw the tousled head on the pillow next to hers. She leaned over, to make sure that the previous night hadn't been just another erotic dream, gently lifting the edge of the sheet. The sight of Eb Thibadeaux's naked body, next to her own similarly unclothed form, jolted her wide awake.

What had she been thinking? Sleeping with the mayor of Cypress Key? Worse, sleeping with the mayor of Cypress Key after having sex with him. Lots of lovely, hot, messy sex, at that.

Greer gave herself a mental head slap. Had she really gotten that buzzed off one and a half martinis? And a glass of cheap rosé?

She slid quietly out of bed and crawled around in the dark, looking for her clothes and her phone. After she'd managed to gather up everything, she tiptoed to the bathroom and closed the door before turning on the light.

What she saw in the mirror gave her a shock. Something as round and red as a bullet hole pierced the exact middle of her forehead. Good God. Maybe she really had been drunk. Her fingertips flew to her face and touched the red spot. No pain. She held her fingertip up to the light and found herself staring at a red M&M.

Oh yes. The Chips Ahoy orgy was real too. She found a smeared green M&M stuck to her collarbone. Way real.

Greer dressed hurriedly, tucked her phone in her pocket, and switched the light off again before opening the door.

The lamp on the nightstand was on and Eb was sitting up in bed. His hair was mashed to the side of his face, and in that moment he looked so boyish, so adorable, she could have licked him like an all-day sucker.

Then she gave herself another mental head slap. What was she thinking?

"Where are you going?" he asked, yawning.

The lie slipped off her tongue as easily as honey. "Don't judge, okay? It's just, after sex, I crave ice cream."

He rewarded her with a sleepy smile. "I could do some butter pecan, if you're interested. It's on the far left wall. Top shelf. Get the good stuff, okay? It's on me."

She felt a sharp, bitter pang of guilt. For once, this lie was killing her. She slid her feet into her sandals. "Be right back."

Her purse was on the dining room table, where she'd left it the night before. She hurriedly hooked it over her shoulder, pushed the sliding door aside, and headed down the stairs.

She rushed for the market's front door and let herself out. The sidewalk was slick with rain, which was still coming down, and as she dashed toward the motel she allowed herself one backward glance, over her shoulder. She could see one tiny, dim spot of light coming from one of Eb's apartment windows on the second floor. This had been a bad idea. Time to run from the light.

A block from the motel, her phone pinged. She hesitated, then reached into her pocket to retrieve it.

The text was from the film's production manager.

NO SHOOT IN MORNING, DUE TO WEATHER. MEET AT 6 @SCHOOL INSTEAD.

Eb stood in front of the window, watching the slight form of a woman as she splashed hurriedly down the street, in the rain. Her handbag was slung over her shoulder. This was a planned retreat. He flung the bag of

Chips Ahoy against the wall. It was his own fault. He'd distrusted her from the start, but then had let her looks and charm win him over. What had his dad told him, when he'd first started dating, as a horny, hormone-driven teen? "Never do your thinking with your pecker, son." Advice for the ages, as it turned out.

20

Friday, midmorning, Greer was, as usual, trying to do two things at once. Returning a text
from Phil, the production manager, who
wanted to know when construction would be
complete at the high school gym, where the
next week's scenes were to be shot, and trying to lock her motel room door. She finished
typing, shoved her phone in her pocket, and
turned around to lock the door, only to find
Eb Thibadeaux standing in the doorway of
her room with a stack of clean towels.

It was the first time she'd encountered him
since fleeing the Hometown Market in the
dead of night three days earlier. Every day
since then, she'd regretted that moment, and
tortured herself, wondering how everything
had gone so wrong so quickly.

"Hi!" she said brightly.

"Hey." His eyes were dead. He thrust the
stack of towels into her arms.

She searched for something meaningful to
say. What she came up with was not her best

work. "How've you been?"

"Fine." He turned back to the cart of linens he'd been trundling down the passageway outside her room, and produced a large plastic sack, which he hung on the doorknob of her room.

"What's this?" She picked up the bag and peered inside.

"Couple things. The key to the city, which you left at city hall, and your bra, which you left behind after you snuck out of my place three nights ago."

"Oh." Her cheeks burned with shame — not at having slept with this lovely, decent man, but at her behavior afterward.

"You're welcome." He turned abruptly and pushed the cart down the corridor at an accelerated pace.

She tossed the towels onto her bed, pushed the thumb latch, closed the door, and raced down the hallway to catch up with him. "I noticed you replaced the air conditioner in my room. Thanks so much. I'm sleeping so much better now that I can cool it down."

"Don't thank me. It was Ginny's idea," he said, still in an eerily accurate robot imitation. He knocked on the door he was standing in front of, called out "Housekeeping," and then, after a moment, used his key to unlock the door. She stood in the doorway, watching as he placed another stack of towels on another dresser.

"Eb, look. I'm sorry about the other night. . . ."

He upended the contents of a trash basket into a large plastic bag attached to the laundry cart, then turned to her.

"Sorry you slept with me? Or sorry about afterwards, when you lied and told me you were going downstairs for ice cream — and then just ran away? Do you have any idea how I felt, when I finally realized you weren't coming back? Who does something like that? Was I that terrible?"

"No! You were wonderful. I had fun. Oh God. I don't know what's wrong with me. I just . . . shouldn't have let things go as far as they did. You're amazing, but sleeping with you was a really bad idea. It was totally unprofessional on my part."

He reached into a carton on top of the cart and brought out miniature shampoo and moisturizer bottles and tiny bars of soap, which he slammed down on the dresser.

"What was so wrong about it? We're single, consenting adults. And you said yourself, movie people are notorious for hooking up on movie sets."

"I'm not notorious for it," Greer said, her cheeks burning. "I told you, I don't do hook-ups."

Eb's cheek muscle twitched. "We had sex. And then you left. Wham, bam, thank you Sam? If that's not a hookup, I don't know what is."

"Okay, I didn't handle that very well."

"Yeah, the ice cream ploy was pretty bush league. I expect something better than that from a professional liar like you."

Greer walked out of the room and returned to her own. A moment later she heard him knocking on the next door. "Housekeeping."

21

The call came at 2:00 a.m., Thursday. The caller ID screen read Cypress Key Police Department. Greer sat up in bed and hit the Connect button, her heart pounding, already imagining any number of reasons why the police might be calling her at that hour. None of them were good.

"Hello? This is Greer Hennessy."

"Hey, Miss Greer. This is Chief Bottoms. Look, I'm over here at the PD and we've got one of your people in my holding cell, and he's raising a big ol' ruckus. I think you might want to come over here and talk to him before things really get out of hand."

"One of our people? Which one?" Greer had a feeling she already knew.

"Kregg," Chief Bottoms said, her voice dripping disgust.

"Oh no," Greer groaned. "What did he do?"

"Mmm, reckless driving, speeding, open container, public indecency to start with. And if he keeps running that foul mouth of his,

I'm gonna find a bunch of other stuff to add to the list. I haven't run a breathalyzer on him yet, but I can tell you right now what it'll show. . . ."

"Please don't do that," Greer said. "I'm on my way right now."

She called Bryce Levy on her way to the police station. The first call went directly to voice mail. "Bryce — it's Greer. I just got a call from the police chief. They've got Kregg in custody for speeding and some other stuff. Just thought you should know."

Her phone beeped to signal an incoming call. She ended the voice mail and clicked to connect.

"Greer?" Bryce's voice was gravelly with sleep. "What's wrong?"

"I just left you a message. I'm on my way to the police station. The cops have Kregg in custody."

"Dammit. What did he do this time?"

"Speeding and reckless driving for starters. Possibly driving under the influence too. I think the chief called me as a courtesy. What do you want me to do?"

"Get him out of there as quick and as quiet as you can," Bryce said. "Whatever it takes, okay? We do not need to get this out to the media. Understand? Call me when you know something."

When she pulled the Kia into the police station parking lot, a tow truck was just arriving — trailing a shiny black Porsche Carrera with a vanity tag that read "KILLA."

Arnelle Bottoms looked as though she'd gotten a wake-up call about Kregg, too, because in place of her ever-present uniform she was wearing jeans and an orange and green Florida A&M University T-shirt, and sitting at the station's front desk.

"Mornin'," she said, as Greer walked through the door.

"Thanks for calling me," Greer said. "I just saw a tow truck pull up with a Porsche. Is that Kregg's?"

"Ain't nobody else in Cypress Key driving a car with a $130,000 sticker on the window," the chief said.

"Hey-y-y!" A loud voice echoed from the back of the station. "Hey, cocksuckers, you better cut me loose! When my lawyer gets here, he's gonna sue your asses! You fuckers are goin' down!"

"Hear that?" the chief said, pointing toward a door at the rear of the small reception area. "He's been like that since we put him in there."

"He's a prince of a guy," Greer commented. "What exactly was he doing?"

"Depends on who you believe. Shelley, the bartender at the Crow's Nest, said he and a couple of his homeys rolled in there shortly after midnight. They were drinking shots and

217

beers, and partying pretty good. Your boy got in a verbal altercation with one of the locals, and Shelley suggested they take it outside. At which point your boy —

"Please don't refer to him as my boy," Greer said.

"Right. So, the accused, Kregg, took that to mean he should whip out his pecker and piss right there on the sidewalk outside the front door."

"Oh no, no, no," Greer moaned.

"One of the locals saw Kregg's new Porsche and had some derogatory remarks to make about it, so Kregg, he invited the local to a little drag race. Right down the middle of Pine Street, at one o'clock in the morning. By that time, Shelley had already called nine-one-one, and one of our patrol officers, Balfour, was en route. That's when he clocked the Porsche at one hundred ten miles per hour, as Kregg blew by him — right down the center line of the street."

"I'm guessing Kregg won the race?" Greer asked. "What happened to the local?"

"He peeled off as soon as Balfour switched on lights and siren," Chief Bottoms said. "Doesn't matter. The dumb-ass was driving his work truck with the phone number right on the door. Balfour's on his way over to his house to pick him up."

Greer glanced anxiously around the station. She and the chief were alone. No reporters, no photographers. Thank God.

"I take it no official charges have been filed yet?"

The chief shrugged. "I thought I'd meet with you first. You've been straight up with us since you came to town, and my officers love all the extra pay, doing security work for you."

"And we really appreciate all their hard work," Greer said.

"On the other hand, he . . ." the chief jerked her thumb in the general direction of where Greer assumed the holding cell must be, "is nothin' but white trash. He's been hollerin' to call his lawyer since we brought him in, and you just heard a sampling of the kind of names he's been calling us."

"So sorry," Greer said. "Not everybody in the business is like that, but the ones like Kregg — too much attention, too much money, too little sense — give everybody else a bad name."

"That's the truth," the chief agreed. "All my guys say that Adelyn Davis is a total sweetheart. Poses for pictures, signs autographs, nice as can be."

"Which brings us back to Kregg," Greer said. "Obviously, I'm not a lawyer, and I don't have any real authority to make offers on behalf of Kregg or the production company, but I do know that sometimes, when an actor has misbehaved, we make arrangements for restitution in lieu of formal charges being filed."

"Restitution?"

"Kregg could make a generous donation to the charity of your choice. I would imagine the production company might also be willing to make a contribution."

"I was thinking some community service hours would be good, too," the Chief said. "I bet that boy would look real good in a safety orange vest, picking up trash on the side of the county road."

Greer laughed. "I'd pay money to see that! Unfortunately, I think his lawyer would probably scream bloody murder about that idea. And his bodyguards would probably get in the way."

The chief yawned loudly. "We'll come up with something. Maybe have him film a public service announcement about safe driving."

"Good idea. Do you want to release him to me, or keep him until morning?"

"Get him out of here," the chief said. "And when I get home tonight, I'm gonna burn every single Kregg CD my kids own."

"That's it?" Greer said, trying not to sound incredulous. "No incident report? No charges? Don't you want something in writing from me?"

Arnelle Bottoms winked. "I don't need anything in writing. I know right where you're staying. Later on today, after we both get some sleep, you can tell me how much he's gonna contribute to our Police Benevolent Society."

"Fair enough," Greer said.

"All right then. Lemme go get that piece of garbage out of my holding cell."

The chief's hand was clamped firmly on Kregg's shoulder as she steered him into the front room of the police station.

Kregg's eyes were red rimmed and heavy lidded. He wore tight black jeans and an unbuttoned blue work shirt with hacked-off sleeves. And orange jail-issue flip-flops. He slouched against the counter.

"He's all yours," the chief said, giving him a gentle shove in Greer's direction. "Oh yeah." She brought out a large, sealed manila envelope from behind the front counter and thrust it into Kregg's hands. "Here's your stuff." She stabbed the front of the envelope. "Need you to initial that it's all there."

"It better be." He ripped off the top of the envelope. Two thick gold rope chains, a diamond stud earring, the Porsche keys, and a diamond-studded money clip holding a fat wad of twenty-dollar bills spilled onto the counter.

Kregg picked up the pen Arnelle Bottoms offered, scribbled his initials on the envelope, and tossed the pen to the floor. He slipped the chains around his neck and tucked the cash and the earring in his pocket.

"Let's go," he said, looking directly at Greer.

"In a minute," the chief said. She pointed at the pen. "I'd like you to pick that up."

Kregg shrugged, leaned over, and retrieved the pen.

"One more thing," the chief said sternly. "This lady here, Miss Hennessy? She just guaranteed your Get Outta Jail Free card. She didn't have to get up out of bed and come down here tonight. And I didn't have to call her. But because she is a nice person, I extended her that courtesy."

"Great," Kregg said, sounding bored.

The chief poked him in the chest. "You, on the other hand, are not a nice person. So if you get in any more trouble in my town — and I mean if you so much as spit on my sidewalk — I'm gonna lock your punk ass up. You understand me, boy?"

Kregg rolled his eyes. "Yeah."

"Uh-uh," the chief said, poking his chest again. "You speak to me, it's 'Yes ma'am.' "

"Yes ma'am," Kregg said, smirking. "What about my car?"

"Your car is out in the parking lot, but you ain't driving nowhere tonight, unless you want Officer Balfour to run a Breathalyzer test on you," the chief said.

"How'll I get home?"

"I'll take you," Greer said wearily.

"A Kia?" He looked at the car in disbelief. "I'm supposed to ride in this piece of shit?"

Greer slid into the driver's seat. "You could always ask the chief to have one of the officers take you back to Bluewater Bay."

He turned his head as they passed the Porsche. "They better not mess with my car, man. If there's one scratch on it . . ."

"What?" Greer asked. "You'll sue the police department? After they just let you walk away from speeding, drag racing, and public indecency charges? And without checking your blood alcohol to add driving under the influence?"

"Hey!" Kregg said sharply. "It wasn't all my fault. That dude in the bar, he called me out. What was I supposed to do?"

"Walk away? Offer to buy him a beer? I can think of half a dozen choices that would have been better than running one hundred ten miles an hour down Main Street."

He gave her an appraising look. "What's your name again?"

"Greer Hennessy."

"You're something with the production company, right?"

"I'm the location manager."

"Right. So, thanks, I guess, for getting me out of there before one of those redneck cracker cops decided to pistol-whip me or something."

"Let me give you a piece of advice, Kregg. Lose the phrase 'redneck cracker' while you're in this town. Okay?"

"Sure." He leaned against the headrest. "Shit. What time is it?"

"Almost three."

"You happen to know what time my call is in the morning?"

"Seven. At the beach." She said it with a deeply malicious satisfaction.

"Shit."

He closed his eyes, and Greer thought he'd fallen asleep. They rolled up to the makeshift guard shack at Bluewater Bay and the off-duty cop, recognizing Greer, waved them through the open gate.

Kregg turned and looked at her through bleary eyes. "Hey, uh, we can just keep this between us. We're cool, right? No press, right?"

"You and I are cool, and I'm certainly not about to alert the media to what happened tonight," she assured him.

"Cool." He nodded his head. "And, I mean, Bryce doesn't need to hear about this. Okay?"

"Too late," she said. "I called him on the way to the police station."

"Jesus! Why'd you have to go and do that?"

"Because he's the boss. And he'd find out anyway."

"Did he sound pissed? Jesus, now I'm

gonna have him on my case all over again."

"He didn't sound pissed at me," Greer said. "But I'd imagine he'll want to have a discussion with you tomorrow."

"Great. He'll call my mom, and then the shit will really hit the fan."

"Your mom? Really? How old are you?"

"She's my manager, okay?" He shot her a look.

Greer shrugged it off. "By the way, sometime tomorrow you and your mom-slash-manager are going to want to make a very large, generous contribution to the Cypress Key Police Benevolent Society. And by generous, I'm thinking fifty thousand dollars sounds about right."

"Oh, hell no! Why would I give money to those redneck — I mean, cops?"

She pulled the Kia into the driveway of the rapper's rented house and parked behind the Hummer.

"Call it an expression of gratitude for walking free tonight."

"Fu-u-uck." He climbed out of the Kia, slammed the door, and headed for the house without a backward glance at his chauffeur.

"Nighty-night," Greer muttered.

22

Watching Kregg run lines and block scenes on the beach Thursday morning, nobody would know that he'd had only three hours of sleep after a long night of partying. His eyes were uncharacteristically clear, his voice was strong, and for once he seemed to hit his mark with every shot as Bryce put him through his paces.

Greer, on the other hand, felt and looked like death warmed over, with dark circles under her eyes and a fatigue that no amount of caffeine could assuage. The night before, she'd fallen into her bed for what seemed like only minutes before being roused to start solving problems. Fortunately, since the day's shoot was actually at the beach behind the Silver Sands, she hadn't had much of a commute.

She watched the grips lay a pathway of wooden planks across the soft, white sand, to afford traction to the camera dollies, and pitied the crew working in the high-nineties heat.

When Bryce finally called for lunch break, it was nearly one. She dragged herself over to the catering tent and was picking at a salad when CeeJay slid onto the chair opposite hers.

"Hey," Greer said wearily.

"Wow," CeeJay said, dipping a carrot into a cup of hummus. "I really love what you've done with yourself today."

"Which do you like best — the hair that looks like dryer lint or the giant bags under my eyes?"

"Why don't you come over to the makeup tent and let me fix you up a little?" CeeJay asked. "You truly look like one of those celebrity police booking photos from The Smoking Gun."

"I don't have the energy," Greer said. "But I notice Kregg looks remarkably refreshed and well rested. Unlike me."

"Thanks," CeeJay said, preening a little. "But looks can be deceiving. I used about a pound of Preparation H on his eye bags, and lots of eyedrops too."

"What did Bryce have to say about Kregg's exploits last night?" Greer asked.

"He was frothing at the mouth after he got off the phone with you," CeeJay said. "Then he put in a call to Anita and things really got ugly."

"That's Kregg's mom?"

"Momager," CeeJay said. "The woman lends new meaning to the phrase 'control freak.' She's absolutely vile. She was threatening to fly down here and sic her lawyers on the Cypress Key cops, but Bryce basically told her if she showed up he'd have her banned from the set."

"Did Bryce have words with Kregg?"

"Oh yes," CeeJay said. "They had a come-to-Jesus first thing, but I don't know what was discussed."

"Must have worked," Greer mused. She looked at her phone, saw the time, and stood. "Back to the grindstone."

Late in the day, between shots, Greer happened to glance back toward the beach and spied a lone figure sitting in the shade of an umbrella on Ginny Buckalew's porch.

She walked toward the porch, expecting to see the motel manager sneaking a smoke break, but was surprised to encounter Allie Thibadeaux, staring intently out at the beach from between some palm fronds.

"Hi, Allie," Greer said, as she reached the porch railing.

"Oh, hey," the girl said. "Is it okay for me to be sitting here? Am I in the way or something?"

"Not at all. Have you been watching long?"

"All afternoon. It's really cool, huh? I can't hear anything from here, but that's okay."

"Some days it's cooler than others," Greer said. "I guess you're a Kregg fan like every other girl on the planet, right?"

"He's okay," Allie said. "I'm a huge Adelyn fan. I've seen *Carry Me* probably twenty times. I like her other movies a lot too, but that's my favorite. I can't believe she didn't even get nominated for an Oscar for that."

"I like *Carry Me,* too, but it was only her second movie, and the subject matter was a little dark for the Academy," Greer confided. "I'm surprised you even know about that movie."

"It's so cool that you're making a movie in Cypress Key. I can't even believe Adelyn Davis ate dinner at the Inn last night. I was totally geeking out when she walked in."

Greer was touched by the girl's enthusiasm. "Well, if you're really that interested, you're welcome to come on down to the set." She pointed toward one of several blue tents set up close to the water's edge. "I've got a chair under the tent down there, but I'm not really using it today."

The girl jumped up from her chair. "Really? Oh my God! That would be so awesome."

"Come on around," Greer said, indicating the gate that led from the patio to the beach.

Allie trailed her across the sand to the tent where Bryce and his assistant were peering at the screen of a laptop, watching the footage

229

that had just been shot.

"Sit here," Greer said, indicating a folding wooden and canvas director's chair with "Crew" screen printed on the back.

"Joe," she told one of the P.A.s who was standing nearby, "This is Allie. She's my guest, if that's okay."

"Sure thing," Joe said. "Let me know if you need anything."

Greer leaned down to give the girl instructions. "Just keep quiet and don't talk to anybody unless they talk to you, and you'll be fine. Okay?"

The girl nodded and beamed her appreciation.

"And if you get hungry or thirsty, go on up to the catering tent," Greer said. "Help yourself. If anybody asks, just tell him you're my guest."

Allie's eyes widened. "You're sure it's all right?"

"Perfectly sure."

The afternoon seemed endless, but whenever Greer glanced toward the blue tent she saw Allie's slight figure, bent over in her chair, intently watching the cameramen and lighting and sound techs.

Shortly after five, Bryce called it a wrap for the day. Greer still had a production meeting with the art director and set designer. When she dragged herself back to her motel room two hours later, she nearly nodded off to sleep in the shower.

She'd just dressed in shorts and a ratty T-shirt, and was trying to decide between a microwaved burrito and a microwaved Hot Pocket, when there was a timid knock at her door. Allie Thibadeaux looked almost surprised when Greer opened the door.

"Hi, um, Ginny wondered if maybe you would want to eat dinner with us. She said it's just baked chicken, and I said you probably wouldn't come, and she said I should ask anyway. . . ." The teenager's words came rushing out in a torrent.

"I'd love to have dinner with you," Greer said, laughing. "Can it wait until I change clothes?"

"You don't have to change. Ginny and me are dressed crummy too," Allie said, blushing furiously when she realized that she'd just insulted the guest.

"Even better," Greer said.

The first thing Greer noticed, with relief, was that the glass-topped table in Ginny Buckalew's apartment was set for only three — meaning they would not be joined by Eb Thibadeaux.

A shallow bowl in the center of the table held a grouping of pink, yellow, and red hibiscus blossoms. "How pretty," Greer said.

She sniffed the tantalizing aroma of roast-

231

ing chicken wafting from the kitchen, sighed, and turned to Ginny, who handed her a cold beer. "A home-cooked meal. You have no idea what a treat this is for me."

"It's nothing fancy," Ginny said. "Allie, would you please check on my green beans, to make sure they're not burning?"

Allie nodded and disappeared into the kitchen.

"I just wanted to thank you for letting her watch today," Ginny said in a low voice. "That girl has always been crazy for movies. I thought about asking you if she could come on the set to watch, but then she made me promise I wouldn't impose on you."

"No imposition at all," Greer said.

Despite Ginny's claims that the menu was "nothing fancy," it was obvious to Greer that the older woman had taken pains with the fare: baked chicken and dressing, gravy, corn cut off the cob, fresh green beans cooked with chunks of ham, biscuits, and a lemon chess pie for dessert.

"How do you two eat like this and stay so skinny?" Greer looked from Ginny to Allie to the half-eaten slice of pie on her own plate.

"We don't eat like this all the time," Ginny said. "But we wanted to do something nice to say thanks for letting Allie go on your set today."

"It was probably totally boring for you,

232

right, Allie?" Greer asked.

"No way! Everybody was so nice. It was amazing," Allie said.

"Ginny tells me you're like me — a big movie buff. Is that right?"

"Uh-huh." Allie sipped her iced tea.

"Even when she was a little kid, she wanted to watch movies, and not just kid ones, either," Ginny volunteered. "Tell her your favorite movie, Al."

"She doesn't care about that stuff, Gin," Allie said.

"Sure I do," Greer said. "I'll tell you mine if you tell me yours. Let me guess — *Hunger Games,* right? Or maybe *Twilight?*"

"Mmm, not really. It changes sometimes, but right now it's *Rear Window.*"

"You're a Hitchcock fan? I'm impressed," Greer said.

"I wasn't so sure she should be watching those scary movies," Ginny said. "I still remember after watching *Psycho.* I didn't sleep for a week."

"Yeah, but *Rear Window*'s not gory scary," Allie said. "It's suspenseful. And I love the way Hitchcock played around with perspective — showing Jimmy Stewart's apartment, and then the apartment that he's spying on. You can never figure out what's going to happen next, and then, when it's about to happen, you're just holding your breath to see if Grace Kelly is going to get out of there before the bad guy comes back."

"I love *Rear Window*, too," Greer said. "Especially Grace Kelly's costumes. My grandmother was a seamstress in the Paramount costume shop, so I guess I pay attention to that kind of stuff."

"You said you'd tell me your favorite movie," Allie reminded her.

"Easy. Has to be *Sabrina*. How could you go wrong with Billy Wilder directing Audrey Hepburn, Humphrey Bogart, and William Holden?" Greer said.

"Oh-h-h. I like that one too," Allie agreed. "Is Billy Wilder the guy who directed *Some Like It Hot*? I loved Marilyn Monroe in that."

"Very good!" Greer said, applauding softly. "You really do know your movies, Allie."

"I'm a total old movie nerd," Allie said apologetically. "We don't have a movie theater here, so I mostly download and watch."

"You should see all the movies on her iPad," Ginny said. "Show her, Al."

"God, Gin. No!"

"Do you like any more contemporary movies?"

"It's not very recent, but I like Amy Heckerling — she did *Clueless*, you know? Super cute, and I like that she wrote it too," Allie confided. "And *Bridesmaids*. Hilarious, right? Kristin Wiig is the bomb."

"*Bridesmaids* was awful!" Ginny put in. "Nasty!"

234

"Don't be such an old lady, Gin," Allie teased. "You know you laughed."

Ginny stood up and began clearing the dishes.

"Let me help," Greer said. "You did all this cooking."

"You'd never be able to find where to put stuff in my kitchen," Ginny said. "You two just sit there and talk about your movies, and I'll fix some coffee."

"I like your aunt," Greer said, when Ginny was gone. "She reminds me of Dearie, my grandmother that I told you about, who helped raise me."

"Gin's pretty cool. You know, I forget she's really my great-aunt. She's more like my mom, kinda."

Greer studied the girl. Her bright blue eyes were sparkling with excitement.

"What do you like best about movies?" Greer asked.

Allie scrunched up her face while she considered the question. "I don't know. I guess — they make me feel a part of things — that I could never really be a part of. At night, in my room, I like to turn off all the lights and watch a movie on my iPad. If it's a good movie — like *The Quiet Man,* or *Moonstruck* — I forget I'm just a kid in this dinky little town. And I'm living in that world — the world in the movie."

Allie used the edge of her hand to sweep

crumbs from the tablecloth and into a napkin, her brow wrinkled in concentration.

She looked up at Greer. "Before I came to live with Gin and Eb, when I was living with my mom in this super-creepy apartment, she worked nights, at Walmart, so she'd buy me all these Disney DVDs, and I'd watch them, alone, in the apartment, like all night, till she came home. I was scared, you know, of being there alone, and TV scared me more, because it showed bad stuff. So I watched *The Little Mermaid* and *Beauty and the Beast* and *Aladdin,* and they were pretty and brave, and they were like my make-believe friends."

"I used to do that, too, when I was a little kid," Greer said dreamily. "In the summer, if my grandmother couldn't watch me, Lise would drop me off at the multiplex in our neighborhood, with five bucks to get popcorn and a Coke. I'd hit all four theaters sometimes. Back to back. All by myself. But I didn't care, because it was the movies, and I thought nothing bad could happen at the movies."

"Did you have a favorite as a kid?" Allie asked.

"*The Goonies,* and maybe *Princess Bride.* And any John Hughes movie, when I hit my teens. I was a weirdo. So, are you interested in acting?"

"Not really."

"Me neither," Greer said. "I wanted to create the worlds I saw."

Allie hesitated. "This is going to sound so crazy conceited, but I really want to be a writer, or a director, or both."

"It doesn't sound conceited at all," Greer said.

"But it's really hard for women, right?"

"Very hard," Greer said. "Hollywood is a boys' club. But some women manage to break through. You've seen Nora Ephron's movies, right?"

Allie nodded vigorously. "Nora Ephron — she's like my god. Did you ever meet her?"

"No, but I wish I had." Greer said, barely managing to stifle another yawn.

Ginny swept into the dining room with a dish towel draped over her arm. "Come on, Allie," Ginny said briskly. "Let Greer go on back to her room to get some sleep now. She can barely keep her eyes open."

"It's not the company, I swear," Greer said. "I had a really late night last night, and a long day today. I wish I could stay and talk movies more with you, Allie. This was fun."

"Me too," Allie said. "Today was unbelievable. Adelyn even said hi to me when I went to the catering tent to get a bottle of water."

"You know," Greer said slowly, "if you're interested, I could probably hire you on as a P.A. Not full time or anything. You have your driver's license, right?"

"Oh my God. Yes! Are you serious?" Allie jumped out of her chair and threw her arms around Greer.

"What's a P.A.?" Ginny asked.

"A production assistant," Allie said. "Joe — he's one — he explained what kinds of stuff he does. It would be, like, my dream job."

"Good," Greer said. "I've got some stuff to do at the production office in the morning. Why don't you meet me there, around eleven?"

"Yes, yes, yes!" Allie chanted. "Thank you, thank you, thank you!"

23

While the crew was breaking down the equipment to move to the next location on Friday, Greer fired off a quick text to CeeJay.

Meet me for lunch?
C U in 10, CeeJay texted back.

"So . . . how's it going with you two?" Greer asked, after they'd found an empty table under the catering tent and piled plates with that day's offerings.

"Great. Really great. Bryce is super busy, but I think he's generally happy with the way filming is going. The house is cool. I love watching these Gulf sunsets."

"Any word about the divorce?" Greer asked.

"Nope. I think he's talked to his lawyer back on the coast a couple times, but I try to stay out of his drama. We're happy, so why rock the boat?"

Greer studied her friend. Today CeeJay wore her hair in a wispy strawberry blond updo, and her eyes were lined with dramatic, shiny black liner and deep turquoise shadow that gave her a modern Cleopatra vibe. She wore a black and white sleeveless striped cotton maxi dress and black platform sandals.

"I'm happy you're happy, but it's weird that we're both working on the same project and we hardly ever see each other except for ten or fifteen minutes in between shots. I miss hanging out with you."

"I know. I miss us, too. I mean, Bryce is awesome, but a girl needs her girlfriends, right?"

"Hey, I've got an idea," Greer said. "What about dinner tonight? One of the grips was telling me about a Thai place over in Ducktown, which he claims is the authentic, real deal."

"That would be amazing," CeeJay said. "Don't get me wrong, the chef Bryce hired to cook for us is fabulous, but after a while you kinda get tired of all that hand-rolled sushi and fancy French shit, you know?"

"I don't know, but I'll take your word for it," Greer said. "If we manage to stay on schedule today, how about I pick you up at your house around seven?"

"It's a date," CeeJay agreed. "Bryce won't miss me. I think he's playing basketball with Kregg and his peeps tonight."

As she spoke, CeeJay's gaze wandered away from Greer. "Speaking of which, who's that with our boy wonder?" CeeJay pointed with a forkful of salad in the general direction of a black golf cart that had rolled to a stop at the edge of the catering tent.

Greer had just bitten into a fish taco loaded with morsels of fried redfish, avocado, tomato, and queso cheese. She swiveled around in her seat to get a look at the subject of her friend's inquiry.

"Oh shit." She frowned when she saw the pretty blond teenager sitting on the front seat beside the cart's driver, Kregg.

"That's Allie Thibadeaux. And that ain't good."

CeeJay bit into her own taco, then delicately wiped the edge of her lips with a paper napkin. "Huh?"

"The mayor's niece."

"Uh-oh." CeeJay eyed the girl thoughtfully. "Cute girl, though. How old?"

"Only seventeen, but she's really a nice girl. Crazy about movies, and thinks she wants to be a writer/director. I just hired her as a very part-time P.A."

"As far as Kregg's concerned, she's total jailbait," CeeJay said.

"Exactly." Greer sipped her iced tea. "And he's, what, twenty-two?"

"Barely legal," CeeJay said. "Or illegal, in his case."

"Kregg better start cleaning up his act," Greer said. "I talked to Chief Bottoms this morning. That matching donation Bryce

241

made to the Police Benevolent Society was a good idea, but I think she's serious when she says there'll be no more free passes for Kregg."

"We'll see." CeeJay nibbled on a cherry tomato, then glanced down at her phone with a sigh.

"I've got five more minutes before time to get him ready for his next scene," CeeJay said. "He's such an entitled little brat. He shows up at least fifteen or twenty minutes late for hair and makeup, every time. He doesn't deign to converse with the likes of a lowly grunt like me. Mostly, he's listening to his own music on his iPod, or he's texting one of his homeys, or he's on the phone with his momager, bitching about being stuck in this godforsaken hellhole."

CeeJay wrinkled her nose. "He also reeks of cheap weed. Even first thing in the morning, and especially after lunch break."

"And he just got out of rehab, like a week ago? Does Bryce know?"

"Bryce chooses not to know," CeeJay said. "If Kregg gets into trouble again and has to go back to that 'spa' in Arizona, after we've already started shooting, it'd cost millions. So, for now, 'Don't ask, don't tell' is our motto."

She wrapped the remains of her taco in foil and dropped it onto her paper plate.

"I better go. God! I can't wait till we're

done shooting these friggin' beach scenes. Kregg's acne has gotten out of control in all this heat and humidity. Yesterday his dermatologist overnighted some kind of goo that I'm supposed to slather all over his body before I apply the self-tanner or the regular makeup. He never says a word while I'm basting him with all that stuff . . ." She looked around the tent, then lowered her voice.

"But it's apparently a turn-on for the little pervert, because he gets a boner. Every single time. Which he makes no pretense of hiding."

"Eww." Greer dropped her half-eaten taco onto her plate. She leaned closer. "So?"

CeeJay placed her thumb and forefinger a scant inch apart. "Just like a real penis. Only smaller."

The two friends had a good laugh over that before CeeJay stood to leave. She stopped only a step or two from the table she'd shared with Greer.

"Oh, look at Romeo and Juliet now. Parting is such sweet whatever."

Greer looked. Kregg had his arm around Allie's shoulder, whispering in her ear.

"Oh shit," Greer whispered.

CeeJay walked away, but Greer stayed seated, trying not to stare at the two. Finally, after what seemed like an eternity, the actor reluctantly peeled himself away from his underage lady love and out of the cart.

Allie slid over behind the wheel. "Call me,

okay?" she heard the teenager say. And then the golf cart was rolling away from the catering tent and the base camp.

Kregg strolled past Greer, pausing to grab half a dozen cookies from a platter on the buffet table. He came close enough to where she was seated that she got a strong whiff. No mistaking it. Definitely weed.

All afternoon she struggled to dislodge the disturbing image of Kregg with Allie. They weren't really doing anything wrong, but Allie was definitely too young to get involved with Kregg.

What should she do? Should she alert Eb to the fact that his niece was getting way too friendly with the star of their movie?

The guy was clearly trouble. And Allie Thibadeaux was only seventeen — a minor with whom Kregg had no business dallying.

She had no idea whether Eb would even listen to anything she had to say.

Maybe, she told herself, as she stood on the beach watching Kregg romp through the waves, hand in hand with his half-dressed costar, she was making too much of what she'd seen at lunch. They hadn't actually been kissing or anything.

Yet.

She shook her head, as though that would clear her conscience. What was that saying Dearie always used to quote? Oh yeah.

"Not my monkey. Not my circus." If she said it enough times, she just might convince herself it was true.

It was ridiculous to be so giddy about a girls' night out, Greer thought, as she stood in front of the tiny closet in her motel room, trying to decide on an outfit from her extremely limited wardrobe.

Finally, she picked out an asymmetrically cut cream silk tank top and black pencil leg slacks. The shoe choices were easier, since she had only red Keds and her one pair of black sandals to choose from.

The major downside to having a best friend who somehow managed to look glamorous twenty-four hours a day was that, inevitably, you could only look dowdy in comparison. Tonight, though, Greer was determined to up her own glam game. She shampooed and conditioned and even blew her hair dry and straightened it with the flat iron, the way Cee-Jay had coached her.

Once her hair was shiny and straight, she carefully applied what she thought of as full-on paint — foundation, blusher, eye shadow, mascara, even lip liner.

Not bad, she had to admit, admiring her own image in the cloudy glass of the bathroom mirror. She wasn't CeeJay gorgeous, but that was okay too.

Greer opened her motel room door a crack

and cautiously peered down the hallway to make sure she wouldn't have another accidental Eb encounter. The coast was clear. She nodded and exchanged greetings with other crew members coming and going from their rooms.

As she passed the pool courtyard, she spotted Ginny Buckalew reclining on a lounge chair, smoking one of her Swisher Sweets. Greer waved and kept going.

The off-duty cop leaned out of the newly built guard shack at the entrance to Bluewater Bay. His name was Ray and he recognized her at once, of course, because she'd been the one to hire him.

"Hey, Greer," he greeted her. He jerked his head in the direction of the quiet street on the other side of the gate. "Are they expecting you?"

"Hi, Ray. Yes, I'm going to pick up CeeJay from Bryce Levy's house."

"Cool. I'll just call up and let them know you're coming."

He picked up the phone and she saw him talking. A moment later he handed the phone to Greer. "She needs to talk to you."

"CeeJay? Everything okay?"

"Oh, honey, I am sick about this, but I've got to cancel dinner. I was all dressed and ready to walk out the door, but Bryce just watched today's dailies on his laptop and he's really upset. I can't go off and leave him like this."

A tiny alarm went off in Greer's brain. "What's wrong with the dailies?"

Silence. "I can't really talk about it right now. Just know I feel awful, missing our GNO. I'll totally make it up to you, I promise."

"It's all right," Greer said. "Stuff happens. I'll take a rain check."

"You better. I'll call you in the morning. 'Kay?"

" 'Kay."

She handed the phone back to the security guard and managed a smile. "Change of plans."

Greer drove away from Bluewater Bay, blinking back tears, hating the way she was overreacting. She'd meant it when she'd told CeeJay she understood. But she'd been looking forward to a night out and away from the set, all day. She glanced down at her carefully pressed pants and touched her carefully pressed hair. All dressed up with no place to go but home, or the closest thing to it. How pathetic was she?

The neon Silver Sands Motel sign blinked in the amethyst-colored dusk. The security guard sitting on a folding lawn chair at the entrance to the parking lot recognized her Kia and waved her in, moving his chair just far enough to one side of the crushed oyster shell drive that she could maneuver into the lot.

It was Friday night, and the crew members and a few of the cast were celebrating a night off after an intense workweek. People splashed in the pool and gathered in knots around a couple of charcoal grills. Loud rap music blasted from the open door of a room that opened to the pool, and one of the grips was handing around longnecks from a red cooler.

They were having a party, but Greer hadn't gotten the memo. Already she could envision herself changing out of her best clothes, slipping into her pj's, and trying to watch a movie or read, above the din from the celebration outside. Or maybe she'd order out and walk the block to the pizza place and eat a slice alone, at one of the tiny tables crammed up against the counter. She could already taste the burned pizza grease and sour tang of the cheap boxed wine.

Or maybe she'd have what she'd come to think of as a solo GNO — Greer's Night Out. She did a quick U-turn, and the guard scrambled to get out of her way. She thumbed her phone and tapped the GPS app for directions to My Thai in Ducktown, Florida.

24

Greer looked down at her GPS, then back at the building she was parked in front of. The tan stucco walls and red tile roof made it look like a Taco Bell from the eighties, and the sickly cactus planted in a bed of white gravel added to that atmosphere. But, sure enough, the sign out front — written in both English and what she presumed to be Thai — proclaimed it to be My Thai, "Now Under New Owner."

One part of her wanted to give up and go back to Cypress Key and wallow in a piping hot bath of self-pity, but some perverse part of her wanted to see if the restaurant's interior matched its exterior. Besides, the parking lot was full, and delicious smells were wafting into the warm night air.

It couldn't hurt to go in, maybe order an appetizer, and check the place out, she decided.

Half an hour later she was nibbling on basil rolls, nam sod, and the best panang curry she'd ever tasted. She ordered a bottle of Phuket beer and settled in to enjoy the schizophrenic ambience. The interior of My Thai was what she thought of as throwback bargain basement Chinese: dusty hanging paper lanterns, red and gold screens, with cheesy gold relief panels of dragons, tigers, and phoenixes dotting the red walls. Ever the location scout, she was dying to pull out her phone and start snapping pictures, but sternly reminded herself that she was officially off duty.

Her waiter was Hispanic, and most of the restaurant's patrons looked like locals from Ducktown, or possibly even Cypress Key. Greer sat at the bar and took her time enjoying dinner, half listening to the swirl of conversations going on around her. CeeJay would have loved this place, she thought. She was busy tending to Bryce's issues tonight, but Greer wasn't so sure Bryce would be a permanent attachment for her best friend. CeeJay was one of the most genuine, giving women she'd ever known, but under ordinary circumstances CeeJay didn't do well with authority figures, even rich, successful ones like Bryce Levy.

Greer was pulling out a credit card to pay the check when she heard her cell phone ding to alert her to an incoming text. She added a tip to her tab and handed the check back to the waiter. She half expected the text to be from CeeJay or somebody else on the *Beach Town* crew, but the area code wasn't a California one, and the number wasn't one she recognized. No wonder.

> Hi Greer. It's Clint. Again. Lise gave me your number. I saw on your Facebook page that you're working in Cypress Key. That's only about an hour or so from where I live, in Alachua. Any chance you could drop by and see your old man while you're down here? Hope so! Dad.

Dammit! Greer threw her phone back into her purse. The mellow buzz of a good meal and an interesting experience was suddenly gone, and she was right back where she'd started the evening. Lonely. Pissed off. Conflicted.

By the time she got on the road back to Cypress Key, it was fully dark. The county road cutting through swamp and woods was twisting and unfamiliar, and it seemed that every other mile her headlights picked up the carcass of a roadkill. Suddenly she was unwillingly channeling every horror movie she'd ever seen that featured unwitting victims driving down a remote rural road. *The Texas Chain Saw Massacre* came to mind, and she hit the automatic door lock, not once but twice. Once, a twisted, moss-hung tree branch reached across the roadway, like the gnarled claw of an ogre, and she flashed back to *The Blair Witch Project.* Each huge bug that splattered itself on the Kia's windshield made her cringe. At every single yellow BEAR CROSSING sign she fully expected to see a raging rogue grizzly bear. Rationally, she knew she was being irrational, but her hands didn't relax their grip on the steering wheel until the Cypress Key city limit sign finally loomed before her.

When she reached the Silver Sands, the parking lot was half empty. She pulled into the lot, moved the orange cones marking her designated parking space, and got out of the car. The moon was half full and the night air was hot and swampy. She was full of a restless energy she couldn't quite describe but knew couldn't be contained in her claustrophobic motel room.

Greer walked down to the beach and stared out at the Gulf. Just at the horizon, in the distance, she could make out slow-moving pinpricks of the lights of what she assumed were shrimp boats. The tide rolled lazily into the sand. She took off her sandals, dug her toes into the still warm, damp sand, and inhaled the scent of salt and decaying seaweed, listening as her own breathing and always rapid pulse slowed, until it seemed to match the rhythm of the waves lapping at the shore.

She closed her eyes and the scary movies images slowly subsided, and beneath her toes she felt tiny coquinas burrowing deeper into the sand.

Greer had never been a stargazer. She'd never had time to ponder the big issues of time and space and mortality. She felt a brief flush of guilt, realizing she didn't even know the names of the constellations spreading themselves out across the blue velvet sky in front of her.

But maybe that was okay. Maybe she didn't have to be able to name them in order to appreciate them.

She kept walking until the beach played out and she'd reached the concrete embankment that marked the entrance to the old pier. She glanced over her shoulder and saw the lights of the Silver Sands. Nothing there for her tonight.

The city park was deserted, except for a lone teenager who rolled slowly back and forth across the concrete plaza on his skateboard. He took no notice of Greer. She found a concrete bench and sat. The heat and humidity settled over her shoulders like a wool shawl, but she tilted her head back and waited, and sure enough, eventually a small breeze whipped a lock of her temporarily straight hair. She could have sworn she felt it as it frizzed out around her head.

The old casino building loomed tantalizingly just out of her reach. As she stared moodily out at it, she realized something was amiss.

A faint beam of light flashed through the wall of broken windows. She sat up and blinked to make sure she hadn't imagined light and movement coming from the abandoned building.

A bank of clouds rolled in, and for a moment she could only make out the dimmest outlines of the darkened building.

But then the beam of light was moving. She could make out shadows, flickering through the windows. She got up and walked over to the boarded-up entrance to the casino.

Now she heard music, a heavy bass beat, and then a high-pitched peal of nervous laughter.

Somebody was in the old casino tonight, and they were having themselves a party.

She strained to hear more, and then was startled by a sudden series of loud pops.

Gunfire? She grasped the chain-link fence, looked down, and saw that the huge padlocks were intact.

A narrow white rocket exploded into the night sky. And then another, this one red, with a blooming chrysanthemum blossom, followed by a blue pinwheel.

Fireworks! Whoever was in the casino was setting off fireworks. She glanced over at her phone. Should she call the police? An errant match or burning cinder could land wrong and burn down what was left of the old building. For a moment, she wondered if Eb Thibadeaux was watching this display from his loft over the grocery store.

But just as suddenly as the fireworks show had started, it ended. She heard the music again, and then silence. Another peal of laughter, and then the high-pitched whine of a motor. A boat? Greer strained to see in the darkness. But it was too dark. The engine tailed off in the direction of the municipal marina, and all she heard now was the steady roll of the lone skateboarder as he criss-crossed the concrete plaza.

Her skin felt hot and prickly and her shirt was sticking to her back. She stood, put on her shoes, and walked briskly back to the Silver Sands.

The pool area looked deserted, but as Greer approached she saw Ginny Buckalew moving slowly around the patio, straightening chairs, emptying ashtrays, and dropping bottles and cans into a large orange recycling bin.

Ginny looked up, startled to see Greer.

"Well hello. You missed the big party here earlier."

"So I see. Where'd everybody go?"

"The Crow's Nest, most of 'em," Ginny said. She pulled a chair away from a round iron table, sat down, and lit up one of her cigarillos. She inhaled, exhaled, and smiled before reaching over to the big red cooler and pulling out a longneck Corona.

"They left all this beer behind. Be a shame to waste it. Care to join me?"

Greer shrugged. "Sure. Why not?"

She sat down at the table opposite the older woman and took the beer Ginny offered. The two women sipped quietly, and they could hear tree frogs croaking in the palms.

Greer slapped at a huge mosquito and could already feel a welt rising on her cheek. Ginny handed her a can of insect repellent, and Greer stepped away from the table before spraying every inch of her body with the stuff.

She handed the can back to Ginny and sat down again. "Don't you need any? I've never seen mosquitoes as fierce as you have down here."

"Honey, those bugs can't chew through this tough old hide of mine."

"Did you happen to see fireworks coming from the casino earlier?" Greer asked.

"The casino? That's supposed to be boarded up tight. You sure they were coming from there and not someplace else?"

"I'm sure. I saw flashlights too, and heard music and voices coming from inside."

Ginny shook her head. "Damn kids. Did you call the police to run 'em off?"

"I thought about it, but it ended almost as soon as it started. Maybe they got spooked. I

256

heard a boat or something speeding away."

"Eb's gonna want the police to check into that," Ginny said. Her eyes narrowed. "You sure it wasn't some of your movie people?"

"I'm not sure of anything, because it was dark. But I didn't send anybody from the crew out there."

"Just asking," Ginny said. She sat back in her chair again and took a long drag from the Swisher Sweet.

Greer waved ineffectively at the cloud of smoke that hung over her head. She looked around the patio area. "Where's Allie tonight?" She hoped she sounded casual.

"She's had to work late at the Inn tonight, and then I think she was spending the night with one of her girlfriends. Courtney maybe? I don't keep up with all those girls."

"Raising a teenager must be hard, even in a small town like this one."

"Allie's a good girl. Stubborn. I guess she gets that from the Thibadeaux side of the family. I hate to think what she gets from her mama's side."

"Do you worry about her — and boys?"

Ginny exhaled another thin plume of smoke. "Eb worries more about her than I do. Maybe that's because he remembers what it was like, trying to get into the pants of every pretty girl in town, back in the day. He keeps an eye on all these fellas coming around Allie."

Greer managed to choke back a surprised laugh.

"Allie knows what's what. One of her best friends since kindergarten, Haylie Bostwick? She got pregnant last year. Had to drop out of school. Her boyfriend's in the Navy now, and Haylie, she and the baby are living in a double-wide trailer with the boyfriend's mama, over in Chieftain."

"That's an unfortunate reality check for a seventeen-year-old," Greer said.

"Allie's not gonna be another Haylie Bostwick," Ginny said. "She's been talking about going to school to be a writer since she was just a little thing. She's taking all honors classes. Eb's been setting college money aside for her since she was a baby."

"Of course he has," Greer murmured.

Ginny gave Greer a coolly assessing look.

"You don't think much of my nephew, do you?"

"I'm sure he's doing what he thinks is right for this town. It's just that I happen to disagree with him."

"Anything else that's bugging you about him?" Ginny took a long sip of beer, then tossed the empty bottle in the vicinity of the recycling bin, where it landed with a loud clink of glass against aluminum. "Come on. It's just us girls talkin'."

Greer laughed nervously. "It doesn't matter what I think of Eb. My job is to help get this

258

film made. When that's done, hopefully, I'll move onto my next project."

"And how is this movie of yours going to make our little town look?"

"What do you mean?"

"You know what I mean. I've got eyes in my head, you know. I've seen what those cameramen are filming around here. The empty storefronts, that sorry-looking old oyster cannery, this motel. You picked Cypress Key because you think it's sad and ugly and depressing. Isn't that right?"

"No!" But Greer knew she'd blown her cover. "We needed a place that looks real. Not like Disney, not like those candy-colored new fantasy towns in the Panhandle. Cypress Key is the real Florida. That's what the director wanted me to find. And that's what I found here."

"We haven't always looked like this. And we're changing, you know." Ginny tilted her head up, her eyes watching the gently rustling palm fronds at the edge of the patio.

"We are so close. When we get that grant money, and get the pier and the casino all fixed up, that'll be the first step back for Cypress Key."

"I hope so," Greer said politely. She took another sip of beer. "It's certainly a beautiful setting, with the beach and the bay."

Ginny's laugh was low and raspy. "You don't know Eb Thibadeaux. He's always been a leader. Always been somebody who could get things done when nobody else could. Or would."

"Has he always had a messiah complex? Always believed he could save the world?"

"I know you think you're being sarcastic, but Eb really did save Cypress Key when he became mayor. And that's not just his aunt talking. You can ask anybody else in town and they'll tell you the same thing."

"And how did he manage that?"

"Living out in California like you do, you probably don't know about the big stink we had in this town. I'll save you the details, but all you need to know is that two years ago our illustrious mayor and two other members of our city council went to prison for taking bribes from the paper company. They were bought and paid for by Peninsula Paper Company, and they sold this town down the same damn river they allowed to be polluted for all those years. The state's attorney came in and did a big investigation, and now all three of those crooks are in the federal prison up at Eglin."

"Wow."

"We very nearly lost our city charter," Ginny said. "Some people in town, they came to Eb, and they basically begged him to run for mayor. After that big scandal, nobody else would touch the job with a ten-foot pole. Eb sure didn't want the job, either. He was thinking about handing his share of the motel back to me and taking a job in Texas, where he'd worked before."

"Why'd he change his mind?"

"He never really said, but I'm pretty sure it was because of Allie. That girl has had a tough time of it. This is the only real home she's ever had, and for damn sure the only stability she's had in her life has been me and Eb."

Greer found herself twisting the beer bottle between the palms of both hands.

"Some people around here think Eb is a soft touch. He bought the grocery a year ago, and it was the same kind of thing. The couple that owned the store, the husband had a stroke and his wife couldn't run it by herself. They were fixing to close it up. That would have been a disaster for us. You know what the closest store is besides the Hometown?"

"Not really."

"There's one of those dollar stores in Chieftain. They sell expired canned goods and some frozen foods from companies you never heard of, and maybe some bread and milk and beer," Ginny said disdainfully. "That's thirty miles from here. We got poor people with no transportation and people on fixed incomes — where would they get meat and fresh vegetables if the Hometown closed?"

"Good point."

"He's made a success of that store," Ginny said proudly. "Hired a proper butcher, opened that little deli counter. He's started buying produce from local farmers, too. You call that a messiah complex? I call that a decent human being who cares about the people around him."

"I stand corrected," Greer said. "But I still disagree with the high-handed way he gets things done."

Ginny stubbed her cigarillo out in the ashtray. "High-handed or not. He gets it done. And that's what this town needs."

Now those gray eyes were studying Greer in a way that made the younger woman squirm in her seat.

"You ever lived in a small town?"

"Not really. I was born and raised in and around L.A."

"Got family back there?"

"Just my grandmother. My mom died two months ago."

"No brothers or sisters?"

"I'm an only child of an only child," Greer said.

"What about your father? Is he still around?"

Greer wondered where this line of questioning was going, but Dearie taught her early never to be rude to her elders. And somehow, that lesson had stuck.

"My parents split up when I was only five.

So I was raised by a single mom."

"But he's still alive, right?"

Greer nodded, thinking about the text she'd received earlier in the evening. The one she still hadn't answered.

"I haven't seen him in years. I think he actually lives not far from here. Alachua?"

"Little over an hour away," Ginny said, nodding for emphasis. "He didn't beat you, did he?"

"No."

"Alcoholic?"

"Not that I'm aware of."

"Criminal?"

Greer laughed. "Now I know where Eb gets his direct way. No. As far as I know, my father isn't a monster. He's just . . . not somebody who's been in my life. Not in a really long time."

"I had a good dad," Ginny mused. "He and my mother were married for fifty-two years. My brother Julian, that's Eb's dad, he was a good man, too. Is still, but he's got dementia now, bless his heart. Allie, she didn't get that lucky. Her dad, Jared? He's just sorry. His mama never could see it, thought Jared hung the moon, but everybody else in this town, they could tell you stories about Jared."

"Does Allie see him?"

"No," the old lady said sharply. "His mama sends him a little bit of money, which he's allowed to use for cigarettes and candy and

263

things like that, but Jared wasn't really in Allie's life before he went to prison, so there's no need for her to see him now."

"Kind of sad," Greer said, barely suppressing a yawn. She stood slowly. "I'm dead on my feet. Thanks for the beer, Ginny. And the company."

"Glad to have you."

"Oh. And I meant to tell you, thanks for getting Eb to replace the air conditioner in my room. The new one works so much better."

"You're welcome, but I didn't know anything about that. He must have done it on his own."

25

It was only eight o'clock on the West Coast. Greer scrolled down her contact list and tapped her grandmother's number.

The cell phone had been Greer's Mother's Day gift to Dearie the previous year. Lise had been apprehensive about the idea. "She'll just lose it, or end up accidentally calling Sri Lanka or something. Just give her some dusting powder or a box of candy, for God's sake."

But Greer had been insistent. Work sometimes kept her too busy to go see Dearie, for weeks on end, and she didn't want to lose contact with her grandmother.

The phone had been a huge hit, instantly upping Greer's stock as favored, if only, grandchild. Not only had Dearie not lost the phone, she'd amazed everybody with her quick adaptation to the technology, sometimes texting Greer photos of her dinner tray, or candid photos of the appalling fashion choices made by her nursing home contemporaries.

Three rings, then four. Greer heard a recording of her own voice. "You've reached the cell phone mailbox for Deidre Kehoe. Please leave a message."

Greer spoke as loudly as she could without shouting. "Dearie, it's Greer. I saw I had a missed call from you. Call me back, but not too late, okay? I'm down in Florida and it's already eleven here."

Her skin felt sticky from the insect repellent, so she showered and scrubbed the war paint off her face, then climbed into bed with her cell phone. No telling when Dearie might call back.

Or maybe Clint would try to call again. She opened Facebook on her phone and found his page. She scrolled down the photos on his timeline for clues about her absentee father's life. Nothing very remarkable here. Clint holding up a large fish, Clint raising a beer toward the camera, Clint and two other men posing in front of his beloved orange Dodge Charger, Clint with more old cars. If there was a constant in her father's life, it seemed to be cars.

The most recent photo, dated a week ago, showed that he was now clean shaven, although he still wore his ever-present ball cap with the bill turned up.

"He's probably bald as a billiard ball," Greer muttered. She noted that his status was "single" and that only a few of the photos he'd posted included women. She scrolled on, past more car and fishing photos, then stopped abruptly when she found one he'd posted nearly a year ago, for Throwback Thursday. The photo was in murky purple tones, but there it was: Clint and Lise seated on a beach somewhere, grinning into each other's eyes, with a blond, diaper-clad toddler seated on Clint's lap.

Greer clicked and enlarged it, then stared down at this family photo she'd never seen before. In the enlarged version she could see the steel framework of the pier in the background, which meant they were at the Santa Monica beach.

The first thing that struck her was how young and happy the adults looked. Lise's hair was pulled on top of her head in a scrunchy. She wore an off-the-shoulder T-shirt, low-cut black bikini bottoms, and huge round-frame sunglasses. Clint wore cutoff blue jeans. He was bare chested and sunburned and rocking a righteous mullet and a full-on Fu Manchu.

And baby Greer? She wore heart-shaped pink sunglasses. Her chubby legs and arms were coated with sand and she was waving a red plastic shovel.

Clint had typed "THE GOOD OL' DAYS" as the photo's caption. Greer sighed and closed out the app.

■ ■ ■ ■

She fell asleep with the cell phone on her pillow, which meant she felt it vibrating before she heard the ring.

Her voice was thick with sleep. "Hello?"

It was Dearie. "Don't tell me you're asleep already."

Greer rolled over and looked at the clock radio on the dresser, then sank back down on her pillow. "Dearie, didn't you listen to my message? I'm in Florida. It's one o'clock in the morning here."

"Sorry." She didn't sound the least bit contrite. "I was watching my shows. *Real Housewives* came on, and I guess I lost track of time. What are you doing all the way out in Florida?"

"Working. Remember, I told you last time I visited."

"Why were you calling me?"

Greer yawned. Sometimes, talking to her grandmother felt like she was Alice in Wonderland, falling down the rabbit hole. "You called me first."

"Oh. That's right. Work going all right? You meeting any nice fellas?"

"Work's good. I don't have time for fellas. Even if there were any nice ones."

"Well, you'll never meet any good ones in the business you're in," Dearie said tartly.

"Not any straight ones, anyways."

"What did you want to talk to me about?"

"Oh. That's right. I was wondering if you could put some more money in my account. I'm a little short this month."

"Are you playing Candy Crush again? I thought we decided that was a bad idea for you."

"*We* didn't decide it. You butted into my business and took it off my phone. But I figured out how to put it back on there."

"Swell. But I promised Mom I wouldn't underwrite your bad habits."

There was a long silence at the other end of the phone. When she finally spoke again, Dearie sounded old and defeated. "Sometimes I forget she's gone. Do you do that?"

"Yeah," Greer said wistfully. "I'll pick up the phone to tell her something, and then I remember." She didn't admit to Dearie that she'd kept half a dozen of Lise's old messages on her phone, and that she replayed them sometimes, just to hear her mother's distinctive low, raspy voice once again.

"What about my money?" Dearie asked, getting back to her own needs. "I seem to remember, back when you were in college, there were lots of months I sent you extra checks to help you make it through the month."

"For things like food and rent and gas for my car. Not stupid Internet games," Greer groused. "Are you going to continue guilt tripping me and calling in the middle of the night if I don't put money in your account?"

"What do you think?"

"Ten dollars. That's all I'm giving you. No more."

"Scrooge. Listen. I better go now. They have bed check in this place."

"Wait," Greer said. "There's something else I want to tell you."

"Are you pregnant?"

Greer hooted. "God no."

"That's good. I'm too young to be a great-grandmother."

"It's about Clint."

She'd halfway expected Dearie to have forgotten her father's name. "What about him?"

"Did you know he and Lise were in touch — before she died?"

"No kidding. She never mentioned that to me."

"Mom was bugging me to call him, after she got sick. She even gave me his phone number."

"Clint Hennessy," Dearie said. "Wonder what ever happened to him?"

"He's living down here in Florida. I think he does something with cars."

"That's not a surprise. He's not still in the business, is he?"

"I don't know. I just know he lives about an

hour away from this little beach town where we're filming."

"How on earth do you suppose Lise got in contact with him?"

"Facebook," Greer said. "I don't know who reached out to who first, but I think they must have talked on the phone. And get this: he's called and texted. He wants me to come see him."

"For what?"

"I think he's got some crazy idea that we'll have a father–daughter reunion."

"You're not gonna go, are you?"

"No. Definitely not."

"Good for you. What's past is past," Dearie said.

"I just don't get why Lise was so insistent I should get together with him. The guy walked off and abandoned us. How is that okay?"

"Well . . ." Dearie's voice trailed off.

"What?"

"That's not exactly how it happened. I mean, they split up, yes, but my recollection is that Lise was the one that did the leaving."

"No. That's not right. Mom always said he took off."

"Not right away, he didn't. He couldn't. He had you to take care of."

Greer gripped the phone so hard her fingertips burned. "Dearie, are you saying Mom left — and didn't take me with her?"

"I don't want to talk about this right now,"

Dearie said, her voice suddenly faint and quivering. "I'm tired. I want to go to bed."

"Don't you dare hang up on me, Deidre Kehoe," Greer ordered. "And don't even try to pull that feeble old lady crap. Answer my question."

"It doesn't matter who left first," Dearie said finally. "It all happened a long time ago. And it was all for the best. Look at you. You didn't end up so bad, even if you didn't have a father in the picture."

"Stop trying to change the subject. Tell me about what happened. When they split up."

"How much do you remember?"

"Not much," Greer admitted. "I was only, what, four or five? I do remember starting first grade, and Lise telling me to tell the teacher that I didn't need to waste time making a Popsicle stick frame for a Father's Day present because I didn't have a grandfather, or a father."

"Oh, Lise, Lise." Dearie said it as a sigh. "Look. They were too young to get married. Young and selfish. Your mother was hell-bent on being a big movie star. Clint? Looking back on it, I guess he wasn't a bad person. He was just all wrong for her. He was a good old boy from Georgia who got hired as a stunt driver on that stupid show . . . what was it called?"

Dukes of Hazzard."

"Stupid show. But Clint was a good-looking stud, no doubt about it."

"I can't believe she fell in love with a guy with a mullet."

"What's that?"

"Nothing. You were about to tell me about their breakup."

"Breakups. Plural. They'd get to fighting, and the next thing I know, she'd tell me he'd gone off to Vegas with his buddies. Or she'd show up at my place in the middle of the night with you and a suitcase."

"What was all the fighting about?"

"Everything. Nothing. She didn't like his friends, he didn't like hers. She didn't like him smoking around the baby, he thought she drank too much. But they'd always get back together after a week or so."

"Until the last time. What happened? What was different about that breakup?"

"Lise never would tell me. I think she was too ashamed of herself. Which she should have been. Look, honey, are you sure you want to hear all this? Your mom's gone now, so what's the difference?"

"I need to hear it," Greer said, her voice steely.

"It was pilot season, February or March, and Lise had a callback for a sitcom on ABC, I think it was. She'd been shut out of so many parts, but this one looked like a real possibility. You'd been sick all winter — nothing serious, mostly ear infections, but oh my Lord, you would be up screaming half the night. I know, because I babysat you a lot on weekends. I thought you'd pop a lung, you'd scream so loud."

"Go on."

"That's really all I know. You had an earache, Lise had an early Monday morning callback. They'd had a fight, and your mom was so mad she threw him out. He stayed gone maybe a week, but when he finally did get home, late on a Sunday night, Lise was gone."

"She left me there . . . by myself?" Greer was stunned.

"No, no. She wouldn't have done something like that. There was a teenager who lived next door. She came over to watch you. Lise just didn't bother to tell her she wouldn't be coming back."

Greer felt her chest tighten with anger.

"You really don't remember any of this, do you, honey?" Dearie asked.

Greer tried to summon up the memories, but it was like that dark, half-hidden road she'd traveled earlier in the evening. The past was out there, bumping up against her subconscious, like bugs on a windshield. She could sense it, but she couldn't see it.

"The babysitter. Was her name Claire? She used to give me Pepsis. And let me stay up late and watch TV, but I wasn't supposed to tell Mom."

"I think her name was Claire, now that you mention it."

"And Lise really just walked off and left me? Because she had an early-morning audition? How long before you knew she'd gone? How long before you came and got me?"

"Maybe a week," Dearie said. "Not that long. Clint finally called and admitted Lise'd left. I think he was too proud to ask for my help before that."

"And how long before Lise came home again?"

"I don't know, Greer. It was a long, long time ago. All that matters is, she did come home. She wasn't perfect, but she loved you, and she did the best she could."

Greer tried again to summon the past. She had dim memories of being upset because, after the divorce, she'd had to leave behind her swing set when they moved in with Dearie. In all the upheaval in her childhood, her grandmother had been the one constant. Dearie couldn't have made much money working as a seamstress in the studio costume department, but somehow she'd seen to it that her granddaughter didn't do without.

"Uh-oh," Dearie said. "I hear the Beast coming down the hallway, rattling door-knobs."

"Who's the Beast?"

"Night supervisor. I've gotta go. You won't

275

forget about my money, will you?"

"I'll transfer the money as soon as we hang up. 'Night, Dearie."

"Good night, sweetheart."

26

Saturday morning was sunny and should have been full of promise, but Greer found the idea of a day off work oppressive. She stared moodily out the window at the glassy waters of the Gulf. Twice she started to put on her bathing suit. A day at the beach was what she needed, she told herself, but the idea held no real appeal.

Her thoughts kept returning to the conversation she'd had with Dearie the night before. At some point she got in the Kia and headed out of town, telling herself she was going out to search for alternative locations for the casino.

She drove north for a half an hour, then abruptly turned east, driving through the lush green swamps and flat pasturelands of the central Gulf Coast. Finally, she pulled into a gas station and typed "Alachua" into her phone's GPS. According to the map, the route would take her through Gainesville, a big university town, where she might decide to go shopping.

But when she reached Gainesville, she kept going. She lived in Los Angeles, California, where she could buy anything, any time she wanted, although she rarely did.

The Alachua city limits sign gave her pause. Was she really going to do this?

Maybe she would drive past his house, just to satisfy her own curiosity.

The problem with the drive-by strategy was that she didn't know where Clint lived.

That was easily remedied. She typed "Clint Hennessy" and "Alachua, Florida," into her phone's search engine and quickly came up with an address on a county road. According to her GPS, the address was only five miles away.

She found a convenience store, used the restroom, bought a bottle of cold water, then sat in her car, tapping her fingertips on the steering wheel, torn with indecision. Why was she doing this? What could be gained by looking up a man she didn't really care to see again?

But the glowing dot on her GPS called out to her. She was so close now, what was the sense of turning back?

The county road led her through a rural area of dilapidated houses, stretches of pastureland with grazing white, humpbacked cattle, and scattered trailer parks. Not exactly the promised land. And to make matters worse, what houses she saw were haphazardly numbered, if at all.

Finally she spied a mailbox with the street number matching Clint's address. There was no actual house in sight, just a sandy road that wound through a lane of oak trees and underbrush. On an impulse she picked up her phone and snapped a few photos.

As she was snapping, her phone dinged to alert her to a text. It was from CeeJay.

Sorry about last night. Meet up at the Coffee Mug and I'll explain all?

She was so intent on typing out a response that she momentarily forgot where she was. Until a sudden tap on her car window startled her so badly she dropped the phone.

She looked up into the face of a stranger, who was bent down, staring into her window. But this stranger had a familiar face: square jaw, sharply planed high cheekbones, bushy white eyebrows, brown eyes the same shade as her own, with a fine network of crow's-feet extending to his hairline.

"Can I help you?" The stranger leaned in closer, and now a slow smile spread across the weathered face. "Greer? You're Greer!" He gripped the Kia's door handle and she saw that his hands — large, chapped, and banged up, with a network of scars and cuts — were violently shaking.

"I'm Greer," she said finally.

"Well, what are you doing sitting in the car? Come on up to the house, okay?"

"I really can't stay," Greer said feebly.

His smile faded. "Aw, c'mon. Please?"

Ten minutes, and then I am so out of here.

"Son of a bitch," he said under his breath. "Son of a bitch. Sorry, but I just can't believe you're really here. Son of a bitch."

They were seated in the living room of his trailer, or double-wide, as he referred to it.

He'd removed his baseball cap once they were in the house. Clint Hennessy wasn't bald at all. He had thinning but still wavy silver hair.

Thank God the mullet is gone.

His living room was small but tidy. Shag carpet, a flat-screen television, a shiny leather recliner, leather sofa, and coffee table and end tables, all matching.

All screaming "I bought all this furniture for less than a thousand bucks!"

Clint was seated on the recliner. Greer was on the sofa, with her hands folded in her lap, wondering just how long she would have to stay.

"You sure I can't get you something to drink? I got beer, sodas. Or I could make some coffee. . . ."

"No thanks. I'm fine." The end of the sentence trailed off. She couldn't bring

280

herself to call him Dad, but she wouldn't hurt his feelings by calling him Clint. So she wouldn't call him anything at all. She would leave just as soon as common courtesy allowed.

"You're as pretty as Lise said you were," Clint said, his gaze fastened on her face.

"Lise was always given to exaggeration," Greer said.

"No. You're beautiful. You were a pretty baby, but you're beautiful now. Just like your mom."

Greer felt herself squirming under the intensity of his stare.

"This is nice," she said, gesturing toward a picture window that showed a small backyard with a brick patio, barbecue grill, and picnic table. "Have you lived here long?"

"I moved to Alachua twelve years ago, after I finally got fed up with California. Four years ago, I found this place. This trailer was already here. I bought it for the land, and the fact that there was a barn big enough for the cars."

"You keep your cars in a barn?"

What kind of redneck has a barn full of cars but lives in a trailer?

"Oh yeah. I can't have them out in the weather."

"Why's that?"

"Those cars are my bread and butter. Didn't Lise tell you about my business?"

281

"No. She just told me you guys had reconnected."

"Facebook," he said eagerly. "That's how I found your mom again, you know. We talked on the phone, too. Right after she found out, you know, about the cancer."

"She mentioned it," Greer said stiffly.

"Uh, well, I wanted to come to the funeral, you know."

But you didn't.

"It was small. Just a few old friends."

But no MIA ex-husbands.

"It's hard for me to travel that far, all the way to California, me running a business and all. I got a couple guys who work for me part time, doing body work and painting, but I do most of the long-hauling myself, delivering cars to locations."

Greer tried desperately to think of an excuse to leave. She'd done what she came to Alachua to do. She'd seen Clint, talked to him. Her obligations had been met.

"How come you don't do Facebook?" Clint was asking. "I thought everybody your age was into that. You don't even hardly have any pictures of yourself on there."

"I have a professional page, for my scouting business, but I don't bother with a personal page," she told him.

Clint's face lit up at the mention of her location scouting business. "How about that? You're the third generation in the business.

Guess you could call that a dynasty, right?"

She shrugged. "I guess. Unlike Dearie and Mom, I never was an actress."

He started to say something, hesitated, then started again. "Good old Dearie. Is she still as full of piss and vinegar?"

"Definitely."

Clint grinned. "She never liked me. And I probably gave her good reason not to. She thought I was some redneck hillbilly. But I always admired your grandmother. In a town full of liars, phonies, and ass kissers, Dearie was the real thing. You always knew where you stood with her."

"To say the very least," Greer agreed.

Must leave. Must leave. Must leave.

"I'd probably better get going. It's an hour drive back to Cypress Key, and I'm sure you have stuff you need to do. It was probably bad manners of me to just drop in on you like this."

"You're leaving already?" Clint's shoulders drooped. "I was hoping maybe you'd let me buy you lunch and we could spend some time catching up."

As if a hamburger and a Coke could bridge a gap of more than three decades.

"Maybe another time," Greer said, sounding deliberately vague. She stood up.

"Let me just show you around the place before you leave," Clint said. "You haven't even seen my cars."

"Okay, maybe just a few minutes," Greer said. "We've got a production meeting this afternoon."

Humor him. He doesn't know it's your day off.

She followed him down the worn wooden steps and through the overgrown, grassy backyard, down a well-packed sand driveway that ended in front of a huge, industrial-looking prefab metal warehouse.

He was shorter than she'd remembered, maybe five ten, and skinnier. His jeans bagged in the seat and were too short, showing off white athletic socks and black tennis shoes with Velcro fasteners, and his gait was stiff-legged.

Just another sad old man. Nothing to me.

Clint took a set of keys from his pocket, unlocked a heavy steel door, and flicked on a light switch.

"My inventory," he said proudly.

The warehouse was full of cars and trucks and dozens of vehicles of every description, their paint gleaming under the glare of overhead lights. She spotted an antique cherry red fire engine, a rusty old Ford pickup truck with a wooden stake bed, a flashy pink 1950s Cadillac with flaring fins, even a vintage yellow school bus.

Holy shit. My father is a car hoarder.

"What is all this?" Greer asked, mystified. "Do you drive all these cars?"

"Oh, hell no," Clint said. "I guess Lise

284

didn't tell you. I'm still in the business, too, in a way. All these vehicles? They're picture cars. I rent 'em for television and movie productions. Some print ads too."

"Really?" Greer felt herself drawn into the warehouse, as though by a magnet.

At the end of the first row she saw the car she'd been wondering about: the orange Dodge Charger with the Confederate battle flag painted on the roof.

"Is that —"

"Yup," Clint said. He walked over to the Charger and gave the hood a loving pat. "The General Lee. This is the same car I drove for *The Dukes of Hazzard.*"

"It's not a replica?" Greer asked. The car had no windows. She walked around to the passenger side, leaned down, and peered inside. The padded tan dashboard appeared to have been spray painted. Looking up, she touched a chrome roll bar.

Clint reached across and leaned on the horn, and the first twelve notes of "Dixie" blared so loudly she jumped backwards.

That horn. "Dixie." Suddenly she was four again, sitting on her daddy's lap

Do it again. Again. Again. Please, Daddy.

Until Lise came out of the house and yelled at him to cut it out before the neighbors called the cops.

"A replica? Not on your life," Clint said. "We used hundreds of Chargers during the life of the series. This was one we wrecked doing a stunt jump for an episode at the end of the third season, in 1981. I bought it, restored it, and for years I'd take it around to car shows all over the country."

"Does it run?"

"They all run," Clint said, gesturing around the barn. "Some of 'em I bought as is, others I restored myself. That's what I've been doing since I quit driving — buying, selling, and restoring cars."

He rested a hand lightly on Greer's shoulder. "This one I'll never sell. Do you remember it at all?"

Lise's voice, shrill, on the phone with Dearie. "Goddamn General Lee. Yeah. The car has a name. He has a kid he can't support, but he treats that car like it's his baby."

Greer closed her eyes, thinking back to that long-ago day. "I have a vague memory of you coming home with an orange car. But that one, the front end was bashed in. I remember you let me sit in it, and we'd honk the horn, but Mom wouldn't let you take me for a drive because she said it wasn't safe."

"God, she hated this car." Clint's laugh was wheezy. "I had a herniated disc, you know, from work. I was getting workers' comp, but I was bored as hell, hanging around the house, so I bought it without telling her."

"You did what? You paid seventy-five dollars

286

for that piece of shit? Jesus, Clint!"

"Seventy-five dollars," Greer whispered.

Clint stared at her. "That's right. I paid seventy-five dollars for it. But how . . ."

She shook her head, as if that would shake off the memory. "I better get going. My meeting . . ."

His face crumpled like an old brown paper sack, dry and creased. "Son of a bitch. You must have heard us fighting that day. Right?"

Greer took a deep breath. "I heard her yelling 'Seventy-five dollars!' over and over."

"We thought you were sleeping," Clint said. "Money was tight. We had all these doctor bills because you kept getting ear infections. And it was pilot season, and she wanted a new outfit to go out on callbacks. But I'd spent every spare dime on this thing." He ran a gnarled hand slowly over the windshield.

"I had a plan, you know. The way I saw it, the General Lee was an investment. All it needed was some bodywork. I was gonna fix it up, then rent it back to the studio for the show. But Lise thought that was just some wild hare of mine. She was furious."

"I'd never heard Mom cry before," Greer whispered.

Clint patted her shoulder awkwardly. "It didn't occur to me to tell her what I was doing. I was the man of the family, right? Why should I ask her permission?"

"When I woke up from my nap, you were

287

gone," Greer said accusingly.

"She threw me out. Told me to take my gee-dee car and never come back. Looking back now, I can't say I blame her." He smiled sadly. "It wasn't just the car. I was a young hothead. It hurt my pride, knowing she didn't believe in me, in my ability to support my family."

Greer's heart was beating wildly, like a trapped rabbit's. For a moment she was back in her tiny bedroom, huddled under the pink and green quilt Dearie had made her.

Lise was in a towering rage. In between her mother's sobs she heard dresser drawers opening and slamming, the muttered curses. Heard metal clothes hangers scraping on the closet rod. The front door opened and closed, again and again, as Lise made multiple trips from the bedroom to the front yard.

"I drove around town for a while, just to cool down. I slept in the car that night," he said sheepishly. "I figured, we'd had fights before, one of us would leave and things would blow over. But when I got home, she'd thrown all my stuff in a big pile in the yard. All my clothes, tools, everything. So that was when I knew it was over."

"I have to go," Greer said abruptly.

No more toxic strolls down memory lane for this girl.

"Okay."

Clint followed her back to the trailer, and then out to the Kia. He circled the car slowly, evaluating it as though it were a horse he was thinking of buying.

"Is this a rental?"

"Yes." She fumbled around, trying to find the seat belt, which had retracted back into the door.

"How's it handle on the road?"

"It's okay. Not the smoothest ride." She started the ignition. But he still had his hand planted on the car's roof. As though that hand could hold her there, keep his daughter from her determined retreat.

He leaned in the open door. "I came back, you know. Two days later. But she'd left you with the babysitter, Claire. The kid who lived next door."

Greer clamped both hands over her ears. She swore she could feel the searing heat, the agony of that long-ago infection.

Clint gently pulled her hands down. "I'm sorry your mom is gone. And I know you don't want to hear this. But you need to know the truth. I didn't just walk off. I came back. I came back, and it was Lise who stayed away. You were sick, and I took you to the doctor and I got your medicine and fed you and gave you your bath and your ear drops. A week! She stayed gone a week. Finally, I didn't know what else to do. I had to go back to work. So I called Dearie to help out."

289

His face was pink with agitation, his voice hoarse. "Lise always told you I was the one who walked out. I bet you never knew I came back. Nobody ever told you that, did they? I came back, dammit."

Greer's jaw was clenched so hard it ached. She closed the door and gripped the steering wheel, trying to calm herself. Just before she put the car in reverse, she rolled the window down and turned to the sad old man with the hollow eyes.

"But you didn't stay, did you?"

She did a neat 180-degree turn in the sandy yard and drove away.

27

Vanessa Littrell's Sunday morning text was brief but intriguing.

Hey! Big news. Can u meet me @Coffee Mug @10?

It was 9:30 and Greer had just returned to her room from a run — two laps of the island equaled five miles. She peeled off her sweaty clothes and jumped into the shower.

As soon as she'd lathered up with the pathetic sliver of hotel soap, she instantly regretted not stopping in Gainesville, at a real store, to buy some decent toiletries. She cursed the cheap hotel soap that left her skin dried out and ashy, and reserved a special curse for the scent memory that would now, forever more, be associated with her ill-advised assignation with Eben Thibadeaux.

Vanessa had snagged a table on the patio at the Coffee Mug, away from the prying eyes and ears of the dozen or so people who were seated inside the café. Greer paid for her coffee and a blueberry muffin, and sat down at the table with her back to the street.

Vanessa noted Greer's wet hair. "I hope I didn't wake you up. I always forget not everybody gets up at six to take out the dogs."

"With my job, six a.m. is the equivalent of sleeping in. I was actually just coming back from a run," Greer said, stirring sweetener into her coffee. "What's the big news?"

"Are you still interested in the casino?"

"Of course. We're dying to use it. The director is still dogging me about it." She held up her phone to show Vanessa the half dozen texts Bryce Levy had sent, urging her to get the casino location nailed down. "Has Eb Thibadeaux changed his mind?"

"We don't need Eb's permission," Vanessa said. "After that farce of a city council meeting last week, I asked my lawyer to go over the old lease one more time. There has to be a loophole, I told her, that could get us out of it. And there was. I don't know why it never struck me before, it's so obvious."

"She found a loophole? What is it?"

Vanessa smiled and nibbled at a bit of muffin. With her sleek, dark hair and pert, upturned nose, she reminded Greer of a self-satisfied Cheshire cat.

"The city hasn't used the casino for a municipal entertainment facility since they boarded it up, back in 2011."

"So? What difference does that make?"

"It changes everything. Their lease specifically provides that if the property is not being used for purposes stated in the lease agreement, they are in default, and the lease is nullified."

"Huh?"

"Standard real estate boilerplate," Vanessa said with a chuckle. "Which I guess is why we all overlooked it. Until yesterday, when Sue Simpson, my lawyer, got her teeth into it. The clause is very clear. The city is in default. Their lease is history. And I can do whatever I want with *my* property. I can blow it up or burn it down, and there's nothing they can do to stop me."

"That's great!" Greer set her coffee mug down on the table.

"I know." Vanessa was beaming. "I've got Sue working on a lease agreement for you guys. She thinks she can get it drafted by tomorrow afternoon."

"Oh. Well, the studio has a standard agreement we use, but I can take a look at what she's done, and I'm sure we can come up with something that will work," Greer said cautiously. "But are you sure we're in the clear with this? I mean, isn't there some process we have to go through?"

"Not as far as I'm concerned," Vanessa said. "Sue will send the city a certified notice first thing in the morning, telling them that their lease has been nullified. And in the meantime

I'm going home to find my daddy's old bolt cutters. As soon as we've served the city, I'm cutting those locks off and going in there. Are you in?"

"Absolutely," Greer said. "I can't wait to let Bryce know. He'll be thrilled. I'm thrilled. I can't thank you enough, Vanessa."

"The pleasure's all mine," Vanessa said. "Or it will be, especially when I see the look on Eb Thibadeaux's face when he finds out he's not the boss of the free world."

"He seems to feel pretty strongly about the casino. Are you sure he won't keep fighting you, maybe take you to court or something?'

Vanessa shrugged. "Let him. He can't win on this one."

"Okay then," Greer said. "If you're sure you can get us in there tomorrow, I'd love to take Bryce and the art director and production folks on a walk-through."

"I'll take you around myself," Vanessa said. "I haven't been in there in years. Once the city started letting it go downhill, I couldn't stand to see it deteriorate. As a kid, I thought the casino was my personal playhouse."

"Greer?"

She turned and saw CeeJay standing there with a puzzled expression on her face.

"Hey," she said.

"Hey," CeeJay said coolly.

"Do you know Vanessa Littrell?" Greer turned to her tablemate. "Vanessa, this is my best friend, CeeJay, who just happens to be the best hair and makeup artist in the business."

"Hi," Vanessa said.

"Vanessa owns the casino, CeeJay. She was just telling me we're in the clear to use it for the film. I'm going to try to get Bryce and Alex in there tomorrow, so we can get working on it."

"How nice for you," CeeJay said. She turned, without another word, and disappeared into the coffee shop.

"Something I said?" Vanessa said, watching CeeJay walk up to the counter.

"I don't know," Greer said slowly. "I've never seen her act that like before."

Vanessa stood. "Well, I have to run. Literally. As soon as I hear from Sue tomorrow I'll get with you about that walk-through."

CeeJay sat at a small Formica-topped table, her hands folded around a steaming mug of chai tea.

Greer pulled a chair from an adjacent table. "Are you mad at me about something?"

CeeJay lowered her eyelashes and sipped her tea. "What makes you think that?"

"You were kind of rude out there to Vanessa just now."

"Oh? Was I rude to your new best friend? So sorry. Maybe it has something to do with the fact that, after standing me up for coffee yesterday, you end up here all cozy with her."

"Stand you up? What are you talking about?"

"You didn't get my text yesterday? Telling you I wanted to meet you here?"

"I got it. And I texted you back that I wasn't around so I couldn't meet you."

"No you didn't."

"CeeJay, I did!" Greer pulled her phone from the pocket of her shorts and pulled up her text history. She found the last text from CeeJay, and the response she'd typed — but never sent.

"Shit," she said, sliding the phone across the table. "My bad. I ended up driving over to Alachua yesterday. I was right in the midst of texting you when I got interrupted."

"Where's Alachua? What were you doing there?"

"It's about an hour from here. On the other side of Gainesville. I, uh, decided to go see my father."

"Wha-a-at?" CeeJay's kohl-rimmed eyes widened. "What prompted that?"

"It was totally a guilt trip. Lise kept nagging me about calling him, after she got sick. They'd reconnected on Facebook, and she even gave him my contact information — including my phone number. Wouldn't you know it, he lives not that far from here, and he'd seen on my Facebook page that I was working in Cypress Key. He called and texted a couple times, but I never responded. Yesterday morning I was at loose ends, and I got in the car, and the next thing I know I'm parked in his driveway, texting you. There's a tap on my window and I look up — into the face of dear old Dad."

"Lise wanted you to get in touch with your old man? I thought she hated his guts."

"So did I. For years she wouldn't even say his name. She referred to him as 'the sperm donor.' Then, on her deathbed, she decides maybe he's not that bad."

"Weird."

"Creepy," Greer corrected her.

"How was the visit?"

"Different. Let's talk about something else. Like why you decided to stand me up for dinner Friday night. I was kinda ticked, you know?"

CeeJay nodded. "It was a lousy stunt. I broke the sacred golden rule of girlfriends, ditching you for Bryce. I'm sorry. I suck."

Greer smiled. "Hold that thought. I need more caffeine."

When she got back from the counter with her refill, she leaned back in her chair. "You were saying how much you suck?"

"It's just, Bryce has been so moody, all week. We get here and he's all pumped up about the film, staying up half the night, working on rewrites, giving notes to Kregg and Adelyn, firing off e-mails to everybody."

"Including many, many midnight texts to me," Greer pointed out.

"I know. Then Friday he's in this huge funk. He knows Terry's drinking again, because the script is totally only half finished, and he's been watching the dailies and I think it's just occurred to him that Kregg can't act his way out of a paper bag, and he's worried about this casino thing. . . ."

"The casino thing is now officially taken care of," Greer said. She leaned closer. "What else? What aren't you telling me?"

CeeJay stared down into her mug. "He uh, well, this morning he asked me to move out of the house. I actually just came from the motel. Looks like we'll be almost roomies."

Greer grabbed CeeJay's hand. "Why?"

Tears sprang up into CeeJay's eyes. "He says he's just feeling crowded. That it has nothing to do with me, or our relationship. He's stressed and he just needs his space."

"Jeez!" Greer slapped the tabletop. "What a cliché. He can't come up with anything more original than that?"

"Guess not," CeeJay said. She dabbed at her eyes with a paper napkin. "He swears this won't change our relationship. Says he still loves me, and once the film is finished we'll be right back where we were. Only better."

"Blah. Blah. Blah," Greer said with a sigh. "Men suck."

CeeJay nodded. "They really do."

"Which room did Ginny give you? Not one of the ones by the pool, I hope. The drinkers and smokers hang out there all night, and you can hear every word they say."

"Ginny?"

"The manager. She also co-owns the motel, with the mayor."

"Huh. Eb Thibadeaux checked me in. He was really sweet, too. Helped me carry my stuff in, gave me extra towels."

"Did he give you the towels that feel like extra-fine sandpaper?"

"I guess. I know you think he's a dweeb, but you know who he kind of reminds me of?"

"I can't imagine."

"Remember that old show, *Gilligan's Island*? Don't you think he looks exactly like the Professor?"

"No." Greer shook her head vigorously. But CeeJay had struck a nerve. With his tousled hair and glasses, he did kind of look like the Professor. Damn. Another image of Eb Thibadeaux which she would really rather forget.

28

Monday morning's shoot hadn't gone as planned.

The old elementary school auditorium was being used as a stand-in for a courthouse. What should have been a tense, emotion-packed confrontation between the fictional judge and the character of Kregg's lawyer had been interrupted half a dozen times by problems big and small. A garbage truck backing up on the street behind the school could be clearly heard. There was a wardrobe malfunction when somebody noticed the lawyer's white dress shirt bore a huge coffee stain. Finally, when it was clear after dozens of takes that the actor playing the judge had not memorized the long monologue the scene required, Bryce Levy lost his cool.

Greer was standing out of camera range, at the back of the courtroom set, but she clearly heard everything.

"What the fuck?" Bryce exclaimed, striding up to Michael Payne, the elderly character actor playing the judge. "Michael! It's twelve lines. Twelve fucking lines that you've had weeks to work on."

Payne stared straight ahead, while the other actors looked away in embarrassment.

Bryce whirled around to address one of the key grips. "And Jesus, Kevin, can you do something about the glare in here? We've got light bouncing all over the fucking room."

"I'll take care of it right now," Kevin said.

"Break for thirty minutes, then everybody get your asses back in here and do your fucking jobs," Bryce snarled.

Her cell phone rang. It was Zena, calling from the house where interiors and exteriors for the next day's shoot were scheduled.

"Hey, Greer. We got problems over here on Manatee. The dude that lives down the block threatened to call the cops on me because some of the crew were parked on the street in front of his house."

"Were they blocking the guy's driveway, or otherwise on his property?"

"No! The guy's just a jerk. He's been raising hell since we got over here," Zena said.

"He can call the cops if he wants, but we're fully permitted to shoot over there," Greer said. She glanced down at her watch. "In the meantime, round up all of our people and tell them to move their cars over to the base camp. I'll rent some more golf carts and we'll

301

start shuttling people and dropping them off. Okay? I'll get over there as soon as I can, or I'll send somebody else to deal with the locals."

On her way to the catering tent, Greer called Island Hoppers, one of the local golf cart rental places, and arranged to have four more carts delivered to the base camp.

She found CeeJay seated under the tent, peeling a tangerine. "Wow. Bryce really is in a foul mood."

"Makes me glad I won't be around tonight," CeeJay said somberly. "When he gets like this, he's totally irrational."

"I'm not looking forward to tomorrow, when we shoot at that tiny house," Greer said, thinking ahead. She was looking around the area as she spoke, and she spotted Allie Thibadeaux leaning up against a brick wall, flirting with Kregg.

The two were so intent on their conversation that they failed to notice Bryce's determined approach until it was too late. The director grabbed Kregg's arm, and she could tell by both men's body language that the conversation wasn't pleasant.

Allie drifted away toward the table lined with soft drinks and snacks.

"I hate to see Allie get mixed up with a guy like that," Greer said. "I tried to talk to Ginny, to sort of warn her that Allie's playing with fire, but she just said Allie is smart enough to know what's up."

"Seventeen? Ha!" CeeJay said. "When I think about the shit I was getting into at that age? I'm amazed I made it to twenty."

"Me too." Greer watched while Allie plucked a can of Red Bull from a tub of ice. "I'm gonna go talk to her," she resolved.

"And tell her what? Stay away from asshats like Kregg?"

"Mmm. No, I'm just going to give her enough stuff to do that she hopefully won't have to loiter with the cast."

"Why do you care so much about this girl?" CeeJay asked.

"I don't know," Greer admitted. "Maybe I see a little of myself in her."

"Go for it then," CeeJay said.

Greer sidled up to Allie, who was watching Kregg on the receiving end of the director's bad mood.

"Hi, Allie."

"Hey," the girl said, keeping her eyes on Bryce and Kregg. "Wow. Bryce is really PMS-ing, huh?"

"Mondays are always tough, and there's a lot going on," Greer said. "Zena just called from the house on Manatee, where we're shooting interiors tomorrow. Do you maybe know Edith Rambo?"

"I did, but um, she's dead."

Greer laughed. "I realize that. I've rented

her house from her son, who lives in Tampa. But Manatee is a really narrow street, and all our trucks are going to block that street, which is already starting to piss off the locals. You could do what I call neighbor triage."

She riffled through the forms on her clipboard and came up with the one she needed, handing it to Allie.

"That's a letter notifying the neighbors that we'll be filming tomorrow on their block and asking for their cooperation. It also lets them know that, once we start, security won't let any cars pass Mrs. Rambo's house. So they'll need to plan ahead and leave before or after we start filming, at nine o'clock."

"Okay," Allie said.

"Take this form over to our production office. It's in the old bookstore downtown. You know the place, right?"

Allie nodded eagerly.

"Ask for Betty. I'll let her know I'm sending you over. Ask her to make twenty or thirty copies of this letter. Then, take one of our golf carts and ride over to Manatee Street and hit every house on Mrs. Rambo's block. Both sides of the street. Knock on doors, give them your sweetest smile, and tell them about the filming tomorrow morning, starting at nine."

"I can do that. I know a lot of people who live on that street."

"Excellent. Be polite, be deferential. My

cell phone number is on the letter, and you can tell them they can call me, anytime, if they have questions or concerns."

"Cool. But what if some people are pissed off?"

"Some people will be," Greer assured her. "It's my job to handle them. Zena, the assistant location manager, is over there now. Get her to give you the gift cards we had made up, for the pizza place. You'll give one of those to every house on Mrs. Rambo's block. As sort of a bribe."

"What should I do after that?"

"Do you have a cell phone?"

Allie pulled an iPhone from the pocket of her shorts. Greer took it and programmed in her own cell number, then put Allie's number in her own phone.

"Call me. We're going to need to move all the crew cars off that street, so I'll probably get you to shuttle people from the base camp back over there, after they've moved their cars. Have you got all that?"

"Yes," Allie said.

"One more thing," Greer said gently. "I need for you to be really professional while you're working for me." She gave Allie a knowing look. "No messing around with the cast during working hours. You get me? If your being around the set is going to be a distraction for either you or Kregg, I'll have to find somebody else to help out."

"I understand," Allie said, looking her straight in the eye.

"I'm taking kind of a chance with you, Allie. We don't usually hire high school kids as P.A.s, but you seem more mature than most girls your age. And I can tell you're a hard worker, so don't let me down."

"I won't," Allie promised. "You'll see."

29

By the time Greer made it over to the city
pier Vanessa Littrell was already unloading
her arsenal of tools from the back of a red
Jeep: pry bars, a hammer, a crowbar, and a
huge, lethal-looking pair of bolt cutters.

It was a blazing hot June afternoon. The
city beach was crowded with families and
teens lolling in the sand or swimming in the
calm turquoise waters of the Gulf. Farther
out in the surf, pleasure boats skimmed
across the water, and on the horizon, three or
four shrimp boats trolled back and forth,
their nets lowered for fishing.

Greer mopped perspiration from her neck
and eyed the bolt cutters. "Do you think the
city got your lawyer's termination letter?"

"I know they got the letter," Vanessa said.
"We sent everything certified mail. Anyway, I
had a hot e-mail and a phone call from Eb
an hour ago."

"How did he take the news?"

Vanessa smiled sweetly. "I didn't actually

speak to him. If he has anything to say to me, he can say it to my attorney." She grasped the thick padlock securing the chain-link gate.

"Hold this for me, will you?"

Vanessa's jaw tightened in concentration as she clamped the tempered steel cutters around the padlock. Her biceps bulged as she squeezed the levers together. A few seconds later the lock fell to the concrete surface of the pier with a satisfying *clunk.*

"Step one," Vanessa said, as she pulled the gate open.

The two women advanced toward the casino entryway, dodging overturned trash barrels, construction debris, and five years' worth of seagull droppings.

Vanessa stopped short in front of the entry, where vandals had spray painted graffiti greetings, declarations of love, and obscenities across the facade. Mounds of beer cans, glass shards, cigarette butts, and a bashed-in Styrofoam cooler had been swept up against the front wall by the wind.

She leaned down, picked up a single discarded tennis shoe, and dropped it again with a snort of disgust.

"How the hell did anybody get in here to do this?'

"The same way I did, probably," Greer suggested, pointing at the dilapidated boat landing on the north and south side of the casino. "Somebody was out here just last week. I was walking on the beach and looked out and saw lights from inside the building. I could hear a woman laughing, and music, and then somebody was setting off fireworks. I heard a boat engine leaving not long afterwards."

"Surprised they didn't burn the whole place down," Vanessa said.

Their footsteps echoed in the high-ceilinged ballroom. Vanessa paced the wooden dance floor, hugging her arms tightly to her chest.

"Does it bring back memories?" Greer asked.

"Some." Vanessa shook her head. "Roller-skating parties. Movies. Kid stuff. But the past is past. Look at it now. It's a dump." She pointed up at the ceiling, where chunks of falling plaster revealed expanses of lath, and at the bank of broken windows looking out on the Gulf.

"You really don't think this could all be restored?" Greer asked.

"Oh sure. If you had millions and millions to flush down the toilet. But what's the point? A community center? Let the city build one over by the park, on their own land."

"Hello? Anybody home?"

Bryce Levy strolled into the ballroom, followed by his screenwriter, Terry Bodenhimer, and Alex the art director.

"Unbelievable!" Bryce shouted, turning 360 degrees to take it all in. "Terr! Alex! What did I tell you? Is this place unbelievable or what?"

"Fantastic," Alex agreed. He whipped his phone from the pocket of his jeans and began snapping photographs. "It's so . . . authentic."

Terry Bodenhimer walked slowly around the perimeter of the ballroom. He stood in front of the snack bar, looking up at the painted menu board. He climbed the steps to the elevated bandstand, then sat abruptly on the floor, his legs dangling over the edge. He ran both hands through his long, graying hair and closed his eyes tightly.

"Terry?" Bryce looked at Greer, then Vanessa, and winked. He approached the bandstand cautiously, looking up at the prone screenwriter.

"Terr? Buddy? What's happening?" The voice was soft, coaxing.

"I'm thinking," Terry said, lying on his back, eyes still closed.

"About the script?"

"No. About my hemorrhoids. Yes, I'm thinking about the script. This place, it changes everything. Everything. Go away, okay? I'm in the moment here."

"Let's go walk around the outside," Greer said in a hushed voice. "Let me show you the patio, and the boat landing."

They were huddled together under the meager shade of the patio awning, discussing the logistics of filming, when Bodenhimer emerged into the sunlight.

"Let's go," he told Bryce.

"Go where?"

"Back to the house. I've got it now." He tapped his forehead with his forefinger. "It's all up here. The whole frigging story. Nick's ambiguity about returning home after deployment. He's seen war, you know? Death. He's not the same guy. Danielle? She's changed too. She's not the sweet girl he left behind. Hell, she was never sweet. Lying, scheming, cheating little bitch."

"Wait." Bryce looked confused. "The wife is cheating on him? Where is this going?"

"Danielle? She's hooked up with the sheriff. Oh yeah. They're in it together. Trying to make it look like Nick's losing his mind. They're gaslighting him."

"Oh-ka-a-ay," Bryce said slowly. "What's the motive?"

"Sex. Money. Greed. Same evil shit as always," Terry said grimly.

"Money? I thought Nick was down on his luck."

"He was. He was estranged from his family. But now . . . His old man died while he was away. Nick's torn. He doesn't want his old man's blood money. But Danielle does. She wants the money, and she wants the sheriff. And the only way to get both of them is to get rid of Nick."

311

"I'm liking it," Bryce said. "But let me ask you this. An ending. Is there an ending in sight? I mean, you said we needed to blow something up, right?"

"Right here." Bodenhimer waved his arm at the casino. "It all goes down right here." He stomped the concrete with his boot. "Some epic shit. A car chase. Helicopters. And then — an explosion. *Boom!* It's gonna make *Die Hard* look like *Toy Story.*"

He clamped a hand over Greer's shoulder. "This place here? Awesome. A game changer. Not gonna lie to you. I was struggling. Lost in the wilderness. But this place? It's like, suddenly the fog clears and the universe hands you the answer you've been seeking. And it was here all along."

He turned and gestured toward the casino. "Right here."

"Uh, well. That's good news," Greer said.

Bodenhimer squeezed her shoulder for emphasis.

"Let's go," he told Bryce. "I gotta get all this down on paper before my head explodes."

Bryce shot Greer a thumbs-up. "Great stuff. Let's get the crews over here and start cleaning it up so we can start construction. Stephen will let you know what he needs."

Vanessa and Greer watched while Bryce, Bodenhimer, and Alex climbed onto the waiting golf cart driven by Bryce's assistant.

"Did you understand any of that?" Vanessa asked, as she gathered up her tools.

"Not really."

"So, that guy Terry. He hasn't even finished writing the script yet? But you're here, shooting? How does that work?"

"Sometimes it does, sometimes it doesn't," Greer said. "That's the film business."

"Crazy. Did you get the lease agreement we e-mailed you?"

"The company's lawyer is looking it over. So far, they haven't raised any red flags. Like Bryce said, we're going to start working on building the set out right away. I know for sure they'll want to get started cleaning it up and painting out all the graffiti. In the meantime, if it's okay with you, I'll get a new lock for the gate. And we'll see about posting a security guard to keep away the vandals and partiers."

"I love it," Vanessa chuckled. "Cleaning and painting and building, just to blow it all up in a few short weeks."

Greer thought they were about to make a clean getaway. She was helping Vanessa load her wrecking tools back into the Jeep when she spotted Eb Thibadeaux's lanky figure striding down the pier in their direction. She sucked in her breath.

Vanessa saw him too. "Wonder what took

him so long?"

The mayor wasted no time with formalities. He barely acknowledged Greer, saving his ire for Vanessa.

"I see you've been busy breaking and entering."

"It's not breaking and entering if you own the property, which I do. The city's rights as a tenant are terminated, Eb. The minute the casino ceased to be used for its stated intent, the minute the city boarded it up, they nullified our agreement. You know real estate law as well as I do."

"This isn't the end of it. We'll ask a judge for a temporary restraining order."

"But you won't get it. Why waste time and taxpayer dollars — my taxpayer dollars, by the way — fighting a losing battle?"

He fixed both women with a cold stare. "And what happens after this movie gets made? After you've blown up a landmark and made a fast buck and we're left with an empty crater at the end of the city pier?"

"We'll see," Vanessa said. "For years now I've had to turn away developers because the property was tied up. Now it's mine again. I'll put out some feelers, and then I'll start entertaining offers."

A muscle in his jaw twitched. "Nothing on this pier can be developed without the city's approval, you know."

"And you'd block me, just out of spite."

"Not out of spite. The pier and the casino are the centerpiece in our master plan for redeveloping the waterfront. I have an absolute obligation to my constituents to see to it that we have an attractive, viable, environmentally sensitive building on this pier."

Vanessa smiled prettily. "I'd be happy to entertain an offer from the city to buy the casino outright, you know. At a current, fair market price, of course."

"I just bet you would be," Eb said. He shook his head and frowned. "I really don't understand you, Vanessa. The casino — that's not just a Cypress Key landmark. It's your heritage. Your great-grandfather built it, your grandfather and father built it up and kept it going. And you'd destroy all that and walk away. Because why? You're greedy? Bored? Which is it?"

"None of the above. And don't even try to make me feel guilty about my motives, Eb Thibadeaux."

"Oh, believe me, I know guilt doesn't work on you."

"Damn straight," Vanessa shot back. "I'm a businesswoman. I'm on my own in this world now, in case you haven't noticed it. If I have an investment that's not performing, I do my best to turn it around. And if I can't turn it around, I sell. That casino?" She flapped her hand in the direction of the pier. "It's not my flesh and blood. My family is cold and in the grave. The way I see it? Their monument is a headstone. Everything else is negotiable."

She slammed the tailgate of the Jeep, got in the driver's seat, and drove away.

30

Eb Thibadeaux muttered something unintelligible under his breath. Then he stooped down to pick up the snapped padlock Vanessa had left behind. Without a word or a backward glance, he started walking back down the pier in the direction of city hall.

His gait was so long, his pace so hurried, that Greer had to break into a trot to catch up to the mayor.

"That's it? You're not even gonna yell at me?"

"Nothing left to say."

"I just . . . I just hate it when somebody hates me." She was out of breath.

That slowed him down a step. "Why do you care? Like you said, it's just a job to you. Your job is to get films made. It's not like you're running for Miss Congeniality."

"Sandra Bullock. I really liked her in that, even though the plot was totally improbable."

He quirked an eyebrow. "What are you talking about?"

"Sorry. Movie stuff. I care what people think about me because I'm a chronic people pleaser. It's what allows me to do what I do. I make connections, get strangers to trust me . . ."

"And then you go to bed with them."

Greer felt as though she'd been slapped. "I guess I deserved that," she said finally.

"No." Eb sighed. "That was a rotten thing to say. My mother would say I was raised better than that. I'm angry at Vanessa, and I took it out on you, which is unfair."

"You're still pissed about the other night, right?"

"The other night? Yeah. That I do take very personally."

Greer's face flushed.

"I don't regret anything about being with you that night," he said, his tone even. "Except for the way it ended."

"And this is why it was a bad idea for us to get together. It complicates an already complicated situation, with the casino and everything else. I just think maybe it's not a good idea for me to get involved with anybody right now. I've got issues. . . ."

"Oh Jesus. You've got issues? Do you know anybody who doesn't have issues? Look at me. It didn't take you a week to figure out that I have a messiah complex."

"Wait. Ginny told you I said that? That was said in strictest confidence."

318

"What can I say? Blood is thicker than water. My aunt doesn't miss a trick. Ginny figured out I was interested in you, and she wanted to give me a heads-up that you had a pretty low opinion of me."

Greer sighed. "This conversation is going nowhere."

"Strictly out of curiosity, what issues do you have that would preclude you from having a relationship?"

"I can't get into all that right now. I've got to get back to the set. Can we please just drop this discussion and agree to a friendly truce?"

"Humor me."

"My last boyfriend left me because he said I cared more about my work than I did about him."

"Sounds like a selfish prick, if you ask me."

"And I have trust issues. Big-time. Sawyer cheated on me. Repeatedly. The last time, I was in Puerto Rico for three weeks, scouting locations for a sci-fi flick, so he started sleeping with his analyst, who helped him rationalize his cheating by telling him that he could never fully commit to me until he explored his attraction to other women."

"Sawyer was a dick, obviously. And his analyst was a self-serving quack who should be reported to the AMA."

"But it's a conflict of interest for both of us," Greer persisted. "You're the mayor. You joke around about it, but I know you take your work as seriously as I do."

"Okay. The casino thing — this was probably inevitable," Eb said. "I've known Vanessa Littrell since we were kids. She's the classic rich girl who always gets what she goes after. If you hadn't come along and dangled this deal in front of her, somebody else would have. I'm going to fight this plan to demolish it — tooth and nail. You say you're doing your job? I'm doing mine. And we'll leave it at that. For now."

31

She was on the golf cart, two blocks away from Manatee Street, when she started seeing the signs.

NO CREW PARKING ON MANATEE OR DOLPHIN.

A block away, she saw another sign.

MANATEE STREET BETWEEN FIRST AND THIRD CLOSED FOR TRAFFIC TODAY, 2–8 p.m.

Greer hadn't directed Zena to put up signs. Had she actually taken some initiative for herself? Greer's day had taken another serious turn for the better.

As expected, the equipment trucks had effectively blocked the narrow, tree-lined street. The off-duty police officer waved her past the metal barrier, and she snugged the cart up tight behind a truck trailering the Royal Restrooms she'd rented.

She found Zena in a heated discussion with the truck driver, who was waving an invoice in her face.

"Talk to this guy, will you?" Zena exclaimed. "He's saying he won't give me the keys to the damned toilets until he gets paid."

"I'll take that," Greer said, extracting the paper from the driver's outstretched hand. She ran a finger down the line items, looked up, and realized that there were only two deluxe bathroom modules on the truck, even though she'd ordered a third module, to be used only by cast members.

"All right," she said calmly. "We've got a problem, because you've shorted us a module. I specifically told your people we need three bathrooms."

"I don't know nothing about that," the driver argued. "I load what they give me, at the warehouse in Gainesville. I deliver, but I don't leave until I get paid."

"We need that third module," Greer said.

"You ain't getting it today," the driver countered. "It's two hours to Gainesville and back, and it's after three now. The warehouse closes at five."

"Okay. Here's what we'll do. If you'll go over to our production office on Main Street, the bookkeeper will cut you a check for half this amount. I'll call your boss and let him know the situation. But I need you to unlock those bathrooms right now, and I need a promise from somebody that we'll get another toilet here first thing in the morning."

"I just pick up and deliver," he repeated.

"Give me five minutes."

Greer scrolled through the contacts on her phone, found the number for the event rental company in Gainesville, and made her call. Three minutes later she handed the phone to the driver, who listened and nodded through the brief conversation.

He handed the phone back to Greer, then withdrew an envelope with the key to the restrooms from the breast pocket of his work shirt.

"Hey, uh, somebody told me Adelyn Davis is in this movie. Is she actually here?"

"That's her, right over there." Greer pointed to a huge oak tree, where Adelyn was seated on a folding chair in the shade while CeeJay dusted her face with powder.

The driver stared at the actress for a long moment. "She's a little bitty thing, ain't she?"

"Very petite," Greer said. "But very nice. She's the one that extra bathroom is for, you know."

"Nobody tells me anything. In the morning, when I drop off the other unit, you think I could get a picture made with Adelyn? She's my little girl's favorite, since she was in that Disney Channel show."

"I'm pretty sure we can arrange that," Greer said. She glanced at the driver's name, which was embroidered over his breast pocket. "And listen, Billy. Is there any way you could get that module here first thing in the morning? It's really awkward for Adelyn to have to use the same bathroom as all the other crew members. She's super sweet, but you know how it is."

"I don't clock in until eight," Billy said.

"Lucky you. I'll be over here before five tomorrow."

Billy looked around at the set. "Pretty interesting seeing all this. I never delivered to a movie set before."

"Have you had lunch?" Greer asked. She pointed to the caterer's tent. "I'd love for you to be our guest."

"The fried chicken's pretty good," Zena offered. "And the barbecue."

"Okay. Sure, why not?" Billy started to wander away.

"See you first thing tomorrow, right?" Greer called.

He smiled and waved.

"Greer, you know Adelyn has her own RV with a bathroom, right?" Zena asked.

"I know it, but Billy doesn't," Greer replied. "And we need that third module before things get funky over here tomorrow. Before I forget, can you get an autographed head shot of Adelyn to hand over to our new friend when he gets here tomorrow morning?"

"Consider it done."

She looked around at the set and the small village of trucks, trailers, and people who, overnight, had quadrupled the population of

Manatee Street.

"Everything else all right?"

"So far. Hey, the new girl, Allie? Where'd you find her?"

"She's the mayor's niece. Never hurts to score points with the authorities. Right? Do you think she'll work out?"

"Oh yeah. You know that nutball neighbor, Steve, I forget his name? The big fat guy with the Sasquatch beard. Lives two doors down from the set. He's the one who's been raising hell all week. A little while ago he came up to me and offered to let me park in his driveway."

"That's the same guy who set his pit bull on you last week because you were legally parked at the curb?"

"Same dude. But today he's all hearts and smiles. Apparently, your girl Allie took him a box of doughnuts this morning, and now we're all best friends. Did you tell her to do that?"

"I would have if I'd thought of it. Damn! I'm officially impressed."

"Me too," Zena said.

Greer's cell phone rang.

"Greer? It's Allie Thibadeaux."

"Hi, Allie. Zena was just telling me you've been doing some fence-mending on Manatee."

"Huh?"

"Bribing the neighbors with doughnuts.

Great idea."

"Oh. Well, that's what Ginny always does when guests at the Sands are pissed off about something. She just drops muffins off at their room."

"I'm going to remember that one. What's up?"

"Zena was saying we should try to move the caterer's tent, because there isn't any shade where it is, and it's super hot right now. This lady I know, Mrs. Witchger, she lives at the end of the block. She's going to be out of town for the next week, and she said we could set up in her front yard. They can put the generators in her driveway too."

"Perfect," Greer said. "You can tell Mrs. Witchger we'll pay her two hundred fifty dollars a day, too."

"Oh. Okay. I think she'd be okay with us using it for free though. She was my kindergarten teacher, and she's a nice lady."

"I'll drop by and see her in a few minutes. I'll take her one of our written contracts, and offer her one hundred dollars a day."

"Cool. I got the golf cart, like you said, so unless you need me for something else, I guess I'll just keep picking up and dropping off the crew between here and the base camp."

"I'll catch up with you later," Greer said.

Two hours later, Greer spotted Allie Thiba-

326

deaux standing in the backyard of Edith Rambo's house, peeping out from behind an overgrown azalea shrub, watching the cameras roll as Bryce Levy directed Kregg and Adelyn in a scene being filmed on the brick patio.

She could tell by Allie's body language that she wasn't much enjoying the spectacle of Kregg doing take after take of soul-kissing his costar.

Greer walked quietly up behind Allie during a break in the filming. "It's just acting, Allie."

The teenager whirled around, embarrassed at being spied upon while spying.

"Adelyn is a total pro. She's been in movies since she was a child. And if it makes you feel any better, she's engaged."

Allie blushed, then giggled. "Okay. Yeah, that does make me feel better."

"It's none of my business, but do Ginny and Eb know you're seeing Kregg?"

Allie's smile faded, replaced by a more typical teen expression. "We're just hanging out. He's teaching me a lot about movies and stuff."

That better be all he's teaching you about, Greer thought.

"But he's five years older than you are."

"Everybody says I'm way more mature than most kids my age. Even you said it," Allie said.

"But Kregg's from a whole different world. He's a millionaire many times over, has owned his own house since he was sixteen. And once he's done filming here, he's gone. In three weeks he heads out on a twenty-two-city tour."

Allie tossed her hair. "I told you. We're just hanging out having fun. It's no biggie."

Greer knew she should let it go, but she couldn't. Not yet.

"Did Kregg tell you he was just released from drug rehab? Literally, he flew here direct from the rehab in Arizona."

"Yeah, he told me. It's not like he's a junkie."

"So, most mornings when he reports to work, he's already buzzed on weed."

"It's legal in lots of places."

"But not in Florida. Kregg's already gotten arrested last week for drag racing. Chief Bottoms isn't going to give him another break if he gets caught for possession. Or for furnishing alcohol to a minor, which is what you are. And neither is your uncle. Just think about your family, okay? If you get in trouble with Kregg, it's going to put Eb in a terrible position."

Allie's carefully made-up eyes narrowed. "I'm not a baby! And I'm not going to get in trouble. Okay? And I would really appreciate it if you would not go narcing me out to my uncle for hanging out with Kregg. Just because my dad, you know, did some stuff, Eb stays up in my grill all the time. And I'm sick of it!"

Greer reached out her hand to the girl's shoulder, but Allie shook her off. "I gotta go to work at the Inn now. You won't tell Eb about me and Kregg, right? I swear, Greer, I'm not gonna get in trouble. Anyway, weed gives me, like, a fierce headache."

"How about beer?" Greer asked.

"Just don't rat me out," Allie persisted. "Please? Kregg is really cool. He's not like people think he is."

Greer sighed. "I won't tell, but don't make me regret hiring you. Or trusting you to know right from wrong."

"Thanks! I'll be good."

She watched as Allie sped off through the backyard. "You better be," she muttered.

32

Shooting on location on a residential street was always fraught with potential hassles, and Thursday morning was no exception to the rule.

The incoming text was from Zena, and it was terse but to the point.

Trouble on Manatee. Better get over here.

Greer spotted the source of the problem the moment she turned the corner onto Edith Rambo's block. Or rather, she heard it. Earsplitting, bass-booming rap blared from loudspeakers set up on the front yard of the troublesome neighbor Zena had nicknamed Sasquatch.

Sasquatch himself was seated in a folded lawn chair at the foot of his driveway, with what she hoped was only a toy BB gun stretched out across his knees.

Across the street and over two houses, crew members milled around, obviously idled by the unwanted concert.

She found Zena standing in the front yard at Edith Rambo's house, talking on the phone, but she disconnected as Greer approached.

"I hope you were calling the cops," Greer said. "How long has this been going on?"

"For the past forty-five minutes. I've called the cops three times, and they sent a unit over, but they say there's nothing they can do. The guy's on his own property."

"They don't have a noise ordinance in this burg?"

"They do, but as long as he's not playing loud music and disturbing the peace after ten p.m., they say he's not breaking any laws."

"I thought you said we'd made peace with the guy. I thought Sasquatch invited you to park in his driveway, and be best friends."

"What can I say? He's a psycho. Everything was good until this morning. Apparently somebody tipped him to the fact that we're paying the people directly across the street a fee, because the exteriors of their homes are in camera range."

Greer nodded. "I see where this is going. He wants to be paid too, right?"

"I explained that his house isn't in camera range," Zena said. "I gave him the last pizza certificates I had. Allie went to the bakery and brought back two dozen doughnuts, but he wouldn't let her on the property."

Greer was gazing at the neighbor. His dark

beard hung down to his chest, and his hair fuzzed out below an orange and blue sun visor, which did nothing to hide the softball-sized bright pink bald spot on top of his head. He was decked out in bright orange polyester basketball shorts, which hung down to his knees, and an extra-extra-extra-large sleeveless blue tank top, which barely covered his huge, distended white belly. He was sucking from a quart-size Slurpee cup and glaring out at the world. An old-school boom box rested on the ground by his feet.

"A guy like that, I can't believe he couldn't be bought off with doughnuts," Greer mumbled.

"Maybe he's glucose intolerant," Zena offered.

Greer looked over her shoulder at the idled cast and crew. "What's Bryce saying about the interruption? Did he blow a gasket?"

"The good news is, he left before the concert started. I think he went over to check out the progress on the casino."

She was studying Sasquatch again. His shoulders were tensed and his chubby white legs were firmly planted two feet apart, while his fingers caressed the stock of the rifle. Greer had seen that look, or variations on the look, before. The man was itching for a fight.

"The police didn't tell him to put the gun away?"

"Nope."

"Damn."

"Adelyn's terrified. She's hiding in her RV, and she says she's not coming out until the gun goes away."

"Where's Kregg?"

"I saw him sneaking down the alley with one of the grips a few minutes ago. I get the feeling his morning buzz is probably wearing off."

"You know about that?"

"Everybody knows about it," Zena assured her. "What are we going to do about Sasquatch? We're already behind schedule."

"What's his real name again?"

Zena consulted a small notebook that she kept in her back pocket. "Steve Woods."

"How much petty cash do you have?"

"Maybe a couple hundred?" She pulled a worn white business envelope stuffed with twenty-dollar bills. Greer pulled out a similar envelope and did a quick total.

"That's eight hundred twenty dollars." She looked anxiously over at Steve/Sasquatch, whose eyes were closed while he bobbed his head in time to the music. "You don't think that gun's loaded, do you?"

"The cop told me it's only a BB gun. Anyway, he's not gonna shoot you in broad daylight, in front of all these witnesses. Probably."

As she and Zena were conferring, Allie Thibadeaux walked up timidly. "I really did try to make friends with him, Greer. But everybody in town knows you don't mess with Mr. Woods."

"Every neighborhood has a Mr. Woods," Greer said. "Crazy, cranky, unreasonable whack jobs. But I'm gonna go over there and see if I can reason with him."

Allie's eyes widened. "For reals? Can I go too?"

"You sure you want to? This could get ugly."

"I kind of want to see how you handle him," Allie admitted.

Greer took a moment to gather her thoughts before crossing the street. It was another scorching Florida morning, temperatures hovering in the low nineties, humidity at around the same range.

She took a deep breath and cautiously approached the home of Steve Woods, with a bright, nonthreatening smile on her face and peace in her heart.

He was really getting into the music now, his eyes still closed, and she could see the aluminum chair slowly swaying from side to side.

"Okay, Allie," she said under her breath. "Think of this as a sort of hostage negotiation. The key to success here is listening, empathizing, more listening, and a willingness to help him decide to help us out."

"Hi, Mr. Woods," Greer called out, still

standing on the sidewalk, carefully avoiding stepping onto the subject's actual property. She had to shout to make herself heard above the din.

He opened his eyes and stared at her. "What?"

She used her cupped hands as a megaphone. "My name is Greer Hennessy. I'm the location manager for the production company filming here this week. I was wondering if I could talk to you for a minute."

He shrugged. "Talk's free."

"Could you turn down the music a little? I can hardly hear you."

He frowned, but then picked up his boom box and fiddled with the volume.

"Okay, talk."

"My associate seems to think you're pretty upset with us. Is that right?"

"Hell yeah. Your people fucked me over royally. You shut down the street. I can't park my truck out front. Can't get out to go to the store. And then you call the cops on me, for listening to a little music. What about my property rights?"

"It must be a big inconvenience, and I'm sorry about that."

"You ain't sorry enough to pay me for my trouble, are you?" he sneered. "Try and buy me off with a certificate for a crappy pizza? C'mon."

"Yeah, that was my fault. Dumb move. I

apologize for that. But we'd like to make things right with you, if it's not too late."

"What kind of rube do you take me for? Send some kid over here with doughnuts? You shut down my life for almost a week and then insult me by offering me food?"

"Again, that was my fault. I hope you won't blame my associates. I take full responsibility for our shortsightedness. In fact, that's why I'm here. I wanted to see if there is any way I could, you know, compensate you for your time and trouble."

He looked wary. "Compensate, how? I know you paid the Fleishmanns and the Erwins five hundred dollars." He pointed across the street, at Zena. "That chick over there tried to tell me she couldn't pay me because my house wouldn't be in the movie. Which is bullshit."

"I totally agree," Greer said. "This was a major failure to communicate. But I'd like to make amends now, if you'd allow me to."

He sat the BB gun down on the driveway. "What'd you have in mind?"

They strolled back across the street in blessed silence. "I can't believe you gave that dude eight hundred twenty dollars," Allie whispered. "You won't really be able to see his house in the movie, right?"

"Right," Greer said. "But now he's happy. The music is history and we can get on with

336

the show. It's called the cost of doing business."

"You straight-up lied to him," Allie said. "That was awesome."

Greer glanced over at the girl and had a sudden, unfamiliar qualm about the life lesson she'd just imparted to this impressionable teen. And then she shook it off.

It's just business.

33

When Greer got back to the production office, she found Friday's call sheet on her desk, which explained why Bryce had left the Manatee set for the casino.

The shooting schedule showed morning calls for Adelyn's character, Danielle, and the sheriff, at the casino. The casino already? She'd assumed construction and set dressing would take another few weeks.

As she approached the pier on her golf cart, she spotted Vanessa Littrell's red Jeep heading in the opposite direction. Vanessa waved, pulled over, and rolled her window down.

"Oh my God! Have you seen what they've done out there?"

"Just headed that way," Greer said.

"Wait until you see. It looks just like it did in the old pictures in the family scrapbooks. Absolutely uncanny. Hey, when you get a night off, call me and let's go out for drinks, okay?"

"Love to."

True to Vanessa's word, in just a few days' time, the casino had been transformed — or reborn, she wasn't sure which. Workers were hammering away on a deliberately aged new tin roof, painters on scaffolding were spraying the stucco facade a shade somewhere between nectarine and faded coral, and on the ground, electricians were wiring up a vintage-look rusted neon sign with scripted letters.

SUNSET CASINO — DANCE TONIGHT!

Greer found Bryce inside, seated with the production designer at a round folding table, going over sketches for the space. He seemed oblivious to the whine of power tools and the chunks of plaster raining down around him as workers patched the old ceiling.

"Greer!" He gestured around at the room. "What do you think? Isn't it unbelievable?"

"It's fabulous," Greer said. "Stephen, I never dreamed you could have it this far along this fast."

"Overtime," Stephen said, with a grimace. "Bryce had the vision, I made it happen."

"But how are you going to get enough done to start shooting tomorrow, Bryce? I thought we were still shooting over on Manatee."

"I've reshuffled the schedule," Bryce said. "Terry has been writing like a fiend. He's been up two nights straight, and the pages have literally been flying off the printer. All genius stuff. It gives the story a whole new gravitas."

"There's a new treatment?" Alarms went off in Greer's mind. "Can I read it? I'm dying to know what he's come up with."

"It's still in process," Bryce said. "Anyway, about tomorrow. We're just going to do some exterior tight shots with Danielle and the sheriff, standing right in the doorway here. We won't do the establishing shots until the entire facade is finished."

"We've rented every potted palm within a hundred mile radius of this place," Stephen said. "We're going full-tilt Old Florida. The painters should be done this afternoon, and my sign guy says he can have the neon up and working before dark."

"Okay," Greer nodded. "But what about security during the shoot? It's getting harder and harder to keep the rubberneckers and the press away. Yesterday, we caught a photographer from *Us Weekly* sneaking around in the backyard over on Manatee with a telephoto lens, trying to get a shot of Adelyn and Kregg together. I think they've cooked up some half-baked story about a set romance. If we're shooting outside here tomorrow, I need to start lining up off-duty cops."

"Adelyn and Kregg?" Stephen hooted. "Oh please. I hope she has way better taste than that."

"Kregg doesn't have any scenes tomorrow," Bryce said. "I want him at home memorizing all the lines for the new scenes Terry's written for him."

Good luck with that, Greer thought. She'd spent the past week watching the neophyte actor struggle mightily just to deliver the lines he'd been given months ago.

"I'll still have to get a security detail," Greer said. "Adelyn's almost as big a draw with the kids who still watch that old Disney series of hers."

"In the meantime," Bryce said, "We're going to need a place that looks like a military facility. I don't know what you call that — an ammunition warehouse? Like a place you'd lock up explosives?"

"Is this part of Terry's new treatment?"

"Yeah. Wait until you see the dark place Terry is taking Danielle. Adelyn has read some of the new pages, and she's ecstatic about finally getting to play a character with some real depth and nuance."

"Bryce, I still don't understand the whole explosive thing. I thought we were shooting a love story — Navy SEAL comes back to his hometown, broken and scarred from a tour in Afghanistan, discovers the marriage he thought was irreparable before his tour is now salvageable. Right? Danielle and Nick get back together. I mean, didn't we just shoot their lovemaking scene over on Manatee this week?"

"All a clever ruse on Danielle's part," Bryce

said, with a faraway look in his eye. "She just wants Nick to think they're getting back together. The reality is, Danielle is a cold-hearted, two-timing schemer who's looking to cash in on Nick's inheritance."

"What inheritance? I thought these were two kids from working-class families. Wasn't Nick's father a fisherman?"

"Not anymore," Bryce said. "Terry's still working out all the details, but now Nick's father was from an old money New England family — like the Rockefellers — but Nick has long been estranged from them. It's perfect when you think about it. Nick joined the Navy in a deliberate attempt to establish his independence, once and for all. He's turned his back on his elitist family. Same thing for his marriage to Danielle, who seems to be a sweet but dumb blonde. He loves her, but part of her attraction is that she's defi-nitely several notches below Nick's family's social and economic stature."

Greer was struggling to keep up with the plot Bryce described.

"So where does this ammunition dump come into play?"

"The original script had Nick coming home from the war, suffering from anxiety and night terrors, sort of post-traumatic stress syndrome. He's struggling to fit back into his old world. That part is still true. Only now, Danielle and the sheriff are deliberately gaslighting him — making Nick think he's going nuts. He's seeing a shrink, right? Trying to work through all his issues. Which fits into their plans to set him up."

"Set him up how?"

Bryce waved his hands impatiently. "Terry's working that out. Just know that Danielle and the sheriff are going to make it look like Nick got his hands on some explosives — which they actually steal from the military — to blow up the casino."

"What's the motivation for that?" Greer asked.

"It's become a symbol to Nick — of his life. This is where he met Danielle. At a dance. As his world crumbles — or seems to — it's a metaphor for all that's gone wrong in his world."

"So we're really blowing up the casino? I mean, I know that was the original idea, but that's pretty extreme, isn't it?"

"Extreme is how you make drama," Bryce said. "Back to the military base. I need you to get that locked down — like yesterday. Shouldn't be a problem, right? I mean, Terry looked it up. There are all kind of military bases in this part of the state."

Greer could, right off the bat, think of dozens of reasons this idea wouldn't work. But she wasn't sure Bryce wanted to hear any of them.

She chose her words carefully. "The thing

about the military is — it's the military. These guys invented red tape. We'd need endless requisitions, authorizations, ad nauseam, which would probably have to go who knows how high up the command chain. Maybe all the way to the Pentagon. It would take months. And there's no guarantee they would actually approve our request. Especially since we don't have a finished script they can read."

Bryce shrugged. "So scrub that idea. You'll just have to find us something that *looks* vaguely official and military. Stephen's guys can do the rest. I mean, look what they've already accomplished right here."

"Bryce is right," Stephen chimed in. "This should be a no-brainer for you, Greer. You get us the real estate. Once you spray something Army drab green, or camouflage, that automatically telegraphs military."

What else could she say? "What's the time frame?"

"Immediately," Bryce said. And she knew he was dead serious. At least now she had a good idea of where to start searching for this abandoned military installation: her favorite local real estate agent.

34

She was just emerging from the shower after the end of another long, hot day, when her phone rang. Greer dove for her cell, which was on the nightstand.

"Hey," CeeJay said. "I'm at La Parilla, that Mexican take-out place on the other side of the bridge. I thought I'd make it up to you for missing girls' night out last Friday night. Dinner's on me. The usual?"

"You're a lifesaver!" Greer said, flopping down onto the bed. "I was just trying to decide whether my dinner entrée would be Cheez-Its or cottage cheese, because I'm too damn lazy to go find some real food. Yes, the usual, please."

"I'll pick up some wine or margaritas, too. Your place or mine?"

"How hot is it outside now?"

"Mmm. It's cooled down some, and there's probably a breeze coming off the water. You want to eat by the pool?"

"Sounds good. It's too depressing eating in

my room."

"See you in fifteen," CeeJay said.

Greer and CeeJay's favorite cheap Mexican restaurant back in L.A. was Candela Taco Bar on LaBrea, which they referred to as Dollar Taco, because they usually met there on Wednesdays, otherwise known as Dollar Taco Night.

CeeJay unloaded Styrofoam containers and foil-wrapped packets from a plastic bag onto the concrete patio table by the pool. It was after eight, and the only other guest in sight was a buff male swimmer making endless laps across the shimmering turquoise waters of the pool.

"They had your fish tacos," CeeJay said, peeling back the foil on one of the packets. "But they looked at me like I was crazy when I asked about a creamed corn one. So I got you a chicken special."

"Chips and guac too, right?"

"Of course," CeeJay said. "Green salsa for me. And," she said, with a triumphant flourish, "premixed margaritas!"

She placed a container that looked like a waxed milk carton on the table and produced two plastic cups. "Sorry. They've got some crazy liquor laws in this county, so this was the best I could do."

Greer couldn't speak, because her mouth was full of fish taco. Instead, she nodded

346

enthusiastically. "Not bad," she said, when she'd finished chewing. "I'd kill for a Candela spicy shrimp taco. But then, anything's better than Cheez-Its. Again."

CeeJay poured them each a cup full of the margarita mix, then attacked her own dinner.

They were both so hungry they didn't even start gossiping until both had destroyed their first tacos.

Greer dabbed at a bit of sour cream on her lower lip. "How's it going with Bryce? Have you been together at all?"

"You mean have I slept with him this week? No. But he texted me while I was at the restaurant. He wants to have me over to dinner tomorrow night, which probably means he wants to have me. Which is okay with me. How's your week been?"

"Nuts. Bryce and Terry have apparently trashed the original script — what there was of it. Now, they've gone in a completely different direction. Bryce loves what he's seen so far, so I guess that's good. Except for me, since I just found out late this afternoon I've got to magically come up with a military-looking location for the new script."

CeeJay picked apart her vegetarian taco, separating out all the onions with her fingernail. "Speaking of Terry, did you know he's running around with April, in wardrobe?"

"I hadn't heard that. I can't believe he can find the time. Bryce told me he's got Terry on lockdown until the script is finished. He claims Terry's pulled all-nighters at least two nights in a row."

"Hmm." CeeJay arched one eyebrow in a knowing expression. "Well, I saw the two of them sneaking out of the wardrobe trailer last night, and it looked to me like Terry's wardrobe had recently been hastily removed."

"Yuck." Greer giggled and scooped up a glob of guacamole with a corn chip.

"Do you know how many calories are in a tablespoon of that glop?" CeeJay asked, pushing the bowl of guacamole away. She had her phone in her hand and was scrolling through e-mails and her Twitter feed.

"No, and I don't want to know, either," Greer said, licking her fingers.

"Uh-oh." CeeJay looked up from her phone. "Oh shit."

"What?" Greer took a sip of the premixed margarita and grimaced. "Ugh. This stuff tastes like battery acid."

"Take a look at this," CeeJay said, handing over her phone.

Greer found herself staring down at a grainy color photo the size of a postage stamp. "TMZ? I can't believe you read this garbage."

"I'm easily amused. Anyway, I have to keep up with world affairs."

"What's this picture supposed to be?"

Greer squinted, and now she could see that

the image was a side view of a couple on a Jet Ski, skimming across the waves. The male driver had very short hair, was bare chested, and had a distinctive tattoo on his bicep. A girl clung to the back of the Jet Ski, her arms wrapped tightly around the driver's waist. She wore only a pair of tiny bikini bottoms, and her face was obscured by a pair of oversize sunglasses and a floppy hat.

"Oh God. That's Kregg, isn't it?"

"Yup," CeeJay said. "I wonder who the lucky lady is."

Greer groaned. "Please don't let it be who I think it is."

"Who?"

"Allie Thibadeaux."

"Gimme that." CeeJay took the phone and squinted down at the image on the phone. "I can't tell from this tiny picture. Hang on. I'm gonna go up to my room and get my laptop."

Five minutes later, CeeJay placed the laptop on the table. Her expression was serious. "Sorry, but I think you're right. It's gotta be Allie."

Greer looked at the screen. "Oh God." She shook her head. "This is not good."

"It gets worse," CeeJay said. "You haven't even seen the item that goes with this picture. TMZ makes everything sound so . . . smutty."

She pulled the laptop back and started reading aloud.

" 'Kregg's Flick Does Trick for Topless

Chick.' "

"I feel nauseous already," Greer said.

" 'Bad boy rapper turned actor Kregg was spotted zipping around the Gulf of Mexico this week in Cypress Key, Florida, with a long-legged mystery lady who was apparently airing out some of her lady parts during a Jet Ski romp.' "

Greer slapped her hand on the tabletop. "No. No. No."

" 'Kregg is in Florida doing a star turn in director/producer Bryce Levy's upcoming action movie *Beach Town,* which is being filmed on location. As usual, Kregg is making waves on the set. Word is he was recently detained for drag racing in the predawn hours, and locals say when he's not in front of the camera he parties hard with his entourage in local bars, and with his lovely lady friend, whose name we didn't catch.' "

"At least they didn't print Allie's name," Greer said.

CeeJay closed the cover of the laptop. "No, but I guarantee, they will. They have spies everywhere. And I hate to tell you this, but if TMZ is running this now, you can bet that Perez Hilton and *Entertainment Tonight* and all the tabloids will be running the same pictures and story."

"Oh God. We caught a photographer from *Us Weekly* skulking around the set on Manatee Street earlier in the week. I thought they

were working on a story about Kregg and
Adelyn. If only."

Greer crumpled the half-eaten remains of
her taco into its foil. Her stomach felt sour.

"If Eb finds out about this, he is going to
go ballistic."

"Eb?" CeeJay eyed her friend.

"The mayor. And Allie's uncle and guardian."

"I know who the guy is. I was just thinking
that the way you said his name just now
sounded pretty cozy."

Greer blushed and looked away.

"Why, Mary Ann! Are you getting cozy with
the Professor here on Gilligan's Island?"

"Shut up."

"I knew it!" CeeJay said with a cackle. "I
can't turn my back on you for a second,
Greer Hennessy. Tell me this. Have you done
the nasty yet?"

"None of your business," Greer said. She
busied herself packing the rest of the dinner
wrappings into the plastic sack. "I don't know
what Allie was thinking. I tried to warn her
about Kregg this week. I told him he was too
old for her, too sophisticated. I pointed out
that he's just out of rehab, yet he's in the local dive bars drinking until all hours, and
obviously getting high every morning before
he gets to the set."

"And how did she take that bit of friendly
advice?" CeeJay asked, sounding skeptical.

"About the way you'd expect. She claims she and Kregg are just 'hanging out.' "

"Yeah, I saw what she had hanging out on the back of that Jet Ski."

Greer glared at her best friend. "It's really not funny. Kregg is bulletproof. Being a bad-ass is part of his persona. He'll leave here in a month and go on to the next town and the next silly little girl. But Allie is stuck here. When this photo gets out to the locals, her reputation will be shot. And Eb and Ginny will be devastated."

"What are you going to do?"

"I don't know what to do. It's not like I'm her mom or something. The thing is, Allie's way more mature than most girls her age. You should see her at work. She takes initiative, she's resourceful and hardworking. She's like one of the best P.A.s I've ever worked with. And she's only seventeen. I hate this for her. And I hate that somebody that smart has such poor judgment when it comes to a guy like Kregg."

"Sound like anybody we know?"

"What's that supposed to mean?" Greer demanded.

"Nothing. I was just thinking about some of your recent significant others. Sawyer comes to mind. That's all." She coughed delicately. "Douche bag."

"And your dance card is full of winners too? Like your landlord, who wanted you to do him in the elevator of your building in return for a dedicated parking space? And Bryce? Who isn't actually divorced yet, and makes you live above the garage?"

CeeJay gave her a sad smile. "Yeah. We're a pair, aren't we? We really know how to pick them."

"You and I are adults. We've been around the block, and we've lived with the decisions we've made. Allie's so young! And Cypress Key isn't L.A. She should be studying for her college boards, not flashing her boobies for every perv in the free world to get a peek at on TMZ."

"I agree. But again, as you said, you're not her family. Speaking of, where are her parents? Is she like an orphan or something?"

"Not exactly. Her parents split years ago. Her father, Eb's brother Jared, is in prison for running a pill mill. The mother apparently drifts in and out of Allie's life and shows up whenever she feels like it. According to Allie, Eb stays on her case all the time, because he's afraid she'll end up like her parents."

"Are you going to tell Eb about this?"

"I don't know. He'll find out sooner or later, like you said. But Allie made me promise I wouldn't rat her out to him. Of course, she also promised she'd make good choices and stay out of trouble."

"Then she's welshed on her end of the

bargain and you can consider the deal's off. And it's better for him to hear it from you than to be blindsided by somebody else."

"And that's another thing," Greer said. "Eb's not just Allie's guardian. He's the mayor. He and the police chief are buddies. What if Eb decides to have Kregg arrested for contributing to the delinquency of a minor? Worse yet, if he wanted, he could probably pull all our filming permits and shut the whole set down."

"You don't think he'd actually do that, do you?"

"He adores that girl. He and Ginny both do. You can't blame him for wanting to protect his niece. I think if I were Eb, I'd give Kregg the beat-down of his life. And then I'd toss his skinny white butt on the next plane out of here."

"If that happens, we're all out of a job," CeeJay pointed out. "Bryce got the financing for this flick based on Kregg's marquee appeal. If he's out, the film doesn't get made. And I don't know about you, but it looks like when I get back to L.A. I'm gonna be looking for a new place to live."

"No more Garage Mahal?"

"We'll see." CeeJay's gaze shifted toward the pool. The lone lap swimmer had climbed out of the water and was leisurely toweling off, with his back to them. His bronzed skin gleamed in the reflected light of the pool. He had wide, muscular shoulders and narrow hips, and the wet swim trunks that clung to his body left little to the imagination.

"Hey. That guy is one of our extras. I'd know that body anywhere. Wonder what his name is?"

She craned her neck, trying to get a better look. "No wedding ring."

"Claudia Jean!" Greer stood up. "You are incorrigible."

"Just keeping my options open," CeeJay said. "Where are you headed?"

"I guess I'd better go see the mayor."

35

Greer tapped lightly on the door of the motel manager's apartment. There was no answer, but she could hear music coming from inside, so she walked around the corner across a stretch of beach, and stepped up to Ginny's gated back porch. The music, which sounded like soft jazz, was louder here, and although no lights shone, she could see the glowing tip of a lit cigarillo among the luxurious greenery on the manager's porch.

"Ginny? It's Greer. I'm looking for Allie. Is she here tonight?"

She heard the scrape of a chair on the concrete porch floor, and then Ginny's head popped out between the fronds of a large potted fern.

"Hi, Greer. Allie's working at the Inn tonight. Want to sit and have a drink with me?"

"Thanks anyway, but I've got some stuff to do."

Ginny leaned over the wrought iron porch

railing. "Anything special you need to see Allie about? Is her work for your people going all right?"

"Allie's doing a great job as a production assistant. She's a natural at it. Something's come up that I need to discuss with her."

The older woman frowned. "Nothing serious, I hope."

Serious? Yes, Greer thought, *this is fairly serious.* Should she tell Ginny the truth? Was this even any of her business? She silently cursed herself for ever getting involved with Allie Thibadeaux's personal life.

The iron patio gate scraped open and Ginny stepped out onto the beach. "Greer? I think maybe you better come up here and tell me what's going on."

Ginny handed Greer a cold longneck. "Whatever it is that's worrying you, I wish you'd just tell me," she said. "I'm old, but believe me, there is nothing you can say that will shock me. And whatever is going on with Allie, I need to know about it."

Greer clutched the icy bottle between both hands. "I'm lost here, Ginny," she admitted. "I confronted Allie about some . . . behaviors earlier this week. She promised me she'd be careful, and in return I promised her I'd keep my mouth shut and not alert you or Eb. I'm in a bad spot, and I honestly don't know what to do."

Ginny exhaled sharply. "Good Lord. What kind of a mess has that child gotten herself into?"

"I don't want to betray her trust. But I'm afraid things have gotten out of hand."

"For Pete's sake, Greer. Just spit it out." Ginny leaned forward and studied Greer's face in the flickering light of a citronella candle burning in the middle of the table. "This is about that boy, isn't it? Kregg — the boy who's here making the movie?"

"Yes. No. Okay, yes. It's about Kregg — our male lead. I don't think he's a good influence on Allie. She's too young, for one thing, and for another, well, let's just say he's no Boy Scout."

"I knew something was going on with that girl," Ginny said, shaking her head. "Every time I look up lately, she's running out the door. She tells me and Eb she's working all the time, but I'm guessing that's not true. So she's messing around with that Kregg?"

Greer felt miserable ratting Allie out, and she felt even more miserable at the thought that she'd allowed things to go too far between Allie and Kregg.

"She told me they were just hanging out. Having fun. She said it wasn't serious."

"She lied," Ginny said flatly. "Didn't she?"

"I don't want to jump to conclusions," Greer said reluctantly. "That's why I wanted to talk to her tonight."

358

Ginny stood up.

"Where are you going?" Greer asked.

"I'm calling Eb," Ginny said firmly. "We'll put a stop to this right now."

"No! Wait. Please let me talk to Allie first before you get Eb involved."

Ginny's lips were set in a firm line. "Too late for that now."

Eb stared down at the oversize image on the bulky old computer monitor on Ginny's living room desk. His eyes narrowed and a muscle in his tightly clamped jaw twitched.

"God damn it. I'll kill that little bastard."

"Eb . . ." Ginny cautioned. "We don't know for sure that it's Allie." She leaned over and again examined the picture. She sighed. "But it sure enough looks like her."

"Only one way to find out." He glanced at his watch. "It's almost ten now. She should be getting off work any minute. When she gets home, we'll have it out."

"She's not coming home," Ginny said. "She and the other girls are spending the night at Courtney's. I told her it was all right if she went right there from work."

"Which is probably a lie," Eb said. "She's probably planning on sneaking around with that little shit."

Greer cleared her throat. "Hopefully not. Bryce told me today that Kregg is supposed to be staying in, learning the lines for some

359

new scenes."

"Does Bryce know about this picture, and this story?" Eb tapped the computer screen.

"I texted him about it before I came over here."

"And what was his response?"

"I didn't hear back from him," she admitted. "But we've got a seven o'clock call in the morning, and we're shooting at two different locations tomorrow, including exteriors at the casino, so Bryce is probably asleep already."

"Asleep at the wheel," Eb said. He grabbed his phone and tapped a number and waited. He frowned and looked over at his aunt. "Voice mail."

"She might still be doing her side work at the Inn," Ginny cautioned.

Eb shook his head and spoke curtly into the phone.

"Allie? Your spend-the-night party is canceled. I want you back here at Ginny's, now. And if you're not home in the next fifteen minutes, I'm calling the chief and she'll have a patrol car sent out to drag you back here. Understand?"

"Was that really necessary?" Greer asked quietly.

He fixed her with a long, cold stare. "Do you have any better ideas? My niece's topless photo has gone viral on the Internet, thanks to you people. God knows what she's been up to with that degenerate. She's lied to me, she's lied to Ginny, and she's lied to you. This has gone far enough. I'm not about to let her get away with that, and I'm not about to sit back and let her ruin her life with that loser, the same way her parents ruined their lives. So yes, I do think it's necessary to take extreme measures here."

Greer gripped the seat of her chair with sweaty hands, fighting her strongest instinct, which was to cut and run. What was she doing here, anyway? She was a location manager, not a family therapist. This was none of her business.

But she couldn't run. This mess was her fault. She should have warned Eb and Ginny that Allie was getting involved with Kregg, and she should have asked Bryce to intervene. And she should never have trusted the word of a starry-eyed seventeen-year-old, no matter how mature that teenager seemed in her work life, and no matter how much she actually liked Allie. Greer should have remembered from her own personal history just how headstrong and devious a teenage girl could be.

"I don't understand what this TMZ thing is, anyway." Ginny was scrolling down the site, shaking her head, reading aloud the lurid headlines about celebrities she'd never heard of.

"We had movie magazines when I was a kid, coming up. They'd have stories about who Elizabeth Taylor was marrying, or which bullfighter Ava Gardner was dating, but nothing like this. I can't believe they can print this stuff and get away with it. And these pictures! Lord have mercy!"

"Unfortunately, this is the norm these days," Greer said. "TMZ, Gawker, Perez Hilton . . . There are dozens of gossip sites online, and they're all competing to be the first to break any scrap of sensationalistic gossip or scandal. The more hits or page views they get, the more money they can get from companies that advertise on their sites. And if they can run a photo with a story, that's huge for them."

"Revolting," Eb said. "If I knew who took this picture, I'd haul their ass into court so fast. . . ."

"It doesn't even have to be a professional photographer anymore," Greer said. "Anybody with a cell phone can take a picture or shoot a video, and if it's of a hot celebrity like a Kardashian or Beyoncé, they can sell it and name their own price."

The front door of Ginny's apartment flew open and Allie stomped inside. She was still wearing her hostess name badge, as well as a very, very pissed-off look on her face.

"What?" Allie took in the three adults staring at her. "For real, Eb? You're going to sic the cops on me? For what?"

"For this." Eb pointed at the computer

monitor.

Allie drew closer, and when she saw the photo, her face paled.

"Oh my God," she whispered, as she sank down onto the nearest chair.

Ginny touched the girl's arm. "Oh, Al. What were you thinking?"

"Who did this to me?" Allie cried, self-consciously folding her arms across her chest, as though that might obliterate the image on the screen of her bare breasts pressed into Kregg's back. "Oh my God!"

"You did it to yourself," Eb said.

"I can explain," Allie said quickly, and the words tumbled out of her mouth in one long, breathless torrent. "We were out on the Jet Ski, and we hit a huge wave, and my top went flying off. I was like, 'Oh my God, don't look,' it was so-o-o embarrassing. And we turned around to go look for it, but I couldn't find it. I mean, it was gone. What was I supposed to do? Kregg took me back to the dock, where I'd left my stuff, and I jumped in the water, and he gave me a towel, and I got dressed." Huge tears welled up in her blue eyes, leaving a mascara-tinted trail on her cheeks.

"Stop it!" Eb said. "Allie, do you think we're stupid? That's the lamest story I've ever heard."

"I can't help it. It's the truth," Allie said tearfully.

"What were you doing out on a Jet Ski with him? These past two weeks, you told us you were working nonstop."

"I *was* working," Allie said. "It was only one afternoon. Kregg got done with his scenes early, so we went to the beach." She looked desperately at Greer.

"Greer, you tell him. Haven't I been working with you? Haven't I been on the set, at the house, and at base camp all this time?"

"I don't know," Greer said, hesitating. "Allie, I'm just really disappointed in you. I thought, after we talked this week, you agreed to cool it with Kregg."

"Wait." Eb's gaze settled on Greer. "You knew about this? Knew she was sneaking around with this joker? And you didn't bother to let me know until now?"

"You ratted me out to Eb and Ginny?" Allie cried. "You promised you wouldn't. I never should have trusted you."

Greer felt the heat rising in her face, but before she could attempt to defend herself, Eb cut in.

"Leave Greer out of this, Allie. She's not the issue right now. The issue is that you lied to us. You lied about where you were, and who you were with, and what you were doing." He pointed at the computer monitor with a look of pure disgust. "And this is the result of your deceit." He scrolled down to the story.

"There are more than eight hundred comments on this piece of crap. Do you want to know what disgusting stuff total strangers are saying about you, Allie? Do you want to know how many people have seen this photo of you?"

"Stop it!" Allie cried. "It's not my fault. How did I know some skeeve would take a picture like that?"

"You should have known better than to put yourself in a position like that," Eb said. "Riding around topless with some guy you'd just met? A twenty-two-year-old, who should be sitting in jail right now for what he's done to you? You should have known better than to lie to us."

"I am not lying," Allie sobbed. "Why can't you believe me?"

"Did you ask me or Ginny if you could go out with a twenty-two-year-old?"

"No! Because I knew you'd say no. And you don't even know Kregg. He's nothing like what you think. He's a nice guy. He's funny and he's sweet — and he doesn't treat me like a baby!"

"Allie, Allie," Ginny said softly. "A nice boy wouldn't sneak around behind your family's back. A nice boy would come to me or Eb and ask permission to take you out."

"Oh right, Gin," Allie retorted. "Like you would've said yes."

"Okay, enough," Eb said wearily. "We're

getting nowhere with all this. Obviously you don't appreciate the position you've put yourself, or us, in. So far, it looks like these gossip sites don't know your name. I can only hope nobody who knows you sees these pictures and recognizes you. In the meantime, here's what's going to happen. You're grounded, Allie. For the rest of the summer."

"You mean, like, after work, right?"

"I mean grounded as in grounded. You're done working on the movie, and you're absolutely forbidden to see or go out with Kregg."

"You can't do that to me," Allie cried. "It's not fair." She threw Greer a pleading glance. "Tell him, Greer. Tell him what you told me, that I'm doing a good job, and that you need me."

"I'll hate losing you, Allie," Greer said, and it was true. Her heart was breaking for the kid. Personally, she thought Eb was being a little heavy-handed, making his niece quit a job she loved, but she was determined to extract herself from this no-win situation.

"Don't even try to pretend you really care about me," Allie sneered.

"Allie!" Ginny's eyes darted from Eb to Greer.

"That's it." Eb leaned across the table and grabbed the girl's arm. "I won't have you disrespecting your elders like that. You're done here."

He released her arm. "Give me your cell phone."

"My phone? Are you kidding me?"

"Not at all. Your phone. Now."

Allie backed a step away. "You can't take my phone. It's mine! Ginny gave it to me for my birthday. Tell him, Gin."

Her great-aunt shrugged and looked away.

Eb held out his hand. "Ginny gave it to you, but I pay your phone bill. Give me the phone please, Allie."

"This is so lame!" Allie took her phone from the pocket of her jeans and tossed it onto the table. It spun across the polished wood surface and landed with a sickening crack on the tile floor. "It's so not fair! Why are you treating me like a criminal?"

"I'm not treating you like a criminal."

"You totally are. You want to take my phone away, make me quit my job, lock me up for the whole summer. Why don't you just put me in handcuffs, Eb? You might as well, because you're ruining my life."

"I don't expect you to understand this, Allie, but I'm trying to save your life, not ruin it. I won't have you running around . . ."

Allie stood with fists defiantly clenched on her hips. "What? Like my mom did? Is that what you were gonna say? You think I'll get knocked up like she did? Or maybe you think I'll end up in jail, like Dad? Admit it, Eb, that's what you think."

"I never said that."

"But you think it. I can tell. You and Ginny want to pretend like Dad's dead, or like he doesn't even exist. Well guess what? Dad's getting out of jail. Surprise!"

"What?" Ginny's voice was strained. "Who told you that?"

"Dad e-mailed me yesterday. He's getting out soon. And when he does, he's coming back here to get me, and won't make up a bunch of bullshit rules like you two."

Allie turned and ran from the room. Her bedroom door slammed.

36

Eb got up and started toward the bedroom, but Ginny put out a hand to stop him. "Just let her be. She's upset right now. I'll wait a while for her to calm down, then I'll talk to her."

"Girls!" Eb shook his head. "And the mouth on her. If I'd talked to my folks like that, at that age . . ."

"You *did* talk to your folks like that," Ginny said. Her hands shook as she pushed back a lock of her silvery hair. "And worse. Remember? I was there. Anyway, it's not her language that's got me worried. Can that be right? Is Jared actually getting out of prison? Could he really take her away from us?"

Eb was grim-faced. "This is the first I've heard of him being released. As for her going to live with him — that's not going to happen, Gin. We're her legal guardians."

"Dear God! I can't bear to think of that child living with him." Her brow knitted with worry. "I'm sorry, Eb, I realize he's your brother, but you know what Jared is like. Always chasing the next big scheme. He'd never stay put here so that Allie could finish high school."

"What I can't figure out is how Jared contacted her," Eb said. "As far as I know, he hasn't written her, and inmates aren't allowed to have e-mail or cell phones."

Greer hesitated. "I know it's none of my business." She picked up Allie's cell phone and examined it. The case was black, with Allie's monogram picked out in girlish pink rhinestones. "The screen is cracked, but it looks like this is still working."

Eb took the phone and clicked over to e-mails.

"Honestly, Eb, this doesn't feel right, spying on the child," Ginny objected. "I did give her the phone. It's such an invasion of her privacy."

"Allie forfeited her right to privacy when she lied to us and deliberately misled us. What should I do? Ignore the fact that she's been in touch with her jailbird dad and in some kind of relationship with a guy who's managed to, at the very least, trash her reputation, if not worse?"

"Well, no, but there must be some other way."

"I'll make a deal with you," Eb said. "I won't read any e-mail unless it's from Jared or Kregg."

"But you can't help but see personal stuff if you read her e-mail logs," Ginny pointed out.

"Fine." Eb held out the phone back to Greer. "You're as close to an impartial party as we've got right now. You take a look. Do you see anything here that we need to be worried about?"

"Good idea." Ginny beamed her approval.

"Oh no." Greer held her hands palm out, as if to fend off the phone. "I've done enough already." She stood up and moved toward the door. "I'm sorry, you two. But this is a family matter. And I've got to be at work early tomorrow."

Eb stood too. "I'll walk you back to your room."

"That's not necessary," Greer protested. "You two have a lot on your plates right now. I can let myself out."

"I insist," Eb said, and his stern expression meant there would be no further discussion. He put Allie's phone in his pocket and guided Greer out of the living room.

She waited until they were in the breezeway outside Ginny's apartment.

"I can't win with you, can I?" Greer gave Eb a sidelong glance in the dimly lit hall.

"You should have come to me the first time you saw Allie with him," Eb said tersely. "You had no right to keep something like that from us."

"Look. I realize that now, but what was I supposed to do? Allie's a good kid. Anybody can see that. I trusted her, and she let me down. I feel horrible about the TMZ story, the picture, all of it."

They'd reached the door to Greer's motel room. The yellow lightbulb in the overhead fixture threw harsh gray shadows on Eb's face.

"Forget it," Eb said, thrusting his hands into his pockets. The hot, sticky air in the hallway was nearly suffocating. Moths and bugs battered themselves against the overhead light. The awkward silence seemed endless.

"I guess maybe I'll see you around."

"Guess so," Greer said, bringing out her room key. She felt numb.

"One more thing," Eb said. "You tell Bryce, and everybody else connected with this movie, if I see Kregg come anywhere near Allie again I'll break both his legs."

37

Friday was the first day of shooting at the casino. Trucks and trailers lined both sides of the pier leading to the old building, and a small city of tents had been erected. Greer had arrived at 4:00 a.m., wearing a baseball cap with a flashlight mounted on the bill, to direct the load-in of equipment.

At dawn, she'd finally had a minute to make her way to the caterer's truck. She was just about to take a bite of a breakfast burrito when she felt a hand clamp her shoulder.

She was already a hot, sweaty mess, but Bryce Levy was serene and composed looking in a short-sleeved white Columbia fishing shirt and his favorite black jeans.

"Everything cool?" he asked, uncapping a bottle of water.

"Think so," Greer said. "We had to move the genny to get it out of your sight line. The guys should be done with that in about fifteen minutes."

He nodded. "Good. How's it coming with

my ammo dump? You got some pictures for me yet?"

Pictures? She hadn't even started looking yet, not that she'd admit that to the producer/director.

"I've seen some possibilities," she lied. "But nothing worth a picture yet. I should have something you can look at by Monday."

"You'd better," Bryce said curtly. He turned to examine the cut up fruits and vegetables arrayed around the gleaming stainless steel Vitamix.

"Um, Bryce, can I talk to you about something?"

"Sure." He held up a lumpy beige root and eyed it critically. "You think this ginger is organic?"

"We specified all organic in the catering contract," Greer assured him. "The thing is, we've got kind of a sensitive issue brewing, and I think it's something you need to address."

Bryce gave a martyr's sigh. "What is it now?"

"It's about Kregg," she said. "Did you happen to see the item about him in TMZ?"

"I never read that crap. You shouldn't either. It's all a load of lies."

"I normally don't read it. But this week they ran a photo of Kregg and a topless girl riding around out in the Gulf on a Jet Ski."

"That guy is a pussy magnet, right?"

Greer winced. "The girl is seventeen years old. She's a minor. And she's Eb Thibadeaux's niece."

"Remind me who Eb Thibadeaux is?" Bryce was loading chunks of papaya and mango into the juicer's feed tube. "Have you had the kale?" He held up a leaf. "Is it local?"

Greer felt herself doing a slow burn. "I don't know about the kale, but Eb Thibadeaux is not only local, he's the mayor of Cypress Key. And he is justifiably upset about his niece having her topless image splashed all over the Internet with the lead of this movie."

Bryce held a biodegradable cardboard cup under the juicer's spigot, watching intently as a thick, greenish sludge oozed out.

He took a cautious sip, rolling the juice around on his palate, then reached for a plastic squeeze bottle labeled Orange Blossom Honey.

"What would you like me to do, Greer? Hire a nanny for Kregg? Get him fitted with a chastity belt? He's an adult. I can't exactly put him in time-out for the duration of this film."

"Could you have a heart-to-heart conversation with him? Allie might be just another summer fling to Kregg, but this is an innocent small-town kid we're talking about. She hasn't even graduated from high school yet. And you might also want to tell Kregg to lay off the weed while he's here. The mayor is gunning for Kregg right now. He'll use any excuse available to keep his niece safe. Including having the cops bust Kregg for possession or lock him up for contributing to the delinquency of a minor."

"Cops?" Bryce frowned. "Cops mean lawyers, and lawyers mean a pain in my ass. Yeah, that's a hassle I don't need. Okay, I'll have a word with Kregg and tell him to keep it in his pants. You can advise the mayor we deeply regret, etcetera. Do we need to get a publicist involved with this?"

"No publicist needed," Greer assured him. "Thanks, Bryce."

By midmorning Greer had moved the generator twice, and the portable bathrooms three times, because each time she'd had them moved Bryce had changed his mind about the direction of his shots with Adelyn Davis and the character playing the sheriff.

She'd also had the off-duty cops positioned in skiffs behind the casino chase off three different boatloads of paparazzi and rubberneckers, who were probably intent on having themselves a Kregg sighting.

The sun was merciless, and despite the sunblock she'd slathered on her neck and shoulders hours earlier, she could feel her skin blistering.

During a lull in activity she wandered over to a tent where CeeJay was applying eyeliner to one of the extras, who were supposed to be milling around inside the casino for a crowd scene.

CeeJay's short hair was done up Rosie the Riveter style in a wide bandana headband. She wore a vintage fifties-style halter top and high-waisted red cotton shorts, with a tool belt full of makeup equipment buckled loosely around her hips.

The extra, a middle-aged man dressed in a garish Hawaiian shirt and baggy shorts, sat perfectly still while CeeJay powdered his bald spot and touched up his comb-over with hair spray.

When he was gone, Greer sank down into his vacant chair. "I'm melting," she said matter-of-factly.

"I've got just the thing," CeeJay said, grabbing a spray bottle of water from a small cooler at her feet. She started spritzing her friend's face, but just then Greer's radio squawked with a call from Zena, who was stationed at the barrier erected across Pier Street.

"Incoming. You know a Vanessa Littrell?"

"Yeah. She actually owns the casino. Why?"

"Says Bryce personally invited her on set today. Okay to send her up?"

"That's weird. Bryce is notorious for insisting on a closed set. But if he invited her, that's all I need," Greer said.

"Who's coming on set?" CeeJay asked, spritzing her own face.

"Vanessa Littrell."

CeeJay's eyes narrowed in suspicion. "Interesting. Two months ago Bryce wouldn't let his own mother come on set. Said it was too distracting for him."

A few minutes later, Zena rolled up on a golf cart to deliver the visitor.

"Hi, Greer." Stepping out of the cart onto the steaming asphalt, Vanessa was a lemonade-tinted vision, with a short, pale yellow sundress that showed off her deep tan, toned legs, and glossy, dark hair. She stood and took in all the activity surrounding them.

"This is so cool," Vanessa exclaimed. "I've never seen a movie being made before. Is Bryce around? He said I should check in with him as soon as I got here."

"Right over there," CeeJay volunteered, pointing at a nearby tent, where Bryce was peering into a monitor with his cameraman.

"See you later," Vanessa said, as she strolled away.

CeeJay and Greer watched with undisguised interest as Bryce greeted the newcomer with a hug. Moments later, a P.A. produced a folding director's chair with "Vanessa Littrell" emblazoned on the back.

"He never gave me a chair with my name on it," Greer mused.

"Because he never anticipated you might sleep with him," CeeJay shot back.

"Well, that kind of hurts my feelings. What? I'm not his type?"

"If you have breasts and a vagina, you're his type," CeeJay said. "It's not that he would mind schtupping you," her best friend explained. "He thinks you're cute. But you're my friend, so that makes you off-limits. Because you might rat him out."

Greer nodded in the direction of the tent, where Vanessa was now staring into the monitor, with Bryce standing directly beside her, his hand on the small of her back.

"You don't seem too upset about any of this," she observed.

"Bryce has the sexual attention span of a three-year-old," CeeJay said with a shrug. "He likes anything shiny and new. What's the story on Vanessa?"

"From what I gather, she's what passes for royalty in Cypress Key. Her family's been here for generations."

"Married?"

"Twice divorced," Greer said. "And actively seeking a suitable man. She says the local pickings are pretty slim for somebody in her tax bracket."

"What about the Professor?" CeeJay had an impish twinkle in her eye. "He seems eminently suitable, if you ask me."

"Nobody did. Vanessa made a run at him

379

years ago, but I don't think Eb was interested."

"Saving himself for something better." CeeJay nudged Greer.

"That was over before it even began. He's currently avoiding me. Which is fine. It never would have worked out. Anyway, I've got enough drama in my life without his and his niece's."

"Oh yeah. I'm guessing the shit hit the fan when he found out about TMZ?"

Greer gave CeeJay a condensed version of her last conversation with Eb Thibadeaux, including the fact that he'd made Allie quit the film and had placed her under semi-house arrest.

"Too bad about the kid," CeeJay said. "But Eb might want to dial it down. Girls that age, you clamp too tight a lid on 'em and you get a backlash that's even worse than what you're punishing them for. I ran away from home the first time when I was only fourteen, after my dad refused to let me get a nose ring. All kids rebel. It's part of growing up. Right?"

Greer's attention had wandered, as she watched the body language between Vanessa and Bryce.

"Hmm?"

"Teenage rebellion?"

Greer's mind flashed back to an incident in her early teens when her own youthful rebellion had nearly gotten her killed. She shuddered. It was a memory she'd long repressed and didn't plan to dredge up again any time soon.

"You seeing what I'm seeing?" she asked CeeJay, nodding at the director's tent, where Bryce's hand was now gently hovering over Vanessa Littrell's posterior.

"Gag me," CeeJay said.

Greer's radio squawked again.

"Hi, Zena, what's up?"

"You've got a guest down here. Okay to bring him up?"

"Looks like it's open house on the set today," CeeJay observed.

"What guest? I didn't invite anybody on set," Greer said.

"Uh, he says he's your dad."

Greer felt the blood drain from her face.

"Stay where you are. I'll be right down."

"Did she just say your dad is here?" CeeJay asked. "Like, your real dad?"

"Alleged dad, is more like it," Greer said.

When Greer arrived at the barricades blocking entrance to Pier Street, she spied Clint Hennessy leaning up against a dusty, late-eighties-looking black and white sheriff's department cruiser, chatting with her assistant. He wore a black baseball cap, black Hennessy Picture Cars logo T-shirt, and baggy, ill-fitting jeans — again with the white tube socks and ten-dollar black tennis shoes. "Dad jeans," CeeJay would have called those pants. He'd hooked his sunglasses over the neckline of the shirt.

Oh my God. This old redneck is my father. I have his DNA. How did he and Lise ever end up together? I don't care. It doesn't matter. She's dead, and he might as well be.

She pulled the golf cart up to the barricade, hopped out, and hurried over to the car.

"Greer, you didn't tell me your daddy was coming to the set today," Zena bubbled. "I could have gotten him a director's chair and put it under Bryce's tent."

"I didn't know he was coming myself," Greer said.

"Hi, honey," Clint said, offering a shy smile. "Surprise!"

"Could I talk to you a minute?" Greer said, taking him by the arm and steering him away from Zena's curious stare.

"Sure thing," Clint said.

She waited until they were several yards away from the barricades and the crowd of girls lined up there, hoping for a glimpse of Kregg.

Greer could feel the sweat rolling down her cheeks, down her back, and between her breasts, but an odd chill settled itself in her chest.

"What are you doing here?" she asked tersely.

"Working, same as you." He turned and pointed proudly at the police cruiser. "That's my 1986 Crown Vic. My graphics guy finished your sheriff's department logo yesterday, so I drove it over here today. I couldn't believe it when I got the call from your transportation guy Monday, telling me they needed a picture car for *Beach Town.* What a coincidence, huh? They needed a Crown Vic, not too new, not older than mid-eighties, for a sheriff's cruiser, and I got two of 'em. I said, 'Hell, my daughter is working on that movie. Greer Hennessy.' And that fella, he told me you're the location manager and they think a lot of you. I almost never do the deliveries anymore. I leave that to my guy Wally. But there was no way I'd miss out on seeing where my kid is working. Not when you're practically working in my backyard."

"Great. Now you've seen it, and now I have to get back to work," Greer said.

I sound like such a bitch, but I am a bitch. And he needs to go.

"That's it?" Clint pushed the baseball cap to the back of his head. He wasn't cool enough to hide the hurt. "I thought maybe we could grab some lunch or something. It wouldn't take long."

Greer felt the cold, clenching feeling in her chest. She could hear Lise's voice: "Call him. What could it hurt?" It hurt a lot, seeing him.

She sighed. "Why are you doing this? Do you really think after thirty years you can just show up in my life and everything will be all good and happy?"

He took off his cap and turned it around and around in those big, chapped hands. The stubble on his weather-beaten cheeks was gray, and his hair was plastered to his head. "You showed up at my house. You did. I thought maybe . . . I don't know. I guess I hoped maybe we could figure things out, between us. Maybe, if we spent some time together, you'd see I'm not such a bad guy."

"I don't think you're a bad guy," Greer said, and even to her own ears that sounded like a lie. "I don't think anything about you, because I don't know you. And the reason I came to your house — the *only* reason — is I promised Lise I would see you. I still don't understand why she wanted me to, but she did, and I did."

"Okay," Clint said. "Fair enough. You got work to do, I got work to do." He turned and walked slowly back toward the barricade and his Crown Vic. He got a few yards away, then came back.

He jammed the hat back on his head. "You want to hear something, Greer? Lise made me promise too. I told her you probably wouldn't want anything to do with me, but she said I had to try. Your mom and I had some good talks, those last few months. I wanted to come see her but she wouldn't let me, said she didn't want me to see her sick and skinny and old."

"Just go, please?" Greer swallowed hard and swiped at her eyes with the back of her hand.

His gait was slow and bandy-legged, and he held his right arm stiffly out to one side, like a sailor who'd lost his sea legs. When he reached the barricades, Zena stopped, smiled widely, asked him something. He shook his head and kept on walking.

As soon as the casino scenes were shot, by midafternoon, Greer and Zena directed the move of all the equipment, trucks, and personnel to the nearby Veterans Park, where the call sheet dictated a 4:00 p.m. shoot time.

As the day progressed, the crowds behind the barriers grew, until Greer estimated there were probably at least two hundred fans straining to catch a glimpse of Kregg and Adelyn.

Twelve hours into the day, with no end in sight, Greer was in no mood for diplomacy when she spotted Kregg, in costume, toss a lit cigarette butt into a flower bed that the set dressers had just finished planting with multiple flats of daisies, geraniums, and ferns.

"Hey," she said, approaching him, as he slouched against a bench. "Please don't do that."

"Do what?" He looked up from lighting another cigarette and appraised her with glassy, red-rimmed eyes.

"That was a lit cigarette," she said, leaning

down and retrieving it. "There are trash barrels right over there." She pointed to an area not more than five yards away.

"Sorry!" he drawled, in a tone that conveyed the complete opposite sentiment. "Hey, uh, what happened to your cute little P.A.? I haven't seen her around in a couple of days. And she doesn't answer my texts. She like . . . disappeared."

Greer glanced discreetly around. Bryce and his assistant director and cameraman were huddled together on the opposite side of the park, blocking out their next shot.

"Her uncle grounded her for life after he saw the topless photos of her with you on that Jet Ski on TMZ."

Kregg grinned. "Yeah. Girl has a rack on her, right?"

Greer's temper flared. "You're a pig, you know that?"

He blinked. "What's that supposed to mean?"

"It means, Kregg, that that cute little P.A., whose name is Allie? She's only seventeen. A minor. Her uncle is the mayor. And his best friend is the chief of police. Right now he's said that if he catches you anywhere near Allie Thibadeaux he will see to it that you end up not just in the jailhouse, but in the hospital."

"Christ," Kregg muttered. "First Bryce, now you. Everybody should just chill. We were just messing around."

He exhaled and blew a smoke ring in her face, then pinched the butt and tossed it at her feet.

"Find somebody your own age to play around with." Greer bent down, picked up the still smoldering butt, and nimbly flicked it at his face. "And pick up your own friggin' mess. I'm the location manager, not your maid."

38

Sunday morning was finally, and inescapably, laundry day. Greer pushed the wobbly-wheeled Hometown Market shopping cart slowly down the corridor at the Silver Sands Motel. On her second trip between the motel's laundry room and her own room, she spied Ginny Buckalew.

Ginny was wearing a pair of shapeless white painter's pants, a long-sleeved cotton shirt, and an ancient-looking canvas safari hat. She was standing outside her patio garden, whacking away at a palm tree with a pair of long-handled pruning shears.

Her broad, pink face broke into a smile when she saw Greer approach.

"Well hey there, Greer. You doing laundry for everybody in the whole motel?"

Greer laughed ruefully. "It sure feels like it. This is every stitch of clothing I own." She gestured at her own peculiar ensemble: a pair of jeans so old and faded they'd worn to the consistency of a crumpled Kleenex, and a black T-shirt from a long-forgotten TV series for which she'd scouted locations.

"I've been putting off this day for three weeks, but now I am officially out of clothes."

"You're not working today?"

Greer leaned against the shopping cart. "Not supposed to be. But in between loads, I've been doing research on the computer."

"What kind of research?"

"We need a military-looking building for a location this week. But everything I've come up with is either too far away or tied up in red tape." She hesitated. "I was going to call Eb and ask him for suggestions, but I think he's officially not talking to me."

Ginny gave her a sympathetic smile. "He'll get over it. I will say that he's been pre-occupied the last few days with all this business about Jared."

"Oh-h-h. Can I ask? Is his brother really getting out of prison?"

Ginny used her shirtsleeve to wipe the sweat from her brow, leaving a faint stripe of dirt on her forehead. Her gray eyes clouded over.

"I'm afraid it's true. The Department of Corrections website shows Jared's status as prerelease, which means he could be released as early as this Wednesday. But our lawyer says it's never really official until right up until the day."

"Has Eb talked to Jared?"

"No. Inmates don't have access to phones or e-mail, and the boys have been more or less estranged since Allie came to live with us." She shook her head in dismay.

"What will happen with the custody issue?"

"Nobody seems to know. It's so frustrating! Our lawyer doesn't think a judge would award custody of Allie to Jared, but nothing is certain. All we can do is be prepared for the worst."

"How is Allie? We all miss having her on the set."

"I'm sure she misses being there as well. But she's not speaking to me or Eb. It's the old silent treatment. I used it on my mother, may she rest in peace, and I'm sure you used it on yours."

"Definitely," Greer agreed.

"She's just so angry! It's not like Allie. She works her shift at the Inn, comes home, and goes right to her room here.

"She doesn't see her girlfriends?"

"No. Not even Tristin, her best friend." Ginny sighed. "I wish Eb would let up a little. But he's just as stubborn as she is."

"I hate this, for her and for you guys," Greer said. "I feel responsible for allowing Allie to get mixed up with that character."

"It's not your fault. You had good intentions. Anyway, you mentioned you need to find — what? A military base? Maybe I could help with that."

"I'd love to hear any suggestions."

Ginny set her pruning shears on top of a wheelbarrow full of faded palm fronds. "Well . . . there's the old Cross City Army Airfield, that's not too far from here. It used to be a pilot training base during World War II, but I heard they knocked down all the old barracks and hangars. Maybe the only thing that's left is the airstrip."

"Interesting, but I need an actual building for the film."

"What about the old National Guard Armory, over in Ducktown?"

"That sounds promising," Greer said.

"It's been closed for years and years, since our local Guard unit was folded up into the unit in Gainesville. You can see the main building on Ducktown Road. It's concrete block, nearly covered over with kudzu. And there used to be an old, rusty tank parked out front, but I haven't been over that way in a long time."

"Even better. You say it's closed? Who owns the building?"

"I'm guessing the county does. Eb would know. I'll call him."

"Oh no," Greer said, but Ginny was already headed back into her apartment.

She emerged a couple of minutes later, holding out her phone. "Here. He wants to talk to you." Ginny went back into the apartment, a not-so-subtle signal that Greer could speak to her nephew in private.

"Hi there," Greer said. "I didn't mean to bother you."

"It's no bother," Eb said. If his voice wasn't exactly warm, it also wasn't anywhere near as arctic as it had been during their last encounter.

"Gin says you might be interested in the Ducktown National Guard Armory?"

"Maybe. Her description sounds intriguing. Can you tell me anything about it?"

"The county actually owns the property, and it's been for sale for a while. I'm looking at their surplus real estate website description right now. Hmm. Sits on three acres, most of which is floodplain, which is why nobody wants to buy. This says the parcel includes the eighty-thousand-square-foot armory building, a vehicle maintenance barn with bays, and three other outbuildings."

"Wow. That could be exactly what I'm looking for. Can you send me a link to that website? I might take a ride over there this afternoon."

There was a long pause on the other end of the phone. "I can do better than that. If you want, I'll take you to Ducktown myself."

"Really?" Greer couldn't hide the surprise in her voice. "Thanks, but I don't want to take up your Sunday. If you just send me the link —"

"It's not a bother. From the photos, the

place is in really bad shape. I realize you're no stranger to breaking and entering, but it's probably not safe to wander around there by yourself."

"Ha-ha," Greer said weakly. "Okay, if you're sure you don't mind. This is part of yet another last-minute script change, and I promised Bryce I'd have something for him by tomorrow."

"How soon can you be ready?"

Greer looked down at her ensemble, and back at the shopping cart full of clean but unfolded laundry. "Give me twenty minutes?"

Eb pulled his truck onto the shoulder of the narrow two-lane blacktop called Ducktown Road. Beyond a narrow stretch of newly mown grass and a dank-looking drainage ditch was a chain-link fence with a faded FOR SALE sign.

Just beyond the fence sat the tank Ginny had mentioned. It was rusting and nearly covered over with flourishing green kudzu vines. Just beyond that rose a boxy, flat-roofed building. A thick tangle of bamboo, vines, and sapling trees obscured her view of the rest of the property.

"The tank is awesome," Greer exclaimed, jumping down from the truck. "Just the right touch of military might." She eyed the fence. "But how do we get in?"

He held out a key. "I stopped by the as-

393

sistant county manager's house before I picked you up."

He joined her on the shoulder of the road, where the grass and weeds were knee high. "When I was a kid, it was considered big fun to come over here and spray paint the tank with obscenities. Just as soon as we got done, the Guard would repaint it Army drab green. All those layers of paint are probably the only thing holding it together."

He handed her a can of insect repellent. "Here. Better give yourself a good coating. I doubt the county's mosquito control trucks bother to come over here. Plus, there are probably wood ticks."

"Ticks?" She grabbed the can and nearly emptied it on every inch of her own exposed flesh.

"I thought you love nature," Eb said dryly.

"I draw the line at insects that want to suck my blood."

She walked over to the fence and started snapping photos with her phone, while Eb dealt with the padlock. He swung the gate open, but when Greer started through it he grabbed her by the shoulder. "Just a minute."

He went to the truck and came back with a sturdy walking stick and a heavy-duty flashlight. "Snakes," he said, in answer to Greer's puzzled look.

"You're just saying that to scare me," she said, but she hung back a few steps as he beat the shrubbery with the stick while they advanced on the armory building.

She quickly forgot about the threat of bloodsucking bugs and poisonous snakes as her mind switched into location scout mode.

"Have to get a landscape crew in here to cut back all the overgrowth," she muttered, as bamboo branches slapped her face and arms. "Would the county be okay with that?"

"They'd probably send in their own crews to do it, if the money's right," Eb said. "The place is sitting here empty. The county manager told me he'd be happy to make a deal, which I've been authorized to broker."

Greer nodded. "Can we see the inside?"

He brandished another set of keys and fiddled for a few moments before opening the heavy steel double doors on the brick building.

He stepped inside and Greer followed. The air was rank with the smell of mildew and dust. Eb played the flashlight over the walls. They were in a sort of entry hall, off of which were half a dozen doors that led to small offices. A second set of steel double doors hung partially open, leading to a huge room that resembled a high school gym.

They walked around the room, with Eb shining the flashlight and Greer snapping more photos. "It's pretty dark, but this is good enough to give Bryce an idea of what's here," Greer said.

"According to the county's website, the vehicle maintenance barn is back here," Eb said, unlocking yet another door at the rear of the assembly hall.

They walked out onto a cracked gravel parking lot grown over with more weeds and saplings.

"That's the maintenance barn," Eb said, pointing to a long, low, concrete block building with a flat roof.

He yanked on a set of steel double doors, which finally rolled open with an echoing squeal. They stepped inside and Eb played the flashlight around bare block walls streaked with decades of grease and dirt. A dusty green Army jeep on rotted tires squatted in the corner.

"Perfect," Greer said, snapping pictures of the exterior. "Not that I've ever seen an ammo dump, but if I had, this would look like it."

She glanced around at a vast, overgrown field that stretched out for what looked like two or three acres. "Plenty of room to get all the trailers and equipment in here, too. No neighbors to complain about a night shoot. It's better than I could have hoped for."

Eb nodded. "Seen enough, then?"

"Yep. Did your guy have an idea of what kind of fee he's hoping for?"

"He didn't, but I'm thinking a flat fee. How's five thousand?"

"And the county will come in and mow and clear the grounds?"

"Yes. What's your time frame?"

Greer laughed. "According to Bryce, we need it immediately. According to him, *everything* has to happen immediately. But as far as I know, the shoots at the casino and Manatee Street should take most of this week. But in the meantime, if the set dressers and painters and art department can start getting in here ASAP, that would be great."

"I don't think that's a problem. I'll let my guy know he has a deal, so he can get the county's landscaping crews over here."

"Great. I'll e-mail you our standard leasing agreement. Can you take it from there?"

"I can," Eb said.

The conversation in the truck on the drive back to the motel was short and businesslike. Greer kept sneaking sideways glances at Eb, hoping to see some softening in his demeanor. But his jaw was set and his eyes stared straight ahead at the blacktop road.

Finally, out of desperation, she decided to try to bridge the widening gulf between them. "We really miss Allie on the set. Ginny says she's giving you guys the silent treatment."

"If she thinks I'll fold on this, she doesn't know me very well."

"Just FYI, Bryce had a talk with Kregg. And so did I. He's gotten the message to stay away from her."

"He'd better have," Eb said.

He swung the truck into the Silver Sands parking lot and pulled around to the parking space in front of her motel room.

"Okay," she said helplessly. "Um, thanks again for setting it up so I could see the armory. That's a huge load off my mind." She hesitated, then put a hand on his arm. "I really appreciate it, Eb."

He shrugged. "It's a business deal. The county can use the money. And I'll get a small commission, which will help, with all the attorney's fees it looks like we'll be racking up."

She sensed a tiny sliver of daylight between them.

"Family issues can suck the life right out of you, right? My mother's been dead for more than two months, but it seems like, even from the grave, she won't let go."

"Hard to believe anybody could get somebody like you under their thumb."

"You never met Lise. If they gave Academy Awards for button pushing, she'd have a shelf full of naked golden men."

"What's she pushing your buttons about?"

Greer shook her head. "Never mind. You've got problems of your own. You don't want to hear my drama."

"Try me."

"It's complicated."

"I'm an engineer. And a real estate broker. And a politician. And I own a supermarket. I can do complicated."

"You're not just saying that to be nice?"

"I'm not all that nice," he reminded her. "In fact, Ginny says I was a real asshole to you."

"You kinda were, but I guess I deserved it."

"How about if I make it up to you and buy you lunch?"

"It's nearly three o'clock," Greer said.

"Have you had lunch?"

"No. And I'm getting pretty sick of eating Pop-Tarts and watching one of the three television channels in my room."

"Okay. We can call it early dinner if you want." He shook his head. "Dammit, I keep forgetting it's Sunday. The only decent place that's open is the Inn, and I don't feel like having Allie giving the both of us the evil eye while we eat. How about if I cook?"

"You cook?"

"I'm a great cook. Okay, I'm a decent cook. And one of my buddies just brought me a couple quarts of headed-out Gulf pinks."

"Is that a fish?"

"Shrimp. Trust me, you'll like it. I'll head home and make some calls to set up your deal for the armory. Come over in about forty-five minutes, if you want."

"I want," Greer assured him.

39

Greer wound her way through the cramped aisles of the Hometown Market and climbed the stairs to the second floor. She rapped cautiously on the door of the apartment, and from inside heard the sound of enthusiastic barking.

"Come on in," Eb hollered. "It's open."

Gunter met her inside the door. He barked and pawed at her ankles, and when Greer bent down to scratch the elderly dachshund's ears, his entire body wriggled in delight. "Hey, buddy," she cooed. "Long time no see."

"Don't pick him up," Eb called from the kitchen.

She looked down at the floor and, sure enough, spotted a telltale puddle. She walked into the kitchen, where she found her host standing at the sink, peeling shrimp.

"Too late." She set down the six-pack of craft beer she'd picked up on the way to the market and snagged a handful of paper towels.

After she'd wiped up the mess, she returned to the kitchen, with Gunter at her heels. She peeked over Eb's shoulder at the dishpan full of shrimp.

"Those are some big Gulf pinks."

"And they're right off the boat." He nodded toward the beer. "Thanks for that. My hands are kinda shrimpy right now. Wanna open one for me?"

She twisted the metal cap off one of the bottles and handed it to him, then helped herself to another before stowing the rest in the fridge and taking a seat at the counter.

"Need any help?"

"Not right this minute."

Eb Thibadeaux moved from one task to another with ease and efficiency, chopping a slab of thick bacon and tossing it into a large skillet, which he placed on the stove's front burner. While the bacon sizzled, he diced an onion and a green bell pepper, along with some celery and garlic, occasionally turning back to the skillet to poke at the bacon with a wooden spoon.

When he was satisfied the bacon had rendered enough fat, he added the chopped vegetables to the skillet and turned the heat down a notch.

"Smells great," Greer said, sipping her beer. "Don't think I've ever had shrimp and grits."

"We're just getting started," Eb said. He opened the door of a battered oak Hoosier cabinet to reveal a row of cans, and picked out a couple.

"What have you got there?"

"Ro-Tel tomatoes with green chili peppers. There isn't much a can of this won't improve." He held up a can with a blue label. "This one's chicken stock. Sometimes, if I'm getting fancy, I'll use vegetable stock or canned seafood stock instead, but I don't have any up here, and I don't feel like going downstairs to the store to get some, so chicken broth it is."

"I wouldn't want you to get fancy on my account," Greer said.

He gave her a wry smile. "That didn't come out the way I intended. You know? I'm, uh, I'm trying to find a way to say I'm sorry for being such a dick, as Allie would put it."

"It's okay. I get that you were trying to protect her. That's a good thing."

"She's almost eighteen. Ginny says it's too late to protect her from all the bad stuff in the world. But I can't seem to make myself stop trying."

Greer hesitated, then got up and brushed her lips against his cheek. "That's what I like about you."

She noted that Eb didn't kiss her back, but he also didn't try to fend her off with the wooden spoon in his hand.

"Really?"

She sat back down at the counter. "That,

and your adorable dog."

Eb poured the chicken broth into the skillet, releasing a cloud of fragrant steam into the air. He stirred vigorously, then dumped in the can of tomatoes and stirred again, before turning the heat down.

He lifted the lid on a large pan on the back burner and looked inside.

"Now I could use your help."

Greer moved over to the stove.

"Can you watch these?" he asked.

She looked down into a pot of bubbling white grain. "What am I watching for?"

Eb handed her a wooden spoon. "Just keep stirring and don't let the grits burn. We had a nice lady who used to cashier in the store for years. Sweetest little old gal you'd ever meet. One night, Thelma was fixing supper, and she got a phone call from her mama in Tallahassee. She asked her husband to watch the grits. But when she came back into the kitchen, sure enough, the sorry slacker had wandered off to watch the ball game, and let 'em burn. Thelma dumped the whole pot on his head and walked out the door and never went back."

Greer eyed him suspiciously, but kept stirring. "Is that some kind of local folk humor?"

"Absolutely not."

While she stirred and stared at the grits, Eb set the table with thick white restaurant plates and shallow soup bowls. He tossed together a salad of romaine lettuce and blood red tomatoes with cucumbers and purple onions, and whisked together a quick vinaigrette.

"Homemade dressing. Looks like you *are* getting fancy on my account," Greer said.

"No. Fancy would be if I ran downstairs and got buttermilk to make ranch dressing," he corrected her. "This is just easy. And good. How are my grits coming?"

She held up the wooden spoon for him to inspect.

He nodded approval. "Almost there. Keep stirring."

Now Eb moved over to his side of the stove and added the peeled shrimp to the pan of gravy.

"Three minutes," he advised. "Just three minutes on the heat, until the shrimp tails have barely begun to curl up."

Greer scraped up the last bit of grits and gravy with the side of her fork and sighed happily as she pushed her chair back from the table. "So, so good. Where'd you learn to cook like that?"

"Here and there," Eb said, sipping his beer. "My mom taught school, and she didn't have any daughters, so she taught Jared and me enough so we could start dinner before she got home from work most nights. I also make a mean pot roast and a decent lasagna."

"And what did Jared make?"

"Excuses." He stood abruptly and started clearing their plates. Gunter stayed right on his heels, until Eb tossed him a dog biscuit from a jar on the countertop.

"Let me do the dishes, since you cooked," Greer said.

She filled the sink with hot, soapy water and dumped in the dishes and silverware while Eb leaned against the counter and supervised.

"How about you? I know your mother was an actress. What was that like? Did she do normal mom kinds of stuff with you? Cooking and all that? Or maybe you had maids and a chef, since she was a big star?"

"No."

"No, what?"

"No, there was nothing normal about how Lise raised me. No, she didn't teach me how to cook. After my dad left, we moved in with Dearie — that's my grandmother. She worked, too, so we ate a lot of tuna noodle casserole and take-out Chinese. And no, sorry to burst your Hollywood fantasy bubble, but we never had a maid. Lise's stardom lasted just long enough for her to move us into a bungalow of our own before the show got canceled. I became the maid. And the chef."

"You mentioned your dad. Is he still living?"

"Actually, he's living right here in Florida, in Alachua. I saw him last weekend, for the

405

first time in nearly thirty years."

"How did it go?"

"Swell. He wants to buy me a pony and take me to Disney World for my birthday."

Eb took the skillet from her. "Here, let me do that. You'll ruin your manicure."

"Too late." Greer held up her hands, with their short-clipped, workmanlike nails. But she stepped aside and let him take over.

"Seems like you're still pretty angry at your folks," he said, plunging the skillet back into the sink. "You're thirty-five, right? Isn't it time for you to let go of all that crap?"

"That depends on your point of view. Most of my life, my mother let me believe my father was a deadbeat dad who walked away from his family responsibilities when I was five. He never paid child support, that I knew of, and aside from a couple lame visits at Christmas and birthdays while I was still a kid, he never attempted to see me.

"Then, shortly before she got sick, for reasons I still don't understand, Lise and Clint — that's my dad — befriended each other on Facebook. She started dropping heavy hints that she wanted me to contact him, and being Lise, she even gave him my contact information. He texted and called me, and finally, last Sunday, I dropped in and saw him."

"And?" Eb prompted.

"And nothing. I granted Lise her deathbed

wish. As far as I'm concerned, I've done my duty. Clint apparently hopes for more. He showed up at the casino shoot on Friday."

"Kind of a nice gesture, wasn't it?"

"He has a picture car business — he supplies oddball vehicles for film and television shoots, and he was delivering an old Crown Vic for *Beach Town.*"

"And you weren't exactly thrilled to see him, I take it?"

"I was in the middle of working a twelve-hour day and he wanted to take me out to lunch. Besides, he wants what I can't give."

"Forgiveness?"

"I just can't . . . conjure up warm and fuzzy. Not after all this time."

"Still, isn't he about all the family you have left?" Eb asked.

"Dearie's alive and kicking. That's plenty of family for me," Greer countered. "Anyway, what about you? You're, what, forty-one? Why are you still so mad at your brother?"

"Who says I'm angry? Jared is who he is. I accept it. I deal with it. There's no anger."

"When did you last talk to him?"

"I don't know. We're not pen pals."

Greer found a dish towel and began drying the plates and bowls. "Allie seems to think her dad was framed, or railroaded. Is that possible?"

"No." Eb shook his head vigorously. "We saw the video. The undercover FDLE guy had film of Jared writing scrips for OxyContin, Percocet, Vicodin, in exchange for a fistful of twenties. It was a pill mill. They nailed him dead to rights. Which is why Jared pled out in exchange for a lesser sentence. After he ratted out the real doctor supposedly running the clinic."

"Does Allie know that?"

"She was only twelve when he was arrested, and thirteen when he went away. It wasn't something we wanted to get into with her at the time. She'd been traumatized enough, getting handed back and forth between her mom and dad and her grandparents, like a cast-off pair of shoes or something. Ginny and I wanted her to have some stability in her life. We told her Jared had committed a crime, and left it at that. She didn't ask a lot of questions."

Greer thought back to her own childhood and teen years. She'd never asked Dearie or Lise many questions about her parents' marriage, because even at six she sensed the subject was taboo. But that had never stopped her from wondering. And brooding. And blaming.

"Were you and your brother ever close?"

"I don't know." He held up the skillet and examined it, then plunged it back into the water, mounting a renewed attack with the steel wool. "Why does it matter?"

"I'm just trying to understand the family

dynamic here. I was an only child. I used to ache for a big brother or a little sister. One year, I told my mom I wanted Santa to bring me a baby. That's all I asked for. A baby."

"And what happened?"

"That was the year Lise told me there was no Santa. And then she went on to explain in graphic detail where real babies actually come from. I was eight."

"That's messed up," Eb said. He scraped out the last of the grits into the trash, then set the pan in the sink. "We'll let that soak."

He went to the refrigerator and brought out two more bottles of beer, uncapping both and handing one to Greer.

They sat back down at the kitchen counter. Greer sipped her beer and waited. Gunter waited too, sitting upright, his pudgy body quivering with anticipation.

"Jared was always the golden boy," Eb said finally. "He never had to work at anything. He was smart, a gifted athlete, and sharp as a tack. He'd get into trouble, but he could always manage to talk his way out of it. It was always somebody else's fault. And everybody bought that, including my parents, because Jared could make you believe the sky was green, when you knew damn well it was really blue."

"He was the favorite? Did you resent him?"

"He was my big brother. I idolized him."

"Until?"

Eb reached down and picked up the dachshund, who'd been sniffing his ankles. He rubbed the top of the dog's head, and stroked his long, silky ears.

"I was in ninth grade. My parents went away for the weekend and left Jared in charge. He was supposed to drop me at school in the morning and pick me up after football practice. He did drop me at school, but that was the last I saw of him. He ditched school, ditched me. I had to walk three miles home, after running drills in ninety-plus heat for three hours. When I got home, he was gone. In my mom's car. I didn't know what to think. Hell, I thought maybe he'd been in an accident or something. All weekend I was terrified he was dead."

"Obviously not. Where'd he go?"

"He and his buddies went to Gainesville, to a frat party. Jared was only a junior, but he was already being recruited by every school in the SEC, including UF. When he got back home that Sunday, a couple hours ahead of my parents, the whole front end of my mom's car was bashed in. He and his buddies had gotten hammered, and he'd managed to rear-end another car at an off-campus bar. Of course, he persuaded my parents that somebody had backed into him at the mall."

"Somebody else's fault," Greer said.

"Eventually, I figured out there was something really wrong with my brother. One day

I went to the library, and somehow I found a book called the *Diagnostic and Statistical Manual of Mental Disorders*. DSM, it's called. They wouldn't let me check it out, so I sat there all afternoon, and I read that thing front to back, until I figured out that my big brother was a classic sociopath."

Greer winced at the description.

Eb's long fingers massaged Gunter's head. The dog rewarded him with a lavish slurp on the chin.

"You said Jared went to med school?"

"Offshore. He'd bounced around to several colleges, dropping out or flunking out. We never got the straight story. My parents wrote the checks and Jared cashed 'em. They totally believed every lie he ever told them. Right up until he went to prison."

"That must have broken their hearts."

"It broke my mom's heart, for sure. Dad had already started showing signs of dementia, so I'm not sure he actually understood what was going on."

"How did he and Allie's mother end up together?"

"Amanda hooked up with Jared when he was home on one of his 'breaks' from school. When she found out she was pregnant, Jared flatly denied the baby was his, claimed she'd been sleeping with his best friend — which, by the way, was true. Of course, once Allie was born, and it was obvious she was a

411

Thibadeaux, he changed his tune. They got married when Allie was four, but by the time she was five, the marriage was over."

"The same age as me, when my parents split," Greer blurted.

"The difference is, you had a mother who stayed put, and raised you," Eb said. "Amanda had zero maternal instincts. And *her* mother had even less. Allie ping-ponged between Amanda and her relatives for years."

"Until you moved back to Cypress Key and took her on as one of your projects," Greer said. "Like the store, and running the town."

"Allie isn't a project," he said sharply. "I'll admit, I was terrified at the prospect of raising a kid, especially a little girl. Sarah and I wanted kids, but then she got sick." He shook his head. "I'm not perfect, and neither is Ginny, but we're doing the best we can for Allie."

"From where I sit, you've done a great job," Greer said. "But she turns eighteen . . . when?"

"Two weeks," Eb said, his expression grim. "And then she's a free agent, if she wants to be."

"I guess you'll just have to trust that you and Ginny have given Allie the tools to make good decisions for herself. If her dad is as big a jerk as you say, she'll figure that out, right?"

"Trust? Us messiah complex guys aren't really good on the trust thing. The only people we trust to do the right thing is ourselves."

Greer reached across the table and gave his hand a sympathetic pat. "Let it go. Isn't that what you told me?"

Before Eb could reply, Gunter hopped down from his lap, sat up on his haunches, and gave a sharp, commanding bark.

"Okay, buddy," Eb said. He took a leash from a hook by the door. "Let's get you walked before you flood out my kitchen floor." He turned to Greer. "Feel like a stroll?"

"I've got to get back to work," Greer said. "Thanks for dinner, though."

"No time for dessert?" Eb's eyes glinted mischievously.

Greer's mind flashed back to the last dessert she'd shared here with Eb Thibadeaux, and simultaneous erotic sensations — condoms and cookies — drew a deep flush to her face. "I thought you decided 'dessert' was off the menu for us."

"Stupid, stupid, stupid," Eb muttered, leading the dog toward the door.

40

On Monday Bryce called for an early lunch break to allow for time to inspect the potential ammo dump.

A pair of work release inmates in bright orange jumpsuits pushed lawn mowers back and forth in front of the opened gates of the former National Guard Armory on Ducktown Road. Behind the gate, another orange-garbed inmate was astride a riding mower, while three more men attacked the dense underbrush with chain saws and weed whackers.

A uniformed sheriff's deputy leaned against the fence, his shotgun propped on his shoulder, his eyes hidden behind polarized sunglasses.

The heavy air smelled of freshly cut grass and gasoline fumes.

Bryce Levy rolled down the window of his black Navigator, leaned out, and inhaled deeply. "Oh yeah." He turned around to address the occupants of the backseat, gesturing toward the tank, which had been shorn of its overcoat of vines and dead leaves. "This is definitely it. Come on, you guys. How cool is this?"

"Very cool," Alex, the art director, said obediently.

"Even better than the pictures," the set decorator echoed.

"I can't wait to see the inside," Bryce said, opening the driver's side door.

"Wait." Greer handed him the can of insect spray.

By the time they'd finished touring the main building and the maintenance shed, Bryce had used up all his superlatives and was merely recycling *awesome, fabulous,* and *unbelievable.* Repeatedly.

"You nailed it again," he told Greer as they climbed back into the Navigator. "Honest to God, it's like you knew exactly what was in my head, when even I didn't really know what was in my head."

"Uh, thanks," Greer said. "I just got lucky this time around. The county had it listed as surplus real estate, and Eb Thibadeaux managed to get it for us at a rock-bottom rate."

"The mayor," Bryce said thoughtfully. "Are we all good with him now? I mean, I told Kregg in no uncertain terms to keep his pecker in his pants and his hands off the mayor's niece."

"I've been mending fences," Greer said. "So I think we've reached a truce."

"Good. Excellent. We're going to need him in our corner when we demo the casino."

"So it's definite — the explosion?" Greer asked.

"All systems are go," Bryce said. "Terry finished the last scene, like right at dawn Friday. He sent me the pages and I was blown away." He swiveled in his seat. "Right, guys? This shit is genius. Am I right?"

"Unbelievable," Alex and Stephen agreed.

"This scene? It's insane. And I love it so much, it's sick. I mean, I gotta tell you, I was about ready to cut Terry loose with all these last-minute changes and delays. I was literally shopping for another screenwriter to finish up the script. But when you read it, Greer, you'll absolutely agree, the words come jumping off the page. He's found a way to bring all the subplots to a full boil. This new ending, at first it seems like it comes out of nowhere, but when you think about it, everything has been leading up to this. Swear to God, when I read it I had tears running down my face."

"Exactly what happens in this last scene?" Greer asked.

"So . . . Danielle and the sheriff, they've been plotting all along to make it look like Nick, Kregg's character, has lost his shit. Post-traumatic stress disorder. But once the hot lady shrink starts putting it all together, and actually starts to help Nick, that forces their hand. They gotta do something epic. To prove he's batshit crazy. And get rid of him. What better way to do that than to actually blow up the freakin' casino — with him inside it?"

Greer felt her mouth go dry.

"But Bryce . . ."

"Yeah, yeah, now you're gonna give me all the reasons we can't really blow up the casino. Save your breath, okay? Van is totally on board with this. And it's gonna happen. It's gonna be mind-blowing. Literally."

"Van?"

"Vanessa Littrell. Sure, at first she thought it was kind of radical, but then we talked it over and she came around. She's totally green-lighted the whole deal."

"Bryce, the casino . . . you know how the community feels about it. It's an old, historic building. The city has put together a grant proposal to restore it. Surely you don't really have to tear it down."

"Technically, we're not gonna tear it down. We're gonna blow it up. It's the only way, Greer. You'll see when you read Terry's new pages. I don't care how authentic-looking a model you make, or how good the CGI, there is no substitute in this film for the real thing. That's why we're here — in this fuckin' swamp out in the middle of nowhere instead

417

of a nice, air-conditioned soundstage back in L.A. Authenticity, Greer. For this film to succeed, my audience has to be right there, in the action. And that's where we're gonna put them. You and me. We're gonna blow that fucker up, and then, those people in that dark theater? They're gonna be ducking and trying to hide, because they'll absolutely believe chunks of concrete and plaster are raining down all around their seats."

"But Bryce . . ."

He turned the key in the Navigator's ignition. "I realize you're worried that something could go wrong again. I know all about what happened during that shoot up in Paso Robles. The fire? That was bad. But it ain't gonna happen here. Not on my watch. I've already reached out to the best special effects guy in the business. He's on a plane right now. And Van, she had a great idea. We're gonna get the local fire department on our side, let them use the demo for training. Brilliant, right?"

He leaned closer to Greer, challenging her to challenge him. "Right, Greer?"

It was useless to argue with an ego like Bryce Levy's, she knew.

"How soon do we shoot it?"

He gave her a broad wink. "Just as soon as you get everything permitted."

She sighed. "I know you don't want to hear this, but part of my job is to tell you the reality of lining up locations. So I have to tell you that getting the city to agree to allow you to explode a historic building is going to be really, really tricky. We already know how the mayor and some of the council members feel about it. I'll do my best, you know that, but I honestly doubt the city is going to allow this."

The city *shouldn't* allow it, Greer thought. A town like Cypress Key was the sum of its parts, and the old casino, as run-down and dilapidated as it was, was a key ingredient of the town's Old Florida charm.

This was a novel thought for Greer, but she hated the idea of destroying a historic building for the sake of a three-minute moment in a film, all on the whim of a crazed screenwriter who was one drink away from a full-tilt binge.

Bryce pulled the Navigator across the two-lane blacktop and did a three-point turn, heading them back toward Cypress Key.

"Van doesn't anticipate it's going to be that much of a problem," he "But like you said, it's your job to make it happen. Right?"

41

"Ahem." Greer coughed politely, hoping to catch the attention of Cindy, the city clerk, who was intently reading something on her computer monitor. If Greer stretched her neck, which she did, she could see the screen, which seemed to be showing a YouTube video tutorial of an intricate hairstyling technique.

The clerk looked up and immediately clicked off the screen. "Oh, hey," she said. "Something I can help you with?"

"Yes, thanks. I guess I need to see about getting a demolition permit. Can you tell me how long it usually takes to get something like that approved?"

It was Tuesday morning. Greer had spent a sleepless night trying to figure out a way around blowing up the casino, but she hadn't been able to come up with a single plausible solution to her dilemma.

"A demolition permit? I don't think I've ever processed one of those. Around here, we usually just let things deteriorate until they fall down all by themselves." Cindy giggled merrily at her own clever joke.

"Yes, well, for the film, we basically need to speed that process up a bit. Is that possible?"

"I'll check," Cindy said, giving her Farrah Fawcett–throwback hair a dubious shake. She swiveled around in her chair and reached up to a bookshelf behind her desk, bringing down a thick, white loose-leaf binder labeled Permitting and Licensing.

"Everything going okay with the movie?" Cindy asked.

"Just peachy."

Cindy leafed through the pages, running a fingertip down lines of print. "Pretty much what I thought. A permit like that, you'll need to get approval from the city engineer."

She went to a filing cabinet, rifled the contents, selected a folder, and handed it across the counter. "Fill that out, then submit it to the county engineer. Oh, I almost forgot. There's a five hundred dollar application fee, too."

"Okay. Who is the city engineer?"

"Eb Thibadeaux."

Greer rolled her eyes. She should have seen this coming.

"Any idea where he is today?"

"You're in luck. He's in his office." Cindy jerked her thumb in the direction of a door on the right side of the room.

Greer tapped at the door.

"Yes?"

"You never told me you're the city engineer," Greer said accusingly.

"You never asked," he said. "Is that why you're here?"

She tossed the folder with the demolition permit onto his desktop. "It seems we need the city engineer's approval in order to blow up the casino."

Eb scratched his chin absentmindedly. "Come to think of it, I believe that's right. Nobody's ever applied for one before, so I guess it slipped my mind."

"Nothing ever slips your mind," Greer said, flopping down onto the chair opposite his desk.

"Some things do. Birthdays. Vice presidents. Central American capitals."

"This is a farce, right? I fill out the application, write you a check, and then you deny it before the ink's dry. Right?"

He folded his hands on his desktop. "Are you accusing me of some type of malfeasance? Or unfairness?"

"I'm saying there's no way in hell you'll issue us a demolition permit."

Eb opened the folder, studied the contents, and looked up in feigned surprise. "You haven't even filled out the application. How can you assume what I'll do if you haven't even followed official procedures?"

He pushed the papers back across the desk toward her. "Fill out the application, and I swear I'll give it due and proper consideration."

Greer sat back and crossed her legs. "Look, I'm on your side now. I really am. But Bryce is hell-bent on blowing up the casino. And Vanessa's just as determined."

"More determined," he corrected her. "There's a lot of money at stake for her. But those two don't scare me."

She glanced through the half dozen forms and sighed. "Red tape. Okay, I'll get this back to you before the afternoon's out."

"Fair enough," Eb said.

At the Coffee Mug, Greer found a table near a window, ordered an iced coffee, and started reading the application. It was surprisingly straightforward. Address here, proof of ownership there, proof of performance bond there, and a long list of requirements, including name and address of licensed demolition company, licensed material hauling company, and state-approved recycler.

Using her cell phone, she got quotes from local hauling, demolition, and recycling companies to do the work required by the county, cringing at the prices for their services.

She texted Bryce the results, hoping the price tag might change his intentions about the casino's fate.

INITIAL QUOTES FOR DEMOLISHING,
HAULING AND RECYCLING DEBRIS
FROM CASINO ALREADY IN EXCESS OF
$25,000!

His response was immediate, and disheartening.

WAY CHEAPER THAN CALIFORNIA. GET
IT DONE!

"Dammit," Greer muttered.

She called the fire marshal's office, and the production company's bonding agent, to make the necessary arrangements, all the while hoping that none of her painstaking work would come to fruition.

Two hours later she trudged back across the street. The city clerk was on the telephone, but she approached the counter and took the folder and the check Greer offered, without comment, walking it back to Eb's office and then returning.

She put her hand over the telephone receiver. "He's gone for the day."

"Gone, where?"

The clerk shrugged. "He didn't say."

42

Greer sat in the golf cart, staring at her phone, wondering how she was going to break the news to Bryce that the only thing standing between him and his precious demolition permit was Eb Thibadeaux.

Her phone rang. Of course it did.

"Hey," Bryce said. "What's the word on my permit?"

"I just finished filling out the paperwork."

"Great. What's the time frame? I want to get the special effects guys lined up ASAP."

"Not sure. The thing is, it has to be approved by the city engineer. And the city engineer happens to also be the mayor, Eb Thibadeaux."

"Are you kidding me? One guy? The one guy who is clinging to that damned casino like a drowning man — he gets the final say? What kind of kangaroo town is this?"

"Sorry," Greer said. "He did promise that he would give it 'due consideration.' "

"Fuck that," Bryce said. "Enough already.

I'll deal with this." He hung up.

Before Greer could start wondering how the producer planned to "deal with it," her phone rang again. She picked it up and checked the caller ID. It was Eb.

"Hey, Eb," she said. "Are you calling to tell me you've approved the demo permit?" It was her idea of a joke, but it was immediately clear that he wasn't laughing.

"Have you seen Allie?" His tone was urgent.

"When? Today? No."

"You're sure? She hasn't been hanging around the set?"

"I haven't been on set today," Greer said. "And I haven't seen her since you put her under house arrest."

"Dammit," he muttered.

"What's this about?" Greer asked.

"Rebecca, the manager at the Inn, just called. Allie was supposed to work lunch today, and then dinner tonight, but she never showed up."

"Has Ginny seen her?"

"Not since this morning. Allie left there around ten. She told Gin she had to go in early to do some side work. Obviously that was a lie."

"What about her girlfriends? Have you called them?"

"None of them has talked to Allie."

"You're sure? They wouldn't just be covering up for her?"

"They all swear they haven't seen or talked to her. The only one I haven't talked to is Tristin Thomas, her best friend. I drove over to her house, but Gail, her mother, says Tristin has been at soccer camp in Gainesville all week. She texted Tristin to tell her to call, but we haven't heard back from her yet. Gail promised she'd put the fear of God into the kid, so that's something."

"I'll call Zena and ask her if Allie's been around the set," Greer said quickly. "I'll call the office, too."

"Talk to that piece of shit Kregg, while you're at it," Eb demanded. "I swear to God, if he's been seeing her again . . ."

"I'm sure he knows better, but I'll check with everybody, then I'll call you right back," Greer promised.

"I haven't seen Allie," Zena said. "You want me to ask around?"

"Yes, please," Greer said. Before she could say anything else, her phone's call waiting line beeped. "Let me know if you hear anything."

She switched over to the other line. It was Bryce.

"I see I have a missed call from you. What is it now?"

"Sorry, I'll make it short. Listen, have you seen Allie Thibadeaux around the set today?"

"The mayor's kid? No. I thought you said

427

she wasn't allowed."

"She's not. But Eb just called. She didn't show up for work at the Inn today, and nobody else has seen her, either. The mayor is worried she might be with Kregg. She hasn't been with him, right?"

"I'm not Kregg's babysitter," Bryce said. "Anyway, Kregg hasn't been on set today. We've been shooting the scenes with Adelyn and the sheriff all after noon."

"But have you seen Kregg today? At all?"

"No. Look, I gotta go. I've got my guy on the coast on hold."

"Wait! Bryce, I don't have a phone number for Kregg. Could you please do me a huge favor and call and ask him about Allie? The mayor is really upset."

"Come on, Greer. I don't have time to play these games. I told him to stay away from that girl. That's the end of it as far as I'm concerned."

"She's a kid, Bryce. Seventeen years old. And she's missing. This isn't a game."

"One call. I'm making a film here, not running a day care."

"Thanks. You'll call me and let me know what he says?"

"Whatever."

Greer felt helpless. She called her best friend while she steered the golf cart back toward the motel.

"CeeJay? Have you by any chance seen Allie Thibadeaux today?"

"No. Zena already asked me about her, though. What's up?"

"She's missing. Lied and told her aunt she was working at the Inn, but never showed up there. Eb's worried she might be with Kregg. And I've got an awful feeling he could be right. Bryce says Kregg wasn't working today."

"Yeah, that's right. I haven't seen him. What can I do to help, honey?"

"Are you done for the day?"

"Thank God, yes. I was just about to head back to the motel."

"Feel like running a covert op with me?" Greer asked.

"Whatever it is, I'm in," CeeJay said.

"Good. Meet me back at the motel in ten and I'll fill you in on the way. What are you wearing?"

"Why, is there a dress code?"

"No, but it'd be helpful if you looked, um, sexy."

"Since it was one hundred ten degrees in the shade today I'm wearing the least amount of clothes I could legally get away with. Although, I must warn you, I smell like a goat."

"All good," Greer said.

Her phone rang again, and she saw that it was Bryce calling back.

"Kregg's phone went right to voice mail," he reported. "I left him a message telling him he'd better not be with any underage girls. Where are you? I was thinking we could have a dinner meeting at Van's place tonight to discuss strategy."

"I'm still tying up some loose ends at city hall," Greer lied. "Can we meet tomorrow? I've still got a lot on my plate tonight."

"Have you seen tomorrow's call sheet? We're starting at sunup, at the casino. I'll see you then."

CeeJay hopped into the Kia's front seat. She appeared to be wearing an orange tube top that barely covered her assets.

"What's the plan?" she asked, as Greer swung the car on to Pine Street.

"I'm worried that Allie might be hiding out over at Kregg's house. Bryce tried calling him, but he's not answering his phone. So I thought we'd run by there and check it out."

CeeJay hoisted her tube top up so that it was covering one more fraction of an inch of her boobs. "Let me guess. I'm some kind of decoy?"

"Not sure," Greer admitted. "If Kregg's there, and his bodyguards are there, I'll need you to sweet-talk your way in the door, to look for Allie, since Kregg's probably not my biggest fan."

"And if he isn't there?" CeeJay asked.

"Let's play it by ear," Greer said.

When they reached the guard shack at Bluewater Bay, Greer lowered her window to speak to Marvin, the off-duty cop who was working security. CeeJay leaned forward and waved at the guard. "Hey, Marv!"

Marvin smiled broadly. "Hi, Miss CeeJay! Where have you been this week?"

"Oh, here and there," CeeJay said. "Hey, Marvin, do you happen to know if Kregg's at his house right now?"

"I came on duty at two and I haven't seen him go in or out," the guard said. "You want me to call up to his house to check if he's home?"

Greer and CeeJay exchanged a glance. Greer nodded.

"Yes, please."

A moment later Marvin walked out of the shack and back to the Kia. "Nobody's answering on the house phone, but you know that gang of his. They might be out at the pool, as hot as it is today."

"Okay. We'll just run up there and check," CeeJay said.

There were no cars in the driveway at Kregg's leased waterfront home. "No Hummer," CeeJay noted. "Which means the posse must be out."

"And no Porsche," Greer added. "Which

431

means Kregg's not home, right?"

"Probably," CeeJay agreed. "Kregg and his homeys like to shoot hoops at the city park, but they usually don't start playing until after dark, because of the heat."

"Although maybe the bodyguards took the Porsche and the Hummer," Greer said worriedly. "I wish I knew if they were together. Guess we should take a look around back, to see if Kregg's back there in the pool with Allie."

"I'll go check it out," CeeJay volunteered. "If Kregg is there, I'll just tell him Bryce sent me over to deliver a message about tomorrow's shoot. I doubt he realizes Bryce and I are no longer an item." She pointed to the vacant house next door, with the large FOR SALE sign in the front yard. "Park in the driveway over there and play lookout, okay? If the guys roll up while I'm still back there, call my cell."

She plucked her phone from her pocketbook, tucked it into her cleavage, and climbed out of the car.

Greer pulled into the circular driveway at the vacant house, parking with the Kia pointed in the opposite direction, on the off chance that Kregg's bodyguards might notice a strange car parked there.

It was after six, but still ferociously hot, so she kept the Kia's motor and air conditioning running. She trained her eyes on the road, hoping no cars would approach. After fifteen minutes, she started to worry. What was taking CeeJay so long? What if Kregg was in the pool, or in the house? Would he believe whatever pretext CeeJay came up with? And if he didn't believe it, what would he do?"

She felt sweat beading up on her neck, dripping down her back. After thirty minutes, she felt so anxious she knew she had to do something. She drove slowly up the driveway at Kregg's house, so that CeeJay would have a fast getaway, if need be. Her heart thudded in her chest, and the palms of her hands were slick with perspiration.

Greer was glancing in her rearview mirror for the hundredth time, when the passenger-side door opened and CeeJay slid onto the seat.

"Let's go," CeeJay said calmly.

"What took you so long?" Greer fretted. "I was afraid you were being held hostage or something."

"I was being thorough," CeeJay said. "I went up to the deck, just to see what I could see, and I noticed that the French doors were unlocked. I might have thought I heard somebody tell me to come on in. And I might have looked all over the house, just to check it out."

"You broke into Kregg's place? What about Kregg's bodyguards? What if one of them had walked in on you? Not to mention, I think that house has a security system. What if the cops showed up?"

"I thought he invited me in," CeeJay said. "Turns out I was mistaken. Nobody was home. No bodyguards. As for the cops, I was in and out in five minutes. But Kregg better hope the law doesn't show up at his place. He's got bongs and weed scattered all over the place, and a cute little coke stash in his medicine cabinet."

"You checked his medicine cabinet? Are you insane? I just wanted you to check for his car, I didn't ask you to do a search and seizure."

"I had a headache, and I went looking for an aspirin," CeeJay said airily. "It's not my fault if the guy has absolutely no imagination. Or discretion."

"Did it look like a teenage girl might have been there earlier?"

"I didn't see any Taylor Swift CDs lying around, if that's what you're asking," CeeJay said. "It just looked like your typical piggish man cave — beer cans and pizza boxes all over the place, the biggest flat-screen TV I've ever seen, a weight bench, like that."

"Slow down," CeeJay said, as they approached Bryce's house. "I want to see if Miss Richy McBitchy's Jeep is there."

Both women craned their necks as they passed the house. But the driveway was empty. "Nobody home," Greer commented.

"Hmm," CeeJay said. "Maybe I should run inside and ransack his place, too." She sighed dramatically. "Probably not necessary. I know he's sleeping with her."

Greer gave her a sympathetic glance. "I thought you were over Bryce."

"I am. Totally. Okay, semi-totally. I knew he was a player when I hooked up with him, but like the dumb bunny I am, I talked myself into believing that true love and great sex could make Bryce change his ways."

"Not so much, huh?"

"Players gonna play," CeeJay said. "To tell you the truth, I'm mostly bummed because it means I've got to move again, when we're done with this gig."

"Since you brought it up," Greer said, "Bryce wanted me to meet with him for dinner at Vanessa's house tonight, so we could discuss our strategy for getting the damned demo permit for the casino."

"What did you say?" CeeJay asked.

"I lied and told him I had some other loose ends to tie up for tomorrow's shoot," Greer said.

When they reached the security gate, Marvin waved and stepped out of the guard booth. Greer rolled the window down and he leaned in.

"Hey, Miss CeeJay, Dooley, the guy who works morning shift, just came by to pick up his paycheck, and I asked him if he'd seen

Kregg or his bodyguards today. He said Kregg left out of here before nine. He was alone, and driving the Hummer, and he thought that was kinda odd, 'cuz since he bought the Porsche, his bodyguards usually drive the big car. Kregg hasn't been back all day."

"Thanks, Marv," CeeJay gave the guard a finger-wave.

"Well, that was fun," CeeJay said brightly, as Greer pulled into the parking lot at the motel. "Almost like high school days with my tight girls, rolling past the head cheerleader's crib. All we're missing is some toilet paper and shaving cream."

"Maybe we can TP Vanessa's house when this shoot is over," Greer promised.

"Where are you headed now?" CeeJay asked. "You're not gonna just drive around town looking for the kid, right?"

"No, but I can't just sit in my room, waiting to hear something," Greer said. "I'm going over to Eb's place to see if he's heard anything."

"Let me know," CeeJay said.

When her phone rang again, she snatched it up.

"Have you heard anything?" Eb asked. "Have any of your folks seen her?"

"No and no," Greer said. "Kregg wasn't on

set today, and CeeJay and I just drove over to Bluewater Bay. No sign of her at Kregg's house. . . . Has Allie ever done anything like this before?"

"No! But then, she's never been this pissed off at us before. God, this is like a nightmare."

"Did you check her room, to see if there's anything missing? I mean, if she's really run away . . ."

"Allie's room is your typical teenage rat nest," he said. "It looks like a bomb went off in there, but that's how it always looks. Damned if I can tell if there's anything missing. Ginny says Allie's suitcase is still in the closet. And her iPod is still on her dresser, if that means anything."

"How about her purse? And her phone?"

"I took her phone away, remember? Anyway, Allie usually carries a little backpack thing. It's not at Ginny's."

"How about her computer? Does she have a laptop?"

"Her laptop is at Ginny's."

"Does Allie have any money? Or a credit card?"

"No credit card. We'd talked about getting her one, once she buys a car, just for emergencies. As for money . . . yeah, she's been saving her money from waitressing for two years, for a car. I'm cosigner on her bank account, and I went online and checked — she hasn't made any withdrawals. But she also

437

hasn't deposited her last paycheck, which was for about one hundred fifty bucks. She also has tip money, which she usually keeps in a jar and uses for walking-around money."

"So she's got a little money, but not a lot." Greer hesitated. "Eb, you don't think . . . I mean, there's no chance, right, that something really bad has happened?"

"I called Chief Bottoms as soon as we realized Allie was gone," he said abruptly. "She's got patrol cars out looking for Allie. We've never had anything like this happen around here. This is Cypress Key, for God's sake. Who would take her? And why? We're not the Rockefellers. . . . I still think she's with that son of a bitch Kregg."

"She's not with him right now," Greer said. "CeeJay kind of let herself into Kregg's place. She walked all around the house and checked and didn't see any sign a girl had been there."

"Breaking and entering? I like her style," Eb said.

"We also talked to the cop at the guard shack, and he said Kregg left there around nine this morning in the Hummer. Alone, and without his usual posse."

"If I get my hands on that punk . . ."

"I don't blame you," Greer said. "Have you talked to Allie's best friend yet?"

"I just called Gail. Tristin is on the way back from Gainesville, and their bus should be dropping the girls off at the high school

any minute now. Which is where I plan to be.
I better go. I need to keep this line open, just
in case Allie calls."

"I understand," Greer said.

43

It was nearly seven when she drove alongside Eb's pickup truck in the parking lot at the high school. He stood leaning against the hood, arms folded across his chest. He wore jeans and a collared golf shirt. He raised one eyebrow as she got out of the car and walked over to join him.

"I thought maybe I could help," Greer said shyly. "I hope you don't mind."

He shrugged.

"If Allie really has gone off with Kregg, I feel responsible."

He pushed his glasses off the end of his nose and sighed. "What did you have in mind?"

"Maybe let me talk to Tristin? I mean, you're the mayor, and Allie's uncle, and you can be kind of an imposing authority figure. I was thinking we could play good cop/bad cop."

"I'm the bad cop?"

"Somebody has to be." Greer leaned up

against the bumper. "Any thoughts about where Allie would have gone? If she actually is with Kregg?"

"I hope to God I'm wrong," he said grimly. "I think she might have gone to Starke."

"The prison? Where her dad is?"

"Was. Ginny had the same idea. She checked with the state corrections department. Jared was released at noon today."

Before Greer had a chance to process that thought, a short yellow school bus rumbled into the parking lot. A few minutes later the doors opened, and two dozen tanned and chattering teenage girls started spilling out into the concrete lot.

Eb pointed to a pretty girl with blond-streaked brown hair worn in a ponytail. She wore a sleeveless white T-shirt and bright green gym shorts that showed off long, lean legs. She had a Cypress Key High School logo gym bag slung over one shoulder and earbuds dangling around her neck. "That's Tristin."

The girl started walking toward a green VW Beetle.

"Hey, Tristin," Eb called. "Can we talk to you for a minute?"

Tristin approached slowly. "Hey, Mr. Thibadeaux," she said, her voice meek. "I, uh, kinda have to get home. My mom's waiting on me." She adjusted the strap of her gym bag.

"This won't take very long," Eb said. "I

think you know why we wanted to see you. Allie's missing."

The girl's expressive brown eyes widened. "For reals?"

"She didn't show up for work today. Do you know anything about that? Do you know where she's gone?"

"No sir," Tristin said quickly. "I've been at soccer camp all week."

"She didn't call or text you to tell you her plans?"

Tristin stared down at her feet. She wore bright pink Havaiana flip-flops, and her toenails were painted neon green to match her shorts. "Um, no."

"Tristin, could you look at me, please? This is serious. I need to know where Allie went today. Is she with Kregg?"

"I don't know," Tristin said. Her eyes darted from Eb to Greer. "Allie doesn't tell me everything."

"Come on," Eb said bluntly. "You two talk on the phone ten times a day. You're texting each other constantly. I don't believe she wouldn't tell her best friend if she was planning something like this."

"Like what?" Tristin flipped a strand of hair behind one ear. Her fingernails were painted green, too, with tiny white smiley faces etched on each one. "Anyway, she couldn't call me, because you took her phone. Right?"

Eb gave a snort of frustration. Greer shot

him a warning glance.

"But maybe Allie got a new phone," Greer said gently. "Maybe Kregg gave her one?"

"No. I mean, I don't know." Tristin shifted her weight from one foot to the other. "I really have to get home, Mr. Thibadeaux."

Greer decided to take another tack.

"Tristin, we know you're trying to be loyal to Allie. You're her best friend, right? You don't want to rat her out. We get that. But we think she's really in a dangerous place right now. How about this? We'll tell you what we think is going on, and you just tell us if we're right. Okay?"

"I don't know," Tristin said. "I mean, Allie didn't tell me all that much. We're kinda broken up, you know, as friends, because of him."

"You mean Kregg?" Eb asked.

Tristin nodded. "He's kind of a douche canoe, you know. And I told her that, too. Which made her all mad at me and stuff."

"Kregg did give her a phone, right?" Greer asked.

"An iPhone 6!" Tristin said. "It was supposed to be like this big secret."

"Has Allie talked to you about going to see her dad?" Greer asked.

"Um, yeah. She was kinda obsessed with him, you know?"

"How did she get in contact with him?" Eb

asked. "Inmates aren't allowed phones or e-mail."

Tristin's gaze wandered to a group of three girls standing beside a nearby red Camaro. The girls were whispering among themselves and making no secret of their interest in Tristin's conversation with the adults.

"Tristin?" Greer said.

"Allie got a post office box," Tristin said. She looked at Eb. "She knew you had this family feud with her dad, and you didn't want her talking to him." She hesitated a moment. "And sometimes her dad would call her, too. Like you said, guys in prison aren't supposed to have phones, but Al said sometimes a guard would let him use theirs."

"For a bribe," Eb said, his tone dripping with disgust. "How long has she been in contact with Jared?"

"Mmm. Not that long. Maybe three months?" Tristin clapped a hand over her mouth. "Oh my God. I totally swore to keep that a secret. Al will kill me."

"Never mind that," Eb said. "We figured out most of this already. And we know Allie's dad was released from Starke today. Is that where she's gone?"

Tristin nodded.

"Kregg took her?" Greer asked.

"I told her not to go with him," she blurted. "Kregg's, like, obsessed with meeting Allie's dad. He thinks it's awesome that he's an ex-con. He says he might want to make a movie about her dad's life."

"Do you know anything else, Tristin?" Greer asked. "Were they coming right back here?"

The girl shrugged. "Seriously, that's all I know. Allie's pissed at me. Because I told her it was a dumb idea. I mean, she knew you would totally put her on restriction forever, but she said she didn't care." She shot Eb a sympathetic look. "Because she turns eighteen this month, she gets to decide where she wants to live, and she said her dad wants her to live with him, so that's what she's going to do."

Eb snorted and stomped away.

Maybe, Greer thought, it was better this way. Now they could talk girl to girl. "Tristin, have you talked to Allie today? Is there anything else you're not telling us? I promise, we won't let her know you talked to us."

"I texted her, earlier, after my mom called to say Mr. Thibadeaux was looking for her, but she hasn't answered me back," Tristin said. "I swear, that's everything I know."

Greer had one more question, and she wasn't at all sure Tristin would tell her the truth. Still, she had to ask.

"Do you think Allie is having sex with Kregg?"

Tristin blushed violently. "No way! Gross! I mean, Al said he was getting kind of . . . you

445

know — especially after her top came off on the Jet Ski. But she told him no. Allie likes him and all, but one of our other friends at school got pregnant last year and had to drop out. Plus, her mom got pregnant with Allie when she was only eighteen, so Al is like this super virgin."

Greer realized she'd been holding her breath, waiting for the answer to her last question. Now she exhaled slowly. "Okay, that helps. A lot." She reached in the pocket of her jeans and brought out one of her business cards. "If you do hear from Allie, no matter when, would you call me and let me know?"

Tristin took the card and studied it, and then studied Greer.

"Can I ask you something now?" Tristin said.

"Of course."

"Why do you care about any of this? I mean, you're not related to Allie, right?"

Greer had been asking herself the same question. She glanced toward the truck, where Eb was sitting behind the steering wheel with the windows rolled down and the motor running.

"I care because he cares," she said softly. "And because I like Allie, a lot."

Tristin nodded. "Mr. Thibadeaux is pretty upset, huh? You know, everybody always thought Allie was so lucky, because her

446

uncle's usually pretty chill, and Aunt Ginny, she's pretty cool for an old lady. Plus, Allie gets to live in such cool places. I totally don't get why she wants to go live with some dude she doesn't even really know." She hesitated. "Especially somebody who just got out of prison. Allie says her dad only went to prison because some judge had it in for him. But still. Prison. That's hard core."

"Tell me something, Tristin. Are your parents together?"

Tristin looked taken aback. "Yeah. Sure. Why do you ask?"

"My parents split up when I was about the same age as Allie was when her parents got divorced. And my dad was never really in the picture after that. I used to envy my friends whose parents were still married." She looked directly at Tristin. "I fantasized what it would be like, you know, if they were still married. Like, if my dad worked in an office and my mom stayed home and baked cookies. Like some television sitcom family."

Greer patted the teenager's shoulder. "I guess Allie wants to believe her dad is really a good guy. And that he loves her and wants to take care of her. That's probably what we all want. Right? To have somebody love us enough to take care of us?"

"I guess. Okay if I go now?"

"Sure thing."

Eb was on the phone when she reached the truck. He covered it with his hand. "I'm on hold, waiting for the chief. I want her to put out a warrant for Kregg's arrest."

"For what?" Greer asked, alarmed.

"Anything she can think of," Eb said, his expression grim. "Contributing to the delinquency of a minor, you name it."

"That's kind of drastic, isn't it?"

"Not from where I'm sitting. He's absconded with a seventeen-year-old girl whose guardians forbid him to see her, or her to see him," Eb said.

"And if the chief agrees to that, and they manage to find Allie, how do you think she'll react to the fact that you sicced the police on her? Come on, Eb. You're upset, and I don't blame you, but get a grip! Putting Kregg behind bars won't solve anything. He'll get a lawyer and bond out in fifteen minutes. And in the meantime you will have alienated Allie for good. She'll hate your guts."

He clenched his jaw. "I don't need her to like me. I'm not her friend. I'm her guardian, and I'm responsible for her safety. You've never had kids, so you wouldn't understand that."

Greer felt stung. She swallowed and tried to think of another way to get through to this stubborn man.

"You're right, I don't have kids. But I was a teenage girl once, and I still remember how furious I was the one time my mother tried to discipline me. I don't even remember now what the issue was. But I vividly remember sneaking out of the house at two in the morning, with the idea of hitchhiking to my grandmother's house. A fifteen-year-old hitchhiking all the way out to the Valley! A truck driver pulled over to give me a ride. He gave me a beer from a cooler he had on the seat. I thought I was so grown up. Five minutes down the road, I looked over and realized he'd unzipped his pants. . . ."

Greer's heart pounded, recalling the terror of that long-ago moment. "He slowed down at a red light and I jumped out. I fell on some broken glass, but I didn't even notice. I ran for what seemed like a mile, to an all-night gas station. I called Dearie, and she came and got me and took me right back to Lise. It was a miracle I didn't get raped . . . or worse. I never told Dearie or my mom what had happened, just that I got scared and chickened out."

"Is this supposed to make me feel better about my niece riding halfway across Florida with a guy who's nothing but trouble?" Eb rubbed his jaw. "God knows if he'll even take her to Starke. They could be shacked up in a motel somewhere. . . ."

"I've got news for you, Eb. If she wanted to sleep with him, she could do that right here in Cypress Key. He's got that big house on the water. . . ."

"Jesus, Greer! This is my niece we're talking about here."

"I know. And I know it's hard for you to hear, but it's the truth. The thing is, I really believe Allie was telling the truth when she said she and Kregg weren't doing anything bad. She doesn't strike me as somebody who lies easily."

"Up until now, she wasn't," Eb snapped. "All that changed when you brought this damned movie to town."

"Tristin says Allie isn't having sex with him. Or anybody else. Apparently she's a 'super virgin'."

"She's Allie's best friend. She could be covering up for her."

Greer shook her head. "I don't think so. Is it really that hard for you to believe the best of your niece?"

"I want to," Eb said. "But she's changed this summer. We used to be best buddies. She'd go out in the boat fishing with me, or stay up late Saturday nights watching *Star Wars* movies with me. She actually laughed at my jokes. Now? Half the time, I don't know who she is."

"She probably isn't sure herself," Greer said. "Weren't you a pain in the ass as a

450

teenager?"

"Major," Eb said.

"Hate your parents?"

"Sure. Everybody hated their parents."

"Did you ever smoke weed or drink under age?"

He nodded. "Who didn't?"

"Have sex with your girlfriend?"

He gave her a wary look. "Are you planning on sharing this information with Allie when she gets back here? If she makes it back?"

"I'm just pointing out that the stuff you want to throw her in jail for is normal stuff for kids her age."

"So, what? I just sit back and hope Kregg brings her back here safely?"

"I happen to know he has a seven o'clock call in the morning," Greer said. "Kregg's a sleazebag, but he's not going to ditch work."

Eb clicked the cell phone to disconnect it. "Okay. I'm probably going to regret this. So. No cops."

"Am I allowed to give you one more piece of advice?" Greer asked.

"Go for it. Doesn't mean I'll take it. I got nothing better to do while I wait to see if Allie makes it back home. With or without her deadbeat dad."

"That's what I'm talking about," Greer said. "You heard Tristin. Allie really believes her father was some innocent victim. I think

451

the only way she finds out differently is to be around him. She's a smart girl, Eb. She'll figure it out for herself, without you harping on what a loser he is."

"No. You don't know Jared like I do. He'll dazzle her with his bullshit, the way he has everybody else. And Ginny's right. Jared's not going to want to hang around Cypress Key. I can't risk letting him take Allie away from here. I'll risk her hating me, but I won't risk letting him ruin that girl's life."

He threw the truck into gear and drove away.

44

Greer kicked off her shoes and sank down onto the bed in her motel room. It was nearly eight o'clock. She was simultaneously sweaty, grubby, hungry, and tired, but she had work to do if she was going to comply with Bryce's orders to move ahead with the demolition of the casino, pending approval of the demo permit.

She grabbed her laptop and began firing off messages: to the fire marshal, the demolition, hauling, and recycling companies, and Frank Norris, the production company's accountant back in L.A., to get authorization for the added expenditures.

Fifteen minutes later her cell phone rang. She grabbed it, hoping Eb was calling to tell her that Allie had arrived home safely. But when she glanced at the caller ID she was disappointed to see that it was only Frank Norris.

"Hi, Frank," she began.

"Hey, Greer. I got your e-mail, and forwarded it up the line, but we've hit a snag."

"Oh?" She sat up straight on the bed.

"Twenty-five thousand to blow up a building? That's nuts."

"I know, Frank. But Bryce is insistent that it has to be the real, authentic big bang."

Norris let out a prolonged sigh. "I don't think I'm gonna be able to sell this. Bryce hired Jake Newman to do the blast — you know that, right?"

"This is the first I've heard of it," she admitted.

"Jake is the most expensive special effects guy in the business. We're talking $125,000, plus first-class travel. To light a fuse. Crazy town. And you people are already seriously over budget. I mean, two million over. You didn't hear it from me, but I understand Seelinger is flying out tomorrow. And she ain't bringing champagne and roses."

Sherrie Seelinger was an executive vice president of the studio. A visit from her was not good news.

"Does Bryce know?" Greer asked.

"Not sure," Norris said. "But for now I can't authorize the extra twenty-five thousand. No hard feelings, okay?"

"None at all, Frank. Just business, right?"

And then she deliberately tried to temper her optimism. Frank Norris's refusal to let her cut checks for the demolition didn't actually mean it couldn't still happen. And Sherrie Seelinger's drop-in didn't mean Bryce would have to scale back his plans for a big explosion. After all, there was a chance — a very slight chance — that Eb would actually approve the demolition permit for the casino.

She went back to work, staring at the small print on her laptop until her eyes burned and her belly growled. It was almost ten.

Greer stood and stretched, trying to work the kinks out of her tense shoulder muscles. She grabbed a handful of change from a jar she kept on the dresser, and her room key, and headed down the corridor to treat herself to a healthy late-night repast of Diet Coke and overprocessed, Day-Glo orange cheese crackers from the vending machine.

But as she walked toward the machines she noticed the lights were on at Ginny Buckalew's unit. All evening long she'd kept one eye on her phone, hoping to hear about Allie. Eb hadn't called, but maybe Ginny had some news.

She tapped lightly at the motel manager's door. A moment later Ginny stood in the doorway. She had a lit cigarillo in her hand, and a weary expression.

"Sorry to bother you this late, but I was wondering if there's any word about Allie."

"Come on in and see for yourself," Ginny said.

The television was on, the volume turned up

high. Allie Thibadeaux was perched on the arm of a faded navy blue recliner, holding a PlayStation controller in both hands.

Jared Thibadeaux — or the man Greer assumed was Jared — looked up briefly from his seat in the recliner, then went back to the black controller he held in his hand. He was staring intently at the television, where he and his daughter were playing *Grand Theft Auto.* The cardboard carton for the PlayStation sat on the floor, near the flat-screen television, a sixty-inch HD model that still bore the manufacturer's sticker on the screen.

Greer could see the family resemblance between Eb and his older brother — and Allie, for that matter — especially in profile. The chins and cheekbones were the same, the noses similar. But Jared's eyelids were heavily hooded, and he had a broad, high forehead and receding hairline. His hair was straight, gray-streaked, and thinning across the top, fastened in a narrow braid at the back of his neck. Even while he was seated she could see that he was taller and more powerfully built than his younger brother. His biceps bulged beneath the short sleeves of his dark purple Kregg concert T-shirt, and he wore dark blue jeans and leather flip-flops.

Ginny gestured at her guest. "Greer, this is my nephew Jared. Allie's dad."

He looked up from the game again and gave Greer a coolly assessing stare. "Hey," he said.

"Greer is the location manager for the movie," Ginny added.

"Oh, hey," Jared said, jumping to his feet. He took her hand in both of his and pumped them vigorously. "That is awesome. So you're the one responsible for the whole movie thing here, right? Very cool. Hey, maybe if you're not too busy, since you're in the business and everything, I could pick your brain a little bit."

"Maybe," Greer said, being deliberately noncommittal. "It's nice to meet you."

Allie pointedly declined to make eye contact.

"Allie!' Ginny said sharply. "Where are your manners?"

The girl shrugged and looked up. "Hey."

"Hi, Allie," Greer said. "Glad you made it back home. You had everybody pretty anxious today."

"Crazy kid," Jared said, reaching over and ruffling Allie's hair. "I told her she should have let Ginny and Eb know what she was up to. But it's all good now, right, Gin?"

"I suppose," Ginny said, clamping her lips together.

"Dad!" Allie held her controller up. "Come on."

"They're too busy playing this stupid game to be polite," Ginny said, annoyed. "Come on out to the patio and have a beer with me, Greer."

457

Jared raised an empty bottle. "How 'bout a refill for me while you're at it, huh, Gin?"

Ginny went into the kitchen and returned, handing her nephew another beer, wordlessly exchanging it for the empty bottle, which she dropped noisily into a recycling bin just inside the patio door. She took two more from the refrigerator and Greer followed her outside.

The older woman sank down into a wrought iron chair and took a long drag on her cigarillo, exhaling slowly.

"I thought you didn't smoke in front of family," Greer said.

"It was this or slit my throat," Ginny said. She tapped ash into a plastic cup on the tabletop. "This has been one of the longest days ever. And it's still not over."

"The good news is that Allie's back in one piece, right? How did that happen?"

"Allie and Jared just showed up here, a couple of hours ago. That horrible Kregg drove up and dumped them off, and the two of them strolled in, acting like nothing had happened. They'd actually stopped at Mc-Donald's, if you can believe it. Jared sat there and ate two Quarter Pounders and two orders of fries and drank three beers. And then they unpacked that stupid PlayStation and the TV They've hardly spoken to me since they switched it on."

"That looks like a pretty expensive setup,"

Greer remarked.

"A welcome home gift from Kregg," Ginny said.

"What was Eb's reaction to all of this?"

Ginny shook her head. "I called to let him know as soon as they got here. He still hasn't seen them. He's been out of his mind with worrying all day."

"I know. I was with him earlier this evening when he intercepted Tristin coming back from soccer camp."

"He told me. He also told me you talked him out of sending the police after Allie. Thank God."

"I'm surprised he hasn't been over here to confront Allie. And Jared."

"He said he was too keyed up to deal with her tonight. I think he was afraid he might say something he'd regret. So maybe that's a good thing. I do happen to know he paid a visit to Kregg tonight."

"Oh?" Greer raised an eyebrow.

Ginny sighed and took a sip of her beer, then gestured with her bottle toward the patio door. "I'd like to throttle that one."

"Jared?"

"Who else? He's been here a little over two hours and he's already on my last nerve. He's worked his way through a six-pack and bummed four cigarettes from me. I had to remind him twice that he couldn't smoke in the house. I don't even smoke in there, usually."

"Is he staying here with you?"

"Good Lord, no. There's an efficiency unit right next to the laundry room that I usually don't rent. I can't subject paying guests to the heat and the noise, so I mostly use it for storage. But I told him, flat out, he can't stay there permanently."

"How did he take that piece of news?"

"Typical Jared. He's already got some grand scheme cooking. Which does not involve him finding a paying job, naturally."

"What's his plan?"

Ginny waved her beer in the air. "He and Kregg are going to write a screenplay together and make a movie. About Jared's unjust imprisonment, and some other nonsense. A collaboration, Jared calls it. I can't even listen to his wild-hare schemes. But of course Allie's right there, hanging on his every word. That's what really worries me."

"It does all sound pretty far-fetched," Greer agreed. "I don't know about Jared, but Kregg doesn't strike me as somebody with any kind of writing skills. He doesn't even write his own rap lyrics."

"Well, if making up lies counts for anything, Jared can do the heavy lifting," Ginny pointed out. "He's been living in his own fantasy world for years."

"But Jared's not talking about leaving

Cypress Key and taking Allie with him, right?" Greer asked.

"Not so far. That's the only good thing about him having no money and no real prospects. And it's the only reason I'm letting him stay here at the motel. As long as he's here, Allie's here."

Greer sat back in her chair and looked up at the sky. It was a clear night, and the stars spun out across the horizon. She heard waves lapping at the sand, and the sweet scent of jasmine wafted from the vines surrounding Ginny's porch railing. For such a peaceful-seeming place, there sure was a lot of drama in the air.

She took another sip of beer. "I think Kregg's only here for another couple weeks, and then he's supposed to go out on his summer concert tour. It'll be interesting to see if he can make a movie at the same time he's trying to write one."

"Pipe dreams," Ginny said with a snort. She took another drag of her cigarillo, then tilted her head back to watch the smoke slowly dissipate in the humid night air. "I like you, Greer, but right now I wish you and the rest of your movie people had never heard of Cypress Key."

45

It was still dark when Greer carefully picked her way across the snaked cables and wires crisscrossing the pier parking lot in the predawn hours of Wednesday. The flashlight mounted on the bill of her baseball cap showed dozens of shadowy crew members scurrying around, getting ready for the day's shoot at the casino.

A light breeze was blowing off the bay, and as she came closer to the row of trailers holding the portable toilets, she picked up the scent of a disaster.

She wrinkled her nose as she grew closer, and tossed the cup of hot coffee she'd been clutching into a trash barrel. The door of one of the units opened and a young grip hurried out, fastening the zipper on his cargo shorts. "Hey, uh, you might not want to use these," he warned, pointing to the door he'd left ajar. "It's rank. No toilet paper, no paper towels, no soap. And the women's side is just as bad. I know, 'cuz I checked."

"Thanks," Greer said. She climbed the steps to the men's side and quickly discovered the grip hadn't exaggerated. She checked all three of the trailers, with mounting disgust.

Her contract with the portable bathroom people specified that each of them would be "refreshed" daily — meaning that a pumper truck would arrive at the end of the day to pump out the sewage tanks, thoroughly clean and sanitize each bathroom, remove trash, and restock each one with toilet tissue, paper towels, and soap.

It was painfully obvious that none of that had happened. She pulled out her phone and dialed the number of the bathroom people in Gainesville, but only managed to leave a voice mail.

Next she got on her radio to her assistant location manager. "Zena!"

"Hey, Greer. What's up?"

"I'm over at the bathrooms. They're disgusting. What happened? Why didn't they get serviced last night?"

"I didn't know they hadn't," she said. "I'm inside the casino. I'll head over there right now."

Zena clapped both hands over her nose. "Oh man. This is bad. What are we going to do?"

"Obviously, we can't use these today," Greer said. "I left a message for the rental company, but until they can get somebody

463

over here, we'll have to make other arrangements."

She turned and looked around the pier and spotted the municipal bathhouse on the opposite side of the pier, near the beach playground. "I'll check to see if, by some miracle, the city bathrooms are unlocked. In the meantime, you go over to the seafood restaurant and the ice cream shop and the T-shirt store. They won't be open this early, but maybe they'll have an emergency number posted on their doors. See if you can get ahold of the owners to ask if they'll rent us out their bathrooms for today."

"Okay." Zena nodded her head dutifully.

"Offer 'em, um, two hundred dollars apiece, and uh, invite them to have breakfast and lunch at the catering truck if they'll come down right now and open up for us," Greer added.

"I can do that."

"And Zena?" Her voice was sharp.

"Yeah, Greer?"

"Weren't you supposed to check on those bathrooms last night, before leaving the set, to make sure they'd been serviced?"

"I was, but I went to the dinner meeting with Bryce to talk about the casino demo, since you couldn't make it."

Greer didn't miss the smugly accusatory tone in her assistant's voice.

"Fine," she said. "After you put up Out of

Order signs on the porta-potties and make arrangements for us to use the bathrooms at the shops, I'd like you to take your golf cart and head over to the Hometown Market. Buy paper towels, toilet paper, soap, and hand sanitizer. And some rubber gloves and a gallon of Pine-Sol."

"What am I supposed to do with that stuff?" she protested. "I'm no janitor."

"No," Greer said pointedly. "You're *supposed* to be the assistant location manager. But if you can't do that job, you'll have to play janitor. You can take the soap and paper supplies to whatever bathrooms we manage to rent. We can't do anything about the sewage holding tanks until they send the pumper truck. But we can do something about cleaning these things up in the meantime. And that's where you come in."

"Thanks a lot," Zena muttered.

"You're welcome," Greer said.

At first Greer mentally chided herself for her treatment of Zena. But then she shrugged it off. As a woman working in the male-dominated film industry, she'd done every nasty, menial on-set job that arose, and not just when she'd started out as a production assistant. Why should Zena miss out on all the fun?

When she reached the city bathhouse, one tug on the restroom door told her the sad

465

truth. They were locked. She pulled out her phone and scrolled through her list of contacts. She called the city's director of public works, Renfroe Jackson.

"Hey, Miz Greer," the always affable Renfroe said. "What can I do you for this morning?"

Greer smiled despite her sour mood. "Oh, Renfroe, how come everybody can't be as nice as you when I call them at the butt-crack of dawn?"

"Guess everybody isn't as blessed as me."

"I'm in kind of a pickle this morning down on the pier," she confessed. "Our rented porta-potties didn't get refreshed last night, and I'm desperate for bathrooms for the crew. Do you think you could get somebody to unlock the city bathhouse for us?"

"I've got a man not two blocks from there. He can swing by city hall and pick up the key and take care of that for you," Renfroe said.

"Thank you so much," Greer said. "You are my hero."

An hour later, as pink streaks creased the morning sky, Greer finally had time for breakfast. She was spooning sliced strawberries onto her Greek yogurt when CeeJay sat down at her table at the catering truck.

"Did you see that our star made it back to town last night," CeeJay asked, nodding toward Kregg, who was strolling past with a burly black-clad bodyguard. Despite the early-morning temperatures in the mid-eighties, the hip-hop star wore jeans and a black hoodie. "I'm hoping that means Allie came home?"

"Yep. She and her dad got back around eight last night."

"So, what happened to Kregg? Did you see his face just now?"

Greer whipped her head around, but the rapper was out of sight.

"No, I couldn't see his face because of the hoodie."

"He showed up in makeup this morning with a busted-up nose and a black eye," Cee-Jay said. "It took me an hour to get the damage covered up. What happened? Did they get in a car wreck?"

Greer grinned. "I think Kregg's face must have collided with Eb Thibadeaux's fist."

"Poor baby," CeeJay said. "Not."

She was just out of camera range, watching the scene under way at the casino, when she felt her phone vibrating in her pocket.

Greer walked away from the set and saw that the caller was the Royal Restroom company.

"Ms. Hennessy?" It was the woman she'd made all the rental arrangements with.

"Hello, Cecilia." Greer's voice was frosty. "Did you finally get my messages?"

"We did, and you have my deepest apologies. Believe me, we want to make this right. I've got three of our brand-new Ritzy Rest-Stop units en route to you right now. The driver should be dropping them off around four, and he'll take the old units back to us. And we'll adjust your invoice to reflect the inconvenience."

"Mind telling me what happened? I've got a pretty unhappy bunch of cast and crew members over here, having to run off set to use a grungy bathroom in an ice cream shop."

"I'll tell you, but you're not going to believe it. The tanker driver hit a bear."

"No way. A for-real bear?"

"On the county road," Cecilia said. "It was right at dusk. The poor thing came running across the road, and the next thing my driver knew, he was in a ditch. He thinks he only grazed the bear, though, because it ran back into the woods. But my tanker is right messed up. Which is why we couldn't get to you last night."

"That's some story," Greer said.

"I know it sounds far-fetched, but it's the truth," Cecilia said. "Be sure and call me back if you don't see those units by four."

"Don't worry, you'll hear from me."

Bryce Levy called for a break while the camera, sound, and light techs changed the location of their equipment inside the casino.

When she got back to the set, she stepped inside the building and was taken aback by the transformation.

Strings of lighted paper lanterns had been strung from the roof trusses, with a mirrored disco ball dropped down from the middle, and all the lights were reflected in the newly polished wooden floors. Clusters of round wooden tables and delicate gold ballroom chairs were placed in a semicircle around the dance floor. At one end of the room, an ornate, heavily carved antique bar had been installed, backed with a cloudy mirror. Rows of dusty liquor bottles lined the shelves, and extras, costumed in gaudy eighties club wear, lounged on the bar stools and at the tables.

At the other end of the room, the snack bar had also been restored, with a functioning popcorn machine and racks of period-appropriate candy bars and soft drink cans.

Up on the raised bandstand, clunky mike stands stood in front of a drum set and guitars belonging to the band that would perform during the flashback dance scene about to be shot.

Greer let her fingers trail across one of the tables as she headed for the door, and she was struck again with a pang of regret about the old building's fate. She knew it was only temporary movie magic that had transformed the place — truly a feat of smoke and mirrors — but it was still a damned, dirty shame.

She was almost at the door when Bryce caught up to her. He'd forgone his usual cargo shorts and fishing shirt and was dressed today in tailored slacks and a linen shirt. He looked unusually harried. She braced herself for a tongue-lashing over the bathroom issue.

"Greer," he called.

"Hi, Bryce. The place looks amazing. How did this morning's shoot go?"

He shrugged. "It went. Can you meet with me in my trailer during lunch?"

"Sure. Any special agenda?"

"Very special. The studio sent Sherrie Seelinger down yesterday. She's got her panties in a wad about some budget overruns. She's especially unhappy about the cost of the casino demo. So I need you to show up and help me sell her on it."

Greer tried to act surprised. "Me? Bryce, I don't think I'm the appropriate person for that. I still haven't seen the actual script changes. Why not have Terry explain it?"

He ran a hand through his hair, which left it worse for wear. "Because Terry is in no shape to talk to anybody right now. Especially Sherrie Seelinger. He's, uh, had another slip. When I find out who's smuggling Dewar's to him, I'll fire their ass. But in the meantime, you're up. Come at twelve thirty, and bring your A game. Got it?"

"I'll try."

470

■ ■ ■ ■

Bryce and Sherrie Seelinger were seated across from each other at the wood-topped dinette table. Plates with half-eaten salads had been pushed aside, and the tabletop was littered with water bottles and computer printouts.

"Sit here," Bryce said, indicating the bench beside him. She could already sense the tension in the crowded trailer.

Greer seated herself and Bryce made the introductions.

She'd seen plenty of photos of the studio's most feared executive, but Greer had never met her before. Sherrie was petite, probably not even five two — though it was hard to tell, because she was seated. She was in her early fifties, dressed in an expensive suit, though she'd ditched the jacket in the Florida heat, and she wore a platinum Rolex Oyster watch on her left wrist. In other words, she was imposing, even seated, even in a Winnebago.

"Right," Sherrie said, returning to the topic at hand, which was obviously the budget. She tapped a sheet of paper, which Greer recognized as the check request she'd submitted. "Bryce was just making a very persuasive argument for this big explosion scene he has planned for the casino. It sounds riveting,

471

but as I was explaining, I can't in good conscience approve expenditures like this when you're already dramatically over budget."

She paused. "We can easily simulate the explosion you've envisioned, back in the studio, for next to nothing. Models, blue screens, and of course the CGI technology is amazing these days. Or you could just get Terry to write another, less expensive scene. I understand he hasn't actually finished the script yet, right?"

Bryce's face flushed. "Terry's polishing the ending, even as we speak, Sherrie. That's why he's not here today. I don't dare disturb him when he's working. Anyway, Greer here can do a better job of laying it all out. Right, Greer?" He turned and flashed her a beseeching look.

Sherrie shook her head. "You're not hearing me, Bryce. It's not just these costs. It's Jake Newman's salary and expenses, too. Flying him down here business class? That's absurd. And I understand he has three more of his special effects staff planning on joining him here before the week's out? You're already at three hundred K, and the meter's still running."

She turned to Greer and tapped the printout again. "Are you telling me these costs are all-inclusive? Nothing additional?"

Greer shifted uncomfortably on the hard

vinyl bench. "Well, to be honest, there'll be some additional expenditures. We'll have to hire off-duty firefighters — I haven't had time to get with the fire marshal on what they require, but I'd say a minimum of six. Also, added security, off-duty police officers. We'll have to rent more barriers, though that's not all that expensive." She hesitated. "Also, it just occurred to me this morning, because the casino sits right on the bay, I'm pretty sure we'll have to erect some kind of safety netting to keep the debris from blowing out into the water. I won't know for sure, though, until the demo guys do their walk-through."

From the corner of her eye Greer saw Bryce scowl.

"And what about insurance and bonding?" Sherrie asked. "Three years ago, on a shoot in Atlanta, we blew up an old convenience store and a chunk of concrete struck a man in the head — three blocks away from the blast site. We're still paying his hospital and rehab bills."

Greer glanced over at Bryce. "I haven't talked to the lawyers yet about insurance."

"That's what I expected," Sherrie said. She started gathering the papers on the table, stuffing them into a slim black Hermès briefcase. "I'm sorry, Bryce, but you have got to get a handle on your budget. You can see for yourself, this little plot twist of Terry's can easily add close to a million dollars to production costs. And for what? A boom we could just as easily create with a computer and a blue screen?" She slid out from the bench and stood, and Bryce scrambled to join her.

Greer was struck by just how short Sherrie Seelinger was. Bryce towered over her by a head and a half. But the studio exec didn't seem the least intimidated by his height advantage.

"We can cut costs in other areas," he pleaded. "Sherrie, I really, really believe we can't sacrifice the sense of verisimilitude we'd get, bringing down the casino. Let me just crunch some numbers. . . ."

"Crunch away," Sherrie said, her hand on the doorknob. She consulted the Rolex. "My driver should be here by now. Look, Bryce, as it stands right now, I think you'd better put the demo plans on hold."

"Dammit, Sherrie —" he started, but there was a discreet knock at the RV door.

"That's him," Sherrie said. "We'll talk after I get back."

46

Greer turned to follow the studio exec out the open door, but Bryce put a restraining hand on her arm. When she turned to look at him, his face was a study in barely controlled rage. He looked over her shoulder and waited until Sherrie had climbed into the back of the black Town Car.

"What the fuck? Could you have done a better job of sabotaging me with that bitch?"

Greer carefully pried his hand from her arm and struggled to control her own temper, which had been on simmer all morning.

"I'm trying to do my job, Bryce. You wanted a beach town that doesn't actually exist, but I found it anyway. Want to film in a historic building despite the mayor? I found a way to make that happen. An ammo depot? With only two days' notice? Check. You want to blow up that historic building? Hey, I think that's a terrible idea, but I did my job. I spent the day pushing paper and got the application submitted. But I can't do anything about how much it costs to make your big bang happen. And I'm not going to lie to a studio exec about what the demolition will entail, or about what it costs."

Bryce sat back down at the dinette table and stared at his open laptop screen.

"Just go, Greer? Okay? I don't have time for this shit. I've got a male lead who shows up this morning with a broken nose and a black eye, who tells me he ran into a door, studio hacks breathing down my neck, and a screenwriter on a bender. And speaking of shit — I've got a location manager who can't even manage to get me working bathrooms."

Greer started to protest.

"No!" Bryce glared at her. "Spare me the lame excuses. Just do your job. Or I'll find somebody else who can do it. Somebody cheaper. Okay? Jake Newman says he can have everything set up to go by Monday. So that's what we're gonna do, Greer. You're gonna help make that happen. No matter what it takes. Right?"

Greer struggled to control her own temper. "Like I told you, I submitted the application, but I really doubt Eb Thibadeaux is going to approve it."

Bryce closed his laptop and stood. "And like I told you, I'm dealing with that. You call that Mickey Mouse mayor and tell him I want a meeting with him, this afternoon at four, to discuss our permit. Vanessa will be there, and so will her attorney."

"What if he won't come? He's the mayor, Bryce. He doesn't work for you. You can't just summon him to a meeting with, what, three hours' notice?"

"Call him and tell him we're meeting at Vanessa's place at four p.m. today. Maybe suggest he invite the city's attorney too, if they have one. Remind him how many hundreds of thousands of dollars this film is pumping into the town's economy."

Stung, she nodded and beat a hasty retreat from the RV.

When she got back to the casino, she found Zena directing the driver who was delivering the new porta-potties. As promised, they were glistening platinum-silver units, with elegant script proclaiming their status as Ritzy Rest-Stops.

She conferred briefly with Zena, who was still sulking, then hopped on her golf cart to return to the office. Despite her own resistance to the idea, she knew she had to have everything ready for a Monday demolition — or risk being fired. And that was a risk she couldn't afford. Two firings in a row could mean the end of her career.

She was tooling down Pine Street at the cart's top speed when she spotted Eb Thibadeaux walking rapidly down the sidewalk toward city hall. He saw her at the same moment and waved, and for one absurd moment she thought he actually might be glad to see her.

"Hey, Eb. I saw Allie at Gin's last night. I know you're relieved to have her home. I met your brother, too."

"So I hear."

"You're still pissed at me? Eb, you should know I'm already having a really bad day. I just came from a major ass-chewing from Bryce."

"And I just got off the phone with Vanessa Littrell. It seems I've received an imperial summons to meet with her and her attorney and Bryce today to 'chat' about this demolition application."

"So it's a two-pronged offense," Greer said. "Bryce just informed me of the same thing — that I was to 'invite' you to Vanessa's house to talk about the permit."

"I haven't denied your application, you know."

"But you intend to, don't you?"

Eb shrugged. "To tell you the truth, I've been a little too distracted since yesterday to give the casino much thought."

She reached out and caught his right hand in hers, and he winced.

A jagged cut stretched across his knuckles, and the hand was bruised and swollen.

She gently traced the cut with her finger. "I got a look at your handiwork this morning when Kregg showed up on set. CeeJay had her work cut out for her, covering up all the damage you did."

"He's lucky he only needed makeup and not reconstructive surgery," Eb said.

"Not that I care whether or not you beat the living daylights out of him, but just out of curiosity, what were his bodyguards doing while you were punching out Kregg's lights?"

"From the commotion I heard from the back of the house when I pulled in, it sounded like they were having a pool party," Eb said, allowing himself just a hint of a smile. "I rang the bell and he answered. As soon as he saw who it was, the little twerp tried to slam the door in my face. But he wasn't fast enough."

"Kregg told Bryce he ran into a door," Greer said. "So, will you come to this meeting today? And bring the city attorney?"

"The city attorney is on vacation this week. I don't especially like being issued an ultimatum, but yeah, I'll show up. Not that it will make a damned bit of difference on what I decide to do about the casino."

"Nothing like total impartiality," Greer said, laughing.

"Will you be there too?" Eb asked.

"Yep. It's a command performance for me, too. Bryce made it pretty clear my job could be on the line over this issue."

"I'm sorry about that."

"The one good piece of news is that a

woman who's vice president in charge of bean counting for the studio flew in today to try to rein in Bryce's spending. He's already nearly two million dollars over budget, and blowing up the casino doesn't come cheap. The special effects guy alone charges $150,000."

Eb whistled.

"Which is not to say she'll pull the plug on Bryce's plans," Greer warned. "In the meantime, my marching orders are to move ahead and get things done."

"And my job is to do what's best for this community. I'll see you this afternoon."

47

Her radio crackled again, and Greer considered throwing it under the tires of a passing minivan. Since one of the grips had appropriated her cart, she was on foot, en route to her motel room to shower and change before the four o'clock powwow at Vanessa Littrell's house.

Instead, she keyed the radio mike. "What is it, Zena?"

"The pizza guy and the ice cream lady want to get paid. You know, for letting us use their bathrooms."

"So pay them."

"I would, but I don't have access to the petty cash," Zena said. "Also, it looks like somebody maybe broke one of those concrete benches in the park."

"Somebody? Somebody on our crew?"

"Maybe. Anyway, it's broken, and since nobody else but us has been in the park since we started filming, I thought I better notify you."

"Okay." Greer pivoted and began walking back toward the pier. "Take a photo of the damaged bench and e-mail it to me. Ask the pizza and ice cream people if they can give me an invoice. Handwritten is fine. I'll stop at the office for petty cash and be there in ten minutes to pay them. Anything else?"

"That's it for now."

She paid off the ice cream lady and then hustled over to the pizza shop. Marco, the owner, was lifting a huge pie out of the oven as she pushed through the glass door. The mingled aromas of garlic, onions, tomatoes, and sausage assaulted her nostrils.

Greer waved the envelope. "Hi, Marco. Thanks so much for helping us out today."

"No problem," Marco said. "Hang on a minute." He drew a rotary cutter through the steaming pizza, lifted out a huge slice, and transferred it to a paper plate, which he presented to her with a flourish. "Here ya go. I'm calling this the *Beach Town* pie. All your guys love it. I bet I did two hundred dollars in extra business today, just with your crew coming in here to take a whiz."

"I'm glad," Greer said with a smile.

"Go ahead, taste it," he urged. "Nobody likes cold pizza."

What could she do? She bit into the pointed end of the slice and felt the boiling sauce sear her tongue and the roof of her mouth.

"Oh-h-h." She had to clamp her lips to-gether to keep from crying out.

"Too hot?" He handed her a bottle of water.

She took a long gulp, but the damage was done.

By the time she walk-trotted back to the Silver Sands, it was five till four. No time to shower or change clothes. Greer climbed into the Kia and drove as fast as she dared in the direction of Seahorse Key.

The dogs ran out to greet her as she drove on to the Littrell property. Four other cars were lined up in front of the house: Vanessa's Jeep, Bryce's black Navigator, Eb's pickup, and a gleaming silver Lincoln with Florida license tags. It was ten after four and she was undoubtedly the last arrival.

Greer flipped down the visor and checked her appearance in the mirror. She found a crumpled Kleenex in the cup holder and used it to mop her sweaty face, applied some coral lip gloss, and attempted to finger-comb her out-of-control mop of blond curls. There was no time to do more. She took a deep breath and stepped out of the car, and the dogs began barking loudly to announce her arrival to their mistress.

Vanessa met her at the door. She was dressed in a sleeveless pale pink scoop-necked dress and looked as fresh and cool as a scoop of strawberry sorbet

"We were starting to get worried about you," she said, as Greer followed her inside. Her eyes swept over Greer, taking in her disheveled appearance: the faded denim shorts, the sweaty white T-shirt, the red Keds. "Is everything okay?"

"Fine. I'm just having one of those days. Everything is a crisis, you know?"

"Mmm-hmm." It occurred to Greer that there was no crisis in Vanessa Littrell's life that could keep her from looking poised and polished — twenty-four hours a day.

"Everybody's in the dining room," Vanessa said. "And let me say how glad I am to have another woman in the mix. There is a *lot* of free-flowing testosterone in that room."

"I'll bet."

"I really don't get why guys have to get so hostile when somebody challenges them," Vanessa went on. "You should have been here five minutes ago. I thought Eb was going to throttle Sawyer when he told Eb he doesn't have the authority to —"

"Sawyer?" Greer clutched Vanessa's arm. "Did you say Sawyer?"

"Yes. He's the lawyer I hired to get this casino thing settled. It was Bryce's idea. He knew Eb was never going to give us that permit. . . ."

Greer felt the blood drain from her face. "Not Sawyer Pratt, right? Not my Sawyer."

"Your Sawyer?" Vanessa frowned. "You

know him?" She studied Greer's panic-stricken face. "Oh-h-h. That's right. You did tell me you'd had a relationship with an attorney. And his name was Sawyer. Oh my God. I'm just now putting it together. I bet it is the same guy. I mean, how many attorneys from L.A. are named Sawyer Pratt? Right?"

Greer couldn't trust herself to speak. When was the last time she'd seen him?

Was it the morning she'd arrived home two days early from a location shoot in Colorado and interrupted Sawyer and his shrink sharing a tofu scramble in the kitchen of his Hancock Park apartment at 9:00 a.m. on a Saturday? She could still remember the sight of Erica — the redheaded shrink — sitting at the kitchen table dressed in Greer's striped bathrobe.

Since then, she'd encountered Sawyer a few times at industry events, across the room at parties and screenings. Once he'd even been ahead of her in line at the movie theater at the Grove. With another woman, who definitely wasn't Erica. As soon as she'd spotted him, Greer had slunk quietly out of the theater lobby. Somehow, she'd always managed to avoid having to speak to her ex. Until now.

"You two are on friendly terms, right?" Vanessa asked breezily. "I mean, it's all very civil, right?"

"Right," Greer said weakly.

Civil? No. The end had been anything but civil. Bitter tears, angry accusations.

Somehow, Sawyer had made it her fault that she worked long hours and neglected his needs. Somehow, she was to blame for his needs being met by another woman. He had called her needy, selfish, childish, naive, and suffocating. Greer had called him a low-life, scum-sucking whoredog. And then she'd burned every single item he'd ever given her and mailed him a box containing the ashes of their relationship. It was probably safe to say she was not on friendly terms with Sawyer Pratt.

"Here's Greer," Vanessa announced. The four men were seated at one end of the long mahogany dining table. File folders and documents were scattered across the polished tabletop. All four heads turned as she entered the room, but only Eb Thibadeaux stood.

"Sorry to be so late," Greer murmured. She could feel the heat rising in her cheeks. "Complications on the set."

Bryce gave her a curt nod, then turned back to the document he was reading.

Sawyer sat back in his chair, his hands resting loosely on the arms. His dark eyes sparkled with barely disguised amusement.

"Hello, you," he said. Now he stood and brushed his cool lips against her cheek. "Good to see you again," he murmured in her ear. "It's been too long."

He smelled expensive, like the inside of a new Jaguar. His coal black hair, shot through with silver, curled against the collar of his jacket. His chin had a trendy line of dark stubble, and he wore dark denim designer jeans, an olive green silk shirt, and a slubby linen sport coat.

Bryce looked up. "You two know each other?"

"Old, dear friends," Sawyer said smoothly.

"A long time ago," Greer added, disengaging from Sawyer's embrace. She took a seat at the table. "Where are we?"

On cue, Sawyer slid a piece of paper across the table toward her. "I was just reminding the mayor here that the city's lease of the Cypress Key Casino is terminated, because the city hasn't used the property for its stated use in three years. If he reads the lease agreement, he'll see that it specifically states that the lessor's rights are terminated if the building goes dark."

Greer pretended to study the lease, sneaking a sideways glance at Eb, whose jaw was firmly clenched. He took off his glasses, polished a lens with his shirt sleeve, and rubbed the bridge of his nose.

Sawyer handed another set of documents around the table. "Mr. Mayor, this is a copy of your city ordinances governing the issuance of building and/or demolition permits.

I'll save us all time here by pointing out that there is absolutely nothing in these ordinances that would give you cause to deny the demolition permit Ms. Littrell and Beach Town Productions have applied for."

Eb shook his head. "That's your interpretation of the ordinances, Mr. Pratt. As city engineer, and as the mayor of Cypress Key, I can tell you that I find plenty of exceptions that would justify denial of this application."

"Name one," Vanessa cried.

"Public safety interests," Eb shot back. He tapped the demo application with a pencil. "There's nothing in this application that gives me any assurances that the firm hired by the production company can guarantee the proposed demolition will be done in a safe manner."

"Certainly there is," Sawyer said. "You're being deliberately obstructionist. You know it, and everybody at this table knows it."

"Let's get this over with," Bryce said, tossing a sheaf of papers onto the tabletop. "We've danced around long enough. I've got a film to make."

Sawyer shot Bryce a look and a barely perceptible shake of his head. He reached into a briefcase at his feet and brought out yet another document, which he slid across the table to Eb.

"This is a writ of mandamus, which I'm prepared to file with the circuit court in this county, first thing tomorrow, compelling you to issue a demolition permit without further delay."

Eb glanced at the document, then shoved it aside. "Fine. File it. Do what you need to do."

But Sawyer wasn't done. "I understand you're the mayor of Cypress Key?"

"I am."

"And that's an elected position?"

"Yes." Eb looked bored.

"But you're also the city engineer? And that's a salaried, appointed position?"

Eb gave Sawyer a hard look. "My salary, as you refer to it, is five hundred dollars a year. And I've never cashed that particular paycheck. What's your point?"

"My point is that it's a conflict of interest for you, as mayor, to also appoint yourself city engineer," Sawyer said.

"It's fuckin' nuts, is what it is," Bryce muttered.

Vanessa clamped her hand on top of his, a not-so-subtle warning gesture.

"I didn't appoint myself," Eb said, leaning forward. "And I don't appreciate your inference that the appointment is somehow shady or unethical."

Sawyer dug yet another document from his briefcase. "This is a copy of the minutes of the Cypress Key City Commission meeting where you were appointed city engineer two years ago." He tossed it toward Eb. "Does that look familiar?"

Eb picked up the sheet of paper and scanned the print. "Yes. And if you've read it, you'll see that Rev. Maynard, the mayor pro tem, made the motion to appoint me city engineer, and that I abstained from voting on that item."

Sawyer smiled. Greer was painfully familiar with that particular facial expression. It was his version of "Gotcha, sucka!" Sawyer was clearly enjoying himself. She wished she could have warned Eb about what would come next, but it wouldn't have done any good.

"Oh, I saw that, all right," Sawyer said. "And while I was at it, I noticed that you seconded the motion. Pretty cute little joke, huh?"

"We joke around a lot at meetings. It's a small town and a small board of commissioners," Eb said.

"Seconding the motion to appoint yourself to a salaried city position is a clear conflict of interest, and of the notion of separation of power in that city," Sawyer said. "Any judge who takes a look at these minutes is going to rule your appointment improper. And every single permit or application you've approved or denied over the past two years is going to be invalidated."

Eb stared down at the minutes he'd so

casually brushed aside moments earlier.

"This is nuts. The city attorney was at that meeting. He's at all our meetings. He didn't say anything."

"Your city attorney is a joke!" Bryce said.

Sawyer gathered the documents he'd just arranged around the table, packing them into a neat stack.

"Here's my point, Mr. Thibadeaux. I don't want to have to file a writ of mandamus with the circuit court here. I also don't want to have to ask a judge to vacate your appointment as city engineer. Frankly, that's all bush league stuff. It takes up my time, and it's gonna cost the city money to defend those actions, which you're not going to win. You're just not."

"Give us our demo permit," Bryce said. "Today. That's all we want. Time is money, and we're running out of both."

Eb looked from Vanessa, to Bryce, to Sawyer, and then back to Vanessa.

He grabbed the file folder with Greer's completed demolition application, opened it, and scribbled his name at the bottom of one of the forms. Then he stood and slapped it down on the table in front of Vanessa.

"Here's your permit. You always get what you want, don't you, Vanessa? Doesn't matter who it hurts or what it costs, you'll do whatever it takes."

"I did warn you, Eb," Vanessa said. "This is

a business decision. There's no need to take it personally."

Eb's eyes met Greer's. She blushed and looked away.

"Don't take it personally? I've been told that before," Eb said. "But I've found that whenever people say that, what they actually mean is, 'I won. You lost. Get over it. Don't hold me personally responsible for whatever selfish, destructive actions I've rammed down your throat.' "

"You're impossible," Vanessa said, her voice cold.

"So I've been told."

Sawyer stood now, too, and extended a hand to Eb. "Thanks for coming today. Sorry about the way things worked out, but I think, in the end, you'll see this will all be to your advantage. Great meeting you."

Eb ignored the gesture. "Fuck you, too."

48

"Fantastic!" Bryce reached across the table and high-fived Vanessa.

"Excuse me," Greer said. She hurried out of the house and caught up with Eb as he was getting into his truck.

"What? You want to shake my hand, too, and tell me it's nothing personal?" he asked.

"You know this is not how I wanted things to go," Greer said. "I had no idea you'd be sandbagged like that."

"Whose idea was it to fly in your old boyfriend? That *was* Sawyer the lawyer, right?"

Greer took a step backwards. She felt as though she'd been slapped in the face. "You can't really believe I had anything to do with that. I haven't talked to him in over two years. I feel just as ambushed as you do."

"No, you don't." Eb climbed onto the front seat and stuck the key in the ignition. "Maybe it was a little awkward for you, running into him this way, but you'll get over that. You don't have any real skin in this game. You never do, right? Like you keep telling me, it's your job."

"That is totally unfair," Greer said. "But I guess I should have expected it. You really want to believe the worst of people, don't you? Because then you can go on feeling morally superior to everybody around you." She pushed his door closed and turned and went back toward the house.

She heard soft laughter and the clink of ice and glasses as she stood in the hallway of Vanessa's house. They were drinking, celebrating their rout of Eb Thibadeaux. But she didn't have the stomach to join in the party.

One of the golden retrievers was sprawled out on an Oriental rug in the entryway, his muzzle resting on his paws. She wasn't sure if this was Luke or Owen. The dog turned and regarded her with mild indifference. She kneeled down on the floor and scratched his long, silky ears.

When she heard footsteps, she looked up. Sawyer stood there, a bemused expression on his face. "If you like dogs so much, why didn't you ever get one?"

"I don't know. I travel so much, it wouldn't be fair to a dog to leave it all the time."

"You could get a dog sitter."

"And then what would be the point of me having one, if I'm not going to be the one to take care of it?" She didn't get up, just kept scratching the dog's ears.

"Hey," he said softly. He extended a hand. She took it and stood.

He reached over and plucked something from the front of her T-shirt and held it up for her to see. It was half of a tomato-smeared pepperoni. "Late lunch?"

So she'd just sat through an entire business meeting with half a pizza hanging off her boob. She felt her face begin to burn. Damn him for having that effect on her, for always making her feel unbalanced and inferior.

"I was sorry to hear about Lise," he said. "I left you a message on your phone. Did you get it?"

Greer stared down at her red Keds. "Maybe. I don't know. So many people called, and sent cards. The whole experience was surreal. It's a blur to me now."

"Your mother was a trip," Sawyer said, grinning. "The world's a duller place without Lise Grant in it."

"She liked you a lot," Greer said. "But then, she was always a sucker for a pretty face."

"Dearie wasn't so hot about me. I never could quite win her over to my side."

Greer shrugged.

He jerked his head in the direction of the dining room. "Bryce and Vanessa want to take us out to dinner. To celebrate. You coming?"

"Don't you have to get back to L.A.?"

"It's too late to get a flight out today," Sawyer said. "Come to dinner. Okay?"

"I'm a hot mess," Greer protested. "I've been up since dawn, and now I'll have to work double time to get everything lined up to shoot the explosion at the casino."

"One dinner," he said. "What could it hurt?" He lowered his voice. "We can get a drink together after. Just the two of us. Catch up."

She thought about things — not about Sawyer standing here, begging her to go to dinner, but flashing back to the scene a few minutes earlier: Eb Thibadeaux hurling one last accusation at her. How could she really have thought his opinion of her would change? And why was his approval something she so desperately needed?

Funny, she'd felt that way about Sawyer once. Pined for him, really. Every time he'd pushed her away it had made her want him more. How sick was that?

"Greer?" Sawyer glanced over his shoulder, toward the dining room, where they could hear Bryce and Vanessa chatting.

"I've missed you. Crazy, huh?" He touched a strand of her hair, let it curl around his little finger. Sometimes, when they were in bed together, just before he dropped off to sleep, Sawyer would coil her hair around his fingers.

What was crazy was the fact that right now he was standing there, touching her, telling her he missed her. And she felt . . . nothing. Not the searing rage that had burned in her chest for months and months after the breakup, not the bone-bruising sadness and sense of loss. She felt nothing.

"How's Erica?" Greer asked.

He quirked an eyebrow, then shook his head. "I suppose that's fair. I haven't seen Erica in over a year."

"I guess she must have healed you, huh?"

"You probably don't want to hear this, but Erica actually helped me a lot. Helped me understand myself, what drives me, why I have problems connecting with people."

"You didn't seem to have any problem connecting with her that morning I walked in on the two of you," Greer said.

His face changed and the charming mask slipped, just a little. "I see you haven't changed. Still want to point fingers, lay blame. Okay. I get it. I guess that's the reason you're alone. Why you'll probably always be alone."

"How do you know I'm alone?" she asked, surprised.

He took a step backwards. "Forget it. I thought maybe there was a chance for us. My bad."

"No, seriously," Greer said. "What? You were checking me out?"

"I saw the stories in the trades, heard the talk. After that fire up in Paso Robles. I actually felt bad for you. And then I saw Lise's obituary. I really did call, you know."

"Okay. Thanks, I guess."

"Never mind." He made a dismissive gesture. "Run along after Mayor McCheese."

"Don't call him that," Greer said.

He raised that eyebrow again. "So it's like that. Wow, Greer. What? You've gone native?"

"Maybe. Maybe I've finally got some skin in the game."

49

Eb pounded the steering wheel with his fist. He'd blown it with Greer. Again. And why? Because he was angry and disgusted — at himself, for failing to see the handwriting on the wall. At all the Vanessa Littrells and Bryce Levys of the world. And especially at all the slick-haired Sawyer the lawyers of the world.

He could still see the stung look on Greer's face, as though he'd hauled off and slapped her, back there on Seahorse Key.

Why had he insinuated she'd known her old boyfriend would be at the meeting? He'd seen her face when she encountered him. Her face had gone pale and still, two bright pink spots blooming on her cheeks. Almost like that first morning in her room at the motel, when she'd spotted the roach on her pillow.

So why lash out at her? Why blame Greer when he was the one to blame? Clearly he'd been outgunned back at Vanessa's house.

He pounded the steering wheel again, glanced at the speedometer, and realized that in his anger he'd floored it and was now doing nearly eighty. It wouldn't do to have one of Arnelle Bottoms's officers pull him over for speeding.

Eb eased off the gas pedal, but he couldn't stop thinking about Greer.

50

Greer was so absorbed in the legal complexities of the city's fire code that the sharp rapping on her motel room door caused her to literally leap off the bed.

"Hey, it's me," CeeJay said in a low voice. "Let me in, okay?"

She unfastened the chain latch and CeeJay pushed her way inside, closing and locking the door behind her. She was dressed in her bikini, with a towel wrapped around her waist.

"Can I hang out in here for a while?"

"What's going on?" Greer asked.

"Just some creeper hitting on me," CeeJay said, moving over to the window, where she parted the venetian blind slats to peer out into the corridor.

"Creepers hit on you all day, every day," Greer said.

"Right. Usually, I handle this stuff. I either shut a guy down or, sometimes, I just roll with it, to see if he can come up with something original. But this guy would not let up."

She closed the blind and stepped back from the window. "Okay, he's gone. I just saw him leave on a golf cart."

"Who was it? Somebody on the crew?"

CeeJay moved to the bathroom, where she was combing her damp hair. "I don't think so. I've never seen him around before. I was swimming laps, hoping my new fella would happen along and decide to join me. Minding my own business, right? And I got the sensation that I was being watched. But there was nobody around. And then I saw the guy. He was on one of the chaise lounges, in the corner by that one big clump of palm trees, and he was sitting there, watching me, drinking beer. He'd drink one down, throw the bottle in the bushes, then open another one. I could hear the bottles clinking as he tossed 'em.

"It spooked me so bad I kept swimming, hoping somebody would come along. Finally my legs were cramping up, so I got out of the pool, and this guy is standing there, holding my towel, like he's going to dry me off."

"Eww," Greer said.

"I tell him no thanks, and then he starts rubbing my back with the towel!"

"Double eww."

"I take my towel and walk over to the chair where I left my stuff, and he's right there, hitting on me, offering me one of his beers.

Wants to know if I'm working on the movie, if I'm staying here. I'm giving him no information, of course, just being vague. I tell him I'm waiting for my boyfriend to join me, but he still doesn't take the hint. Finally, the guy is acting so sketchy I tell him I have to go because I have an important business call to make. I grab my stuff and start heading for my room, then I realize he's following me!"

"So you lead him to my door?" Greer asked. She went back to the window and peeked outside, but the corridor was deserted.

"Sorry. I didn't know what else to do. I figured he wasn't going to break in on two of us."

"What did he look like?"

"Big, muscle-bound type. With a little pigtail. Like, in another life, somebody who's not me would consider him good-looking." CeeJay shuddered.

Greer sat back down on the bed where she'd been working. "That's Jared Thibadeaux."

"Eb's brother?"

"And Allie's dad. He's staying here. I wonder if I should let Ginny know he was bothering one of the guests here?"

"No," CeeJay said quickly. "It's no biggie. . ."

She sat down on the only chair in the room and pointed at the cardboard pizza box on the dresser. "I thought you hated the pizza place."

"I do, but this was a desperation dinner. After the meeting at Vanessa's today, I'm so behind on work it's pathetic."

"How did it go?"

"That depends on your perspective. If you're Bryce and Vanessa, it went great. They got everything they wanted, and more. If you're Eb, it went lousy."

"But how was it for you?"

Greer uncapped a bottle of water and took a drink. "It was . . . different. I knew Vanessa had hired a lawyer from L.A. that Bryce recommended. What I didn't know was that it was Sawyer."

CeeJay whipped her head around. "No way!"

"Way."

"I would have liked to have seen that," Cee-Jay said with a chuckle.

"It wasn't pretty. I nearly wet my pants when I got to the house and Vanessa casually mentioned his name. It was all I could do to pretend I was cool. And then it got worse. Sawyer basically mowed Eb down, buried him in a blizzard of legalese — writ of mandamus, conflict of interest, lease termination. He did everything but slice Eb up and serve him on a platter with a slice of lemon."

CeeJay was fastening a bath towel around her damp hair. She looked like a movie star.

She always looked like a movie star.

"How did Eb take it?"

Greer shook her head, remembering the way he'd looked at her back at Seahorse Key. "He thinks I had something to do with bringing Sawyer out here to humiliate him and get that damned demo permit."

"Oh man," CeeJay said. "That sucks." She sat down on the bed next to Greer and crossed her legs Indian style. She nudged Greer in the ribs. "So. How did he look?"

"Eb? He looked like he'd been run over by a bulldozer."

"No. Sawyer."

"He looked okay. Some gray in his hair . . . just enough to make him look distinguished."

"Knowing that weasel, he probably has it colored that way."

Greer laughed. "He wanted me to go to dinner. I begged off."

"Good for you. What else?"

"He told me he's not with Erica anymore but that, thanks to her, he has a whole new level of connectedness."

"Whole new level of bullshit, more like," CeeJay said. "What a waste of a penis that guy is."

"It was good on one level, though," Greer said. "It made me realize how over him I am."

CeeJay patted her on the knee. "That's my girl. But what about Eb?"

"Nothing. The good news is I'm over

Sawyer. The bad news is I have a schoolgirl crush on a guy who won't give me the time of day."

"Oh, honey. He'll come around. How could he resist a package like you?"

"Same old story. I am *so* messed up." Greer gave her best friend a crooked smile. "Hey. Maybe I should call Erica. I bet she could help me feel connected and fix me right up."

"Ha!" CeeJay flipped the lid on the pizza box, looked inside, and shuddered. "Enough of this moping around about boys. Let's go get some real food. I'll even buy."

"I can't," Greer said with a sigh. "I've got a ton of paperwork to do before the demo scene."

"Bryce is really going to blow up that cool old casino, huh?"

"That's what he says. Thanks to Sawyer, it looks like it's going to happen. Vanessa is calling the shots. Eb signed the permit. Jake Newman is here, checking it out for the big blow."

"What about Sherrie Seelinger? I thought she was threatening to shut off the money fountain."

"As far as I know, the blow is a go."

The yellow fluorescent light in Eb Thibadeaux's office in the Hometown Market flickered and buzzed. He had a stack of invoices to check, and e-mails about city business that needed to be answered, but instead he'd been researching historic preservation guidelines on the Internet, grasping at some straw that might help save the casino.

"Eb?" Bobby Stephens, the store's assistant manager, stood in the open doorway. He was young, not even thirty, but Bobby was a local kid who'd worked his way up from bag boy to management. Right now he looked supremely uncomfortable.

"Hey, Bobby. What's shaking?" Eb motioned for the manager to sit down, but Bobby darted forward and placed a stack of cash register receipts on the desktop, each with a hastily scrawled signature on the bottom.

"What's this?"

"Uh, well, your brother Jared's been coming in this week, buying groceries, and he, uh, said he'd cleared it with you to just sign the receipts. He said your family always had a house account here. Roseanne, she didn't know any different, so she's been letting him do it, but I thought maybe I should check with you."

Eb leafed through the receipts. His brother's purchases came as no surprise. Four cartons of cigarettes, lunch meat, bread, Doritos, deli stuff, and three cases of beer. Imported beer. In all, Jared had managed to charge nearly three hundred dollars' worth of supplies in just a few days' time.

He felt a slow burn in his gut.

"Thanks, Bobby," he said finally. "I'll handle this. But let Roseanne and the other girls know, the next time Jared comes in here, we don't have house accounts, and there's no credit. If he has any questions, tell them to send him to me."

"Right." Bobby nodded and backed out the doorway.

He was in the back room, using a box cutter to open cases of canned goods that had come in on the delivery truck earlier in the day, when he heard his cell phone ringing in the office. Eb hurried to the desk, and he felt a flutter of happiness when he saw the caller ID screen. Allie Thibadeaux.

"Hey, Al," he said.

"Hey, bro. Sorry, it's me, not Allie. How 'bout giving me a ride home?" His brother's voice was thick, the words slurred. "The damned golf cart ran out of juice and I'm kinda stranded."

Eb's first impulse was to disconnect. If Jared was stranded, let him stay that way. Maybe he'd wander away and never find his way back.

"Where are you?"

"Aw hell, I'm not sure. Lemme see. It's been a long time since I was home, you know? Okay. Yeah. I'm standing in front of Old Man Crowley's house."

"Crowley? You're over on Palmetto? What are you doing way over there?"

"Shit. I dunno."

There was a pause. Eb heard the phone drop, and the line went dead. A moment later, Jared called back.

"Sorry. Had to take a leak. Look, if you're gonna get all pissy about it, I'll just call Gin."

"No. Stay right there," Eb said. "I'm on my way."

Palmetto was a narrow street, and the live oaks on either side made a thick canopy of branches that threatened to blot out what little moonlight seeped through the leaves.

Eb's headlights picked up the shadowy image of a golf cart pulled over on the dirt shoulder of the asphalt. He parked the truck behind the cart and walked over. Jared was draped over the steering wheel, passed out, snoring.

Eb shook him by the shoulder. "Jared! Wake up. Let's go!"

Jared raised his head slowly. A trickle of drool made a trail down his meaty chin. "Hey. Gimme a minute, can you?" He yawned expansively, and Eb had to step back from the blast of beer breath.

He grabbed Jared by the elbow and pulled him from the cart. Jared stumbled on a tree root, cussed, regained his balance, and pushed away the arm Eb offered. "I'm fine.

Just a little tired is all."

"You're drunk is all," Eb shot back. He opened the truck's passenger-side door, and Jared stood there, not moving.

"Come on, dammit. I don't have all night."

"What about the golf cart? Who's gonna drive it?"

"I'll come over in the morning with a new battery and Gin can ride it back to the motel."

"No, man," Jared protested. "Somebody will rip it off."

"Just get in the truck, okay?"

Eb went around and got behind the wheel and Jared finally followed suit.

"If somebody rips off that cart, I'm not taking the blame," he persisted.

"This is Cypress Key, not the Starke correctional institution," Eb snapped. "The only person ripping anybody off around here is you." He started the truck.

"What's that supposed to mean?" Jared said.

"It means you managed to charge three hundred bucks' worth of beer, bologna, and smokes in my store this week," Eb said.

"Hey, I'm good for it," Jared said, leaning back against the headrest. "We're family, right?"

"Right," Eb said, glancing at his brother.

Jared had the window rolled down.

"Where were you going tonight?" Eb asked.

But he had a feeling he already knew.

"Just for a ride. Change of scenery. Fucking boring hanging out all day at the motel."

"Maybe you could try actually working, instead of lounging around sponging off Gin and me," Eb said.

"Whatever. I am working on something. Something big." Jared brought a cheap steno notebook from his hip pocket and waved it at his brother. "It's all right here."

"Oh yes," Eb said, his voice dripping sarcasm. *"The Jared Thibadeaux Story: Justice Denied."*

"Fuck you, bro." Jared pointed. "Do me a favor, turn here."

For reasons he couldn't fathom, Eb made the turn. He slowed down, and finally, in the middle of the next block, he pulled to the side of the road. It was after ten. Most of the houses on the street were dark, but behind some windows he could see the blue-white blur of a television screen.

The houses on this block were modest cottages, wood frame with asphalt shingles and single-car garages. They'd been built after the war, by returning veterans who were starting families and building new lives. It was not the fanciest street in Cypress Key, but it wasn't the worst, either.

He turned and looked at his brother, who was hanging halfway out of the window, staring into the dark.

"You were trying to find the old house?"

Jared's shoulders lifted briefly. His voice was muffled. "Yeah. I guess." He turned and looked at Eb, and tears glittered in his bloodshot eyes. "Those were good times, you know? The old man burning steaks on the grill on Sundays? Mom, you know, cooking. Me and you throwing the ball around in the front yard. I miss that."

Jared gestured toward their old house. "Would you look at this place? It shrunk!"

The house needed paint and the yard needed trimming. A bicycle and a yellow and red plastic ride-on toy leaned against the front porch. The vehicles in the driveway were at least twenty years old — a white Toyota Corolla and a rusting brown pickup with a boat trailer hitched to it.

Jared started to open his door, and Eb reached across the bench seat and hauled his brother back by the belt on his pants.

"What?' Jared protested. "I just wanted to see the old house. Man, it's gone to seed. Remember, Pop would make us mow every Saturday, come hell or high water. I wonder what kind of white trash lives here now, lets it get like this?"

Eb clenched the steering wheel with both hands. He started the truck and eased down the block.

"Place looks like shit." Jared was still looking backwards at the old home place.

"The new owner is a clammer. His name is Sosebee. He's got three kids and he's also a volunteer fireman." Eb said. "I sold him the house, if you want to know."

"Maybe I'll buy it back, when I sell my screenplay. That'd be righteous, huh? Surprise Mom and Dad, get their old place back for 'em?"

Eb clamped his lips together. It was a waste of breath to explain to a drunk that nearly all the proceeds from the sale of their parents' home of thirty years had gone to paying off Jared's legal bills. Why point out that their dad could no longer push a mower or wield a paintbrush? Or remember his sons' names.

He heard a soft snore. "Yeah, bro," Eb muttered, glancing over at his slumbering sibling. "Keep on dreaming."

51

"Jared!" Eb stood beside the open passenger door. His brother slumped sideways onto the seat. Eb shook him by the shoulder. "Wake up! Come on. We're home."

"Huh?" Jared sat up and yawned another blast of stale beer breath.

Eb yanked at his brother's arm. "Out! We're back at the motel."

Jared jerked his arm away. "I'm coming. Ease up, would you?" He swung his legs out of the truck and had to hold on to the truck bed to get his balance.

"*You* ease up," Eb said tersely. "I've had a long day, and I've got a longer one tomorrow. And I'm tired of babysitting you."

"Fuck you, asshole!" Jared yelled. His voice echoed across the empty parking lot. "Just go the fuck away, okay? I don't need a baby-sitter!"

A moment later the light snapped on in front of the manager's apartment and Ginny Buckalew came flying across the parking lot.

She was dressed in a cotton bathrobe and slippers, and she had fire in her eyes.

"Quiet down, Jared," she ordered.

"Sorry, Gin," Jared said in a loud stage whisper, giving her a dopey grin. He looped an arm around her shoulders. "You're not mad at me, are you, Gin-Gin?"

She shrugged off his embrace. "You're drunk," she said flatly. She glanced over at the truck, and then at Eb. "Where'd you find him? And what did he do with my golf cart?"

"Out of juice!" Jared hollered, leaning against the pickup bed. "No more juice for Gin!"

He started to walk away, but Eb grabbed him by the belt. "Where do you think you're going?"

"Left my cooler over by the pool. I need a beer, man."

"It's not your beer, it's mine. And you're done for the night," Eb said. He turned back to his aunt. "He ran the battery down. I had to leave the cart over on Palmetto, a couple blocks from Mom and Dad's old place. We can take a battery over there in the morning and bring it back here," Eb said. "In the meantime, let's get him to his room before he wakes up everybody in the motel."

He turned to take his brother's arm, but in that moment Jared danced away, just out of his reach. He took off fast, in the direction of the pool and patio.

"Go get him, please, Eb," Ginny pleaded.

Jared stood over the large red cooler, up to his elbow in ice water. "Hey, man," he hollered, his voice echoing over the pool and the concrete patio. "Who took my last beer?"

A light snapped on three doors down, and a head popped out the door. "Shut up, asshole," the man called. "People are trying to sleep."

Eb caught up to Jared and clamped his arms on the big man's shoulders. "Come on, Jared, let's go. No more beer tonight." But Jared was bigger. And drunker.

"Hey, motherfucker!" Jared shook him off and started down the walkway toward the man who had called. "Did you take my beer?"

The door slammed and they heard the metallic sound of a dead bolt ramming home. Jared pounded on the door. "Talking to you, asshole!"

The voice from inside the room was muffled. "I'm calling the cops."

Eb threw an arm around Jared's neck and tightened it across his windpipe. He put his lips against his brother's ear. "When the cops come, I'm turning you over to them. Drunk and disorderly. You can go back to jail, and I'll be damned if I'll bail you out."

He squeezed and Jared gasped for air.

"Okay," Jared wheezed. "Leggo."

Eb released the pressure, but shoved his

brother away from the door.

Ginny hurried down the corridor. "Get him out of here," she said, keeping her voice low. Suddenly, the fight had gone out of Jared. He slumped against the block wall.

"Jesus," Eb said, his voice thick with disgust. "He's passed out cold again."

Greer heard the commotion coming from the courtyard. She opened her door, looked down the corridor, and saw Ginny Buckalew and Eb half walking, half dragging the unconscious Jared Thibadeaux in the direction of the laundry room.

She ran down the corridor. Ginny was a head and a half shorter than her nephew, and his body nearly engulfed hers.

"Let me help," Greer said breathlessly. She took Jared's arm and slung it over her own shoulder, and Ginny stepped away. Jared swayed and then listed to the right, throwing most of his weight on his brother's shoulder.

"I've got him," Eb said, frowning.

"Don't be a jerk," Greer said. "He outweighs you by at least eighty pounds. Let me help you get him to his room."

They heard a door opening behind them, and footsteps.

Allie Thibadeaux's eyes were wide as saucers. She was barefoot, dressed in an oversize Cypress Key High football jersey. "Dad!"

"Allie, go back to the apartment," Ginny

said quickly.

"What's wrong with him?" Allie darted in front of them. She touched her father's cheek. "Dad?" She glared at Eb. "What happened to him? Did you beat him up, like you did Kregg?"

"Come on, Al," Ginny put an arm around her great-niece's shoulder. "He'll be okay. He just needs to sleep it off."

Jared's head jerked upright. "Hey, Allie baby," he said softly.

Allie's body stiffened. "You're drunk."

"Naw," Jared protested. "Just a little buzzed, that's all." He straightened. "Your uncle and I were out on the town. We went by the old house, just catching up on old times." He slid out of Eb's grasp, and then Greer's. "Right, bro?"

"Right," Eb said.

Greer glanced from one brother to the other, holding her breath to see what would happen next. Jared swayed, then righted himself.

Allie leaned in, sniffed her father's breath. "You reek." She backtracked a step. She pointed at the crotch of Jared's jeans, and a large, spreading damp stain. "Oh my God. Did you wet your pants?" She made a soft gagging noise and turned away.

"Go on to bed, Allie," Eb said wearily. "We got this."

■ ■ ■ ■

Somehow, between them, Eb and Greer managed to drag Jared down the corridor, in the direction of his room.

"Wait," Jared stopped. He patted his pockets. "Lost my key."

"I've got a master," Eb said. Jared slouched against the wall while Eb unlocked the door. Greer took Jared's arm and led him into the darkened room.

Eb turned on the light. The room was tiny, with room for a single bed, a desk, a chair, and a dresser. The bathroom had the usual fixtures, plus a dorm-size refrigerator topped with a toaster oven. Greer was taken aback by how neat it was. She'd assumed a sloppy drunk made for a sloppy guest.

There was a single cheap suitcase standing in as a nightstand beside the bed, which was made up with a flat pillow and a blanket. Hooks on the back of the wall held a pair of jeans and a couple of shirts. The linoleum floor was swept clean, and a pair of inexpensive tennis shoes was lined up at the foot of the bed.

Jared sank down onto the bed and turned toward the wall.

Eb stood, looking down at him, shaking his head in dismay. He jerked the blanket from beneath his brother's feet and draped it over him.

"Let's go," he said, turning to Greer.

"You don't want to try to undress him . . . or anything?"

"I've had enough of being my brother's keeper for one day," Eb said. He held the door open, Greer stepped into the corridor, and he snapped the light off and closed the door again.

They walked down the narrow corridor, just a few inches apart. When they came to the door of Greer's room, Eb cleared his throat.

"Uh, listen. About what I said earlier today, out at Seahorse Key? That was a really crappy thing to say. I saw your face when you walked in the room and saw that guy. Sawyer the lawyer. You were blindsided. Same as me."

Greer nodded. "I was. But I understand. He really piled it on you."

"Looked like he was enjoying himself," Eb said.

"Trust me. He was having the time of his life, beating you down. It's just the kind of thing he gets off on."

He gave her a look that was almost shy. "Would you want to go get a drink, and maybe something to eat? I never had any dinner."

"It's after ten," Greer reminded him. "You Cypress Key folks roll up the streets pretty early."

"I could probably cook something. . . ." Eb said, his voice trailing off.

"Tell you what. I've got half a cold, greasy pizza in my room, and a bottle of almost drinkable red wine."

"I couldn't eat your pizza. . . ."

"Final offer," Greer said. "If it's any consolation, this is the worst pizza in the world."

"Since you put it like that," Eb said.

She puttered around the room, finding a plate to heat up the pizza, bringing plastic cups and the corkscrew she'd bought at the liquor store where she'd gotten the wine. He sat back in the same chair CeeJay had used earlier, watching her.

"This is kind of weird, being in your room like this," Eb said, trying to make conversation. "Seeing as it's where we first met."

Greer laughed. "Yeah, no wonder we've had such a rocky time. I really made a great first impression, didn't I?"

She opened the wine and poured him a cup.

"You weren't so bad. And I loved your outfit that morning."

"My outfit?" That's when she remembered she'd run out of the room in an oversize T-shirt and not much more, screaming at him to get the cockroach.

"Oh." Her face went pink. The microwave dinged and she was glad to have an excuse to switch into hostess mode. She slid the pizza onto a paper plate. He took a bite, chewed, stood up, and unceremoniously dumped the entire plate into the trash.

"I should speak to the chief about shutting that joint down. Cite them for impersonating an Italian or something. The frozen Tombstone pizzas I sell at the market are better than that crap," Eb said, taking a gulp of wine to wash away the taste.

"Pretty sure that crap *is* frozen," Greer said. She hoisted her cup in a toast of agreement and drank. "I walk by there on the way to the office all the time, and it just struck me today that I've never seen anybody in there touching anything that looks remotely like pizza dough."

"We'll look into it," Eb said gravely.

"I'm really kind of surprised there aren't more decent restaurants in town," Greer said. "The Inn does a great business, and Tony's is always crowded, so it's not like the demographic couldn't support another good place."

"That's another one of our challenges," Eb admitted. "Bringing in new businesses. In the past couple months I've shown a young couple from Orlando half a dozen downtown spaces that would be great for a restaurant they want to open. They're both professionally trained chefs, and they've got a good concept — healthy Southern seafood. But the problem is, they can't afford what the landlord wants to charge."

"Who's the landlord?" Greer asked.

"Littrell Limited," Eb said, with a sigh. "Vanessa owns or controls nearly two blocks of prime commercial property on Pine Street. She won't fix up the properties, and the price she's demanding for rents are prohibitive. Tenants come in, open a business, make whatever improvements they can afford, but none of them can sustain themselves paying those kinds of exorbitant rents. They stay six months and then it's 'Peace out.' "

"You'd think it would be in her own best interest to do whatever it takes to keep her properties rented," Greer said, sipping her wine.

"You'd think that, but you'd be wrong," Eb said. "Vanessa's a bottom-feeder, pure and simple. The churn works in her favor. Businesses are paid up on their rent, lots of them make improvements with plumbing, electrical, whatever, then they close up shop. She gets to keep the rent — and the improvements. And she can show a loss on her taxes. She's got no incentive to do business any other way."

"Except this is her hometown, and she's part of this community," Greer said. She poured herself some more wine.

He frowned and shook his head. "Not really. And that's the problem. Vanessa was picked on as a kid, so her parents sent her away to boarding school, and then she went out of state to college. I don't believe she really feels any connection to Cypress Key. Except as a revenue stream."

"She told me that, after she had a nose job, the girls all hated her for being cute, and the boys loved her, so the girls had all that much more to hate her for," Greer volunteered.

"Vanessa told you that?"

"Female bonding," Greer admitted. "When I first arrived at Cypress Key and we both thought we could help each other out. We were united in our contempt for Eb Thibadeaux."

"Me?" He laughed and did a mock bow. "I'm not worthy."

"I got the feeling she had a crush on you and it was not reciprocated," Greer said. "Which could explain why she now wants to squash you under her heel. Like a bug."

"Like a cockroach?" Eb took his glasses off and polished them on the hem of his shirt.

"Don't do that," Greer said sharply.

"What?" Eb looked down at his glasses, then put them on again. He peered over at her. "I can't clean off my glasses? Is this some fetish you have, like the bug thing?"

"No." She sat up straight on the bed, feeling just the slightest bit tipsy.

"What is it?"

She shook her head. "It's nothing. Stupid. Forget I said anything."

Eb set his cup of wine down on the night-stand. He moved over to the bed and sat down, only inches away from her. She took another sip of wine. He took the cup from her hand and carefully placed it on the night-stand. She looked at him, shook her head helplessly.

He leaned his forehead against hers. She closed her eyes. "Tell me you don't want me," he whispered. "Tell me to go home and forget about you."

His breath was warm on her cheek. He stroked her cheek, kissed her ear. She'd had just enough wine to tell the truth. She opened her eyes and stared into his pale gray ones. "I can't," she said, shaking her head nervously. "God help me, I don't want you to go."

52

Eb went to the door, locked it, and fastened the dead bolt. He switched off the overhead light.

"What are you doing?" Greer asked. She turned on the lamp on the nightstand and took another gulp of wine. He sat down beside her on the bed and put his arms around her.

He kissed her and nudged her backwards until she was flat on the bed. He propped himself up on one elbow and smiled down at her. "If we're really doing this, I don't want you running out on me in the middle of the night." He traced the outline of her cheek with his fingertip. She caught his hand in hers and kissed it.

"No second thoughts this time?" he asked.

Greer took a deep breath. "None. But what about you?" Before he could answer, she pulled him down and kissed him. He worked his knee between her legs, and tugged her T-shirt upwards. She slid her hands up under his shirt and rested the palm of her hand lightly on his chest, feeling the steady beat of his heart. He reached around her back, fumbling with her bra.

"Um . . ." Greer stopped.

"What?"

She giggled nervously. "It's just that we're not at your place. Remember? I don't keep a stash of condoms here. Or cookies."

Eb rolled over on his left hip and took his billfold from the pocket of his jeans. "Not a problem." He shook a foil-wrapped square onto the bedspread.

"For me?" Greer pulled him toward her. "That's so sweet."

"After the last time, I put one in there. You know, just in case." He chuckled. "I think that's the first time I've carried a condom around in my billfold since I was fifteen years old."

She kissed his ear. "And did you ever get to use it?"

"Not that one. Unlike my brother, I was sort of a late bloomer. I think it disintegrated from old age by the time I finally got around to needing one."

"Let's hope this one doesn't suffer the same fate," Greer said solemnly. She reached past him and turned off the lamp.

They kissed and touched and got tangled in the sheets. Finally, Eb rolled away from her, and she heard the rip of foil.

She sat up in bed and ran a finger down his spine. She kissed the back of his neck and he leaned against her. "I just thought of something."

"I'm not going for ice cream," he said, his voice husky.

"If you've been carrying that condom around with you, that means you thought there'd be a next time."

He turned and gently pushed her onto her back. "I was hoping." He kissed her collarbone. "Counting on it." He cupped her breast and ran his tongue across the nipple.

"I thought you hated me. You basically told me you did," Greer said, running her hands down his smooth back.

He parted her legs with his knee and slid into her. "I lied."

They both dozed off, wedged in together on the lumpy double bed. Sometime around one they heard a door open and close down the corridor. Eb jumped out of bed and ran to the window, peeking out through the venetian blind slats.

Greer sat up. "That wasn't Jared, was it?"

He turned and crawled back into bed. "No. I was afraid of the same thing, but it was just the woman in number twelve, with a puppy on a leash."

"I didn't know you allow pets," Greer said.

"We don't, but that puppy is probably a whole lot less trouble than my brother."

Eb sighed and rolled onto his back, and Greer rested her head on his chest.

"What are you going to do about Jared?" she asked, knowing it was on his mind.

"Not sure, but we're going to have to do something. He can't stay here much longer. Not after tonight."

Greer sighed. "I wasn't going to tell you this, but earlier this evening Jared was hitting on CeeJay, to the point it made her really uncomfortable. She actually came in here to hide out, because she didn't want him knowing which room was hers."

"Dammit. I'm glad you told me, though. We can't have him harassing our guests. Ginny was afraid something like this would happen."

"I'm sorry," Greer said. "CeeJay said she was swimming laps and she got that creepy feeling that she was being watched. She finally saw him sitting on a chair under that big clump of palm trees. She said he was drinking one beer after another, then pitching the empty bottles into the shrubbery."

Eb stroked her hair for a while.

"I was so pissed at him tonight, when he was hollering and carrying on out there, I came this close to choking him out. Maybe I should have."

She turned to look at him. "You wouldn't

have done that. He's your brother."

"He's a career fuckup," Eb said bluntly.

"He's only been out of prison a week," she pointed out. "He's probably just cutting loose. Maybe he'll change after all this."

"Never. This is who Jared is."

Greer was silent. With her head on his warm chest, she could feel his heart beating. But once again she couldn't really understand how he could love Allie so deeply and at the same time hate his own brother so thoroughly.

"I get that he messed up," she said finally. "But he went to prison. He must have done something right there, to earn early release. And don't forget, he did give you and Ginny custody of Allie."

Eb's voice was low but hard edged. "Jared may have paid his debt to the state but he'll never repay my parents. They paid for his lawyers, for the appeals, the private investigators, all of it. It broke them, financially and emotionally."

"I didn't know," Greer said.

"He was headed over to our folks' old house tonight, when the golf cart's battery died," Eb said. "He was drunk and couldn't even find his way to the house we lived in for thirty years. The ironic thing is, if it hadn't been for Jared, my parents might still be living there."

"What do you mean?"

"They owned the house free and clear, but after Jared's arrest Dad mortgaged it. Plus they spent nearly every dime in Dad's retirement account. I managed to sell the house for them, but they owed more than it was worth."

"So sad," Greer said. "For all of you."

"That's why they're living in a crappy one bedroom 'villa' hours away from their lifelong home and their only grandchild. That, and the fact that my mother couldn't hold up her head in Cypress Key when it was all said and done. She was so ashamed of Jared."

"Surely people here wouldn't judge them by what happened with Jared," Greer said. "Didn't you say he was arrested clear across the state?"

"Doesn't matter," Eb said. "At the trial, his teachers, our neighbors, my parents' minister, his football coach, they all showed up to be character witnesses. And they were all set to tell the judge what a good, solid citizen Jared Thibadeaux was. But then they sat in that courtroom and watched the video. They saw their hometown boy stuffing twenty dollar bills in his pockets like any other two-bit hustler. They were sitting there when Jared pled out. He stood up in court, stared at his shoes, and admitted to everything he'd already sworn he didn't do."

They heard a door open and close down the hallway again.

Eb sat up abruptly. He went to the window and looked out into the corridor one more time, his shoulders tense.

"Just the lady with the puppy again," he said. "And that's another reason Jared's got to go. I'm sure Gin isn't getting any sleep tonight, either, wondering what he'll do next."

He went into the bathroom and came back a moment later with two cups of water. "Thanks," Greer said, sipping hers.

"You know," she said, pulling him back down beside her, "everybody else's family issues always look so uncomplicated, compared to mine. I should know better by now."

Eb slipped his arms around her and nuzzled her neck.

"Before she died," Greer said, "my mother insisted I should contact my dad. She was ready to forgive and move on. She *had* moved on. Clint told me this week she'd been planning a trip out here to see him, before she got sick."

Greer thought back to one of the last conversations she'd had with Lise about Clint. The hospice nurses had set up the apartment with a hospital bed and all the other depressing equipment needed to keep the dying woman comfortable, including a morphine pump that her mother could activate when necessary.

A couple nights before the end, Greer had been dozing in a chair beside the bed. She'd assumed Lise was sleeping, too, but that night her mother was restless.

"Do me a favor?" she'd asked, turning hollow eyes on her daughter.

"Whatever you want," Greer replied.

"Bottom drawer of my nightstand, there's an envelope. Could you get it for me?"

The envelope was addressed to Lise, with a Florida return address Greer didn't recognize and a three-month-old postmark. Lise opened the envelope and a photograph fell onto the white blanket. She turned it over and smiled, then handed it to Greer.

The photo was one she'd never seen, one of those bad eighties studio specials from Sears, Roebuck. It was a color portrait of the Happy Hennessys: Clint with his gleaming dark handlebar mustache and sideburns; Lise with her poufed-out, bleached, teased, and tangled big hair; and little Greer, wearing a pink dress with a unicorn and rainbow print, and a giant pink bow plunked in the middle of her blond ringlets.

"There is so much wrong in this picture, I don't even know where to begin," Greer said. "The hair, the clothes. My God, are those shoulder pads on your dress?"

"We thought we were very hip, very *Dynasty*," Lise said serenely.

"I can't believe you fell in love with a man who had a mullet *and* a pornstar 'stache. I've

533

never seen this picture before. Where'd you get it?"

"Clint sent it to me, just recently," Lise said. "I'd never seen it either. We went to Sears to have the portrait made but, a couple days after that, we had that last big fight and we broke up. He must have gone back to the studio and picked them up. I'd forgotten all about them."

"Should have forgotten about him, too," Greer sniped.

"No," Lise shook her head. "I don't want to forget him. Those were good times. We had you, a little house. Mostly we were happy."

"And then you weren't, and he walked out," Greer reminded her.

Lise sighed. "I wish you wouldn't keep harping on that. It doesn't matter who was right and who was wrong. I thought it did, back then, but what did I know? I'd give anything to take back all the stupid stuff we said." She clutched Greer's hand. "I'd give anything for you to have gotten to know your dad. It's not too late."

But Greer was sure it was too late. She'd made some vague assurances, and Lise had drifted off to sleep again.

"And what about you?" Eb asked. "Can you be as generous minded as your mother?"

That gave Greer a chuckle. "I wish you could have met Lise. She was not your textbook mom, that's for sure. She was

534

complicated, but amazing. I don't think I ever realized just how special she was, until she was gone."

Eb took her hand in his and lightly kissed her knuckles. "She must have been pretty special to have raised a daughter like you."

Greer turned around to face him. "You're just saying that because you want to get into my pants. Again."

"You don't seem to be wearing any pants," Eb said. "But if you insist, I do happen to have a little something in my billfold."

The alarm on her cell phone rang at 6:00 a.m. Eb's arm was flung over her bare breasts, his leg rested on top of her thigh. She inched toward the nightstand, groping for the phone, but he reached it first and tapped the Off icon.

He kissed her ear and tried to roll her toward him.

"No-o-o," she groaned. "Baby, I've got to go to work."

"It's dark," he murmured. "Can't make a movie in the dark. Don't go."

She kissed his forehead, then swung her legs over the side of the bed. "Believe me, I wish I didn't have to."

He snaked an arm around her waist. "What time do you have to be at the casino?"

"Seven o'clock call, which means I need to be there now."

He flopped back onto the bed, grabbed the pillow she'd abandoned, and propped it behind his head.

"Damn, these pillows are pathetic." He tossed the pillow aside and sat up. "And the mattress is even worse."

"I could have told you that weeks ago," Greer said. She yanked open a dresser drawer and grabbed clean clothes, then moved toward the bathroom.

Eb scooped his clothes from the floor. "Guess I better get going too. I don't want Allie to see me sneaking out of here."

Greer poked her head around the door. "Hey. Look at that. We spent a whole night together and didn't even fight once."

He laughed and kissed her. "I call that progress. Can I buy you dinner tonight?"

"I'll call you when I get off work," she promised.

53

Greer was pacing off the perimeter of the casino blast site with the state fire marshal when her cell phone vibrated in her pocket. She'd set the ring to silent so she could concentrate, and she was annoyed by the disruption. She looked at the caller ID number but didn't recognize it, so she let the call roll over to voice mail.

The fire marshal's name was Samuel Stillwell. He was young, with an earnest face and the thickest Southern drawl she'd ever heard, so deep she had to keep asking him to repeat whole phrases.

"Blay-ust zahn?" she finally said, shaking her head. "I'm sorry. I'm not getting . . ."

"Sorry," he said. "I'm from Savannah, and I always assume folks know what I'm saying." He repeated the words slowly and deliberately, and this time she got it.

"Oh! Blast zone. Of course."

Her phone buzzed again, and this time when she looked at the caller ID screen it popped up as a call coming from Clinton Hennessy. She frowned at it.

"Please, go ahead and take your call," Stillwell said. "I need to call and check in with my office anyway."

He stepped into the shade of the casino, and Greer shrugged and tapped the Connect button.

"Greer? Is this Greer Hennessy?" The voice was male, but it didn't sound like Clint.

"This is Greer. Who's this?"

"My name is Wally Patterson. I work for your dad. I just tried calling you on my phone, but when you didn't answer I figured I'd try on Clint's phone."

"Look, Wally, I'm working right now, which is why I didn't take your first call. Why can't Clint call me himself if he needs to talk to me?"

"Uh, your dad's been in an accident. The thing is, along with some other stuff, he got a pretty bad concussion, and the doctors at the hospital say they need authorization from a family member to run some tests. As far as I know, you're all the family Clint's got."

Greer's knees were suddenly rubbery. She sank down onto a concrete bench near the railing overlooking the bay.

"Where is he?" she asked shakily. "What hospital?"

"Warren Memorial," Wally said. "Here in Williston. I can give you the address."

"No, text it to me, please. I don't have a paper and pencil with me," Greer said.

"So you'll come? Clint was conscious in the ambulance, and he told the EMTs they should try to find his kid."

"It's that serious?" Her stomach lurched.

"I'm not a doctor," Wally said. "Your dad's a tough old bird, but he got banged up pretty good in the wreck. If he comes around, can I tell him you're coming?"

Greer looked desperately around the pier. Her first instinct was to say no. There was so much work still to be done before the Monday shoot. What difference would it make if she didn't go? Let somebody else give authorization for any procedure Clint needed. Hospitals did that all the time, didn't they?

She clenched and unclenched her fists. She didn't need this in her life. This mess, this complication, this . . . annoyance.

"Yeah," she said, reluctantly. "I'll come."

She raised Zena on the radio. "Sorry about this, but I've got a family emergency. My father has been in an accident and I've got to get to the hospital in Williston where he's being treated. You'll have to take over."

"Oh no. Your dad was so cute the other day," Zena said. "Of course. I'll be right there."

"You'll have to finish up with the fire marshal, and make sure you understand everything he's telling you. He'll tell you what kind of notification we have to do with all the businesses and property owners on the pier, and within the blast zone. Then you can get started with that."

"I got it," Zena said. "Consider it done."

According to the Kia's GPS, the hospital was about an hour away. She tried calling Eb but only got his voice mail. She left a message, telling him where she was going and why.

But why was she going? The urgent nature of her father's friend's call had been enough to propel her into the car and put her on the road, but what would she accomplish by showing up at the hospital?

She stopped at a convenience store on the state highway, bought a cold drink, and sipped it while her gas tank was filling. She kept looking at her cell phone, hoping it would ring, that there would be news about her father. He was better, she didn't need to come. Didn't need to get involved.

When the gas tank was full she pulled slowly away from the pumps. She wanted to head west — back to Cypress Key, her job, her commitment there, and most of all, to Eb. Hadn't she promised him she'd stopped running away?

Clint's friend — was his name Wally? He'd said Clint asked the EMTs to contact his kid, his only family, to let her know about the accident.

Funny, in all of this, she'd never thought of Clint Hennessy as *her* family. Oh, technically, she knew it to be true. There was never any doubt that Clint was her biological father. Lise had showed her Clint's baby pictures, and even Greer could see the strong family resemblance. She had his DNA.

But family was not the same thing as biology. For most of her life, Lise and Dearie had been her family. Her only family. She might have yearned for more, but looking back on it now, they had been all the family she needed. Somehow these two strong women had managed to raise her, to clothe and feed and educate her, and to launch her into the world and into a career in the industry they had both loved. With Lise gone, all she had left was Dearie, still feisty at eighty-seven.

Lise. Those last months, watching her die, had been the hardest thing she'd ever gone through. A part of her still felt hollowed out from all the sadness that poured out of her during her mother's illness. Would she be forced to relive that experience all over again — but with a man she barely knew?

Her phone rang and she snatched it up.

"Hey, babe," CeeJay said. "Zena just told me about your father. So, you're really flying to his bedside?"

"I guess."

"Greer? You are, or you aren't. Which is it?"

"I'm on my way to the hospital. His friend said they need some kind of authorization to do more tests, or procedures, on Clint — I'm not even sure which. As soon as that's done, I'm out of there."

"Really?"

"Really," Greer said firmly. "To tell you the truth, I honestly don't know why I'm bothering."

"Keep telling yourself that," CeeJay said.

"What's that supposed to mean?" Greer's eyes darted back and forth on the road, always vigilant for bears. Or any other mammal that might wander onto the asphalt. She'd only been on the road for ten miles and already she'd spotted enough roadkill to fill a zoo.

"It means I think you care more about your old man than you want to admit."

"No," Greer said. "It means I'm afraid Lise would haunt me from her grave if I didn't go to the hospital to check on Clint. So I'm going. And I'll be back tonight." She hesitated, and then decided to throw her friend a crumb of information. "I actually have kind of a date."

"With the Professor?" CeeJay squealed into the phone.

"Calm down. Yes, with Eb. We, uh, sort of made up last night."

"Did that happen to involve makeup sex?"

"I'll never tell," Greer said. "By the way, I

let Eb know Jared was harassing you last night. I think he and Ginny are going to ask him to move out of the motel."

"I can't say he'll be missed," CeeJay said. "Let's catch up when you get back here."

The hospital was the smallest she'd ever seen, no bigger than the elementary school in Cypress Key, and it was even built in a similar architectural style.

She'd forgotten to ask exactly where Clint was being treated, but since she assumed he'd been taken by ambulance to the emergency room, she decided to start there, driving around to a side entrance with a neon EMER-GENCY sign.

A pair of automatic doors slid noiselessly open and she walked into a small, linoleum-tiled waiting area. The room was cold and smelled like antiseptic. A row of hard vinyl chairs faced a ceiling-mounted television, and a very young, very pregnant teenage girl sat on one of the chairs, with a hard-eyed woman on one side of her and a scared-looking boy on the other. The youngsters were holding hands.

A young male clerk in aqua hospital scrubs sat behind a reception desk, typing on a computer terminal. His name tag said "Mr. Gower."

"Hi. I'm looking for Clinton Hennessy? He

was brought in earlier today? He was in a car wreck?"

"Believe it or not, we had two car wrecks today. Was he the older gentleman?"

"Yes. He's uh . . ." Greer blushed. She had no idea how old Clint was. "He's in his seventies," she said finally.

Mr. Gower clicked some keys on the computer terminal, then looked up at her with a sad face. "You're his next of kin?"

Greer felt a stab of anxiety. She swallowed hard, waiting for the bad news. She'd spent a lot of time in hospitals lately and had never heard anything but bad news in one. That antiseptic smell brought it all back to her. All the hours sitting in rooms like this, waiting for test results.

Her mouth went dry. "Yes," she managed. "Is he . . ."

"He's back in curtain three." Mr. Gower pointed toward a set of swinging doors.

She felt suddenly dizzy. And nauseous. She held on to the laminated surface of the counter while the room swirled around her.

Mr. Gower's face was fuzzy. He ran around the counter, took her by the arm, and led her to one of the chairs. "Are you all right? Miss?"

She swallowed, trying to fight off the wave of nausea. Finally the room tilted back into the proper frame. "I guess I forgot to get lunch today."

"I'll be right back," the clerk said, and true

to his word, a minute later he was handing her a Fiber One bar and a Dr Pepper. "Let's get your blood sugar up," he said, sitting down beside her.

Greer chewed the bar and sipped the drink, and the dizziness subsided. "I'm okay," she said weakly. "Really. I've just had a long couple of days. Can I go back and see him now?"

"Let one of the nurses know if you feel dizzy again," he said. "We can't have you in a double room with your dad now, can we?"

The thought horrified her.

When Greer pulled the curtain aside she found a white-coated doctor, who had the darkest skin she'd ever seen, standing beside a hospital bed, taking the patient's pulse.

She assumed the patient was Clint, but it was hard to tell. The top portion of his head was swathed in a large bandage. Tufts of white hair stuck out above the bandage, and his jaws were covered with thick white stubble. An oxygen mask covered the lower portion of his face.

He looked, she thought, small and broken. The neck of his cotton hospital gown had slipped down, and his bony pink chest reminded her of an underfed broiler chicken. His arms and hands were crisscrossed with cuts and scrapes. His head lolled back against the pillow, eyes closed. He was either asleep or in a coma.

The doctor turned and smiled. His hair was a brilliant silver, and he had a tiny clipped mustache. "You're Greer? Clint's girl?"

The accent was foreign, Pakistani maybe?

"I'm Greer Hennessy," she said. He took her hand and pumped it vigorously.

"I'm Dr. Gupta. Nobody here can say my last name, so it's just Doc. I'm so glad you came, Greer. Your father will be very, very glad, too, when he wakes up and sees you here."

"How is he?"

She realized she was holding her breath.

"Lucky to be alive."

"Oh God. It's that bad?"

"No, no," Doc said quickly. "His injuries are not at all life threatening. I didn't mean it to sound like that. He has a concussion and, you can see, lots of cuts from broken glass. Also a cracked rib. If he were a younger man, without the medical issues Clint has, we would have discharged him already."

"What kind of medical issues does he have?"

Doc frowned. "He hasn't discussed this with you?"

"Do you know my father?" Greer asked.

"Oh sure. Everybody knows Clint. We play poker. Well, he plays poker. I sit in sometimes. He's a terrible card player, but a wonderful man. But you already know that."

She shook her head. "The thing is, I don't know that much about him. My parents divorced when I was five, and up until a couple weeks ago, I hadn't seen or talked to him in nearly thirty years."

"What?" Doc glanced over at Clint. He lowered his voice. "But he talked about you all the time. He has pictures of you, tells us about your work on the movies. He was so excited last week, when he went to visit you in Cypress Key."

Greer shrugged. "I guess maybe my mother sent him pictures, recently. We'd been . . . estranged, I guess you'd say. So I really don't know anything about his health."

Doc put a hand on her arm. "Let's go to the coffee shop and talk, shall we? I don't want to disturb him."

They found a table in the tiny coffee shop. Doc drank green tea, Greer had a bottle of water.

"Your father should make a complete recovery from this accident," Doc started out. "He does have chronic obstructive pulmonary disease, because I gather he smoked quite a bit when he was younger."

Greer nodded. She remembered sitting on Clint's lap, as a child, complaining of the tobacco smell that clung to his clothes.

"We're keeping him overnight because he had an irregular heartbeat when he was brought in," Doc said. "And with the concussion, and his age, I want to keep an eye on him."

"Okay," she said. "I meant to ask, how did the accident happen? His friend . . . Wally? . . . said it was a wreck, but that's all I know."

"Oh my goodness," Doc said, shaking his head. "I meant it when I said Clint was lucky to be alive. He pulled out into an intersection, right into the path of one of those huge log trucks. Luckily he was going slowly, for once in his life, and the truck was, too. Otherwise your father would be dead."

Greer looked down at the hand holding the water bottle. It was shaking.

"Wally said you needed me to sign some kind of authorization? For a test, or a procedure? What was that about?"

Doc smiled ruefully. "Well, I'm afraid that was a bit of subterfuge on my part. I didn't feel right, letting Wally know about your dad's confidential medical information, but I had to be sure you would come today, so I can impress upon you how serious Clint's condition is."

"But . . . you just said he should make a complete recovery. I don't understand."

"Clint is losing his eyesight," Doc said gently. "That's what caused this accident. He has macular degeneration."

54

Greer was holding her breath again, waiting.

"Clint's known about this for some time now," Doc said. "I told him he had to stop driving but, well, he's a car guy." He reached across the table and patted her hand. "I'm sorry this is all such a shock to you. I had no idea you and Clint weren't close."

"I've heard about macular degeneration," she said, trying to assimilate the barest facts she could recall. "It means he's going blind, right?"

"Maybe not totally blind. I'm not an ophthalmologist, but basically what you need to know is that there are two kinds of macular degeneration. Your dad has the rarer variety, wet MD. It's where you develop tiny blood vessels that leak fluid and cause your macula to degenerate. Right now, Clint tells me, he can see some things, but it's as though there's a large blot in the center of his field of vision. The blot is growing larger. There are some treatments that may help slow the progression of the disease, but there is no cure."

"He never said a word," Greer said. "I didn't have time to talk to him last week, when he delivered that car to the set. But earlier, when I went to his house, he didn't mention it."

"I think he's still in denial," Doc said. "This wreck he had today, it's not the first. He's had a couple of small fender benders in the past year. And I noticed, on poker nights, that he seemed to have cuts and bruises on his arms and his shins. Finally I flat-out asked him about it, and he admitted he was having vision problems. I referred him to a specialist at Shands, and they made the diagnosis."

"Shands?"

"I forget you're from California," Doc said. "It's the teaching hospital at the University of Florida, in Gainesville. They're one of the leading research institutes in the field. He's lucky they're so close by."

Greer picked at the paper label on the water bottle. "What happens next? I mean, he'll be blind, right? But how will he live? Who will take care of him? He can't keep living alone, right?"

Doc shrugged. "I can't answer those questions. People with visual impairments do live alone, and independently, and that includes people with macular degeneration. Fortunately, your father is fairly healthy. He's active, and he's lived alone for some time now, right? Also, he has you in his life now. Right?"

"I don't know." She shook her head. "This is a lot." Her eyes welled up with tears. "I live in L.A. I travel all the time for my job. I don't know anything about him. Thirty years he's been gone. I can't tell you how old he is, or his birthday. . . ."

"There's time for all that," Doc said, his voice gentle. "He should have been moved over to a room by now. Shall we go check?"

Clint had been moved to a bed in a private room. He was still sleeping. She sat down in a pleather recliner near his bed and glanced down at her phone.

There was a text from Bryce.

Zena told me about your dad. Hope he's ok. Don't worry about shoot. Zena doing great job.

And another one from Eb.

Call me when you get a chance.

She laid her head back and closed her eyes. When she opened them again, the room was in semidarkness. She yawned and looked around.

Clint was looking right at her, sipping water through a straw.

"Hi," she said. "You're awake. How do you feel?"

"Like I got T-boned by a gee-dee log truck," Clint said, laughing at his own joke.

"Does your head hurt?"

"Yeah. But I'll live. Thanks for coming. I guess Wally called you, huh?"

"That's right."

"I probably shouldn't have done that. You got work and all."

"It's okay," Greer said. "My assistant took over for the afternoon."

"She seems like a real nice girl," Clint said. He gestured toward the window. "Getting dark out. Hadn't you better get back to Cypress Key?"

Greer had been thinking the same thing. She dreaded the night drive down that spooky two-lane country road. But how could she just walk away and leave him in the hospital like this?

"I can stay a little while," she said, standing up and stretching. "Do you need anything?"

His laugh was wheezy. "I could use a lot of things. Did they tell you anything about my truck? I mean, was it totaled?"

"You really *are* a car guy," Greer said. "Your friend . . . Doc? He told me you were sideswiped by a log truck. He said you were lucky to be alive. Do you remember that?"

"I remember looking up and thinking, 'Aw, shit. There goes my insurance premiums.' " His chest heaved with the effort of laughing, and his face twisted in sudden pain.

"You've got a cracked rib," Greer said. "I bet it hurts."

"Like a sumbitch," Clint agreed. "All those years of stunt driving I did, back in the day before air bags and safety harnesses, I probably don't have a rib that ain't been cracked." His fingers groped his chest, beneath the gown. "Feels like I'm wearing a girdle under here."

Greer smiled. "How do you know what a girdle feels like?"

He tapped his head lightly. "I got imagination." Now his fingers probed the bandage around his head. "Did Doc say I've got a concussion?"

"Yes." She paused. "He also told me you've got macular degeneration."

Clint's face crumpled a little. "Gee-dee old tattletale. What ever happened to doctor-patient confidentiality?"

"He said you've known for a while. And that you shouldn't be driving. I guess that's why he wanted me to come to the hospital."

"To gang up on me and take away my car keys," Clint said with a sigh. "Is that why you're here?"

"Me?" The question startled her. "No. I didn't even know about your eyes until Doc told me."

"Why did you come, then?"

She smiled. "I've been asking myself that same question."

"What'd you come up with?"

"Wally said you asked the EMTs to call me. Because I'm your next of kin. He said the hospital needed me to authorize a test or a procedure, but that was really just a pretext Doc used to get me here. So he could tell me about your eyes."

"If we didn't need him for poker nights, I'd sue him for malpractice," Clint groused. He turned his head toward the window.

"How much can you see?" Greer asked.

"I can see the edges of things, mostly. It's like there's a dark hole in the middle of the picture. I can tell that it's getting dark outside, I can see some of you. I was watching you sleep just now."

"That must have been fascinating," Greer said.

"I was thinking how I used to watch you sleep, back when you were little. The first time Lise left me alone with you, I was terrified something might happen. I pulled a rocking chair up beside your crib and stared at you the whole time, until she got home. I remember I went and got a shaving mirror and put it right by your mouth, to make sure you were still breathing."

He tilted his head away, and Greer was surprised to see a single tear slide down his cheek.

"I used to sing to you," he said.

"What? The theme song from *Dukes of Haz-zard*?"

He shook his head. "You weren't really into that. When you were about five you liked that song from *Golden Girls.*"

She shook her head. "I don't know that one."

"Sure you do." He coughed, then launched into a raspy high falsetto. " 'Thank you for being a friend . . . travel down a road . . . something something, friend and a confidante.' "

He looked at her hopefully. "Remember? They got the reruns on television here non-stop, because this is Florida and it was set in Miami, but that show was actually shot in L.A."

She had a dim memory of sitting in the front seat of his classic red Mustang, and of him singing to her while they went to Carl's Jr. for burgers and milk shakes. She loved Carl's, and she loved riding in the Mustang.

More vivid was the memory of Lise scream-ing at her father for being an irresponsible idiot and not putting her in a car seat. *Ah, yes. Good times.*

"Do you remember the time I took you to the *Dukes* end-of-season wrap party? And they gave you your own little director's chair that the whole cast signed? You'd have been four. I didn't drive the last season, 'cuz I'd hurt my back."

"Not really," she said, shrugging. Greer knew that her father wanted her memories of their life together to be like that dress in their Sears studio portrait, all rose tinted, with rainbows and unicorns, flavored with milk shakes and sitcom theme songs, tied up with a big, floppy pink bow. But that was his version, not hers.

He was watching her, expectantly.

"I'm no good at this," she said helplessly. "It was all a long time ago. I'm sorry, Clint, but I can't . . ."

"You should go on back to work," Clint said after a while. "I don't want you getting in trouble on the job because of me." He closed his eyes again. "My head's hurting. I think I'm just gonna take a nap now. You go on back to Cypress Key. Don't worry about me. Doc said I can go home tomorrow. Wally can come get me."

She waited until his breathing was regular, then tiptoed over to the side of the bed. The hospital room was so cold. She unfolded the blanket at the foot of his bed and pulled it up over his sleeping form. He didn't stir, so she carefully moved his hands to put them under the covers.

Clint had blue-collar hands. His nail beds were rimed with grease, the fingers were calloused, and the knuckles and backs of both hands were networked with old scars and with recent cuts from the shattered glass of the wreck. For the first time, she noticed he wore a narrow gold wedding band on his left hand. She was fairly sure he hadn't been wearing it before. She tucked the blanket up under his grizzled chin and absentmindedly patted his shoulder.

Greer found a nurse in the hallway and told him that her father was sleeping, and that she had to get back to work. "Okay. I'll look in on him in an hour or so," the nurse promised. "He's due for his pain meds at nine, and then he should sleep through the night."

She unlocked the Kia and slid into the driver's seat, humming, then remembering snatches of the verses.

And if I threw a party . . . the biggest gift for me. . .

55

The damned *Golden Girls* song. It was an earworm, and she was certain Clint had deliberately planted it in her subconscious.

Thank you for being a friend
Traveled down the road and back
   again . . .

Greer couldn't shake it. Fifteen miles down the road she made a U-turn.

The hospital was eerily still. The nurse at the charge desk looked surprised to see her. "Visiting hours are over."

"I'm his daughter. He doesn't have anybody else," Greer said. "I thought I'd stay with him. Just for tonight."

"I'll get you a pillow and a blanket," the nurse offered.

The recliner was shockingly uncomfortable, even for a hospital. She burrowed beneath the blanket and tried to sleep. Clint's breathing was raspy but even. She heard carts rolling down the hall outside, the low murmur of voices, the squeak of rubber-soled shoes on linoleum. Her phone buzzed. It was Eb.

"Hi," she whispered. "Can't believe I forgot to call you. I'm staying over at the hospital tonight. I'm in the room with him now, so I can't really talk."

"That's fine," Eb said. "I got a little worried when I didn't hear from you."

"You were worried about me? That's so sweet."

"I'm a sweet guy. You'll see."

She smiled as she tucked the phone back in her pocket.

The overhead light flickered on, bathing the room in a harsh blue-white wash. Clint sat on the edge of the hospital bed, his skinny legs dangling over the side.

"What's wrong?" Greer jumped up from the recliner.

He grimaced. "I gotta pee. Bad."

"I'll ring for the nurse," she said.

He shook his head. "Just help me get to the bathroom, please?"

"Are you supposed to be walking?" Greer looked longingly toward the door, willing it to be opened by a calm, competent health professional.

"Dammit, I gotta go," Clint rasped. He slid off the bed, and faltered. His gown bunched at the waist and Greer looked away, but not before glimpsing something she knew she could never unsee.

Out of options, she wrapped her arm around Clint's narrow waist and steered him toward the bathroom. He was lighter than she'd imagined. She turned on the overhead light, positioned him in front of the commode, and stepped out of the room just in time. Whatever else was wrong with him, it certainly sounded like the old man had a healthy bladder.

Afterwards, she helped him back to bed. His face was pale from the effort and he was breathing heavily.

"I'll ring for the nurse," she said, punching the buzzer attached to the side rail of his bed. Clint didn't argue.

The nurse took his pulse and heartbeat, checked his bandage, administered his next dose of pain meds, and admonished the patient and his hapless helper for the bathroom excursion. She picked up a plastic jug–looking device from the cart next to the bed. "Next time, use this."

Clint coughed and Greer looked away, already plotting her exit strategy.

Luckily, he fell asleep again almost immediately. Greer had no such luck. At six, she tiptoed out of the room and made her way to the hospital coffee shop, where she sipped terrible coffee and a vile-tasting vending machine pastry while checking her phone.

There were three texts from Bryce. He'd

sent the first one around 10:00 p.m.

When will you be back here? Jake Newman
wants to do walk-thru for demo scene.

The second text was transmitted at 10:30 p.m.

Need answer asap on your eta.

The third had been sent at 5:45 a.m.

Never mind. Zena on top of things. But still
need ETA

Zena on top of things? Greer's eyes narrowed as she considered the implications of this turn of events. Was the girl maneuvering herself into Greer's job? The idea was laughable on the surface. Zena was cute and friendly, and if you gave her a clearly marked list of instructions, she could get things done. But there was no way she had the imagination, initiative, or intelligence to manage a big-budget film location.

Greer's fingers flew over the phone's keyboard.

Father should be discharged this a.m. Back
by noon.

Clint sat in the wheelchair. He was dressed

in the clothes his friend/employee Wally had delivered to the hospital that morning. A striped golf shirt, baggy-butt dad jeans, white socks, black tennis shoes, and a Hennessy Picture Cars baseball cap.

The nurse handed him a clipboard. "These are your discharge instructions. These are your prescriptions for the medications the doctor wants you to have. Doc wants to see you in a week to check the sutures on your head wound. Any questions?"

"What about his concussion?" Greer asked. "Anything special he needs to know about that?"

"No driving, no operating heavy machinery." The nurse glared at Clint. "You got that Mr. Hennessy?"

Clint glared right back at her. "Can I go now?"

"As soon as you sign all those forms." The nurse glanced over at Greer. "Try to keep him from doing too much these first few days he's at home."

"Me?" Greer looked from the nurse to Clint, who was scratching his name on the bottom of all the paperwork.

"Aren't you staying with your dad?"

"No, she's not," Clint tossed the clipboard onto the bed. "I don't need a nursemaid."

Despite his protests that she should just drop him off and get back to work, Greer helped

Clint out of the car and into the double-wide.

It was stifling inside, so she turned the air down and helped settle him into the brown leather Barcalounger that faced his big-screen television in the living room.

She placed his prescriptions on a table near the chair, then took his phone and plugged it into the wall to charge it.

"How about food? Can I go to the grocery store for you?"

"Open up the freezer in the kitchen," Clint said. She did so and saw that it was completely filled with an astonishing array of frozen dinners. "Check out the cupboard there beside the stove, too," Clint said. The pantry was stocked with rows and rows of canned soups and vegetables.

"Do you ever eat any fresh foods?" she asked.

"Wally will stop at the store and get me some milk and bananas and salad stuff," Clint said. "You know, I appreciate what you're trying to do, but I can take care of myself. I lived alone for thirty years."

Greer couldn't resist the temptation. "What about the years with Dirty Debbie?"

"Who?"

"Your second wife?"

"Good God!" Clint laughed, then clutched his cracked rib in pain. "That sounds exactly like Lise. I kinda forgot about old Debbie after all these years."

"Maybe you could look her up on Face-book," Greer quipped.

Clint grinned and shook his head. "You do have your mother's wicked tongue, don't you?"

"I'm afraid so," she admitted. "It's gotten me in trouble over the years, for sure."

"That's one of the things I loved best about Lise. She had a mouth that could blister the paint off a barn, and the face of an angel." He sighed and looked around the room. "You wanna see something?"

"Maybe another time," Greer said apologetically. "I need to get back to work now."

"Just this one thing," he insisted. "It's on the dresser, in there." He pointed through the doorway.

She walked into his bedroom. The blinds were drawn, and it was dark. She turned on the light and immediately saw what he wanted her to find.

It was a framed photo, of a much younger Clint and Lise. She took it out and handed it to him.

"Bet you never saw this before."

The colors in the photo had faded over time, but it showed Lise, with long, very blond hair, staring into the eyes of her beloved. She was dressed in a white cotton minidress, holding a bouquet of daisies, and wearing a broad-brimmed straw hat. Clint's hair was wild and bushy, and he appeared to be wearing a cowboy shirt and bolo tie.

"Is this what I think it is?"

He nodded. "Our wedding picture. We got married on the beach down in Cabo. Spent one night there in a motel, then headed back to L.A., because we both had jobs the next day."

Greer trailed her finger over the photo. "I didn't know this was Mom's wedding dress." She looked over at Clint. "She kept it all these years. In fact, I have it. I wore it to dinner just the other night."

"I'll be damned," he said softly. "I'll be damned."

56

She had to put Clint Hennessy and his needs
and the ghosts of old memories on the back
burner. Twenty-four hours away from Cypress
Key meant she was basically at least forty-
eight hours behind with work. Greer stopped
by her room to shower and change out of the
clothes she'd been wearing for the past day.

Her golf cart wasn't where she'd parked it,
in back of the office on Pine Street. Zena,
she thought, had usurped both her job and
her vehicle. But not for long. Despite the
punishing heat, she walk-jogged down to the
pier and the set.

Bryce was rehearsing Kregg and Adelyn's
scene on the seawall by the kayak rental
kiosk. She could hear him berating the two
actors as she approached the cluster of
camera and sound techs.

"No, dammit! Danielle, you've got to make
Nick absolutely believe he's only imagining
the voices he hears outside at night. Sell it! If
he for one minute doubts what you're telling

him, the whole plot with the sheriff falls apart. Understand?"

Adelyn nodded. She was dressed in a bikini top and board shorts, with a light cotton shirt thrown over her shoulders to prevent sunburn. The sweat-soaked shirt clung to her back, and her face was already pink.

"Good," Bryce said. "Run the lines for me."

Adelyn rested her hands on Kregg's shoulders and started to speak.

"Stop, stop, stop," Bryce hollered. "Who told you to touch him?"

Greer couldn't hear Adelyn's response, or Bryce's, but a moment later she saw the actress storm off in tears, in the direction of the air-conditioned pop-up tents.

"See what I mean?" Kregg said, shaking his head in disgust as his costar disappeared. "She's a friggin' diva. Won't listen to anything I suggest."

"Take a break, everybody," Bryce called, and he and Kregg walked away, their heads bent together in discussion.

CeeJay walked up just then. "Hey. Just getting back?"

"Yeah. Looks like it's been a tough morning," Greer said. She nodded toward Bryce. "Who pissed in his Cheerios?"

CeeJay smiled widely. "Good ol' Sherrie Seelinger. She's cutting off the cash pipeline. Looks like the casino demo is a no go."

"When did that happen? Bryce was texting

me last night wanting me to hustle back here to get stuff lined up."

"I guess word must have come down this morning. One of the paint crew guys heard him on the phone in his RV at base camp this morning. He was apparently making a last-ditch effort to try to raise the money on his own, but one of the transpo guys took Jake Newman to the airport in Gainesville around lunchtime, so he's out of here. I heard Newman wanted half the money up front to do the explosion."

"Oh wow. I bet Vanessa was livid when she got the news," Greer said. "After all the expense they went to, flying in Sawyer and everything. That is not a cheap oops."

Just then, Bryce walked up. "Ceej, Addie's gonna need some damage control on her face after her latest temper tantrum. So how about you get back to work?"

"Fuck you," CeeJay said sweetly.

Bryce watched her go and shook his head, before turning his attention back to Greer. "I guess you heard that bitch Seelinger nixed the casino explosion. So we have to retool, and fast. The word's come down from on high. No more money, no more time. They want everything here wrapped up next week, by midweek. Whatever we don't get here we finish up back in L.A."

Greer felt her jaw drop. "I thought we had at least another week and a half here. How are we gonna get it all done?"

"Terry's working on a new ending," Bryce said. "I've seen the first few pages, and I think it'll work. It's nowhere near as good as the casino explosion, but at this point we gotta punt and hope for the best."

"Can you give me any idea of what he's planning? I'll need to start figuring out logistics."

Bryce looked around to make sure nobody was eavesdropping. *Paranoid to the end,* Greer thought.

"He's thinking about a boat chase. High-speed cigarette boats. Like the ones they used to have on *Miami Vice,* back in the day? Bobo's already lining 'em up. He says he can have 'em here by tomorrow, no problem, so the stunt guys can start practicing with 'em."

Greer's brain was spinning. "How soon can I get some pages?"

"Soon," Bryce said.

"Can you give me an idea of the starting and ending point?"

Bryce furrowed his brow while he thought about it. "When you first got down here, you sent me some pix of an old boathouse-looking place. That'd be good, especially if we do some night shots."

"The mayor owns that," Greer said. "I'm pretty sure he'd be willing to lease it to us."

"The mayor who's still frosted over the casino?" Bryce looked dubious.

"He'll get over it," Greer assured him.

"For the end of the chase, I'm thinking right out here." Bryce turned and pointed toward the pier and the bay. "I want to shoot it with the casino in the background."

"So . . . start early in the morning at the boathouse? And then move back over to the pier?" Greer asked.

"That'll work," Bryce said. "We'll put a splinter unit on top of the casino to do long shots of the boat chase."

Greer nodded. "We'll need security on boats out in the bay, and here on the pier. If we start early enough in the morning at the boathouse, we won't need as much security, because it's in sort of a commercial area"

Bryce took his phone from his pocket and stared down at an e-mail. "Uh, you might want to run that by Zena. She, uh, has been working on this since yesterday."

"Zena?" Greer's eyes narrowed. "Zena the assistant location manager?"

"Whatever," Bryce said. "I just want working bathrooms and no rubber-neckers screwing up my shoot. You girls settle the turf war amongst yourselves."

"Girls?" Greer scowled at Bryce's retreating back.

A few minutes later, her radio squawked.

"Greer?" It was Zena.

"Hi, Zena."

"I heard you're back."

"That's right."

"Thank God! The air conditioner in tent one isn't working. Addie is literally having a meltdown up here."

"Sorry to hear that," Greer said.

"Um, so, you'll come up and fix it?" Zena said.

"Um, no. Bryce just told me you're handling things today," Greer said. "You want to be a location manager? Here's the secret, sweetie: you have to actually manage."

Greer turned her radio off and started walking toward the catering truck in search of food that didn't come from a vending machine. When she saw her golf cart parked at the curb, with the key tucked in the cup holder, she climbed aboard and rolled off.

57

It was Friday night and the Cypress Key Inn was jamming. Eb had texted her that they had an eight o'clock dinner reservation, but she'd arrived thirty minutes early, telling herself it was so she could nab a seat at the bar. Who was she kidding? She'd been thinking off and on most of the day about seeing Eb.

Greer snaked her way through the throng of people waiting for tables in the restaurant and managed to claim what amounted to twelve inches of unclaimed space at the bar. The bartender rushed up, took her order, and promptly disappeared. Greer leaned with her back to the bar and surveyed the crowd, which appeared to consist largely of the cast and crew of *Beach Town.*

She felt a tap on her shoulder. "Hey, movie lady." It was Jared Thibadeaux, miraculously — and temporarily, she was sure — cleaned up and sobered up. He was sitting to her right, jammed shoulder to shoulder with Kregg.

"Oh, hi, Jared." She nodded politely to his companion. "Kregg."

"Can I buy you a beer?" Jared asked, raising his arm to motion for the bartender.

"I already ordered a glass of wine," she said quickly. "But thanks."

"Kregg," Jared said, "do you know this nice lady? She's staying at our motel."

Kregg gave Greer a sour look. The black eyes had faded to a bilious shade of yellowish green, and it appeared that he was using professional-strength foundation to cover the other damage he'd incurred in the beat-down Eb had administered. "We've met," he said.

Greer looked around the crowded room. "Where's your posse tonight, Kregg?"

"He's with me," Jared said. "Nobody's messing with my boy Kregg while I'm around."

Jared poured himself a shot of Jagermeister from the bottle on the bar, drank it, and slid the bottle over to Kregg, who did the same.

"Tell me your name again, movie lady?" Jared said.

"Greer."

He pulled a narrow steno pad from the pocket of his jeans and held it up for her inspection. "Me and Kregg, we're collaborating on a screenplay together."

"That's fascinating." Greer craned her

neck, looking in vain for the bartender and her MIA glass of pinot grigio.

"We're calling it *O-Train,*" Jared went on. "Because of OxyContin. We're thinking it'll be kind of like *Breaking Bad,* but instead of being about a high school teacher cooking meth, it'll be about a doctor unfairly incarcerated for allegedly selling OxyContin."

"Oh, I didn't know you were actually a doctor," Greer said.

Jared shrugged. "Well, not board certified, but I did my time in med school."

Greer kept her eyes on the door, watching for Eb, but it was still early yet.

"And will Kregg play the role of Jared Thibadeaux?" she asked.

Kregg knocked back his shot. "Hell yeah." He pointed at the steno pad. "This right here is some raw stuff. It's the shit."

"He's writing all the music for the soundtrack too," Jared confided. "That's why I'm staying at his place on Bluewater Bay now, so we can really concentrate on the writing, when he's not on set."

Greer was bored. She couldn't help herself. "So you're not staying at the Silver Sands anymore?"

Jared's face darkened briefly. "Ginny decided she needed to rent the room. Which was okay by me, because frankly the place is a rat hole. My cell at Starke was nicer than that room."

"Bryce wants to take a look at the screen-play, when we're a little further down the road, you know, to maybe option, but I'm probably gonna have my agent shop the screenplay around town," Kregg said. "And in the meantime, I'm setting up my own production company, too."

"Sounds like you boys are going to be pretty busy," Greer said. "But Kregg, aren't you going out on tour in a couple weeks?"

"That's right." Kregg nodded.

"Won't it be kind of hard to collaborate on a screenplay when you're doing all that travel-ing?"

"Naw," Kregg said. He slapped Jared's back. "My man Jared is going on the road with me. This here's my newest roadie, the J Man."

"I'm sure you'll be very happy together," Greer said, wondering if her wine would ever arrive.

The door from the street opened and a knot of people swelled forward, but Eb was not among them. The crowd did, however, in-clude Zena, who seemed to be scanning the crowd, looking for a familiar face.

Greer had to grudgingly admit that the girl was strikingly beautiful. Her gleaming, dark hair was pinned up tonight, and she wore a striking black one-shouldered knit tube dress that left little to the imagination.

Both Jared and Kregg, along with half the

men in the bar, had taken notice of Zena's entry. Kregg slid from his bar stool and pushed his way through the crowd. "Hey, Zena," he called. "Zena!"

Her smooth face lit up when she saw she was being hailed by *Beach Town's* male lead. Kregg took her by the hand and steered her through the crowd toward his spot at the bar.

This, thought Greer, is about to get interesting.

When Zena saw Greer, her smile briefly vanished. "Hi there, Greer," she said coolly.

Jared stuck out his hand. "Hey. My name's Jared."

"Zena," the girl said, tossing her hair behind her shoulder. She pivoted and deliberately turned her back to Greer.

The front door opened and Eb stepped inside. He stopped and looked around the room, searching for his date. When he saw Greer, and her companions, he raised one eyebrow and frowned.

Fortunately, the bartender arrived with her glass of wine. Greer put some money on the bar, nodded a farewell to Jared and Kregg, and headed for the door.

Eb slid his arm around her waist and kissed her briefly. "You look nice," he murmured. "What were you doing with those two bozos at the bar?"

"Killing time until the man of my dreams showed up to sweep me off my feet," Greer told him.

The hostess was a slender, middle-aged woman with bright red hair. She showed them to their table on the glassed-in porch, took their drink orders, and promised to send a waitress as soon as possible.

"Allie's not working tonight?" Greer asked.

"She told Gin she wasn't on the schedule," Eb said.

When their drinks arrived, Eb sat back and nodded in the direction of the bar, where Jared, Kregg, and Zena seemed to be having an impromptu party. "What's going on over there?"

"They're just plotting their next movie project," Greer said. "I'm sure Zena will be signed up as location manager."

"Movie." Eb rolled his eyes. "Has Jared got his steno pad with him?"

"He sure does," Greer said. "He told me he's moved in with Kregg, so the two of them can work on their collaboration. Does that mean you kicked him out of the motel?"

"I didn't get a chance," Eb said, chuckling. "Ginny booted him out first thing yesterday morning. Woke him up at eight, threw his stuff in a laundry cart, and told him to hit the road."

"Your aunt is my hero," Greer said.

"Mine too."

The waitress came and took their orders: a New York strip for Eb and seared scallops with a sugar cane and mango salsa for Greer.

"How did Allie take the news that her dad had decamped?" Greer asked.

"She's been pretty subdued. I'm sorry that she had to see Jared that wasted, but on the other hand, maybe that's what it takes to open her eyes to who her father really is."

"Fathers," Greer said with a sigh. "I think every girl wishes she had Atticus Finch — or Gregory Peck — for a father. Unfortunately, most of us end up with somebody who's somewhere between Jed Clampett and Homer Simpson."

Eb casually placed his hand atop hers. "Which did you get?"

"I'm still trying to figure that out," she admitted. "He's not as easy to hate in person as he was from a distance. You know, the picture of Clint that my mom always painted — some larger-than-life, macho redneck — just doesn't seem to gibe with the reality. And maybe that has to do with age. Maybe he's mellowed. Right now, he seems so vulnerable, so desperate for my approval, I just feel sorry for him."

"Is he going to be all right — after the wreck and all?"

"His doctor is one of his poker buddies, who seems to know my father pretty well," Greer said. "He actually wanted me to come to the hospital to let me know Clint is losing his eyesight. He has macular degeneration."

"Oh hell. What's the prognosis?"

"Clint didn't want to talk about it, and I decided not to push it, so soon after his accident. But the doctor said he'll eventually be legally blind. There are some treatments that may slow the progress of the disease, but there's no cure."

"How old is your dad?"

"I don't even know," Greer admitted. "Early seventies, I think. Pretty sad, huh? Even sadder when his doctor tells me he's told all his buddies all about me and my career, even shown them pictures of me."

"He's the one who walked away from you," Eb pointed out. "It's easy for him to brag on you, now that all the heavy lifting has been done — by somebody else."

"Well, that's the thing," Greer said slowly. "Before she died, when she was nagging me to reach out to Clint, Lise said she couldn't remember anymore who left first. And she said it really didn't matter, because they both were in the wrong. Which was news to me. So, the last time I talked to Dearie I specifically asked her what went down when my parents split up."

"Did she tell you?"

"She didn't want to. Not at first. Finally, when I pressed her, she said my parents had been having money problems. Clint couldn't stunt drive, because he'd hurt his back, and Lise wasn't getting any real acting jobs. And

I was sick a lot that year, with earaches. So this one day, Clint decides to spend the last of their savings to buy one of the Chargers they'd wrecked for a stunt on the show."

"Charger? Show?" Eb looked momentarily confused. "I thought you said your dad owned a car business."

"Now. But he was originally a stunt driver. He worked on *The Dukes of Hazzard*."

"For real?"

"I thought I told you that."

Eb shook his head. "No. I think I would have remembered if you'd told me your dad got to drive the General Lee."

Greer stared at him. "That's a big deal to you?"

"Are you kidding? I grew up in the South. Every red-blooded boy in the South wanted to be Bo Duke." He grinned. "And to get into Catherine Bach's Daisy Dukes."

Greer rolled her eyes. "Anyway, Clint came home with this busted-up Charger which he'd bought for seventy-five dollars. Without consulting Lise. He had some grand scheme to do all the body work, repaint it, and lease it back to Warner Brothers for the show. Unfortunately, Lise had been planning to use that money to buy herself a new outfit for a callback she had for a television pilot. They had a huge fight, and Clint left."

She took a sip of her wine. "I don't have a lot of memories of the times they were together, but I do remember the fight that night. I remember her screaming about seventy-five goddamn dollars. And I remember Clint lifting me into the front seat of the Charger and letting me blow the horn."

"Which played 'Dixie,' " Eb said.

"Which made my mother really go insane. After he left she took all his stuff and threw it out into the front yard. The next morning she called our next door neighbor to babysit me, because she had that audition."

Greer took a deep breath. "Here's where the story gets interesting. That first time, when I met Clint at his house, he was totally indignant that I thought he'd walked off. He admits he left that night — to drive around and cool off — but he said when he eventually did go go home, the teenage babysitter had been there all night. Because Lise never came home. And she never called, either. Clint said he kept me all weekend, with no word from Mom. Finally — because, let's face it, he was a guy and he didn't know what to do with a kid who screamed all night because of an earache — he called Dearie and asked her to come help."

"He's saying your mother was the one who took off and left you?"

"Dearie confirmed it," Greer said. "She didn't want to admit what Mom had done, but she finally confirmed Clint's version. She says Lise came home after a few days, never said where she'd been, and after that is when they got divorced."

"Sad story all around," Eb said. "So maybe your dad wasn't Atticus Finch. Most dads aren't."

"But he also wasn't Dr. Evil."

Their food arrived, and they found other things to talk about. They were sipping coffee when Greer noticed Eb looking at her oddly.

"What's on your mind?"

"You won't get mad if I ask you one more thing about your dad?"

"It's about that damned car, isn't it?"

He looked sheepish.

"Go ahead."

"What happened to the Charger? I mean, every once in a while you read about one of those cars selling at auction, for like hundreds of thousands of dollars. Does he still have it?"

"He actually did fix it up and lease it back to the studio. I think he told me his General Lee was used for the last season of *Dukes.* Clint's kind of a pack rat — like you, I guess. He's got the car in a barn at his place, along with maybe three dozen other vintage novelty vehicles — old fire trucks, ambulances, police cars, school buses, like that."

Greer could tell from the dreamy expression in Eb's eyes what he was thinking about. And it wasn't about getting into her pants —

it was about getting into her father's storage barn.

58

"You want dessert?" The restaurant had filled up and was now so crowded it was hard to hear each other over the din of the crowd. Greer shook her head no. She'd placed her phone on the top of the table earlier, and out of the corner of her eye she saw a text message flash across the screen.

At the same time, she caught sight of a familiar face sitting at a table closest to the bar. Two familiar faces, actually. Bryce and Vanessa Littrell.

Bryce held up his own phone.

The text was from him.

Did u ask him about using the boathouse?

Eb saw her reading the text. She flipped the phone around so he could read it too. "What's that supposed to mean?"

"I can't believe we've been sitting here all this time and I forgot to mention it. We're not going to demo the casino after all. The studio exec who flew out here this week killed the whole idea because it's too expensive."

"You're serious?" A slow smile spread across Eb's face.

"Bryce told me himself, after I got back to the set today. That's what this text means. Instead of the big explosion, Terry's writing a new ending with a boat chase. Bobo — he's the transportation captain — is supposed to be bringing in some high-powered cigarette racing boats tomorrow. For the location, we need an old boathouse, which is where you come in. Interested?"

"Why not? Just as long as you don't blow it up."

"Bryce wants to try to start shooting Monday, which doesn't give us much time. We'd need to start setup tomorrow and Sunday."

"Sure. It's not like we're exactly humming with activity. Business is so slow it won't make much difference. I'd have to go in tomorrow, or tonight even, to let my boat owners know. Would I have to shut down over the weekend?"

"Mmm, probably. I'm thinking we'll want to tie the boats up there at your dock, so we need that secure from other traffic. We'd pay you, of course, to compensate for all the lost business."

"I like that plan," Eb said. "Ballpark it for me, would you?"

"How's a thousand a day?"

"I like twelve hundred better."

"You got a deal."

Eb flagged the waitress down and asked for their check. As they were leaving the Inn, Bryce motioned for them to stop by his table.

"Are we good for the boathouse?" he asked Greer.

"He's in," Greer said.

Eb reached over to shake Bryce's hand, and after a second's hesitation, the producer shook it.

"Sorry about all the unpleasantness at your place the other day," Eb said, addressing himself to Vanessa. "I got pretty hot under the collar and said some stuff I shouldn't have. I'd like to apologize to both of you."

"I get it," Bryce said. "No offense taken."

But Vanessa didn't intend to let Eb off that easily. "I guess it's a win-win for you," she said, leaning forward. "You get to save the casino, thereby screwing me over, and you even get to make money off your own property. Nice work if you can get it."

"Weren't you the one who said it's just business?" Eb said.

"The demolition deal might be off the table, but don't think I'm going to let you off the hook that easily on the whole conflict-of-interest thing," Vanessa said.

Bryce patted her hand. "Okay, enough vendetta talk." He addressed himself to Greer. "I'm going to want to start blocking the scenes at the boathouse between Nick and the sheriff as early tomorrow as possible. I saw Kregg sitting at the bar a little while ago, and I let him know he's got a ten a.m. call time. I'll text Nate, too. Bobo said the boats should be delivered before that. Can you text him the address of the boathouse?"

"As soon as we leave here," Greer promised.

They were almost at the Inn's front door when Greer saw the black Hummer pull up to the curb outside. Jared Thibadeaux was at the wheel and Zena and Kregg were climbing into the backseat. They could hear the heavy bass thump from the Hummer's CD player as it sped away from the curb with Zena sitting on Kregg's lap.

"Did you see that?" Greer asked, looking over her shoulder at Eb. "It looks like Kregg found himself a new playmate."

"Good. Now he can be somebody else's headache," Eb said.

59

The alarm on Greer's phone buzzed at 7:00 a.m. She reached across Eb's motionless form to grab it.

He stirred, turned to her, and planted his forehead next to hers. "Don't you ever get a day off? Ever get to sleep in?"

"Not during the last days of a location shoot," Greer said, rummaging in the overnight bag she'd brought the night before. "It gets pretty intense. Total crazy-town."

"Hey!" Eb sat up in bed. "What do you mean, 'the last days of the shoot'? I thought you were supposed to be here for at least another week."

"We were, but along with deep-sixing the casino demo, the studio told Bryce everything has to be finished here by Wednesday. Anything we don't get done by then we'll have to shoot once we're back in L.A."

"What's that mean for us?"

Greer came back and sat on the edge of the bed. She picked his glasses off the nightstand

and gently placed them on his face, then kissed his nose. "I don't know. I haven't even had time to process it yet."

He shook his head and his jaw tightened. "When were you going to tell me you're leaving? Were you just going to go out for ice cream and never come back? Maybe text me from the airport?"

"I'm telling you now," Greer said quietly. "I only found out late yesterday. We had a lot to catch up on last night, remember?" She glanced at the clock radio on the nightstand.

"Can we please not fight about this right now? Can we sit down and talk it out tonight? If I don't get to the boathouse in thirty minutes, Bryce is going to pop a vein."

"Go," Eb, giving an irritable wave. "Wouldn't want to keep the great and mighty Bryce Levy waiting."

She was getting ready to climb into the claw-foot tub when she spotted it on the pine vanity holding the sink: a new, wrapped toothbrush, a bar of rose-scented goat's milk soap, and full-sized bottles of the expensive hair salon shampoo and conditioner she favored. Beside the toiletries was a shiny brass key. She knew it was the key to the loft.

Greer felt like weeping.

Eb had gone to a lot of trouble to figure out what brand of products she used, and to make her feel at home here — in his home — and she'd managed to hurt him again. When

was she ever going to get the hang of this
relationship thing?

He was standing in the kitchen, dressed and
drinking coffee.

"Eb, I'm sorry," she started to say. "I swear,
I'm not running out on you again. I want
this to work. You are the dearest, most
thoughtful, sexiest —"

He thrust a thermal coffee mug into her
hands. "Let's just save it for later. You've got
to get to work, and so do I."

There was no time to brood over their latest
argument. Bryce and the production designer
were waiting outside the boathouse when she
pulled up in the Kia. Eb's truck was already
there, and he was unlocking the door.

While the two men walked the building and
the docks outside, Greer joined Eb in the office. He was already on the phone, contact-
ing boat owners, letting them know the dock
and boathouse would be closed for business
for the next three days.

When he'd finally hung up from one call,
she interrupted before he could start another.
"Anything special I should know about your
neighbors around here?" she asked.

"It's mostly commercial stuff," he said.
"The clam processing plant isn't running
right now, so that won't be a problem.
Green's, the auto body shop to my right, isn't
open on weekends, but he does open early

on Monday. The guy to my left, Cypress HVAC, isn't open on the weekend either. He's got three or four vans that come in and out during the week, though."

"Okay. I don't think the HVAC guy will be a problem for our shoot, but I guess I'll need to contact the auto body guy and see if there's a way to do a work-around with him. If he's using loud power equipment over there while we're shooting, our sound equipment is going to pick that up. And that's *no bueno.*"

Eb rifled through the top drawer of his desk and handed her a business card. "That's Joey Green's shop, and his cell number's on there, too. He's not the friendliest guy in the world, but I guess if you show him the money he'll work with you."

"Thanks," Greer said. She looked out the office window toward the parking lot. "Zena should have been here by now. I wanted her to deal with the neighbors. But I guess it's all me."

It was after ten by the time Greer finished canvasing the block around the boathouse. She'd answered questions from curious neighbors, handed out pizza gift certificates and, along the way, had a phone conversation with Arnelle Bottoms about security for the shoot at both locations on Monday.

"Is Kregg gonna be over there today?" the

police chief asked.

"Yes, they're going to be rehearsing and dealing with the boat stuff," Greer said. "We won't have that big a presence to attract the public's attention; none of the big trucks need to come in until tomorrow. But I guess I should probably have an off-duty officer, if you've got somebody you could spare today and tomorrow."

"How about me?" The chief laughed. "I'm off, and I wouldn't mind getting some of that movie money. And I'll be keeping an eye on that low-down Kregg, too."

As the morning wore on with no sign of her assistant location manager, Greer's irritation increased to the point that her shoulders and neck were knotted with tension. They needed to pack a week's worth of prep work for Monday's shoot into two days, and she felt herself stretched to the point of snapping.

She left phone messages and fired off texts and e-mails to Zena, with no reply.

Shortly before eleven, as she was getting ready to tape off the boatyard parking lot for the equipment trailers, Kregg zoomed up in his black Porsche. He bounded out of the car and headed for the door of the boathouse. A full two minutes later the passenger-side door opened and Zena slowly climbed out.

Greer stood with her hands on her hips, momentarily enjoying the spectacle of her assistant's walk of shame.

Zena's eyes were shaded with dark sunglasses, but she wore no makeup and had a baseball cap jammed over her hair. The usually fashionable girl wore an oversize black Kregg concert tour T-shirt over a pair of ripped and tattered jeans, and a pair of cheap rubber flip-flops that still bore the orange convenience store price sticker.

If appearances meant anything, Zena was experiencing the mother of all hangovers. She was clutching a huge Styrofoam cup of coffee with both hands, as though her life depended on it.

"Good morning," Greer said caustically.

Zena held up her hand. "Don't start. Just. Don't."

"I'm not saying a word," Greer said. She handed Zena the roll of fluorescent tape and the diagram she'd drawn of where everything should be placed. "Just do your freaking job, okay?"

Fifteen minutes later a long flatbed trailer with two sleek speedboats — one a burnt orange with red and yellow racing stripes, the other a dazzling white with a metallic blue deck and green and yellow racing stripes — pulled into the boatyard. Eb directed Bobo, the transportation captain, around to the rear of the yard, where Bobo slowly backed the trailer down a concrete launch. One by one, a power winch lowered the boats into the water.

Greer and the skeleton members of the crew stood around and watched while the boats were unloaded. Eb stood beside her, arms crossed, obviously impressed by the watercraft the transportation captain had rounded up.

"What kind of boats are those?" she asked, glancing over at him.

"Cigarette boats. Big, pricey offshore racing boats for seriously rich guys." He pointed at the logos on the side of both boats. "They're the Top Gun model. I don't know all the specs on 'em, but those are twin five-hundred-twenty-horsepower Mercs on each one. Probably looking at four hundred thousand dollars' worth of big-boy toys there."

Greer eyed the boats critically. "You ask me, they just look like gigantic phallic symbols. Might be a little compensation going on there."

As soon as both the boats were securely tied up along the long dock, Kregg was out of the boathouse, drawn to them like a magnet. Following close behind him were the stunt drivers, a pair of brothers named Patrick and Bubba, and Nate Walters, the actor who was playing the sheriff.

Now Bryce and his head cameraman were standing on the dock, too, along with Bobo. Each of the stuntmen climbed aboard his boat and started the engines. The noise sounded like a 727 on takeoff to Greer. She could see Kregg, standing on the dock, arguing and gesturing with the producer.

"Looks like Kregg wants to take the cigarettes for a ride," Eb said. "But that's a lot of horsepower, if you're not used to it."

"I doubt Bryce will let him do more than stand in them for establishing shots," Greer said. "That's what the stunt drivers are for. It's too much of a liability for Kregg to be allowed to drive one of those things."

But no sooner had she said it than Kregg hopped down into the orange boat. A moment later both boats went speeding away from the dock with a deafening roar, leaving wakes that rocked the pilings under her feet.

She could see Bryce watching anxiously through a pair of binoculars as the boats sped back and forth along the bay, their bows punching effortlessly through the water, crossing and recrossing each other's wakes at speeds that made Greer shiver.

"How fast can those things go?"

"Some of them can top out at over ninety miles an hour," Eb said. He turned and, without another word, returned to his office, leaving her to watch his retreat with an overwhelming sense of sadness. Once again she had managed to screw things up.

At lunchtime Greer sent Zena to bring back

lunch for the cast and crew, from the catfish restaurant down the street. The girl returned forty minutes later with stacks of Styrofoam takeout containers. Her usually tan complexion had taken on an unhealthy greenish glow.

After lunch Bryce started rehearsing the actors playing the roles of the unfaithful wife Danielle, Nick, the returning Navy SEAL, and the corrupt Sheriff Hernandez.

The screenplay had undergone so many changes that Greer had stopped bothering to keep the plot straight, worrying only about what location the ever-changing plot would dictate.

She'd been so busy she didn't have time to stop for lunch until after two, when she sat down on a folding chair to eat a cold barbecue sandwich and drink a warm Diet Coke.

Bryce was explaining the new scene to the three actors while their stunt doubles lolled nearby on more folding chairs.

"Okay, so Nick here finally figures out something's going on between Danielle and the sheriff. One night, after Danielle sneaks out of their house, he follows her here, to the boathouse, and he sees her with the sheriff."

He turned to Kregg. "You can't actually hear what they're saying, but your rage is building, especially when you see the sheriff and Danielle practically humping each other right there on a stack of crates. So, then you can't contain yourself anymore. You rush out of hiding, and there's a fight between you and the sheriff. You land a couple of good punches, manage to knock him to the floor, but then he pulls a gun."

Bryce pointed at Adelyn. "You, Danielle, scream like a banshee when you see the gun, which distracts the sheriff just enough for Nick to kick the gun away. At that point, Nick, you know you have to get out of there. You run out of the boathouse, and you see the cigarettes tied up out there. So you run out, jump in the white one —"

"Why can't it be the orange one?" Kregg asked.

"What's wrong with the white one? I want the audience to see the symbolism — you know, you're the good guy in the white hat and the white boat."

"But the orange boat is bigger. It fits better with my image. I like it better," Kregg said meaningfully.

"Okay, whatever. You jump in the orange boat and take off, then Nate, you jump in the white boat and follow. Addie, you're going to hesitate, and then at the last minute, as the white boat is almost out of reach, leap onto it."

Adelyn frowned. "Not me personally, right?"

"No, of course not," Bryce said. He turned to the stunt doubles lounging nearby and pointed to a young woman who was the same height and build as Adelyn, wearing a blond wig styled the same as Addie's hair. "Courtney there is going to do the jumping."

"Good."

"But I am going to need to shoot establishing and close-up shots with you in the boat with Nate. And we'll probably go ahead and do some long shots of the two of you in the boat, during the chase scenes. Right?"

"Okay," Addie said hesitantly. "But the boats won't be speeding, right? I'm kind of a wimp when it comes to that."

"We'll go slow," Patrick volunteered.

"Listen, Bryce," Kregg piped up. "At least let me do some of my own driving. Patrick checked me out on the Top Gun, and I can totally handle it." He turned to the stunt driver, who shrugged noncommittally.

"Forget it. That's not some rowboat out there. Bobo tells me they've got five-hundred-twenty-horsepower twin engines," Bryce said. "The water on the bay here where it's sheltered might be calm today, but I checked the weather report for Monday. There's a front moving through, which means increased wind and waves and chop. And, that afternoon, we're shooting in the open water near the pier. It'll be much rougher there."

"I grew up on boats. I've been around 'em my whole life."

"Oh, you've driven a forty-foot offshore racing craft?"

"Well no, but at home I've got a twenty-nine-foot Yellowfin with twin three hundred Mercs. Let me just go out this afternoon and me and Patrick will open it up and see how I do."

"Not now," Bryce said, but even Greer could see he was wavering. She balled up the foil containing the remains of her sandwich, threw it in a trash barrel, and went back to work.

60

Greer was pulling into the parking lot at the boatyard when she saw Eb's truck poised to pull out onto the roadway. It was nearly 6:00 p.m. She pulled alongside him and rolled her window down.

"Headed home?" she asked hopefully. "I finished up prep work over at the pier, and as soon as I finish up a couple things here I'm done for the day. I was thinking maybe I could cook dinner for you tonight." She waggled her eyebrows in a way she hoped looked suggestive.

"I'm headed to the market," Eb said. "Bobby Stephens just called. He's got a sick kid at home, and Paulette, who usually works till closing, just tried to slice her thumb off with a box cutter."

"Oh no," Greer said.

"He took her to get stitches, but that means I'm two people short on a summer Saturday night, which means I just appointed myself head cashier."

"Could we do a late dinner?"

Eb shrugged noncommittally. "It's up to you. I might not get done counting out the registers and making the bank deposit until after ten."

"It sounds like you don't care whether you see me tonight or not," Greer said. "Is that the message you're sending, Eb?"

"The message is that I have to work late. You work late all the time, right? So is it a big deal if I have to run my business tonight?"

"I understand that you have a business to run," Greer said, trying not to sound as hurt as she felt. "But we've got some pretty important issues to discuss, I think."

His eyes were hard and flat, and she knew there was anger there, and that it had been on simmer since early that morning.

"Is discussion going to change the facts?" he asked. "You're heading back to L.A. on Wednesday. I'm staying here in Cypress Key. Has any of that changed since this morning?"

"No," Greer said, feeling heat rising to her cheeks. Eb pulled the truck forward an inch, as if to dismiss her. But she had to make one more stab at making things right with him. She kept thinking of that faded wedding photo her father had been keeping on his dresser all this time, of the years of longing and regret he'd kept bottled up inside.

She got out of the Kia and walked over to the truck. "Please," she said, leaning in, get-

601

ting right in his space. "Can we please get together, tonight or in the morning? I don't want this to end like this. I know we can figure out how to make this work. If you want it. Do you?"

His phone rang. It was sitting on the seat beside him. He glanced over, saw the caller ID screen. "This is Bobby. I gotta go. I'll call you after closing."

Although she'd left Zena with a long list of prep work that needed to be accomplished before the next day's rehearsals and setup, Greer quickly saw that only half the items on the list had been executed, and Zena herself was long gone.

"Tomorrow, I fire her ass," Greer muttered, as she set up the pop-up tents that would be used as temporary green rooms for the cast and crew that would be assembled the next day. She lugged furniture, set up tables and chairs, and unpacked coolers full of soft drinks, bottled juice, and water, as well as the coffeemaker from the downtown production office, for the first arrivals. There hadn't been time to arrange for a catering truck for the morning, so she'd arranged for the Coffee Mug to bake muffins and pastries for delivery.

The high-ceilinged metal boathouse held the day's heat like a convection oven, and the work was dirty and heavy. By eight she was so exhausted she had to drag herself out to the Kia.

Back in her room at the motel she showered, pulled on her favorite sleep shirt, and collapsed into bed. She'd been trying not to think about Eb, wondering if he'd call. She switched the television on and found a documentary about native tree frogs on the local educational channel. Greer had a lifelong aversion to anything that hopped or slithered, but she was too tired even to get up and change the channel. She struggled to stay awake, still hoping Eb would call.

The sound of a door opening and closing down the corridor woke her up. It was still dark, except for the glowing blue television screen. She got up and turned the television off, wondering what time it was. She reached into the pocket of the shorts she'd worn the day before, but her phone wasn't there. She tried to think about the last time she'd used it, but finally decided she'd track it down in the morning. She dropped down onto the bed and fell asleep almost as soon as her head hit the pillow.

She'd overslept. It was Sunday morning, and bright sunlight filtered through the bent slats of the venetian blinds. She could hear voices outside, crew members on their way to breakfast, or the beach.

603

Greer picked up her shorts and searched the pockets again, but found only the key to the rental car. She rifled through her pocketbook. She looked in the bathroom, even got down on her hands and knees to search for the phone under the bed.

With a sigh she got dressed and went out to the Kia, convinced it must be there, but the phone was not in the car. Had she somehow dropped it at the boathouse yesterday, with all the lifting and lugging she'd been doing?

That's when she remembered. Her battery had been ready to die late in the day, so she'd plugged it into the power cord she'd found in Eb's office. That memory ignited a tiny flame of hope. Her phone had spent the night in his office. Maybe he had called after all.

Greer let herself into the boathouse with the key Eb had given her the day before. She found the phone where she'd left it — plugged into an outlet in his office. She quickly scrolled through the half dozen missed calls, looking for the only one that mattered.

The call had come at 11:30 p.m. and it was 9:00 a.m. now. Eb had left a brief message. "I'm back at the loft. You can come over if you want to talk." That was it, brief and to the point. And there had been no follow-up.

So he'd had the night to fuel his already

mounting anger at her. Was there any point in trying to reach him now, to explain that she'd misplaced the phone the previous night?

She had to try. Friday night was proof of that. Friday night they'd had something wonderful and amazing. Something worth begging for. And she would do that, if Eb gave her the chance.

Greer tapped the callback number. The phone went straight to voice mail.

"Eb? It's me. I missed your call last night because I'd stupidly left my phone plugged in at your office last night and didn't realize it until just now. Please call me back. Please?"

She looked at the other missed calls. Clint had called around nine Saturday night and left a message. Her pulse blipped a little. Had something gone wrong? Was he back in the hospital?

His voice sounded much better, stronger even. "Hey, Greer. Listen, I might be headed over your way tomorrow for a little business venture. I'm feeling a lot better already. Maybe I could take you out to lunch. You're not shooting on Sundays, right? Anyway, call me when you get this. And thanks for what all you did for me at the hospital. I feel like a lucky man, having you for a daughter."

Greer bit her lip at the poignant sound of his voice. At some point later this morning she would call him back to let him know lunch wasn't in the cards for today. For now, she just didn't want to have to deal with disappointing one more person.

She got up and wandered around the boathouse, checking to see that everything was ready for today's rehearsals. She kept glancing at her phone, praying it would ring.

Finally she decided to track Eb down. If he was going to break up with her, he was going to have to do it in person — to her face.

She was headed for the Hometown Market when her phone began to vibrate. She snatched it up before the first ring was complete.

It was CeeJay. "Hey, where are you? I came over to your room with a thermos of cold Bloody Marys and hot gossip, but you're not around."

"I had to go back to the boathouse to pick up my phone. I accidentally left it there overnight. But listen, I'm waiting on a call from Eb, so if my phone beeps and I disconnect, don't get your feelings hurt, okay?"

"I would never get my feelings hurt over a booty call," CeeJay promised. "Before you hang up though, I just gotta share. Have you seen TMZ?"

"You know I don't read that stuff," Greer said. "What now?"

"You're gonna want to read it today. They've got an item saying that Kregg and Zena are an item. A 'hot item' to quote their smutty little story. And they've got the goods to prove it. Somebody has apparently been stalking Kregg's backyard pool with a camera with a very long lens. They must have been on a boat. The photo is of Zena and Kregg, frolicking on a chaise by the pool, wearing nothing but some really ugly tattoos."

That did give Greer a laugh. Her first one of the day. "I bet I know right when it was taken. Eb and I saw them leaving the Inn Friday night in Kregg's Hummer, and they were already getting really cozy. Both of them showed up late for work yesterday, and it was obvious they'd had an all-night rager."

"I've got to say, the girl has a body that is drop-dead gorgeous," CeeJay said. "Even if she is dumber than a box full of rocks."

"Not so dumb she doesn't know a meal ticket when she sees one," Greer said. "Zena is one screwup away from a one-way ticket back to the unemployment line, if I have anything to say about it." Her phone beeped to signal an incoming call. "Gotta go," she said, and quickly connected to the next call.

"Hi, Greer, this is Wally, your dad's buddy? Have you talked to Clint today?"

She felt another stab of fear. "No. He left me a message last night, but I didn't get it until just now. What's wrong? He's not back in the hospital is he?"

"That's just it," Wally said. "I don't know where he is. He called me last night and asked if I could carry him over to Roberta

607

this morning to see a vehicle he'd found on Craigslist."

"Roberta?"

"That's a little bitty town about halfway between his house and Cypress Key, where you are," Wally said. "He found an ad for a 1942 Willys jeep. Unrestored. That's like the Holy Grail for Clint. He's wanted to have one for his picture car inventory for years. I told him I didn't know. My wife, she likes to go to church on Sundays. Her people are foot-washing Baptists, and I kinda promised —"

"Wally," Greer interrupted. "Can you get to the point, please? What are you trying to tell me?"

"When I got out of preaching just now I saw Clint left me another message. He said never mind, he'd figure it out for himself. I thought that meant he'd gotten somebody else to take him over to Roberta. But I went by his place a little while ago, and he's not there. And his Blazer is gone too."

It took a moment for Wally's meaning to sink in. When it did, Greer gasped.

"You think he decided to drive himself, even though he's half blind and he's got a cracked rib? An hour and a half each way? Alone?"

"Yes ma'am," Wally said, sounding miserable. "I don't know what else it could be. I called the other fellas who work for Clint,

608

and his neighbors, but he's not with any of them, and none of them have talked to him today."

"God," Greer moaned. "What do you know about the jeep thing he wanted to see? Do you have the Craigslist ad in front of you?"

"I don't know anything about that Craigslist business. That was all Clint. Your dad, he likes hunting the cars down and buying 'em. I just work on 'em."

"All right, Wally. I'm going to see what I can find out. In the meantime, if you hear from him, will you let me know right away?"

"Yes ma'am. My wife said to let you know she's praying for Clint."

Pray for both of us, Greer thought.

61

1942 WILLYS JEEP. ALL ORIGINAL. SOME RUST ISSUES. READY FOR YOUR RES-TORATION PROJECT. $3,000. Cash Serious offers only. Will not last at this price.

The Craigslist ad was accompanied by a photograph of what looked like the skeletal remains of a jeep, with weeds growing up through the hood.

"Really, Clint?" Greer muttered to herself. "Three thousand dollars for that?" But she was sure she had the right ad. It was the only one for a vintage jeep in the Florida Craigslist ads, and the only one from Roberta.

She'd pulled into a gas station to do a Google search for the vehicle Wally said her father was questing after.

The ad had no contact phone number, so the only thing she could do was e-mail the seller, requesting that he call her immediately about the jeep.

She tried calling Clint's cell phone again, but again it went directly to voice mail. She shook her head in frustration. Two days ago he'd been a sick old man who could barely stand to pee. Now he'd apparently taken off in search of the Holy Grail.

Greer drummed her fingertips on the steering wheel, trying to decide on a course of action. She didn't know for certain that Clint was on his way to Roberta, but Wally couldn't think of any other reason he would have left his house on a muggy Sunday morning.

It started to rain while she tried to organize her thoughts. Just a light drizzle, just enough to drive the relative humidity all the way through the roof.

Her mind ran amok with all the things that could have happened to the old man. He could have been run off the road and been badly hurt, too badly hurt to answer his phone, even. He could have ventured out for groceries, true, but she'd seen at least a month's worth of groceries in his kitchen, and he'd seemed perfectly content with a regular menu of canned soup and frozen Stouffer's lasagna. Even worse scenarios started to haunt her.

Clint lived alone, in a remote rural area. Anybody could have broken into his house and abducted him, taken him away in his own car . . . a terrifying stream of horror movie–inspired possibilities unspooled in her overactive imagination.

"Enough." She typed "Alachua" and

"Roberta" into the Kia's GPS and waited for the map to upload onto the car's nav screen. She started the car and headed off in search of a stubborn, half-blind old man, who was in search of a broken, rust-bucket, World War II–era Army jeep.

Three miles down the road she noticed a distinctive green golf cart pulled over on the shoulder of the road. She slowed down to get a closer look and spotted what she'd expected, a faded Silver Sands Motel bumper sticker affixed to the back of the roof canopy.

In another half a mile she saw a slender teenage girl trudging along the side of the road, a small backpack slung over her shoulder. The girl's hair was plastered to her head. She wore a tank top, shorts, and flip-flops. Definitely not an outfit for a hike in rainy, swampy Florida weather.

Greer pulled alongside the girl, rolled down her window, and beeped her horn.

Allie jumped, and Greer could tell she was poised to run, until she recognized the Kia's driver.

"Hey, Allie," Greer called. "I saw the golf cart up the road. Did the battery die again?"

"Yeah."

"Get in and I'll give you a ride home," Greer said.

"No thanks." Allie kept walking.

"Allie, I know you're mad at me, but it's really not safe for you to try to walk all the way back home. We must be four or five miles from the Silver Sands."

The girl's face took on a familiar, stubborn set of the jaw. It must have been a Thibadeaux family trait. "I don't care. I like to walk." She kept on going, staring straight ahead.

The rain had gotten heavier. Water streamed down the teenager's face. Greer coasted along the shoulder, still trying to persuade the girl. She pointed toward the sky. "Look at those storm clouds, Allie. There's a cold front moving in. That means lightning and thunder."

Allie looked up and, as if on cue, a menacing rumble echoed in the distance. Still she shook her head and walked on.

Greer was losing patience. "Damn it, Allie! Get in this car this minute or I'll call Chief Bottoms and have her send a patrol car to pick you up."

The girl snatched the door open and slid onto the seat, crossing her arms over her chest like a petulant preschooler.

Greer closed her window, wiped away the raindrops that had leaked inside, and drove back onto the roadway.

Allie stared straight ahead, but Greer could see that her eyes were swollen and red rimmed.

"You saw TMZ today, huh?"

"Yes," Allie whispered.

"I'm sorry, but Kregg is a sleazeball. And if

it makes you feel any better, that girl with him in the picture is Zena. And she's a lazy slut."

The girl's facade cracked slightly. She bit her lip. "Zena? Zena who I worked with on the set?"

"That's the one. He was hitting on her at the Inn Friday night, and then they left together. I know it hurts, to find out he cheated on you that way," Greer said.

"You don't know anything," Allie cried. "You don't know what it feels like . . ."

Greer shrugged. The sky ahead darkened and a bolt of lightning streaked across the inky horizon.

Her cell phone dinged to signal an incoming e-mail. She swerved back onto the shoulder again, braked and read the e-mail.

RE: Willys Jeep. Still available. What information can I give you?

Greer typed her number and response as fast as she could.

Please call me immediately at this number. Have reason to believe my elderly father might have contacted you about the Jeep this morning and he has now gone missing. This is not a scam! Thank you, Greer.

Allie watched what she was doing with

feigned indifference. Greer again steered onto the roadway. The storm was moving in. She needed to find Clint before something bad happened. Unless it already had.

"What's going on?" Allie finally asked.

"My father is missing. He was in a car wreck Wednesday and he's half blind and has a cracked rib and is on pain meds. He just got out of the hospital Friday. It's not safe for him to be driving. We think he left his house in Alachua this morning to go look at an old car, but he's not answering his phone."

Greer's phone rang. The caller ID listed an unfamiliar number, but with a local area code.

"Is this Greer?" It was a man's voice.

"Hi, yes! Thanks so much for calling."

"I don't really understand what you want from me. The jeep is legit. I've got registration papers and everything."

"No, I don't doubt that. My father told his friend he'd seen an ad for a Willys jeep for sale on Craigslist. He asked his friend if he'd take him to go see the car this morning, but his friend couldn't do it. Now my dad's car is missing. He just got out of the hospital and he's losing his vision. He's not supposed to drive. At all. Can you just tell me if a man named Clint contacted you?"

"Yeah," the seller said. "He sounded like an older dude. Said his name was Clint and he had cash, but he needed a ride to come see the car and could I wait until Monday maybe. I told him I had another guy coming to look at it this morning, and the first person to show up with the cash gets the jeep. Wouldn't you know it, both guys were no-shows."

"What time did you talk to Clint?"

"Hmm, he e-mailed me last night and I sent him my phone number this morning. Must have been around eight a.m. As soon as I told him I had another buyer on the hook he got all excited and said he'd find a way. That's the last I heard from him."

"It's nearly noon. If he was coming, he should have made it by now," Greer said.

"Yeah, if he was coming from Alachua, he'd have had plenty of time to get here, even if he drives as slow as all the other retired old farts around here."

"Something must have happened to him," Greer said, thinking out loud. "Would you mind texting me your address?"

"I can do that," the seller said. "Now you got me worried about the old dude. Could you let me know when you find him? And, hey, tell him the jeep's still available."

She clicked to disconnect and handed the phone to Allie. "Sorry, but I'm not gonna have time to take you back to the motel after all. Could you please call your aunt and tell her you're with me?"

Allie made the call, and it was obvious from her rapid-fire delivery that she was leaving a message. "Hey, Gin. It's Allie. I borrowed the golf cart, but the battery ran down. Don't worry, though, Greer is giving me a ride back, just as soon as we do some stuff." She disconnected and looked over at Greer.

"What are we going to do?"

"We're going to go look for my father," Greer said, her voice grim. A moment later, her phone dinged to indicate the text message had arrived. "Type that address into the GPS, will you?"

Allie typed rapidly. "Hey, if this car is in Roberta, I know how to get there. One of the girls on my travel soccer team lives there. It's pretty easy."

"Okay, tell me the way," Greer said, glancing at the nav screen. The map was still loading. Rain was slashing hard against the windshield, and the wipers were doing double time.

"It's super simple," Allie repeated. "Up here at the four-way stop, you just make a left onto the county highway."

"The road of doom," Greer muttered.

Allie shot her a look. "What?"

"The first day I drove into Cypress Key, I was on that county road and it terrified me. I was almost out of gas, and it's like wilderness, all pine tree forests and swamp."

"Did you ever see that movie *Wrong Turn*?" Allie shivered. "I don't really like scary movies, but my best friend Tristin loves them. We think they must have used the county road as inspiration for that movie."

"That one was actually shot in Georgia, if I'm not mistaken," Greer said. "But you're right about that road. It freaks me out. I'm a city girl from L.A. That first time I drove it, I was positive that if I ran out of gas I'd be eaten by the bugs or the bears. So, I hear the bears are for real?"

"Black bears. They wander out of the swamps sometimes," Allie said. She pointed at the four-way flashing sign. "Turn here."

A moment later the voice on the GPS screen echoed Allie's instructions. Greer handed her the phone again. "I need to keep my eyes on the road in all this rain. Call that second-to-last number, will you? That's my dad's friend Wally. I need to let him know what's going on."

Allie dialed the phone and then handed it back to Greer.

"Wally? It's Greer. I talked to the guy selling the jeep, and he confirmed that Clint talked to him this morning and told him he was on his way to come see it. That was around eight. You haven't heard from him, have you?"

"No, I haven't," Wally said slowly. "That's not good, is it?"

"I'm afraid something bad has happened," Greer said, trying to sound calmer than she felt. "I've got the address of the place, and

I'm headed that way. My GPS says I'm about fifty miles away. I think I'm going to call the police, too. It's raining hard here, and if he's gone off the road or something, he could be in bad shape."

"You want me to come and help look?" Wally asked.

"No, you hang tight there. There's still an off chance he might have changed his mind and gone someplace else," Greer said. "Do you think you could find out his license tag number? The police are going to want that."

"Sure thing. We lease that Blazer out occasionally," Wally said. "I'll run by the office and call you back with what you need."

Five minutes later the phone rang. Greer handed it to Allie to write down the information about Clint's car.

"You just stay on this road for a while now," Allie volunteered. "You want me to call somebody else for you?"

Greer considered it. She hated to be an alarmist, but on the other hand, she was truly frightened that Clint had met with misfortune. "Check my contacts list and call Chief Bottoms's cell. I wouldn't even know who to call for help out here in the middle of nowhere."

Again Allie dialed and then handed the phone to Greer.

"Chief? It's Greer. I'm sorry to bother you on Sunday."

"No worries about that. I'm headed over to the boathouse right now. What do you need?"

The boathouse. Greer's hand flew to her mouth. She'd completely forgotten she was supposed to have been at work more than an hour ago. But that would have to wait.

"It's my dad. I think he may be in trouble." Greer repeated what she knew about her father's mission and his precarious medical condition. "I'm headed for Roberta now, and I'm wondering who I'd call to help search for him."

"Well, that area could be either or Carlyle County or Magnolia County," the chief said. "Does your dad have a cell phone?"

"He does, but I'm not sure he has it with him. I've been calling, but he doesn't answer."

"If he does have it, they'll be able to locate him through the GPS in the chip. Give me that number and the make, model, and license tag of your dad's car. I can call the dispatchers in both those counties and ask them to send somebody out to look. And part of that area is in the DeSoto Forest National Wildlife Refuge, too, I believe. There's a ranger station about ten miles outside Roberta. They've got ATVs that can go back in those swamps that regular patrol cars can't get into."

"The swamp?" Greer said, choking at the thought. "I can't imagine how he'd end up . . ."

"This happens a lot down here," Arnelle Bottoms said soothingly. "We have so many snowbirds and retirees in Florida. They get confused or disoriented and end up in the damnedest places. But don't you worry. I'll make the calls, and I'll give the dispatchers your number, in case anything turns up."

"Thanks," Greer said. She repeated the information about Clint's Blazer and hung up. The swamp. Unbidden images of Clint, mired in a mud, surrounded by alligators and poisonous snakes and God knew what, sprang to mind. She again cursed her questionable fascination with horror movies.

Allie must have picked up on her terror. "It's not like a real swamp, like the Everglades or anything," she assured Greer. "Mostly the swamp there is like shallow, muddy ditches. And, like, a gabillion mosquitoes."

"Thanks." Greer sniffed and wiped at the tear that was rolling down her cheek.

Five minutes later her phone rang and Allie held it out to her. "It's Bryce," Allie whispered. "Maybe you should just not answer."

Greer shook her head. "No, I need to tell him what's going on."

"Hi, Bryce —" she started.

"Where the fuck are you?" the director shouted. "I've got about a million fans and reporters crawling all over this place after that thing on TMZ this morning. One security guard. This place is a madhouse . . . and you're a no-show?"

"My father is missing," she said. "I'm out looking for him right now, so I doubt I'll make it to the set today."

"You can't send out an APB or something? This is your job here, Greer. You can't just disappear like this the day before a big shoot."

"Sorry, Bryce. He's old and he's hurt and he's family. You'll have to get somebody else to manage the set today."

"Like who?"

"Zena."

"That kid can't manage squat," he said. "Anyway, I already called her. She quit on me."

Her phone beeped to signal an incoming call. "I have to go, Bryce."

"You hang up and you're fired, Greer."

She tapped the Disconnect button and then hit Connect.

"Greer?" It was Eb.

62

"Gin said she had a message that Allie was with you. What's going on?" He sounded angry. As usual.

"Clint is missing. He apparently left his house around eight this morning to go to Roberta, to look at a car he found on Craigslist. But he never made it. I was on the way there to look for him when I spotted Allie walking on the side of the road. The golf cart's battery died."

"Is she okay? It's storming pretty bad here."

"Allie's fine, but I didn't have time to bring her back to Cypress Key."

"Christ, Greer. You should have called me."

"I did call you, this morning, when I discovered I'd missed your call last night. You never returned my call."

His voice was low. "I thought you were blowing me off last night."

"I can't have this conversation now, Eb. Here. Talk to Allie."

She handed the phone to the teenager, then

leaned forward, concentrating on trying to see the road through the waterfall of rain on her windshield.

Allie turned her head away, talking quietly to her uncle.

"I know I shouldn't have taken the cart without asking. I was upset, okay?"

She listened for another minute or two, then handed the phone back to Greer. "He wants to talk to you."

"Tell me where you're headed," Eb said. "I'll meet you there. Have you called the cops?"

"I called Arnelle and she was calling the dispatchers in the counties around Roberta, and the Park Service rangers from the wildlife area there," Greer said. "If Clint has his cell phone with him, they think they can track him that way. I'll have Allie text you the address in Roberta where he was headed."

Greer turned on the defogger to burn off the condensation on the windows. With every mile she felt a mounting sense of urgency, but she had to slow down to twenty miles an hour because of the poor visibility. The county road was flat as a pancake and she was now driving through at least three inches of water that had no place to drain.

She needed something to take her mind off all those frightening images of Clint.

"Allie, where were you going this morning,

when you took the golf cart? Bluewater Bay?"

Allie nodded. "Triss texted me to tell me what was in TMZ today. It was so gross! God! I am so stupid. I should have known something was up. Kregg hasn't called me in a couple days, and he wasn't answering my texts."

Greer glanced over at the teenager. "He gave you another phone after Eb took the second phone away?"

The girl's face flushed, but she nodded.

"Have you been seeing Kregg on the sly?"

"Yeah." Allie's voice was suddenly meek. "Dad told me it was okay. He said Eb wasn't in charge anymore, you know, since Dad got out of prison."

Greer had to bite her tongue to keep from telling the girl what she thought of Jared.

Allie fiddled with the strap of her backpack. "My dad is kind of messed up, huh? I thought it was gonna be so neat, when he told me he was getting out. He said he was coming home and we'd get to live together, like a family again."

"I know," Greer said.

"And Kregg was really into meeting Dad because he thought Dad was a major bad-ass." She shook her head. "I've hardly seen him since he got home. All he does is sit around and drink beer all day, or play *Call of Duty,* and hang out with Kregg and talk about the movie he's writing."

"Not like you thought it would be, is it?"

"No. And I know he's smoking weed with Kregg. He tries to hide it when I'm around, but I'm not a friggin' baby. I can smell it on him. I called him out on it, too. I looked it up on the Internet. Because he's on probation, the cops can make him take a drug test, anytime they want. And if he fails, he goes back to prison."

"What did Jared say to that?"

"He just laughed at me. He said Kregg knows ways to get around that. Some pill you take to make your pee okay. And he told me I should lighten up, because it's not like weed is a real drug, and anyway it helps him mellow out so he can write."

Greer realized Allie was watching to see what her reaction would be to her latest revelation. It probably wouldn't be helpful to tell the kid that her father was an idiot and a loser.

"But you're afraid if he has a positive drug test, he'll go back to prison. Right?"

Allie nodded.

"And you think Jared should care more about staying clean and being with you than getting high with Kregg. Correct?"

"I just want him to be like a normal dad. You know, get a job and buy us a house and come to my soccer games. Like normal families. Maybe help me with my trig homework. He's really smart, you know. He went to med school and everything. He could be a doctor if he wanted."

She swiped at the tears running down her face. "I'll tell you something else, too. You know that little notebook Dad always carries around, because he says he's writing a movie in it? The other day, when he was passed out drunk in Gin's living room, I opened it. It's nothing but scribbles. Seriously. Like I used to do in kindergarten, when I was pretending to be a writer, scribbling in my mom's waitress order book."

So the O-train actually hadn't left the station. Big surprise, Greer thought.

Greer reached over and patted Allie's knee. "My parents split up when I was five. Same age as you were when yours divorced, right?"

"Yeah."

"My dad wasn't around at all when I was growing up. My mom and grandmother raised me. My mom was an actress with some pretty kooky ideas about raising a kid. Definitely not what you'd call normal. And that's all I wanted, too. I finally realized not everybody needs normal." She sighed. "Of course, it only took me thirty-five years to figure that out."

"But you and your dad are tight now, right?"

"Not really. Not the way he wants us to be. I never saw him, except briefly, once or twice, for thirty years. Right before my mom died, back in the spring, she wanted me to reach out to my dad — you know, reconnect. But I didn't want to, because I was still so pissed at the way I thought he abandoned us."

Allie's eyes widened. "I didn't know your mom died. That must suck. I mean, Gin and I fight sometimes, but if something ever happened to her, or Eb, I don't know what I'd do."

"They're really good people, Allie. And they love you so much. I get that Eb went nuts when he found out you were hanging out with Kregg. He doesn't want anything bad happening to you. I know he doesn't think you'll be like your mom or your dad. He told me how proud he is of you, and the way you play sports and make good grades. And what a good person you are."

"I know," Allie whispered. Her eyes filled with tears. "When I was living with my mom, and she was messed up, I used to wish all the time that Eb was really my dad. Pretty sick, huh?"

Greer shrugged. "Who am I to judge? My dad wants to make it up to me now, for all the years he stayed away, but I don't know. Some part of me just won't let go and forgive him."

"But you went to see him in the hospital. And you're out looking for him now, right? You wouldn't do all that if you didn't care about him, would you?"

"Maybe I just feel guilty for not feeling guilty about not loving him." Greer chuckled. "You want to talk messed up? That's really messed up."

Greer glanced down at the car's nav screen. According to it, they were still at least fifteen miles from Roberta. She hadn't seen another car on the road in at least twenty minutes. The pine trees closed the narrow two-lane ribbon of road in on both sides, and the black rain clouds blotted out the sun.

"Spooky, huh?" She pointed at one of the yellow BEAR CROSSING signs.

"Allie, take my phone and try calling Clint again, okay?" She handed over her phone again. "Look under Missed Calls."

The teenager scrolled down the numbers and tapped the one she wanted, for Clint Hennessy. "Put it on speaker, okay?" Greer said.

The phone rang four times, and then went to voice mail.

Greer chewed the inside of her cheek. She felt so useless. "Okay, try it again. Let's just keep trying to call him. If nothing else, if he can hear the phone ringing, he'll know somebody's trying to find him."

Allie did as she asked, and this time, when the automated "Leave a message" recording played, Greer took the phone.

"Clint? It's me. We're looking for you. I'm on the way to Roberta and I'm going to find you. So hang in there, okay? The police are looking too. Don't give up. We're going to find you."

She tapped the Disconnect button. The GPS voice instructed her to turn in a quarter mile. Greer slowed the car and again peered through the window, looking for the crossing. Just as she was about to turn left, her phone rang, and she froze for a moment.

Allie picked the phone from the cup holder and held it up. "It's him!"

She pushed the Connect button and the Speaker button.

"Greer?" The voice was thin and muted, but it was definitely him.

"Clint, it's me. Where are you?"

"I . . . I don't know. I'm lost. I was going to see the jeep. I think I made a wrong turn somewhere." His breathing was loud and raspy. "I pulled off the road, to turn around, but I hit something. A tree maybe. And when I tried to back up I got stuck in the gee-dee mud."

"It's okay. We'll find you. Are you okay? Did you get hurt when you hit the tree?"

"The front bumper's messed up."

"Are there any street signs around? Any houses, or businesses?"

"No, just gee-dee trees and mud."

"Think, Clint. What was the last road you were on, before you made the wrong turn? Was it the state road?"

"Maybe. The one with the bear signs?"

"Right! I'm on the state road now, so I must be getting close to you."

"I turned off that road, made a left and drove a ways, and then turned again. But I couldn't read the sign. I can't remember the name of it."

"Okay. At the first turn you made, was there any kind of a landmark? Anything besides gee-dee trees?"

"A church. A white church with a white sign near the road. It had a big black cross on it."

"I know that church!" Allie said. "It always has these funny sayings on the sign, like 'Highway to Heaven' or 'Prayers Answered Here.' We haven't passed it yet."

"Okay, Clint. We think we know what road that is. Can you see anything at all, out the window of the Blazer?"

"No." His voice sounded weaker, thready. "When I got stuck in the mud, I got out and tried to push. I think maybe I did something to my rib. It hurts real bad. Worse than before."

Had he cracked another rib? Maybe punctured an organ? Greer was terrified he'd pass out . . . or worse.

"I've got an idea," Allie whispered. "Mr. Hennessy? I'm Allie. I'm in the car with Greer. Is your phone an iPhone?"

"What? I guess it is. It has all these apps

and buttons and things."

"Okay. Does your phone have Siri?"

"Who?"

"Siri. It's like a helper app on your phone. You can tap it and ask it things like, 'Where am I'?"

"Oh, her. Yeah, I got her," Clint said.

"Well, if you hang up, you can ask Siri where you are and she'll give you a map, then you can call us back," Allie said, her eyes shining with excitement.

"No," Clint said. "I'm not hanging up. What if I can't get you again? Anyway, I can't see them little bitty maps on a phone." He paused, and his breath got more labored. "I can't see much of anything anymore. I'm a stupid old fool. I ought never have tried to drive all the way over here by myself."

Greer's phone beeped and showed an incoming call from Arnelle Bottoms. "Clint? I'm putting you on hold for a minute. The chief of police is calling me on the other line. I'm not hanging up, so don't get scared, okay?"

She clicked over to the call from the chief.

"Greer? They've got your dad's location and there's a unit from Magnolia County and an ambulance en route."

"Thank God," Greer said. "Can you give me directions? I've got him on the other line, but he's in pain and disoriented, and can't tell me much except that it's off the county road."

"He's about a mile down Alligator Ridge, two miles east of Hawkins Store Road. If you get to Parker's Mill Road, you've gone too far."

Greer turned to Allie. "Did you get all that?"

"Got it," Allie said. "I think we're super close. Hawkins Store should be up here in a mile or two."

Greer clicked back to Clint.

"Clint? I'm back."

Nothing.

"Clint!" she hollered. "Can you hear me?"

She heard a muffled groan, then nothing else. But his phone was still connected.

"Hang on, Dad," she hollered again. "I'm only two or three miles away. And the ambulance is on the way too."

63

"Turn here," Allie directed, pointing to a barely visible road marker. Greer made the turn, and two miles later Allie pointed out the sign for Alligator Ridge. Greer's heart was pounding. She kept looking in the rearview mirror, praying for flashing red or blue lights.

Allie was on the edge of her seat, her face almost touching the Kia's windshield. "I see a car up ahead," she yelled. "See it, back in that bunch of trees?"

Greer leaned forward, too, straining her eyes to see what Allie saw. She turned on the Kia's bright lights and saw a flash of silver, and then red emergency flashers among a thicket of tall pine trees. She pulled on to the shoulder of the road, being careful not to leave the pavement. In a moment she and Allie were out of the Kia and running for the trees.

"I hear a siren," Allie said, but Greer kept running. The Blazer was wedged between two pines, its rear tires mired in muck. She could see Clint's head lolling back against the headrest. His eyes were half open. She yanked the door open. "I'm here, Dad," she said, touching his shoulder. "Right here."

Allie was at her elbow. "I don't think you're supposed to move somebody if they've been in a wreck," she said.

"I won't." Greer kneeled down in the mud, reached in, and unfastened Clint's seat belt. She took his hand and squeezed it. He was cold, but she could feel a pulse. "Can you hear me, Dad? Squeeze my hand if you can." His eyelids fluttered, and she felt the slightest pressure on her hand.

The siren was getting closer, and now they could see the flashing red light, followed by two sets of blue flashers.

"Here's the ambulance, Dad," she said. "You're going to be okay. Everything's going to be okay."

Greer and Allie stood a few yards away from the Blazer, huddled under an umbrella, watching while the medics worked on Clint. She'd filled them in on his recent medical history and the fact that he'd complained of pain after trying to free the car from the mud.

A red pickup pulled on to the shoulder of the road, followed by a black and white Cypress Key police cruiser. Eb climbed out, and Greer realized her knees were shaking with relief. He ran up and gathered both Greer and Allie into his arms.

"How's Clint?"

"They're working on him. They said he's in shock, and because he's having problems breathing, they think maybe he could have punctured his lung with the cracked rib," Greer said. "He's also dehydrated, so they've started an IV, and I saw they've put an oxygen mask on him."

Arnelle Bottoms walked up, greeted them, then went to consult with the EMTs and the sheriff's deputies.

One of the EMTs approached. "Okay, ma'am, we've got your dad stabilized and we're going to transport him to Magnolia General."

"I want to go with you," Greer said, stepping out from beneath the umbrella.

"No ma'am, I'm sorry, we can't do that. You're free to follow us there in your own vehicle."

"Let's pull your car farther over on the shoulder, and then I'll take you to the hospital in the truck," Eb said. "You're in no condition to drive."

Arnelle Bottoms rejoined them. "They've called for a wrecker to get your dad's Blazer. I told them they might as well take it to the garage in Cypress Key, if that's okay with you."

"Thanks," Greer said. Arnelle looked over

at Allie, who was standing close beside Eb. "Allie, how about I take you back to Cypress Key with me?"

"No!" Allie said. "I want to go to the hospital with Eb and Greer."

"Not this time, kiddo," Eb said gently. "We don't know how long it might be. Go on home and fill Ginny in on what's going on. I haven't had time to update her."

Allie gave Greer a pleading look.

"You are an absolute goddess rock star," Greer said. "I never would have found Clint if you hadn't been in the car. You kept calm and kept me from freaking all the way out. But I agree with Eb. Go home and get some dry clothes. I promise we'll call you as soon as we know something."

"You better," Allie said. She turned to follow the chief to her car, then came back and hugged Greer tightly. "He's gonna be okay. I just know it."

The ambulance slowly backed out of the woods. Greer was shivering violently. Eb closed his arms around her. "Come on," he said. "I've got a blanket in the truck."

64

Greer sat hunched over in the plastic chair, her eyes roaming the small waiting room, always returning to the nurse behind the front desk. They'd been sitting in the emergency room for over an hour.

Eb took Greer's hand and held it, but she was too nervous to sit still for long.

She jumped up and returned to the desk again. "Any word yet on my father?"

The clerk shook her head. "They'll call up here when they know something. They were taking him back to X-ray and then to do a CT scan. It might take a little while."

Eb tugged at her hand. "Come on, let them do their job. Let's go get some coffee."

"You go. I need to stay here in case there's any news." She sat back down, facing the desk.

He didn't actually want coffee. He just wanted to find a way to distract Greer. She'd been like a caged animal since arriving at the hospital, pacing back and forth, questioning the polite but beleaguered nurses and clerks.

"What about some fresh air? It's stopped raining. I'll tell the clerk we'll be outside if there's any news."

Greer shook her head. "I just . . . can't . . ." Her voice broke.

Eb put an arm around her shoulder. "I know it's scary."

"This is my fault. I should never have left him at his house. Clint was in no shape to be alone. But he was so damn needy! It felt like these tentacles were reaching out, suffocating me. You should have seen him, Eb. Showing me their wedding picture, talking about what songs he used to sing me to sleep with. He didn't even know any lullabies. What kind of father doesn't know 'Rock-a-Bye Baby'?"

He shrugged, knowing it was useless to tell her everything wasn't her fault.

"This is why I didn't want to see him again. Why I didn't want to get involved with you. It's why I ran away. It's probably why he ran away from Lise and me."

She pounded the arm of the vinyl chair and gestured around the room. "Dammit. I don't want this. Sitting in an emergency room waiting for bad news? I've had my fill of this, after Lise."

"What do you want?" Eb asked quietly.

"I want to be like I used to be."

"And how was that?"

"I was happy, okay? I could take a job and

go anyplace I wanted, and not have to answer to anybody. I was good at what I did."

"You were happy?" Eb looked dubious. "I thought you told me you hadn't had a relationship in two years. And we both know how things worked out with Sawyer the lawyer."

"I meant besides that."

Eb pointed to the ER entryway. "You can have your old life back, if you want it that much. Go on. There's the door. I'll stay here and see about Clint. Go on, Greer. Really. Take my truck. Go back to your job."

Her face flushed and she shook her head. "I can't. Bryce fired me because I didn't show up for the shoot today."

"Why didn't you go?"

She stared at him. "You know why."

"Tell me anyway."

"Clint was missing. All I could think about was that he was in a ditch somewhere in that swamp. I had to find him. You can't walk away and leave an old man. Who would do that?"

"Jared would probably do it," Eb said quietly. "Vanessa would, too. But you couldn't." He took both her hands in his. "Bad news, kid. You love that old man in there. And he loves you. I think you're stuck with each other."

She leaned over and buried her head in his shoulder. Her voice was muffled. "I know."

She pounded his chest with her fist. "Dammit."

He tucked one finger under her chin and turned her face toward him. "So, what are you going to do about it?"

Tears welled up in her eyes again. "I don't know. I'm no good with this stuff. I'm just as lousy at being a daughter as he was at being a dad. I do know he can't stay by himself. Not for a while, anyway."

"Rehab center?" Eb asked.

"Maybe. But aren't those usually short term? What happens when he's ready to go home again? His eyesight isn't going to get any better. He's going to need some kind of help." She smiled crookedly. "God help Clint. I guess that's got to be me. I'll have to figure out the logistics. Eventually I guess we'll have to find a home health-care nurse . . . or something. I do know that I can't stay at his place, not permanently. It's a double-wide. I'll have to find a place nearby."

Eb looked at her and raised an eyebrow. "I have a place nearby."

"You want to rent me a room? Why? Because you feel sorry for me?"

He took off his glasses and wiped the lenses on the tail of his shirt, then put them on again.

"You're doing it again," Greer whispered.

"I don't want to rent you a room and I don't feel sorry for you. I want you to marry me. Because I love you."

He was clutching both her hands in his and holding on for dear life. There would be no running away this time. For either of them.

"I know this is a terrible place for a marriage proposal. I'm sorry about that. When this . . ." he gestured around the waiting room, and noticed out of the corner of his eye that the desk clerk was watching, and listening. "When this is over, we'll go down to the beach behind the Silver Sands, at sunset. I'll get a good bottle of wine and buy you an engagement ring and we'll do it right."

Greer shook her head.

"Okay," he said impatiently. "You're the location scout. You pick the spot. I'll show up with the ring."

"No," Greer started to say.

For a moment, Eb felt like he'd had the wind knocked out of him. But then he recovered. He had to make her listen, and believe.

"Okay. I know there's a lot to think about right now, with your dad and all. And I know I'm not the easiest guy to live with, what with the messiah complex and all. But this morning, when I hadn't heard from you — when I thought you were leaving town for good this week? I wasn't just angry anymore. I was desperate. I knew, no matter what, I had to figure out how to be with you."

"Eb," Greer said, trying to pull her hands away.

"Just let me finish. All this time I've been so busy trying to save the casino and the town and Allie? I was really the one who needed saving. And you did that. You saved me."

"Me? I saved you?"

"I thought I was responsible for fixing everything around me that was wrong. But some things can't be fixed. Jared. Maybe not the town." He shrugged. "I don't care about any of that. I just care about you. Marrying you and making a life with you. On whatever terms you say. If you want, I'll come to L.A. I could get an engineering job again. We can figure it out."

Eb took a deep breath. "Okay. I got it out. Now what were you trying to say?"

She turned around and pointed to the desk clerk. Who was standing just a few feet away, grinning, with a chart in her hand. Obviously she'd heard the whole proposal.

"Miss Hennessy? Your father's back down from X-ray, and the doctor will be out in a minute to talk."

The doctor was an alarmingly young woman, with soft brown eyes and brown hair worn in a ponytail.

"Eleanor Oetgen," she said, shaking Greer's hand. "Your dad is going to be fine. As you know, he had a cracked middle rib from his last accident. Apparently, when he tried to push his car, he punctured the space between the lung and the chest wall, which is the pneumothorax."

"Good God," Greer whispered.

"That's the pain he was feeling," Dr. Oetgen said. "He tells me he thought he was having a heart attack but he didn't want to tell you that, because he was afraid you'd panic while driving and get in a wreck of your own."

The doctor shook her head. "He's quite a guy, your dad. Anyway, we've put a tube in his chest, and he's been sedated, but right now he's awake if you'd like to see him. We'll keep him for a couple days, just to make sure he's healing properly, then you can take him home."

Greer shot Eb a guilty look. He shrugged.

Clint's eyes were heavy lidded. He was semi-reclined, but he struggled to sit up when he saw his guest enter the room. She walked over to his bedside and shook a finger in his face.

"I can't believe you're alive after all that," Greer said, trying to scold her father. "You really do take a licking and keep on ticking."

Clint licked his lips and tried to smile. "You can't kill an old stuntman," he said wheezily. "I've had lots worse wrecks than that."

"No more wrecks, please," Greer said. "You might be tough enough, but I'm not. Promise me, okay?"

"Okay," he said. "Now promise me something. Go on back to work. I ended up here

644

because of my own stubborn pride. You go on back to work. I know you've got a big shoot tomorrow, and I don't need you hanging around this hospital."

"No. I'm staying with you," Greer said.

"The hell you will," Clint shot back. "I've done without you for thirty years, I guess I can do without you for another day or so." He looked over at Eb. "You're her fella, right? Maybe she'll listen to you. Make her go back to work."

"I can't," Greer said. "I got fired. Which is okay, because the producer/director is a royal pain in the ass. I should have quit a long time ago."

Eb coughed discreetly, and both father and daughter turned to him in surprise.

"I don't know if I should tell you this or not, but Bryce called me while I was on the way to meet you earlier. He wanted me to beg you to come back to work. Just to finish the shoot. He's uh, offering you the equivalent of a signing bonus."

"No way," Greer said flatly. "I am done with Bryce Levy and *Beach Town.*"

"It's ten thousand dollars," Eb said. "For that kind of money, *I'll* get a radio and go over there and tell people where to park."

Greer's eyes narrowed. "You think that's all I do on my job?"

"No-o-o," he said hastily. He glanced over at Clint. "Help a brother out here, will you?"

"The man is right," Clint said. "Pride is one thing. Common sense is another. I've been in the movie business for fifty years. You quit a job and leave a director hanging and word will get out that you're unreliable. Flighty, even. That's your reputation, Greer girl. Ain't nothing can fix that. Besides, Hennessys aren't quitters. I know Lise didn't raise you to quit, and Dearie sure didn't, either."

His eyelids fluttered, then he focused on her again. "Go on. Go back and do your job. I ain't going nowhere. I just need some sleep." He waved at them dismissively. "Shoo."

Eb cleared his throat again. "Mr. Hennessy?"

"Clint."

"Um, Clint, there's just one more thing. I was wondering if it would be okay if I married your daughter."

Clint's eyes snapped open. He glanced over at Greer. "I'd say that's up to her. Did you ask her already?"

Eb nodded.

"Did she say yes?"

It was Greer's turn to speak up. "He didn't really give me a chance." She smiled at Eb, who was frowning now, and who seemed to be holding his breath.

Clint regarded Eb with new interest. "He seems like a presentable-enough guy. Well-spoken and all. What'd you say he does for a living?"

"This and that," Greer said teasingly. "He owns a grocery store, and an old boathouse and marina, and half a crappy motel. He's also the mayor of Cypress Key."

"Don't forget I also have a real estate business, too," Eb said helpfully. "I was also, until very recently, city engineer."

"Okay. Just as long as he's not in the movie business," Clint said.

"I can promise you, I have absolutely no interest in making movies," Eb said. "Also, I love her beyond all reason."

Greer let go of Clint's hand and took Eb's. "I love you, too."

Clint leaned back against the pillows and closed his eyes. Greer and Eb exchanged worried glances. Greer took her father's hand. He opened his eyes again.

"Then I guess it's okay with me," Clint said.

"Okay with me, too," Greer said. "I think I'm done with L.A. anyway. With all the film and television projects being done in the South these days, I can just as easily work from Cypress Key as anyplace else."

Eb took her in his arms. She was damp and muddy and her blond curls were full of pine needles. But her kiss was warm and sweet and full of the promise of sunny skies, sandy beaches, and cookies. Lots of cookies.

When they finally pulled apart, Clint

647

seemed to be sleeping.

"We'd better go," Greer whispered.

Clint's eyes opened again. He gave Eb a stern look. "There's just one more thing I need from you."

"Anything," Eb said fervently.

"Seems like you're a sort of jack-of-all-trades. You know anything about cars?"

"I know enough. I change my own oil and I tinker with boats some."

"Good enough." Clint pointed at a large plastic bag hanging from a hook on the back of the door. He took several wheezy breaths. "My billfold is in that bag. There's three thousand dollars cash in there. You go see that fella with the Willys jeep over in Roberta. If that thing is anywhere near what it should be, I want you to buy it. Try to get the price down a little, but if you have to, pay him the money. I been looking for a World War II Willys for twenty years. You get me that jeep, I'll throw in a daughter. Deal?"

Eb clasped Clint's hands in both of his "Deal."

65

She called Bryce on the way back to Cypress Key. Greer's tone was businesslike and direct.

"I'll come back to work tomorrow and finish up the shoot and everything else you need before Wednesday," she said.

"Great. That's great. I knew I could count on you," Bryce said.

"Just a couple of things. I don't know how you're planning on paying me that signing bonus you mentioned to Eb, with the studio breathing down your neck about budgets. That said, this bonus doesn't go through studio channels. It comes from you, personally."

"I can't do that. My own money? You know it doesn't work that way."

"It works that way this time or it doesn't work at all," Greer said. "I'll expect a check from you, tomorrow, when I show up for call time. For the full amount. And just so you know I'm serious, when the banks on the coast open tomorrow, I'll be on the phone with them, making sure the funds are in your account."

"What? You don't trust me?"

"Not especially," Greer said. "Also, with Zena gone, I'm going to need an assistant. Allie Thibadeaux's uncle has agreed to let her come back to work, on one condition. Kregg is not to speak to Allie. He is not to look at her. She'll be paid the same salary Zena was making, for the next three days."

"She's a kid! You want me to pay a kid that kind of dough?"

"Yes. She's twice as hard working as Zena ever was, plus she has a brain. So. Do we have an understanding?"

"Yeah. See you in the morning."

Greer's radio crackled. She switched on the mike. "How's it looking over there, Allie?"

Her new assistant was on a golf cart, troubleshooting between the boathouse, where the morning's shoot would begin, and the pier, where the plan was to move later in the day.

"Bathrooms are here, the tents are going up, and we've got the pier barricaded," Allie said. "The catering guys want to know if you want full hot lunch or if sandwiches and salads and stuff are okay."

"Light lunch," Greer said. "Tell them to make sure we've got plenty of energy drinks and water and fruit." She was running over a mental list, wondering if she'd forgotten anything. She'd been so distracted over the weekend, she was uneasy about her preparations.

"Anything else?" Allie asked.

"That's it. Just remind the security guys over there we need them on the water no later than ten. I don't want any boatloads of reporters and fans zooming in and out of camera range."

"Got it," Allie said.

It had been a tense morning. Bryce had to coax Adelyn Davis to join Nate, who was playing the sheriff, in the cigarette boat for establishing shots, but when he announced that Nate would actually pilot the boat for a few hundred yards away from the boathouse, she flatly refused.

"No," she said, shaking her head. "I don't do boats. It wasn't in the script and it's not in my contract. No boats."

"He won't go very fast," Bryce pleaded. "After this, Courtney will take over for you. But I've got to have you and Nate in that boat for about fifteen minutes."

Adelyn shot daggers at Bryce. "I hate you, dude. I really, really hate you."

Bryce signaled for the driver of the camera boat to pull away from the dock, and a moment later Nate steered his boat away from the dock too. Seconds later, Kregg, who'd somehow won the battle to do his own stunting, followed in the orange cigarette.

Despite his promises to the contrary, as soon as Bryce called "Action" the cigarettes roared away from the dock at full throttle.

The action was repeated six more times, each time with Bryce calling directions over a megaphone.

An hour and a half later, the cigarette boats returned. Adelyn climbed out and promptly vomited all over the dock.

"Cut," Bryce said wearily.

The fight scene between Kregg and the sheriff was shot next. Again and again, the actors and their stand-ins ran through their paces. Adelyn screamed on cue, Kregg and the sheriff cursed and issued threats. Bryce had the cameras repositioned a dozen times.

Greer wandered over to the air-conditioned tent where CeeJay was packing up her equipment to move to the pier for the afternoon's shoot.

"How's your dad?" CeeJay asked.

"Seems to be okay," Greer said. "I talked to him briefly a while ago. He was bitching about being hungry, so I guess that's a good sign." She looked over her shoulder and saw that the tech crews were loading their equipment into the vans. "Hey, um, what's your schedule going to be like in the next few weeks or so?"

"Not sure," CeeJay said. "I gotta find a new

place to live when we get back to L.A. I've got some music videos lined up, and then my agent says he's had some other inquiries. Why?"

"Greer!" Bryce bellowed.

"Coming," she yelled over her shoulder. "I gotta go. I was just wondering how you feel about bridesmaid's dresses."

"Depends." CeeJay's eyes widened. "Don't tell me! You and Eb? When?"

"Soon," Greer said.

"Greer! Dammit, these generators better be over there in ten minutes," Bryce yelled.

"Talk later," Greer said, giving her friend the briefest suggestion of a hug.

As she was climbing onto her golf cart, she saw Kregg and Jared Thibadeaux walking off rapidly in the direction of the Ritzy Rest-Stops. Jared had been hanging around the set all day, and she had a strong conviction that he and the *Beach Town* male lead were taking a detour on the way over to the pier location in order to "mellow themselves out," as Jared would have put it.

Her radio crackled again and she felt thankful that Addie was still several blocks away.

"Greer?" It was Bobo, the transportation captain. "Hey, uh, Kregg just came over and told me that he and his bodyguard are supposed to drive the cigarettes over to the pier. Is that what Bryce told you?"

"That's crazy. Why wouldn't the stunt guys drive the boats over there?"

"I don't know, but the stunt guys already went over to the pier in one of the earlier vans," Bobo said.

"Bryce never said a word about it to me," Greer said. "And I don't think that's such a hot idea. Why don't you call Bryce and see what he says?"

"I tried, but my call went straight to voice mail," Bobo said. "I'll call again. I don't like the idea of those two clowns playing around with nearly half a million dollars' worth of equipment. I'll call my van guy and tell him to bring the stunt guys back. If Kregg and his buddy want to hitch a ride, I guess that's okay."

Greer was poised to pull out of the boathouse parking lot when she heard the roar of the cigarette boats. She shrugged. Not her circus, not her monkeys. She had a location to prep, three miles down the road.

Word had gotten out around town that the *Beach Town* shoot was almost complete. The crowds of bystanders lining the barricades across Pier Street were the largest Greer had seen. Hundreds, if not thousands, stood in the withering heat, hoping for a glimpse of something, or somebody, connected with the film's stars.

Bryce greeted her outside the casino. His

eyes darted around the set, at the air-conditioned tents, the catering truck, and all the equipment vans. "All set?" he asked.

"I am if you are," she said. She pointed toward the roof of the casino, where scaffolding and a platform had been set up for one of the camera crews. "All good up there?"

"All good up there, and the camera boats are getting ready to go out too. Thank God the water's not as choppy as the weather report predicted."

"How's Addie?" Greer asked.

"Green. And very, very pissed," Bryce said with a chuckle. "She'll get over it. CeeJay's got her in makeup right now. And as soon as she's done with Kregg, we'll get started."

"Kregg's in the boat," Greer said.

"What boat?"

"The cigarette. He told Bobo you okayed it for him and Jared to drive the cigarettes over here from the boathouse. They were leaving there when I did, about ten minutes ago."

"What the hell? Kregg is full of shit. That's why we've got stuntmen. We don't have liability insurance for that. Jesus H.! If those two idiots fuck up those boats . . ."

He pulled his phone from his pocket and tapped an icon. "Come on, Kregg," he muttered. "Pick up the phone. Pick it up, you idiot."

They heard the distant roar of two motors and turned to look. Two long, sleek cigarette boats, one white, one orange, raced into view.

"Son of a bitch!" Bryce yelled. He took off running toward the casino. Greer ran along behind him.

Cameramen, sound techs, production assistants, grips, even the chefs from the catering truck were drawn to the pier that ran along the side of the casino to watch the spectacle unfolding before them.

Five hundred yards out, the cigarettes skimmed across the bay at high speeds. They jumped each other's wakes, and each time a boat hit a wake it went airborne for heart-catching seconds before planing out again with a bang and a spume of water.

One of the production assistants looked over at Greer. "Who is that? Are we rolling?"

"It's Kregg and his bodyguard," Greer said grimly. "And no, this is not part of the script."

But Bryce was having second thoughts. "Get a camera on that," he screamed. He turned to an assistant. "Get the second unit on the roof. Tell them to roll and don't quit rolling. Then radio the unit on the boats, tell 'em to get as close to the cigarettes as they can. I want tight shots on Kregg's face. Keep that camera on his face. Got it?"

The boats raced back and forth, jumping wakes, turning around in tight circles, and then heading toward each other again. Each time, they came closer to the casino. Greer felt her pulse quickening. Kregg and Jared were coming dangerously close. Their wake sent waves splashing over the edge of the pier. She looked around for Allie, hoping the girl was busy someplace else, but then her eyes were irresistibly drawn back to the bay.

The roar of the boats' engines was deafening. The cigarettes headed back toward the casino, closing in again, now a hundred yards off, then closer, fifty yards now, this time on an apparent collision course. Now the white cigarette cut in front of the orange boat, and the driver, apparently realizing he was perilously close to broadsiding the pier, veered away. The driver of the orange boat's instinctive reaction was to veer away from the oncoming boat. He cut the cigarette toward the pier, then made a doomed last-minute attempt to swing away. She was holding her breath, until she saw the cigarette's driver jump free.

A second later the boat slid into the pier's concrete pilings with a sickening, high-pitched scream. Greer realized her own scream echoed that of the boat, and that the crowd around her was screaming, too.

She stared at the pier and at the wreckage of the boat for only a moment before running toward the pier. "Get out! Everybody get out!" she screeched.

Cameramen stood, too stunned to move.

"Get the fuck out!" Bryce screamed. "Move

the equipment. Now!"

He pulled the radio from his pocket. "Get those guys off the roof. Get 'em off!"

Greer pulled out her own radio as she ran. "Allie? Where are you?"

"I'm at the catering truck. What was that crash?"

"Stay where you are," Greer said. "Whatever you do, don't move."

CeeJay appeared at her side, out of breath. "We gotta run," she said, grabbing her friend's arm. "C'mon, Greer. I smell gas."

They heard sirens and then, a second later, an ear-shattering explosion.

66

Greer stared in horror at the end of the pier. Where was Jared? Was he in the white cigarette? And Kregg? Was he in the orange boat that had crashed? She'd seen somebody jump free of the boat, moments before the collision. People were shouting, screaming, running. She smelled the gas fumes and understood. She started to run toward the end of the pier, but her legs felt like rubber.

CeeJay appeared at her side, out of breath. "We gotta run," she said, grabbing her friend's arm. "C'mon, Greer. I smell gas." She sped away. Now Greer was running, glancing backward over her shoulder. Eb appeared out of nowhere. He grabbed her hand, started dragging her away.

"Come on, come on. It's going to blow."

"Jared's back there. And Kregg," Greer protested.

"Dammit, Greer —"

The boom was deafening. Eb dove for the concrete and pulled her down with him, covering her body with his. They heard a second explosion, louder than the first, and debris began to rain down around them. Chunks of plaster, roofing tile, wood. Eb was up on his knees, crawling, dragging her with him. "Come on, baby, we gotta get away."

He pulled her toward one of the large metal city trash barrels that had been knocked over by the force of the explosion, upended it, and placed it over their huddled forms as a makeshift shield.

In a matter of minutes, it was over. They heard two, three, four different sirens racing toward the pier. Eb stood up and pulled Greer to her feet. Her knees and hands were bleeding. He was bleeding from a cut near his eye. They stood among the piles of wood and metal and glass and stared at the pier. Acrid black smoke billowed and obscured everything from sight.

"Jared?" Greer's throat was raw from the burning fuel.

"Was he in the white boat?"

Greer nodded. "He was when they left the boathouse."

Eb pointed across the bay. The white cigarette boat rocked violently in the wake from the explosion, but they could see the silhouette of a man standing on the bow.

"Looks like Jared dodged yet another bullet," Eb said.

As they watched, they saw a black and

white sheriff's boat racing across the bay. It slowed a hundred yards from the end of the pier, and an officer in the bow of the boat tossed an orange life preserver overboard. They saw an arm waving from the water. The uniformed officer paused, then dove overboard and swam toward the flailing figure in the surf.

"Looks like Kregg made it," Eb said.

They turned their attention back toward the end of the pier. Through the smoke plumes they saw flames shooting up through blasted-out windows. They heard a sharp cracking noise, and suddenly the tile roof seemed to fold inward on itself. A moment later, the stucco walls collapsed, sending white clouds of plaster into the oily black air. Fire trucks sped past, knocking aside the metal security barricades, and firefighters leaped off and began hooking up hoses to the hydrants at the end of the pier.

But they both knew it was too late. There would be no more dances or movie nights or skating parties for the Cypress Key Casino. No more rock concerts or senior citizens' bridge tournaments.

Greer looked anxiously up at Eb's face, trying to gauge his reaction to the devastation. Eb tightened his hold on Greer's shoulder and turned her gently around.

Arnelle Bottoms met them at the foot of the

pier and waved them toward one of the *Beach Town* tents that had already been commandeered by the EMTs.

"I'm going to find Allie," Eb said.

"I called her, right when they started racing, to make sure she wasn't watching," Greer said. "She was over at the catering truck."

"Let's take a look at your hand," the male medic said, seating her on the edge of a table meant to hold coffee and doughnuts.

"I'm okay," Greer insisted. "What about the splinter crew that was on the casino roof? And the camera crew in the boat?"

"All okay," a young female medic assured her. She made Greer sit still while she cleaned and bandaged her cuts. "We transported one of your guys to the hospital with a broken ankle, and a couple other people had facial lacerations from flying debris. Luckily, nobody was inside the casino when the blast happened."

A thought occurred to Greer. "Where's Bryce? The director? When I saw him, he was running toward the building, right before it blew."

"I don't know," the medic said. "Was that the guy screaming at the firefighters to get out of the way? White dude? Kinda short with wavy gray hair? Waving a movie camera at the fire?"

"Sounds like Bryce," Greer said wearily.

When she'd finally persuaded the EMT that she could walk under her own power, Greer was irrevocably drawn to the end of the pier. The firefighters had commandeered the metal barricades, and a growing knot of people stood quietly behind them. These were not the laughing, jostling movie fans who'd gathered here earlier for a peek at Hollywood magic.

Older couples stood hand in hand, watching as steam rose from the rubble of their youthful memories. Middle-aged couples trained cell phone cameras on the scene, and teenagers exchanged breathless play-by-plays of the big explosion.

She was turning to go when a television news van from the NBC affiliate in Gainesville arrived. An attractive twentysomething black reporter in a sleeveless green dress positioned herself with the still-burning casino in the background and began interviewing the witnesses.

Greer turned to go, but then she heard the reporter announce that the casino's owner, local businesswoman Vanessa Littrell, wanted to make a statement about the fire.

Sure enough, there was Vanessa, pushing her way in front of the camera. Her makeup was freshly applied. She wore blue jeans and a spotless white blouse. And a serious, tragic face for the cameras.

"As the last member of the Littrell family, I am of course heartbroken by the loss of my family's heritage today," Vanessa said, blinking back shiny, perfect tears. "But I thank God that nobody was injured in this unforeseeable tragedy. I pledge to this community that we will rebuild. And the development that will rise in the place of the casino will be a point of pride for everybody in Cypress Key."

Greer felt a wave of bile rising in her throat. She walked another few yards down the pier and spied yet another television news van. This one was from the Tampa FOX affiliate. A shapely blonde who wore a black pantsuit and a serious news expression was poised by an ambulance with flashing lights that was just about to pull away. The rear doors to the ambulance were still open, and an EMT could be seen bending over a stretcher, just before the driver ran around to the rear, slammed the doors, and sped away.

"Sources say that Grammy Award–winning rapper and budding film star Kregg, who was the male lead in the film being shot here today in Cypress Key, was thrown from the speedboat only moments before it crashed into the casino building, in a collision that ended in a fiery explosion," the reporter intoned into the microphone. "I am told that his injuries, while severe, are not life threatening."

The reporter held up her cell phone. "I also just spoke with Kregg's mother, Anita Thompson, who is also Kregg's business manager, in L.A., as she was boarding a private jet in order to be by her son's side. Ms. Thompson said she expects to retain legal counsel to explore the possibility of suing the studio and the producers of *Beach Town,* for forcing her son to perform dangerous and life-threatening stunts for which he had no training or experience."

Greer stumbled away from the scene, knowing only that she had to get away from the noise and the smoke and the confusion.

A golf cart rolled up beside her. Eb was at the wheel, and a tearful, wide-eyed Allie sat behind him.

"Come on," he said softly. "Let's go home."

"I just saw the ambulance leaving with Kregg," she said, glancing over at Allie, who looked away. "They were taking him to the hospital."

"Arnelle talked to the EMTs," Eb said. "He'll live. He's got a broken collarbone and some cuts. And he's missing most of his front teeth."

"Dad's okay, too," Allie said softly. "Just some cuts." She bit her lip. "They're taking him to the police station, though. Chief Bottoms told Eb that he and Kregg are both gonna get their blood tested. For alcohol. And drugs."

"Oh, Al," Greer put an arm around the girl, whose shoulders were shaking with suppressed sobs. "I'm so sorry. About everything."

Allie sniffed. "Me too." She looked at her uncle's profile. "I'm sorry about all of it, Eb. Especially the casino. It's Dad's fault. Dad's and Kregg's."

"It's just a building, Al," Eb said. "Buildings can be replaced. I've got everything I need, right here on this golf cart." He steered the cart off Pier Street and headed for the neon lights of the Silver Sands Motel, where the NO VACANCY sign was blinking on and off.

EPILOGUE

The rowboat rocked gently on the calm waters of the bay. The heat of the day was past, and the horizon was cast in a golden glow.

Eb Thibadeaux uncorked the bottle of wine, filled a plastic goblet, and handed it to his bride. He shifted his weight carefully until he was seated beside her in the bow. She offered him the bucket of popcorn. He took a handful and munched.

"This is really good," he said. "Is it the new line you ordered?"

"Yup," Greer said. "See, I told you the higher price point was worth it." She took the smallest sip of wine, smacked her lips, and handed it to him. "And this is light-years apart from that swill we used to sell."

"Okay. You were right again."

They leaned back in unison against the waterproof cushions Greer had stacked in the bow. Eb looked at his watch, and then again at the end of the pier.

Or to be accurate, the end of where the pier had stood since the twenties. Today, the only thing still standing was a newly poured concrete pad.

"It still kills you to see it gone, doesn't it?" she said gently.

He shrugged. "I'm an engineer. I knew all along the casino wasn't structurally sound. I just always hoped we'd get a chance to fix it. You know, put in new underpinnings, jack her up, and keep going the way we did for eighty-some years. And we could have done that, too, if it hadn't been for my brother and the artist formerly known as Kregg."

"At least they're both alive," Greer said with a sigh. "Allie already had a wake-up call about her father. She didn't need a funeral to remind her just how flawed he is."

"I still can't believe they both walked away without a scratch. While the casino went up in flames and the pier collapsed into the bay," Eb said. "And I really can't believe Vanessa got her way after all."

"I wouldn't call having all your front teeth knocked out and a broken collarbone 'walking away without a scratch,' " Greer said. "Kregg missed half his concert tour. And let's face it, if Bryce has his way the guy really will never work in movies again. And Jared, he'll just always be Jared, won't he? Has Allie heard from him at all?"

"He e-mails, I think. She said Jared swears

he'll be back for her graduation in June. She'd probably talk to you about him more than she would me."

"Al's had to grow up way too fast," Greer said. "But I think she's having too much fun being a senior, thinking about college in the fall, to worry too much about Jared."

"Speaking of graduation, I forgot to tell you," Eb said. "Dearie called me today. She needed some Candy Crush money in her account. And she said to tell you she's definitely planning to come out for Al's graduation."

Greer pointed again at the heavy machinery and the masses of concrete pilings and other materials along the site of the old casino. "At least you got a chance to make sure the new developer's plans fit in with the rest of downtown," she said. "I saw the new set of architect's renderings, and I like the way he's specified stucco and a red barrel tile roof. It won't be the old building, but I think the new one is going to be beautiful."

"Vanessa Littrell wins again," Eb grumbled. "I know I should get over it, but it still gripes me."

"What does she win? More money? Money hasn't brought her happiness before, and it won't now. Love? Bryce Levy left Cypress Key and never gave her a backward glance. I heard she's thinking of selling her dad's house at Seahorse Key and buying one of the new Pierhouse waterfront condos."

Eb gave Greer a funny look. "What would you say about buying Seahorse Key?"

"For an investment?"

"No. For us." He patted the slight mound under her cotton sundress. "You and me and Baby Thibadeaux."

Greer sat up so abruptly the rowboat swayed violently. "You'd give up the loft? Seriously?"

"We can't raise a baby living over the Hometown Market," Eb said. "Besides, I've been talking to Clint."

Greer rolled her eyes. "I can't wait to hear what you and my dad have cooked up between you."

"I think he's tired of having a full-time home health-care aide checking in on him twice a day. I pointed out to him that there would be plenty of room at Seahorse Key. He could have his own small apartment."

"And?" Greer knew there would be an *and.* There always was with Eb Thibadeaux.

"And he could relocate Hennessy Picture Cars to Cypress Key. The boathouse is virtually empty. It's got all the room he'd need for his inventory, plus plenty of room for his guys to do body and paint work. It's a win-win."

"I get it," Greer said knowingly. "Dad gets more room to play with his big-boy toys and you get access to all the toys. Including the General Lee. Is that how this deal shakes out?"

Eb shrugged. And then he slowly, deliberately removed his glasses and cleaned them on the hem of his shirt.

Greer leaned over and kissed him, and the boat swayed so violently it threatened to swamp them both. Finally, reluctantly, she pulled away.

"Your movie's about to start," Eb said. He pointed to the movie screen that had been set up near the site of the old Casino, and at the rows and rows of Cypress Key citizens camped in front of it, on lawn chairs, in convertibles, even golf carts.

"I'm still sad Cypress Key didn't get to experience an old-fashioned Hollywood-style movie premiere," Greer said. "But what delicious irony that Bryce Levy's masterpiece turned out to be just as big a dud as he is."

"Direct to video," Eb said, savoring the words. "I look at it this way. *Beach Town* brought Greer Hennessy to Cypress Key, which brought you to me. We lost a casino in the process, but that's a small price to pay."

She gave him another fond, lingering kiss. "One correction. Greer Hennessy brought *Beach Town* to Cypress Key, not the other way around. But the outcome's the same. A happy ending. And I do love a happy ending."

They heard the opening thumping bass notes of Kregg's soundtrack. Eb started to say something else, but Greer placed a warning finger across his lips.

"Sh-h-h. My movie's about to start."

ABOUT THE AUTHOR

Mary Kay Andrews is *The New York Times* bestselling author of *Save the Date, Christmas Bliss, Ladies' Night, Spring Fever, Summer Rental, The Fixer Upper, Deep Dish, Blue Christmas, Savannah Breeze, Hissy Fit, Little Bitty Lies,* and *Savannah Blues.* A former journalist for *The Atlanta Journal Constitution,* she lives in Atlanta, Georgia.